# Spirit of the Lone Horse

Ani H. Manjikian

*Every story has a beginning, middle, and end.*

The beginning starts with family.
To everyone in mine, love you all.

*The middle is the friends and others who push and inspire you.*
*Three stand out in my mind.*
*For their insight, I am honored and grateful.*

Glen, you taught me that I was an artist,
even before I believed it myself.

Reva and Bobbi, who helped me understand me, so I could share
this part of myself with the rest of the world.

*In the end, the goal is achieved and the dream is realized.*
*Three more answered the call.*
*For their help, I express my deepest gratitude*

Taleena, who read an unfinished manuscript of mine, and inspired
me to take another look at this one.

Rubie and her team over at Unsolicited Press. Without your
enthusiastic yes, this book would still be gathering dust on my
computer.

LividEmerald, your research was invaluable in making the last bits
of this book work. I wouldn't have known where in Montana I was
without you.

*Many others have come and gone in my life as this adventure has unfolded.*
*I can't name all of them because the list would be too long.*
*You know who you are.*
*Thank you, each and every one.*

*Hope* - essence - the reason to keep on fighting when others have given up.

*Enterprise* - boldness - the courage to try something different when doing the same isn't working.

*Creativity* - insight - the intuition to act on the impractical when the practical seems more logical.

*Daring* - audacity - the ability to move forward when others want to take a step back.

*Courage* - heart - the energy to strive toward a goal when obstacles stand in the way.

*Determination* - will - the power to say "Yes" when the easier answer is "No."

*Compassion* - soul - the willingness to care when disinterest and apathy is all around.

# PROLOGUE

A quote from *Henry V* repeats in my head to the rhythm of the brush's strokes through the black mane, *When I bestride him, I soar, I am a hawk: he trots the air; the earth sings when he touches it; the basest horn of his hoof is more musical than the pipe of Hermes.*

Many hooves have touched the sand beneath my feet, but all singing in this ring has been in the form of grunts, groans, and enough swear words to fill a dictionary. If the dark wood rails could talk, they would tell tales of horses and humans learning to understand, anticipate, and respect one another so they can perform together in show arenas around the world. I'm about to be the teacher, or perhaps the student, in one of these lessons.

Throwing the comb in the grooming box, I step back and admire the full beauty of the bay Anglo-Arab stallion hitched to the fence. His height to muscle ratio gives him power without bulkiness. A deep chest means good stamina. The flowing lines from his teacup-shaped head to the long legs of his racehorse body guarantee at least a few points on any judge's scorecard.

If the horse's attitude and abilities are even half his looks, my team has a great chance of winning this year's Championship Series. When we do, history awaits us. I will be the first female captain to raise the International Championship trophy above her head in victory.

My nostrils flare as sadness tugs at my heart. I'm standing next to the horse because I want, and have, to evaluate him. This morning, I found my long-time companion, Day Dreamer, dead in his stall. That left me with no mount for the opening ceremonies of the state preliminaries down in San Diego tonight. If I'm not there, my team will have to wait until next year to make their championship run.

"You ready, Jo?" My brother Jim calls out from his perch on the top rail.

"Almost. I have to check the girth one more time." Girth checks are a normal part of tacking up. They make sure there is a good fit between the horse and the saddle, so there is no slippage during riding.

1

I step to the horse's side, and run my hand between his skin and the leather that connects the strap under his belly with the top part of the saddle. Instead of two fingers that indicate a comfortable and secure fit, I can almost shove in my whole fist.

"You held your breath, didn't you, boy?" I tease the horse. Breath holding is a self-defense mechanism, suggesting that he had a bad saddling experience sometime in his life.

Unhitching him from the rail, I walk Alabaster around the ring to loosen him up. He leads easy with one ear cocked back and the other forward. Every so often, they switch. His tail swishes back and forth in a gentle rhythm. No sighs, snorts, or lip rattles. These are all good indications that he is calm and ready to work with me.

Every so often, I stop and tighten the girth a little bit. The process takes a few minutes, but, in the end, I have a saddle that's snug and a horse that's comfortable.

Licking my finger, I hold it up and check for a breeze. The wetness sits there doing nothing. I rub the moisture away with my thumb. The sun warms the bare skin of my forearms. I look up, and watch a wisp of white float through an otherwise blue sky. Good, we have almost perfect weather. That means if Alabaster does something stupid, it's because I did so first, or he's too high-strung for even pleasure riding.

I chose the name Alabaster because of two rocks. One, the material they make statues out of, and the other, Jim, who is my anchor and counterbalance.

Since birth, we have mirrored each other. We are both stocky with broad shoulders, brown hair, and hazel eyes. Jim is a few inches taller, a few pounds heavier, and a little more laid back than I am. As fraternal twins, we are individuals who need the other to be whole. That's why, even with a few last minute issues to deal with, he sits a shout away, acting as my spotter.

I asked him to watch me ride because Alabaster is an enigma. He appeared yesterday with no official papers, just an anonymous birthday card wishing me all the best. The way he took to a halter and lead rope, grooming, and tacking up suggests he's broke. How well broke, though? How does he interact with a rider? Are there any spots he doesn't like touched? How do unexpected noises and excited people affect him? Can he handle the pressure of competition where split seconds and subtle movements take away or add fractions of points?

Except for the girth problem, I've liked the answers he has given me so far. I still don't trust him, though. I won't until I've had several hours of saddle time on him.

Building a relationship with a horse is like forming one with another human being. It takes time and effort. The difference is that horses have a lot more weight and power at their command than humans, so if things go south, the human ends up getting the bad part of the deal.

More than a dozen other horses fit my riding style and needs. All of whom grew up around me, so I'm familiar with their history and training. Jim rattled off the top three he wanted me to look at as we walked toward the ring. I promised I'd try his suggestions after Alabaster.

All I need is Jim's final okay. If he says no go, I'll respect that. While we both have decent horse sense, his is better than mine in this situation. He still has the objective perspective I lost right after meeting Alabaster.

Leading Alabaster toward the center of the ring, I flash thumbs up at Jim. Unless he sees something I don't, he has no reason to say no.

He points his thumb upwards.

*Yes!* I move to Alabaster's side, check the girth one final time, put my foot in the stirrup, and swing up into the saddle. Settling in my seat, I gather the reins. With a slight pressure of my legs, I ask Alabaster to move out, expecting a slow walk.

He bolts from underneath me.

"Whoa, boy," I say, shifting my weight back and applying light pressure on the reins.

Instead of obeying the simple command to slow, Alabaster pins his ears back, snorts, and launches himself into the air with a powerful thrust of his legs. The bone-jarring landing kicks up a cloud of dust. Fighting the urge to sneeze as much as my mount, I use my weight and legs, as well as the reins, to force him into an ever-tightening circle.

After a few turns, Alabaster relaxes under me. I loosen my grip. Straightening out, he cow hops and lashes out with his hind legs. I lean back. He lunges forward. The surrounding landscape jumbles into an indistinct mass as the speed, ferocity, and unpredictability of his erratic movements increase.

A high, quick bounce sends me flying. I have no time to tuck and roll. Instead, I slam into the ground, stomach first, with an explosive grunt. Sand fills my nose and mouth, scratching my closed eyelids. Breathing in the fine grains, I feel like I'm drowning.

I lie there in a gray, half-aware state, not sure who I am or what I'm supposed to be doing.

An eerie whistle and a shout shock my muddled senses into clarity.

Clawing the dirt, I gain enough of a purchase to push myself onto my side. Sparks of pain light up my mid-section and almost send me back into the grayness. Pushing the discomfort aside, I flip onto my back and open my eyes. Glorious blue sky fills my vision. Air rushes into my lungs. Drinking in all I can, my head buzzes.

Something shuffles near me.

One. Two. Three. Four beats.

The horse's shadow blots out the sun as he rears, his front legs pawing the air.

Rolling, I scramble to my feet. Out of the corner of my eye, I glimpse Jim charging in. Alabaster chases him off with bared teeth and flying hooves. Moving backwards, I watch the chess match between horse and human. The exchange goes on until Alabaster catches Jim with a vicious body slam that knocks him down.

The rogue stallion turns and rushes toward me.

I sidestep. He flies by.

He pivots and lunges again.

Twisting and dodging, I manage to dance away from the berserker's fury.

My ribs scream.

Turn after turn, we circle each other. Pivoting to my right, I spot the fence and safety in my peripheral vision, but don't head in that direction. Jim's still out. Alabaster might attack him once I leave the ring. Most horses wouldn't, but then I've never seen one as insane as this one, except at a rodeo.

Rushing forward, I wave my arms and yell, "Ha!"

Alabaster shies away.

Racing toward Jim, I try to lift him. He's dead weight. I bend over and drag him toward the fence while keeping an eye on the bastard circling us.

We are almost at the rail when Alabaster swoops in and kicks my left leg below the knee. Dropping Jim, I stagger away, hoping the rogue stallion will leave my brother alone. He sniffs Jim once and follows. After a few skips backwards, my knee locks up, tumbling me to the ground.

Alabaster charges toward me.

I throw up my arms to protect my head.

His hooves smash into chest.

He rears again and again, coming down on a different part of my body each time. My bones crack and crunch. My flesh tears with a wet, sucking sound. Every nerve shrieks in agony.

Moments pass as if they are hours.

When I'm nothing more than a pile of mush and screaming nerves, blackness shows mercy by enveloping me in its embrace.

# ONE

# OLD WOUNDS

"Three more transfers, Captain," Vice Captain Ben Harrison, my Executive Officer, states.

"That makes five this week," I protest.

"Six, sir," Ben counters. All superiors in the United States Mounted Band are sirs. Some of my female colleagues want the gender-based honorifics that other military services have. I don't care unless Ben or any of my close acquaintants use the respectful term when addressing me in private.

"Six?" I echo, shaking my head. One every two to four weeks is high, but well within norms. Six in seven days means the department responsible for moving people, animals, and supplies around has forgotten which base serves which purpose. The horses bound for San Fernando pose no immediate concern, but the weapons and ammunition meant for my base do.

Ben places the forms on my desk. No reading on my part needed. Just sign, flip, and repeat. I'm through the mundane chore in under a minute. I do most of the busy work like this here in my bureaucratic office with its soft carpeting, large desk, and pictures on the walls that the civilians expect to see. The real nexus of my command sits two floors and one sub-terrain level beneath my feet.

Handing the papers back to Ben, I notice something on the top sheet that bugs me. Pulling the pages back, I stare at the typed text. Through the first few lines, I don't see anything that should have drawn my attention.

*Origin: Academy Houston.* My cousin Jeff commands that base. He never has trouble with any of his horses. If anything, he and his crew pamper, and almost spoil, their charges. I'll mention this one the next time we talk and see how he reacts.

*Current Location: Joint Forces Los Angeles.* Most of the world associates the USMB with horses and music, but the military part of the organization dates back to its origins in 1850. The Joint Forces, a clandestine division founded in 1976, strengthens the USMB's connections with the various military and peacekeeping forces around the world.

*Destination: Rehab San Fernando.* The base handles the retraining and rehabilitation of minor offenders with two and four legs. The person in charge, Casper Nolan, was a classmate of mine at the Academy.

*Age: 10.* The horse was a yearling when I last rode. Strange, it doesn't feel as if nine years have passed.

*Sex: Stallion.* As a rule, the USMB gelds colts a few weeks prior to weaning them at six months of age. Those with strong bloodlines perform in a limited run of shows before entering the breeding program. Jim's black stallion, Midnight Fury, is a rare exception. He's seven and still performing. Without this policy in place, the sexes couldn't mix during shows and events without the risk of a fight breaking out.

*Description: Bay Anglo-Arab with blaze, four white socks, and black mane and tail.* My last mount was part Thoroughbred, part Arab with almost the same markings.

*Dam: Dreamer's Quest.* One of Double D's many offspring. Given his strong bloodlines, I bred him several times a year hoping for his successor. Never had a chance to train or ride any of them, though.

*Sire: Alabaster.*

The temperature in the room jumps up several degrees. Breathing becomes a difficult chore through my dry and constricted throat.

I dream every night about the bay demon who almost killed me. Relive each moment of those short twenty-four hours that started with a gift from heaven and ended with an infinite moment in hell. Feel every strike of his hooves. Groan at every bite and rip of his teeth. Hear the individual notes of his predatory scream.

The paperwork flutters out of my trembling hand.

Ben's soft tone snaps me out of my shock. "This isn't just another screw-up, is it?"

Not trusting my voice, I nod.

Picking up the papers, Ben reads the sheets. After he finishes, his chocolate brown eyes meet mine. In them, sympathy and understanding mixed with concern. "Are you going to be okay, Cap?"

"Yes." I take a long, deep breath. My heart slows to its normal pace. "As long I don't see him."

"I'll make sure he is the first one loaded."

"Thanks, Ben."

His pudgy form with its balding head turns to leave.

My desktop computer dings three times in a row. "Hang on a second," I say, glancing at the screen and my overflowing inbox. I skip the first two emails, which contain the chow and movie schedules for the week. The third is from my stepfather, Rear Admiral Jason Scott. My eyes shoot down the message.

After reading it through twice, I swear.

"What's wrong, Cap?"

I motion for Ben to take a seat. "San Francisco has been designated the Command Base of the USMB. Its new commander is Commodore Howard Stone."

"Jim and Admiral Scott never mentioned this to you?" Ben's thick, dark eyebrows furrow.

"No, and both of them would have known about it for the last month or so." I shrug. "Yesterday, Jason seemed a little curt and distracted, but not enough to worry me."

"What about Jim?"

"We spoke a week ago, but it wasn't much of a conversation. Something about a mundane procedure security won't implement until next year, I think."

Ben is more than an officer under my command. We became friends at the Academy and have posted to most of the same bases since then. Over the last few years, he's replaced Jim as my confidant and sounding board. Despite having his own family to look after, he makes himself available anytime I need to bend his ear. My six brothers could be just as supportive if I let them, but as the eldest, I'm supposed to be the imperturbable leader of the family.

Decisiveness and emotional control are even more important in my job. As a rare female in a male-dominated leadership position, I'm under constant scrutiny. A stupid career choice adds even more pressure.

Leaning back in the chair, I turn my head to the right. Sitting in the corner, a triangle of flags represents my commands past and present. At the point closest to the door, USMBLA's white banner hangs limp, covering up the black and gold logo. Spinning my chair around, I peer out the window at the same flag.

Catching my ghost reflection in the glass, I pause. My blue uniform, despite the pressed creases and tailored fit, drapes from my stocky frame. Hazel eyes, once so bright and intense, are dull and uninterested. My bottom lip, while not sore, is red from involuntary chewing.

Looking past the image, I continue to stare at my base's pennant, which flutters enough so I can see the gold circle with black horse's head. Once the source of inspiration, the insignia has become another reminder of how much I am, and have, screwed up.

I can no longer claim the steady certitude of a lone stallion standing watch over his herd the design embodies. *What good am I to my crew who looks to me to emulate the ideals expressed in the base's motto, then? Maybe it's time to step down and let someone else who can take over.*

"Jim is the perfect candidate—" I mutter.

"For what?" Ben prompts.

"—assuming command of this base after I resign. He grew up and spent most of his career here, so most of the crew will accept him outright."

"Admiral Scott will find Jim another command. Why do you want to give him this one?"

"I'm tired, Ben, and I owe it to him," I sigh, feeling the wood-paneled walls closing in on themselves. "Go take care of that horse. We'll talk more about this later."

"Yes, sir."

After Ben leaves, I have the choice of stewing in my own self-pity, taking a walk to clear my head, or getting back to work. Both my computer and a small pile of paperwork await my attention, but my gaze and thoughts wander toward the pictures underneath the desk lamp. The right and left ones are individual shots of my parents. They sandwich a family portrait of two adults, six boys, one girl, and a black Lab. In the photo, my youngest brother is still a baby in my mom's arms.

Decked out in his full dress uniform, my father stares out from his frame with a steady gaze that grabs me around the mid-section and pulls me back to the day I received command of the base. I stand at a podium in front of a crowd at the Academy, having just learned about my promotion. On one side of me is Jason, and the other, Jim. Both wear the uniforms of their current positions. The final words of my acceptance speech echo in my head.

*It is my hope that while I command USMB Los Angeles, I will carry on the tradition of excellence established by Robert C. Mason and upheld by those who followed him, including my late father John P. Mason.*

I kept my commitment for a year. Then the mauling happened and excellence, along with my soul and torn up carcass, almost died in the bloody sands of the ring. While my physical body has recovered, the other two remain on life support.

Touching the photo, I swallow back my constant companions of anger, frustration, and self-loathing. "I've dishonored our family, Dad," I whisper, reaching across the eternal divide that separates the living from the dead, hoping he'll hear me. "I wish you could tell me how to make amends."

The phone rings.

Picking up the receiver, I answer with a tentative, "Hello?"

"That's not your usual, efficient 'This is Jo Mason' greeting," a high, thin voice chides.

"Hey, Casper," I smile. "I'm in one of my moods and thought my dad was calling from the grave."

Casper Nolan laughs. "No, just me wondering about another horse we lost to you. He's Alabaster's son."

I pause, bracing myself for another panic attack, but my pinky doesn't even flinch. "Ben's gone down to supervise his loading and departure."

"Good. He's just as crafty and aggressive as his father. I wouldn't want you near him."

# TWO CHOICES, ONE DECISION

The green canopy of the trees filters the bright sun into its individual rays. The soft brown soil squishes in some spots thanks to the overnight rain. Close by, birds celebrate the day with song. Off in the distance, cars whoosh along pavement.

*Ah!* I take a deep breath. The crisp, new smell in the air clears the unsettled thoughts from my head. I am certain. Jim deserves the base. Me, I need to fade into the obscure shadows I've created for myself.

No one in our family has ever resigned from the USMB before. A few were let go because of disciplinary problems. Some broke with tradition and never joined. History won't judge me against any of them, though. My father and great-great-grandfather are the standard-bearers of my family. The former co-founded the Joint Forces division. The latter created the whole organization.

Branches snap. Leaves crunch and crackle.

I try to identify the animal behind the ruckus. I had spotted a few deer tracks near the trailhead, but there's no musky game odor. No whining or barking, either, which eliminates dogs, wolves, and coyotes. Bears and wild cats are higher up the mountain roads. Domesticated felines rely on stealth. Most of the time, birds land on bushes and trees, not destroy them. At least thirty miles and a couple major freeways separate my base from the nearest cattle, pig, and sheep ranches as well as any zoos or wildlife sanctuaries.

That leaves only one other possibility. *Crap!*

Sparks of electricity shoot through my body. My muscles tremble and jerk. Heartbeats thunder in my ears almost drowning out the hoofbeats.

A horse, with a lead rope dragging from his halter, breaks into the open a few feet ahead of me. How escaped from another human's control doesn't matter. His unexpected presence makes me to think something is about to go wrong. Forget the fact that he matches the description of Alabaster's son in every detail, including the height of his white socks.

I freeze, hoping my stillness will blend me in with my surroundings.

The stallion eyes me as if I'm a predator. Snorting, he turns and trots a short distance away. Herd instinct to bunch up in time of fright be damned, I wish he would just go away and get himself caught. Peering over my shoulder at the trail behind me, I slide my foot backwards and then glance at the horse, who remains where he is.

Another step back and glimpse forward. The horse still isn't moving from his spot. Good, he can stay there until someone else comes along.

My heart beats a little slower. As long I'm deliberate and measured in my stride, I can escape unharmed. Can't allow myself to freak out and bolt. If I do, he might attack.

After about half a dozen more shuffles, I stop.

What am I thinking? Am I even thinking? I need to keep backing up. Tomorrow, or the next day, I can go down to the stables and test my bravery.

Not here. Not now.

Then when?

Every day, I plan to do one little thing to ease my uncontrollable, but well-founded, fear of horses. Some lame ass excuse always delays the task until the next day. The next day becomes two or three. A week passes, and somehow turns into a month. The year comes and goes.

Nine have flown by.

This time *has* to be different.

The horse blows a soft huff through his nose. I look up. He stares at me, ears forward, asking a simple question, *Are you friend or foe?*

"Horses and me used to be friends," I mutter, "until your father ruined it for me, boy. Now, I..." I stop, not wanting to admit the next part to myself, or a creature who doesn't care.

He paces back and forth. Every so often, one of his ears flicks in my direction. Stopping in mid-stride, he turns his head and mouths an invisible piece of hay.

Curious, I continue studying his unexpected behavior. Aggressive horses don't make such submissive gestures. *Is Casper wrong about him? No, his father...* I shove the thought aside. Gaining his trust requires me not giving into my fear.

Taking a long, deep breath, I drop my eyes and stare at the ground, saying in basic horse language that I do not want a confrontation.

*This position is vulnerable*, my mind states. I ignore it. My instincts are quiet. They were yelling on the day of the mauling, even when Alabaster appeared half-asleep waiting for me to finish grooming him. *If only I had listened to them...* I shake my head. *No time for any self-inflicted guilt trips. I have to focus and be ready to move just in case things go south.*

More licking and chewing from the horse, but no other movement. Around us, sounds decrease in volume. Objects, other than the horse, become dim and indistinct. I lose interest in all smells, except for the warm richness of his hide.

"He came this way," a voice yells.

I jerk up and out of my trance. *This will not work*, my mind roars. *Yell and grab the voice's attention. They can deal with the demon, and we can go back to our sane and normal life.*

The words yank me to a stop. Neither sane nor normal has described *my* life in a meaningful way since the mauling and, thanks to one particular op, well before that. Everything is the opposite of what it is supposed to be. The creature I once loved terrifies me. I doubt, question, and second-guess my simplest decisions. Everyone around me finds it easier to call me by my rank than my first name. I don't have the will to fulfill my most basic dreams. Forget about the big one of raising an International Championship trophy above my head.

What if it doesn't have to be this way? What if all free-roaming horses have no other intentions than finding a safe place to graze and shelter? What if this one in particular, despite his heritage, fears me more than I do him? Can I afford to let nine more years of my life, my friends, my family, and my dreams slip away from me because of some stupid fear?

Hell, no!

While it would be easier to overcome my anxiety with a horse trained at my base, this one and I have some unfinished business. He needs capturing. I need to know if he's playing me like his father.

My focus returns to the four-legged choice between redemption and damnation standing in front of me. His rigid posture suggests he'll spook at any sudden sound or movement. Given the narrowness of the path, I'll have to pivot on my bad knee to avoid his charge. When I do, I'll pitch forward into danger instead sweeping out of it.

"All right, boy, it's your move." I speak as low and soft as I can manage under the circumstances. "Stay fearful, attack, or trust me. Trust is the best option for both of us."

The horse lowers his head. He begins licking and chewing again. I walk a few steps toward him. My stomach still churns, but the rest of my insides are quiet.

Glancing over his shoulder, the horse sidesteps. Instead of shooing him away, my hands motion for him to come toward me. "Someone is going to catch you, boy, and then where will you end up?" I point to the ground by my side. "With me, you'll always know love and understanding."

Turning, I face him at an angle. My mind offers no objections.

*His move, his choice*, I repeat the mantra until it buzzes in my head. Shutting my inner voice up, I hear nothing, not even the birds. With each beat of my heart, the silence becomes harder to listen to.

The horse inches closer. Stopping just outside my reach, he flicks both ears forward.

We stare at each other.

Heartbeats pass.

Unable to stand the quiet and lack of movement any longer, I consider my options for luring him toward me. I'm not sure how long this little dance has gone on, but it feels like it's almost time for my shift. If I don't check in soon, the base will jump to a security alert status with a great deal of noise and motion that could upset the horse. Given how alone I wanted to be while making my decision, I had left both my cell phone and walkie in my office.

Stepping closer, the stallion rubs a warm streak through the cold sweat on my arm. Instead of grabbing the lead, I stroke the side of his head and neck. As I move along, I feel some uneven, broken patches in his coat. He flinches at my touch, but otherwise remains still. I reach his shoulder. Here the bumps and scabs create a disturbing picture that doesn't make any sense.

Jeff's base has a zero-tolerance animal cruelty policy. This has led to the transfer or demotion of at least a dozen people for minor infractions like not cleaning a stall to established standards. There is no way someone could hit a horse hard enough to break skin multiple times without getting their ass handed to them.

Unless, for some reason, Jeff ignored what was going on or, worse, had a hand in it. Neither scenario seems plausible, let alone possible. He's the most vocal about any kind of unfair treatment in the whole family.

The horse shoves his head into my chest. Tempering my desire to hurt the person who caused him pain, I caress his cheeks and run my fingers down the halter. When my hand touches his lead, a slight tingle spreads up my arm. The unusual, but not alarming, sensation is something I haven't experienced since my last ride on Double D. Not as strong as feeling his mouth through the reins, it still means the horse is an extension of me, and I of him.

Gathering the rope, I step around until the horse is on my left side with my hand a few inches under his chin. A gentle tug, soft cluck, and he falls in beside me.

*Sorry, little bro,* I smile, *you aren't getting this base for at least a few more years.*

# THREE

## BROKEN SLEEP

Palm trees swayed in the slight breeze with a soft swish. The bright sun caressed Bill Mason's bare skin with its warm touch. Beautiful women lounged on the white sand. Perfect white caps broke on the shore.

A vibrating, subtle buzz cut through the air. Cocking his head, Bill listened. *Strange, sound always has an origin point. This one doesn't. Not much reverb or depth either.*

He picked up a handful of sand. As the grains trickled through his fingers, he tried draining the troubled thoughts from his mind.

The hum repeated, but didn't echo.

\* \* \*

*Not tonight. Please, not tonight. Can't I have one night to myself?* Bill groaned, opening his eyes.

Reaching out, he swept the nightstand until he encountered a solid plastic shape. Pulling his cell toward him, he rolled over onto his back. Putting the phone to his ear, he said in a half-dead whisper, "Hello?"

"Bill?" The voice on the other end crashed against the speaker with the force of a panicked horse.

His mind and ears pricked up. The low tone had a feminine flair. He glanced at the bedside clock. Timing was about right, too.

"Jo, is everything okay?"

"I guess." His sister's breathing slowed, but still came in gasps. "I can't get the screams out of my head. They are intense, so is the taste of blood in my mouth."

*Screams and blood? She hasn't gone into this much detail in a few months...* Aloud, Bill prompted, "What triggered this episode, Jo?"

"Another horse bound for San Fernando made an unexpected stop here."

"Is there anything unusual about this horse?"

"Yes," Jo's timbre flattened as if she stood in front of a superior officer giving a report, "according to his records, he's Alabaster's son."

Keeping his inflection neutral, Bill wondered, "You're not thinking of doing anything else but sending him away, are you?"

"Well, I kind of already did," her voice caught before she stammered on. "We met in the woods. At first, I wanted nothing to do with him, but then we clicked and I found myself leading him back to the stables."

Bill's skin tingled. His sister not freaking out during an encounter with a horse was the breakthrough that he and the rest of the family had been waiting for. He just wished it hadn't involved an equine of *that* particular bloodline.

"How did you feel?"

"Like my old self. Now, I'm back to being a limp weenie," Jo whined, "who's scared of her own shadow."

An inadvertent chuckle escaped Bill's lips. The tremors in his sister's voice worried him, but he found hope in her words. She had acknowledged her paralyzing fear of horses, which she almost never did.

"I'm stuck down here in San Diego for one more session." Bill willed himself through the cell towers that connected them, hoping she felt some of his strength embracing her. "Keep holding onto your old self as much as you can until I see you in two days, okay?"

"I'll try," Jo yawned. "I'm going to try and catch some more sleep, if I can. Night."

"Night."

Putting the phone down, Bill fluffed his pillows and leaned into them with a sigh.

Soft moonlight filtered through the window. The digital clock on the nightstand glowed with enough light to read the digits, but not disturb him.

Closing his eyes, Bill waited to disappear.

Not wanting the rivalry between LA and SF to take over their lives during the 2005 Championship Series, Jim decided the family needed some time together before the competition. With Ben's help, he arranged a surprise reunion a week before the competition started. Out of courtesy and respect, Jo's Chief Medical Officer extended Bill practice privileges. In return, he agreed to serve one duty shift at the hospital. He put off fulfilling the commitment until the last possible day.

Bill was the general surgeon on call when his sister's bloody mass rolled through the ER doors. Any other job, any other place, and he would have excused himself for being family. In this case, family was the reason he stayed, and the CMO let him take charge of Jo's treatment.

His sister's medical file read like a textbook of everything that could go wrong with drug interactions. Aspirin acted like sleeping pills. Allergy meds made her hyper. Antibiotics gave her flu-like symptoms. The CMO didn't want to risk his career on someone following established protocol and killing his superior, because they couldn't predict her reaction to the drugs or dosage they prescribed.

At first, Bill tried to care for his sister as both her brother and doctor. When the recovery plan shifted from down and dirty life-threatening injury repair to long-term rehabilitation, his empathy prevented him from being firm and objective whenever she was uncooperative. To keep himself focused and her on task, he started leaving his compassion in the closet every time he put on his scrubs. That habit solidified and added another hardened layer to his calm exterior. He still felt everything, though, and feared the inevitable day his control slipped.

Bill tossed onto his side. A horse's natural instinct was fight or flight. They bit, stomped, and kicked, but only when provoked or spooked. A deliberate attack to maim and kill was rare, almost unheard of, unless the horse was threatened or abused. Jo had done nothing to Alabaster, except ask him to move out. Jim had only tried to save her.

Unlike his sister, his brother had survived the attack unscathed. A busted rib and a broken arm were the extent of his physical injuries. When those healed, he was back training and riding with no hesitation.

Not wanting to spend yet another night trying to solve the mystery of Alabaster, Bill imagined a black hole expanding across his vision. The circle was about the size of a half-dollar when his phone rang again. Opening his eyes, he rolled over, grabbed the cell, and answered with a sharp whine, "You too, Jim?"

The voice chuckled, "Yeah, well, I got hit double tonight, by my own nightmare, and then Jo roaring in with hers."

Bill tightened his lips. Jo and Jim had no problem talking to him or the rest of the family about almost anything. Their conversations with each other focused on status reports and operational procedures. Some emotional topics, like birthdays, holidays, or other celebrations, crept in on occasion. Anything to do with Jo's accident caused at least a week of silence between them.

After a long, deep exhale, Jim stated, "It's not my survivor's guilt, Bill. I'm still having a hard time with losing my command."

Technicalities were a bitch. Jim, a loyal and seasoned officer, had lost out because of one. He was a Captain and two steps below the needed rank for being in charge of a Command Base, but he knew the inner workings of USMB San Francisco better than most. He had been her master for nine of the last ten years; replacing Jo at LA for one during her recovery.

"What about Jason's offer?"

"I'm not taking a command someone hands me by pulling in some favors," Jim snorted.

"Then why don't you join me on my road trip? Meet me in LA and we can the drive back to SF together."

"I have no official reason for going down there."

*Yes, you do. Jo...* Bill stopped himself. Jim didn't need to hear that kind of news over the phone. *I need evaluate the situation, and then bring the rest of them in.* Aloud, he stated, "Family is a great unofficial one, Jim."

No response from the other end.

*Did he just hang up on me?* Lowering the phone, Bill stared at its face. The display showed app icons on lighthouse wallpaper instead of the in-call screen with Jim's picture. *When did family become enough of a curse word to provoke that kind of reaction?*

Thumbing through his address book, he looked for anyone he could talk to. *Jason? Not until he makes his first office appearance in another seven hours. Jeff? A little better, given the two-hour time difference and the fact he's an early riser. Ben? Maybe, but Jo would have called him first. Vince? He might wake up ready to tear into me. Michelle? She's dealing with her own stuff and doesn't need this piled on top of it. Michael, Tyrell, TJ, or John? Maybe John since he's a night owl...* Bill's finger hovered above his brother's image. *Nah, the emotions of the situation will leave him distracted, if not lock him up.*

He threw the phone in the direction of the nightstand. As if mocking him, the device rattled across the wood before landing on the floor with a soft thump.

# FOUR

# CHANGE OF PLANS

The brightness of the day worked its way under his eyelids. Bill stretched and opened his eyes. Rolling on his side, his gaze drifted to the digital clock. *11:30...No, that can't be right.* He raised his arm and checked his watch. *Yes, it is,* he moaned. *Crap.*

The symposium he planned his trip around had finished an hour ago. Some ongoing research out of New York on post-traumatic stress disorder had mapped fear memories to a specific nucleus in the brain. This morning's meeting was to discuss possible drug and non-drug treatments based on the findings.

A few of the participants were attending the gala dinner planned for later in the evening. Given the number of conference attendees, his chances of grabbing their attention were slim to none. Even if he did get lucky, he'd have maybe a second or two to ask one of his many questions.

*Will I get any meaningful answers? No, just a few muttered words, and then they'll move on to someone else. I'm better off emailing the research team when I get home.*

Throwing off the covers, Bill swung his legs over the side of the bed. Outside his window, the midday sun hung over the ocean as surf rolled in and out along the shore. People of all ages played in the waves or sunned themselves on the sand.

Not as pristine or uncrowded as his dream, but water was water and he had already prepaid for another night. There was also the crab shack up the street that he wanted to try. Only open since the first of the year, it had already received a couple of awards for having some of the best seafood south of Seattle.

*A well-deserved mini-vacation, if there is one...* The more his thoughts traveled in that direction, the more his lips twitched upwards.

*I need to find out what's going on with Jo and that horse, though.* Bill's smile dropped. *Jim will kill me if anything happens to her. If I leave now, I'll have some extra spending money, miss traffic, and make LA in a couple of hours.*

He needed to call Jason first. Even if he couldn't talk about the horse with anyone else, he had to mention him to his stepfather.

Scanning the room, Bill picked out every other shape but his cell phone. Bending down, he flipped over his shoes, and found nothing in them. Dropping to the floor, he looked under one bed, then the other, only to see lots of empty rug, but not much else. Reaching around the side of the nightstand, his fingers brushed against a spider web before touching the plastic and metal case.

Jerking back, Bill checked for any bites and found one on the back of his hand.

*That* was going on his comment card.

Standing up, he walked over to the dresser, unzipped the outside compartment of his suitcase, and pulled out a collapsible pointer he used during lectures. Extending the metal rod to its full length, he reversed his grip and returned to the nightstand. With one sweep, the cell popped from its hiding place.

Scooping up the device, he looked down at its face. The battery had maybe a sliver left before dying. Retrieving the charger, Bill plugged it into the closest socket and selected Jason's number from his favorites.

The line rang twice before a crisp, efficient voice answered. "Office of the CO USMB California. Lieutenant Commander Kelso speaking."

"Is Admiral Scott in?"

"I'm sorry, sir, but the Admiral is unavailable."

"This is Vice Captain William H. Mason."

"Sir!" Respect flooded Kelso's tone. "Please hold. I'll let him know you are on the line."

A pause, some canned music, and then a deeper voice tinged with a slight brogue asked, "Bill, what's wrong?"

"Jo and Jim both got me last night."

"They get to you almost every night." Jason, their stepfather, had held out the longest, but the flatness in his tone suggested that even he had given up.

"Why am I the only one who gives a damn about what's going on with those two anymore?"

"We all care, lad," Jason's rebuke was soft and firm, "even Jim and Jo do to some extent."

"Yeah, right. I can't remember the last time they had a meaningful conversation."

"Da may not be sharin' words, lad," Jason's brogue thickened with his passion. "Da still keep an eye on each 'ther, though. Remember Jim's botched rock climbin' trip last year?"

"He got lucky on that one." His brother, while not an adrenaline junkie, couldn't resist a good rock or two. The more difficult the climb, the freer he felt. The particular mountain Jim had chosen to release himself on had the reputation of sending challengers home with at least a few bruises, if not broken bones. A rescue team and its aerial support, training in the area, saved him from that fate.

"Luck 'twas na involved. The lass sent her crew ta shadow him. Jim returned da favor last week. He volunteered San Francisco as da new Command Base so da upper echelon winna take LA away from her."

"*What?*" Jim had talked about the transfer of command for over two weeks with no hint of the sacrifice. That didn't surprise or worry Bill as much as the blatant disregard of tradition by the senior staff. "Why are they questioning Jo's ability to handle her command? Despite her self-confidence issues, the base has maintained operations with a spotless record."

"Maintained is the key word, LA should be setting the standards," Jason stated, his brogue setting back into its softer, almost unnoticeable, range. "They don't want the base to fade into obscurity. Everything started there, after all."

In 1850, the United States government formed the Los Angeles Mounted Scouts as a small, mounted unit that could blend in with the local pioneer and native population. Lt. Colonel Robert C. Mason led the LAMS for eleven years until it split along Confederate and Union lines at the beginning of the Civil War. A Union officer, Colonel Mason transferred his command to the renamed California Mounted Band. The unit's primary duty was entertaining civilians and troops, but it also participated in front line action at the Battle of Picacho Peak in 1862. After seeing the CMB's effect on morale, Colonel Mason petitioned his superiors to create more units like it across the nation. On July 11, 1865, two days after his death, Congress ratified the United States Mounted Band charter.

"Some are also growing tired of perceived favoritism shown to your family. They feel that no one should be above reproach or discipline."

"We don't think that we are above anything," Bill snorted. "Jo's hit a rough spot, that's all. Other than Jim, she's the most qualified to command LA based on her service record and experience, unless they think that—"

"No, no one has mentioned the op," Jason interrupted, "just cited the mauling. A few key people still back her and accepted Jim's proposal of SF becoming the new Command Base of the USMB instead of LA."

"Was there any talk of giving Jim LA for SF?"

"Aye, but that idea was nixed because they didn't want Jo to have any influence on him."

"Jo would have stayed out of his way. She's a good officer who knows her duty. We all do."

"The only way the upper echelon will back off is if Jo and Jim present a united front. I can't, and won't, issue orders thrusting them in each other's lives."

None of his family liked pulling rank on one another. Their level of formality when they were in uniform was as high as the people around them needed it to be. Bill liked the arrangement, most of the time. *Until a situation like this comes up,* he swallowed a majority of his sigh, *when the normal structure isn't there to take care of the business being family cannot.* Aloud, he stated, "I'm headed to LA after I check out. I'll work on Jo."

"Good, so other than those two, why did you call?"

*Say something about the horse,* his mind urged.

*No, I can't add that worry to this new, more pressing concern,* he argued.

"They were the only reason."

# FIVE

## METAL VS FLESH

"That's a good looking piece of horse flesh, Jo!" my cousin exclaims after glancing at the horse.

"Yes, he is."

The stocky, tending toward athletic, Commandant of the USMB Academy appeared on my doorstep this morning without any warning. Jeff never hops the red eye from Houston to LA unless his gut keeps him from sleeping after he talks to me. In this case, he planned the trip as soon as the rumors about me having a horse hit the scuttlebutt network, a little over forty-six hours ago. He couldn't get away from his responsibilities until last night, though.

The horse is no longer just the horse. I now call him Dreamer's Hope or DH for short. Dreamer honors Double D's memory and the secure feeling he always gave me. Hope signifies just that.

As long as DH remains in his stall and another person accompanies me, I can tolerate standing around him. Up close, other horses still scare me, but I can watch them from a distance or on television. It'll be a while before I'll handle DH or another horse in the open again.

The rumors about DH spread so far and fast that even people I haven't heard from in a few years are calling. Five of my six brothers don't even bother with a quick text inquiry.

Bill came up yesterday, a day earlier than planned. We spent almost all night talking about family stuff, Jim's loss of SF, and my horse. He declined my invitation to tag along on this little outing, saying that he needed to do some laundry before heading home. Though he promised not to leave, I expect the house will be empty when Jeff and I return.

I mutter a few choice words under my breath.

"Something wrong, Jo?" Jeff prompts.

"Brother trouble."

"Well—"

My nostrils flare. "Well, what?"

"Nothing that you haven't heard before," Jeff shrugs.

Older than me by five years, Jeff acts more like my big brother than my cousin. Like Bill and Ben, I can call him anytime my fear has a stranglehold on me. His quiet certainty mirrors Jim's laid-back attitude and shields his underlying intensity and sensitivity.

Jeff runs his hand through his deep brown, almost black, hair before offering it, palm up, to DH. My horse sniffs, bares his teeth, and snaps. Jerking back, Jeff taps him on the neck. DH tosses his head.

A familiar warm sensation pulses through my body. Taking a deep breath and pushing it aside, I ask in a calm voice, "What's the real story behind DH, Jeff?"

"What do you mean, *real* story, Jo?" Jeff snorts, "All I wanted to do was see him and congratulate you. I think he might be the horse I transferred to Philly three years ago to help with their breeding program."

"Is he?"

Jeff nods.

"Then how do you explain your actions?"

"Of tapping him on the neck because he tried to bite me?" Jeff's tone jumps half an octave. Settling back down into his normal range, he adds, "I was trying to distract him without scaring him, or have you forgotten that's how you correct a nipping horse?"

"No, I haven't." Pointing to the welts on the side of DH's neck, I sharpen the edge in my voice. "What about those? Are they your handiwork?"

"Of course not!" Jeff growls. "When I find out who's responsible, they'll feel a whip on *their* ass."

"They are at the Academy."

"What are you talking about? Nobody there did this."

Hot power surges forward. "No more lies!" I snap. "According to his records, DH never left Houston before his trip to San Fernando."

"I put him on the trailer to Philly, myself." Jeff backs up a few steps with his hands held out. "The Academy Herdmaster and at least three of his staff were witnesses." Planting his feet, he crosses his arms. His hazel eyes flash, daring me to challenge him.

Raising my chin, I meet his gaze. I'm not backing down. I can't. DH's body and records contain proof that he suffered abuse at the Academy.

Even if Jeff is only a bystander by hearsay, he is still the commanding officer of that base. That makes him responsible for his crew's actions, and therefore DH's suffering.

Captain, I'm sure there is a logical explanation to all this," Ben offers from behind me. When Bill refused, I asked him to accompany us in case Jeff needed to take DH out of his stall.

Keeping my gaze locked on Jeff, I prompt, "How do you figure, Mr. Harrison?"

"Maybe his paper records were never updated. A quick inquiry of Transportation Command, Houston, Philly, or all three will clear the matter up."

"All three," I bark.

Ben relays the request.

As the moments tick by, my innate trust in Jeff begins weighing on me. For as tough as he acts on the outside, Jeff is a tender heart who won't allow anyone or anything to suffer under his watch. I've lost track of the numerous times he has said or done something to protect me and brought harm on himself as a result.

Ben's phone beeps. After a few muttered words, he says, "Cap, Academy Houston confirms Jeff's story. Transportation Command and Philly both deny it."

"It's your call, Jo," Jeff shrugs.

I swear again, this time a little louder. The evidence for each side of the abuse argument stands in front of me. I can't refute either, nor can I choose between them. Chewing my lip and thoughts, I try to devise a logical explanation that balances both. After dismissing all other possibilities because they are too far-fetched, I'm back to my original dilemma.

Lowering my eyes, I turn away. "I trust you, Jeff, but—"

"You still believe I, or someone at my base, may have something to do with hurting DH," Jeff finishes.

I nod. "I'm sorry."

"No need to apologize, Jo. Everything we have points in that direction. I'll find you irrefutable proof that he was hurt somewhere else. Better yet, I'll track down the person responsible."

While the tension has eased between us, I'm still uneasy. I've been living with anger, fear, and frustration for years, internalizing and justifying their negativity because of my failures. Now that they've turned on someone else out in the open like this, I need every ounce of my inner strength to keep from exploding with a few choice expletives.

"Jo, what's wrong?" Jeff prompts.

"A lot of things," I shake my head. "We have fallen apart, haven't we?"

"You could say that. DH is only—"

"The latest symptom of that," I finish. "If I hadn't needed to be perfect and in control when dealing with..." The words sputter and die. They are there, ready to come out, but I'm afraid if I speak them, they will be babbling mush through the tears welling up inside me. Gulping a couple of times, I gasp, "so much pain," before my inner dam bursts.

# SIX

# SURPRISE VISIT

TJ Mason watched his brother pace the length and breadth of the living room, trying to distract himself. Walking over to the stereo, Jim flipped through a few channels before snapping it off. Glancing at the rows of CDs in the entertainment center, he tapped his foot, but didn't reach for any of them. The newspaper lying in a chair was his next target. Then the books on the bookshelf drew his attention.

Growing bored with the spectacle, TJ returned to reading his story. His perusal lasted to the end of the page, when Jim plopped down beside him and began shuffling the magazines on the coffee table. The medium-muscular engineer closed the novel, placing it one inch from the edge of the end table on his right side.

"Look, Jim, if you want to put your energy to good use," TJ said in a quiet and measured tone, "there is a whole load of dishes in the kitchen." Jim picked up a glass and almost dropped it. "Then again, maybe you should leave the dishes for me. Go take a run around the block."

"It's not that kind of energy, TJ." Jim stifled a yawn, adding, "My body is ready for bed, but my mind wants to run a marathon."

"Jo?" TJ prompted. His career choice often forced him to deal with hypothetical non-tangibles. The link between his two oldest siblings fell into that category. Though he could not describe the nature of the connection in terms of mass, weight, and dimension, he had seen its impact on Jim and Jo enough to acknowledge its existence.

Jim nodded. "She's taken me on a roller coaster ride today. Decisiveness mixed with doubt. Fear with calmness. Anger weaved into stillness and peace. The contradictions are as baffling as their intensity."

TJ could rattle off the meaning of the words his brother used, but he kept the emotion behind them away from his logic. Dealing with the chaos that was his family was much easier that way.

Letting some of his control slip, he broached a taboo subject. "What if we transferred to LA? Would being closer to Jo ground you?"

Instead of locking up or storming away, Jim stated in an even voice, "I've considered it, but we are better off staying here. Besides our communication problems, Jo has no room on her staff for three of us."

An assistant outranking a department head was unheard of, so was two department heads having a higher rank than the executive officer. Not to mention, three captains on base, unless two were on a temporary duty assignment. All three scenarios would happen if they joined Jo's crew.

"Those aren't the biggest issue, are they, Jim?"

"The talking one is pretty major, but we are doing enough that we could do our jobs. If Jo switches me with Ben, I'll be responsible for her again, and I didn't do so well with that the first time," Jim admitted. "Her disastrous ride on Alabaster is my fault. There were several regs on horses with missing paperwork I could have invoked to prevent her from getting on him."

"Why didn't you?"

"I saw and felt how she connected with him. He buffered her pain over losing Double D. I didn't want to take that solace away from her."

"What if Double D's death wasn't natural? What if Alabaster was more than a birthday gift?"

Jim cocked his head and stared at him. TJ kept his dark-green eyes steady. Every red-brown hair of his military cut laid in perfect formation. No doubt or question in his tone or seated stance. Logic had put the hypothesis together, and he had to focus on that. The possibilities that branched off the conjecture were too horrific to consider.

"That's a lot of what ifs for you, TJ, but Alabaster being some a plant does explain the odd timing between his arrival and Double D's death."

"This leads me to something a little more  theoretical," stated TJ, shifting his gaze down. "What if someone trained Alabaster to attack Jo?"

A sharp, persistent knock left the question hanging between them.

Jim bounded to his feet and across the room. Swinging open the door, he stepped back and drew himself up. Striding past him, a blue-eyed, gray-haired, stalwart man in a loose fitting blue jogging suit entered. TJ started to rise, but the man motioned for him to remain seated.

"Jason, what's going on?"

"Nothing much, lad," Jason replied.

Jeff and Bill, wearing jeans and long-sleeved shirts, crossed the threshold.

"We weren't expecting you back for a few days, Bill. Jeff, I thought you were in the middle of preparing for finals and graduation." TJ grinned. Between his brother's medical knowledge and his cousin's innate calmness, there had to be a way to siphon off enough of Jim's excess energy, so he could sleep.

"I had some business in LA to take care of that was a little more important," Jeff shrugged.

"LA?" TJ echoed. "Is everything okay?"

"I'd say more than okay, TJ," Bill replied.

"How's Jo?" Jim prompted, swinging the door shut.

"I'm fine," Jo replied, pushing it open further. "More than fine, I'm great."

TJ rose to his feet and stiffened. The white dress uniform that strode into the room demanded that respect, and so did the bearing of his sister.

"Relax, TJ," Jo stated, her warm smile filling the room, "this is not an inspection."

Sitting down, he blinked a couple of times. The figure standing before him did not change, which confused him. Last week, when they talked over Skype, his sister was her usual mixture of nerves, random thoughts, and distracted conversation. Now, she stood ramrod straight with a quietness that couldn't hide an intense and direct focus. Even after hearing her speak, he couldn't decide if the transformation was permanent or temporary.

"Jo, what happened?"

"A lot of healing, TJ. Still have more to do, and I need everyone's help." Reaching into her uniform jacket, Jo pulled out a sealed envelope. "Here are the orders necessary to satisfy the bureaucrats." Glancing at Jason, she added, "No offense."

"None taken, lass."

Laying the paperwork on the closest table, Jo opened her arms, wrapped Jim in them, and buried her head in his chest. He draped his arms over hers. She snuggled deeper into him. Stiffening and shuffling back, he leaned into her arms. She loosened her grip. He exerted a little more pressure. She dropped her hands to his hips. One more wiggle and they'd break apart.

*No, you twits, don't!* TJ yelled in his head, surprising himself with the force of his reaction. Family used to mean something. Holidays, including the small ones like Valentine's Day, were once compulsory celebrations of joy, life, and togetherness. He missed the certainty traditions like that brought to his existence.

*If either one of them blows this opportunity, I'll...* TJ stopped. *What will I do? They expect me to be the cool, logical one. Has logic solved this problem, though? Hell, no.*

He leaned forward, readying himself to intervene should they continue their stupidity.

Jim moved closer to Jo, the tension around them easing. Whatever they had shared in their silent language had been enough. TJ settled back into his seat, his lips curling upwards in a slight, almost shy smile. They were as they should be, and as his family would be soon enough. Whole once again.

# SEVEN

## AS IT SHOULD BE

A large transport capable of hauling horses and motorized vehicles sits on the tarmac. Horse trailers, six cars, and a moving truck form a semi-circle around the gaping maw at the rear. Jim stands at the base of the ramp, directing traffic. He's in the shadows, so I'm not sure if they are casting a funny distortion, but his uniform appears off in some way.

Ben approaches my window. "You want me to check on the status of the horses?"

"Yes, please."

Walking up, Bill puts his hand on my shoulder. "It's good to have them back, isn't it?"

I nod.

My tall, well-built, black-haired, blue-eyed brother wears the logo of my base on his sleeve and the pins of my Chief Medical Officer on his collar. The previous owner of that position retired without much notice or fanfare a couple days ago. I have similar pins to make TJ my Chief Engineer. His predecessor asked for a transfer yesterday. My three youngest siblings will blend in with their departments of legal, supply, and information technology. Jim, I'm still trying to figure out what to do with. He qualifies for only one open position on my staff. That of Academy Commandant, a department head.

I already have a department head who outranks Ben in Michelle Holmes. Michelle received her commission of Captain and Commanding Officer of USMB San Bernardino, ten years ago. She refused the base, citing medical reasons. After receiving command of USMBLA, I offered her Jim's vacated Chief of Security position, which she accepted. This allowed her to keep her new rank. Her twin brother, Vince, took over San Bernardino.

"Jo, are you even listening?" Bill's raised tone cuts through my thoughts.

"Sorry, I was thinking about Michelle. What did you need?"

"Are you going to tell the others about DH?"

"No. I want to wait until I can handle him outside of his stall without any help or supervision."

As long as the stall door remains between us, I can stand around DH for hours at a time without anyone else around. He still flinches when I touch his bumps and scrapes, but doesn't jerk back or snap at my fingers if I pet him anywhere else. Chin scratches and butt rubs are his favorites.

My relationship with my horse is one of many things that have changed in the last week. At night, my nightmares are faded in color and detail. Sometimes they don't come at all. Sleep now means rest, which translates into plenty of energy with deep reserves and a less frazzled outlook on life. I'm able to think things through instead of rushing to judgment or second-guessing myself.

"Jim and you working together to rehab DH will be good therapy for all three of you," Bill suggests.

"I don't want to go splat in front of him," I counter. "Ben has agreed to spot me."

"How long will you need?"

"Not sure," I shrug, "but Jim isn't going to go through the records of every horse on this base looking to see if I have one."

"True. Any more info on how DH ended up here?"

"No, but Jeff has determined the mix-ups started with miscellaneous supplies, about five years ago."

"Shouldn't that have triggered an audit?"

"Yes, on many different levels. That's why, this morning, I made the investigation an official assignment of the Auxiliary Team, and offered Jeff the support of John and Tyrell." Between my two brothers and their intimate knowledge of their specialties, the ghost in the logistic machine doesn't stand a chance.

Command Teams are interdisciplinary units with the authority to work inside and outside the command structure. Their missions involve investigating and fixing problems like the failure within the horse and supply chain management system. My team, the Mason Seven Command, Support, and Auxiliary (CSA) Team, is the only multi-unit CT in the USMB. Most of the time, the team operates as its individual components. Jim, Vince, and Jeff are the unit commanders. I'm the overall one.

The USMB is unique among its military peers in respect to family members and groups of friends serving together. While the organization doesn't encourage the practice, it doesn't limit or ban the act. Instead, they require a few more steps for promotions, transfers, and other actions where favoritism might be perceived. Three notable tragedies have struck units with related personnel, but no one has tried to challenge the stance.

I glance over at several large pallets that dwarf the slight man with light brown hair. Of all my brothers, I'd resign my commission before ordering him into harm's way. The youngest of our family, John needs no instruction manual to operate any piece of technology. Computers sing in any key he wants. Expressing emotions and dealing with people are a little harder for him.

Two mirror images stand by another pile of boxes. One holds a clipboard while the other scans the area around him. Michael and Tyrell are the identical twins of the family with medium-stocky builds and hair a few shades darker than John's. Tyrell is a laid-back, fast-talking logistics specialist who lives with trouble and chaos as his constant companions. Michael, a conservative lawyer, protects Tyrell by knowing all modern day and archaic laws, rules, and regulations.

Among the personnel unloading cargo are a pair of lighter blue uniforms. They belong to Jim's son, James C. Mason, Jr., and his best friend. James Jr., or Jimmy to his family and few close friends, is a taller and skinnier version of his father. Duff Cordero is the same height as Jimmy with a stockier build and black hair.

Gesturing toward them, I ask, "How long are the kids here for?"

"Until the end of the month," Bill replies. "After they didn't make this year's Academy team, they requested a COTC assignment that would have allowed them to compete on the SF team. All their instructors signed off on it, but then the change of command happened and a new team was selected."

The Cadet Officer Training Corps supplements the theory of the classroom learning and controlled exercises with the practical experience of base operations. All cadets, except fourth years, are eligible for the program and hold the rank of Ensigns when on assignment. Ensigns, like new enlisted personnel, don't have rank boards.

That's what's wrong with Jim's jumpsuit! His doesn't have any, either. Boards are optional on a collared shirt worn under a dress or show jacket, but mandatory with every other kit. By defying regulation, he is demanding an immediate decision regarding his position at my base.

I both love and hate Jim for the clearest indication of his feelings in years. He should have asked me in private about my plans. Even with Bill and TJ already having their new positions, they haven't changed. I want to give my brothers a few days to settle in and relax before assigning them any responsibilities.

Throwing open the door, I storm toward the plane with short and pounding steps. I no longer want to climb over the wall that separates me from Jim. Hard to define, it's even harder to understand why it still exists. Last week, we had breached the barrier. Now, the rampart needs to be destroyed, once and for all.

"On my six, Bill," I snap. Though the mauling took away my wings, I still think like a fighter pilot where position corresponds to the numbers on an analog clock. Noon's front, three left, nine right, and six back.

Bill follows me without saying a word.

When we are about halfway to the loading ramp, Ben approaches and says, "Captain, wait."

"Are there any more horses to unload?"

"No, sir." Ben gestures toward Jim. "You and your family need to be a team, we all know that."

"Is that why my command structure shifted in the last few days without notice?"

"Yes, sir. He and I are the last piece in the puzzle."

Removing the pins from his collar, Ben replaces them with those of the commandant position. He clutches the symbols of his former office before rolling his fingers open and holding his hand out with them lying in the middle of his palm.

My heart swells and embraces Ben. He always seems to anticipate my needs, but I never would have asked him for any of this.

"Mr. Harrison, I—"

Ben holds up his hand. "No need, Captain."

Taking the pins, I continue moving. My long and flowing stride eats up the remainder of the distance. When I stop in front of Jim, he draws his shoulders back and assumes a rigid posture.

Undoing one of the boards from my uniform, I fill the empty spot on his shoulder and offer Ben's old pins to him on the flat of my hand. Jim glances between them and me several times. In his eyes, I see clouds of sadness raining upon a gray landscape colored with a few shades of hope.

With my free hand, I take his and place it over mine, saying, "Jim, your place is, and always has been, by my side. Just as mine is by yours."

"I failed you," he protests.

"How?"

".Alabaster—"

"You charged into the ring to save me from him."

"Before that, I—" Jim looks down at the ground.

"What could you have done? I was so drawn to him, I would have overruled anything that prevented me from riding him," I snort. "Yes, the regulations manual isn't one of my favorite books to read, but I am aware of what's in it. Our—no, *my*—handling of Alabaster violated at least half a dozen rules."

Glancing over at the light blue uniforms, I sigh. Jim's ex-wife kidnapped Jimmy the day Alabaster attacked me. The year that followed divided his attention and left him burdened with the responsibly of my base when his complete focus should have been on finding his son.

Taking Jim's chin in my hand and lifting it until our gazes lock, I say, "It's I who should apologize to you."

# EIGHT

# CAT AND MOUSE

The house was as quiet as it could be with five other people sleeping. Jim lay on his bed, enjoying the snores and other night sounds. The squeaks and taps of someone walking downstairs from his left and out the front door was Jo heading out on a late night errand. No alert klaxon, so that meant either someone had blown a minor issue beyond their pay grade, or she wanted to spend more time with Ben.

Rolling to his side, he closed his eyes and willed his body to sleep. While most of his muscles relaxed, his brain kept firing off random thoughts about Jo. Flipping on his back, he counted down from ten. *Ten transfers to write, nine vet appointments to supervise, eight movies to review for language and decency...*

The further he counted down, the more his mind ramped up.

Jim grabbed his tablet from the nightstand. He checked on anything he had forgotten, and any reason for Jo's disappearance. His schedule was full, but not packed. The base's status feed scrolled through the usual mundaneness of the late shift. His hand hovered over the locator app that would pinpoint Jo and Ben's exact location. He tapped on the e-book reader instead.

Losing himself in a world of swords and sorcery, he ebbed and flowed with the story until stumbling in the midst of a battle. *Author chewed the dog with an ex can of beans? No, wait...* He read the sentence two or three times before it made any sense. *Ah, Arthur challenged the dragon with Excalibur!* Putting the tablet down, he yawned and stretched. *One last check on everyone and I'll join you on your quest in my dreams, sir knight.*

Moving between each room, keeping his steps light so as not to disturb the sleepers, Jim peered in on the still forms. Each shape was as unique as the person who made it. In their separate rooms, Michael and Tyrell mirrored each other while the orderliness of their covers reflected their personalities.

Jim started to leave Bill's doorway and move onto Jo's room when his brother whispered, "She isn't back yet."

"Do you know why she is out this late?"

37

"She said she is conducting an inspection."

"Why at night for over a week with Ben?" Jim objected. "I'm her second-in-command."

"Given how big this base is, it might take at least two weeks at odd hours to keep everyone honest. As for why Ben, my guess is they have done so many together, they have an established routine that Jo will teach you."

One of the stairs squeaked. Jim stepped back, pressing himself against the wall. He closed the door until there was a small crack for him to look through. A shadowy form crossed his line of vision. It kept going straight instead of turning toward him. *Good, Jo's returned from wherever she was.*

Jim waited until she closed her door before emerging from his hiding spot. An unexpected odor tickled his nose as he approached her room. Sweet saltiness suggested that she had just gone through something strenuous. A warmer, heavier scent inspired comfort in most people, but in her, panic. No bitterness of fear, though.

Returning to Bill's room, Jim asked, "Does Jo have a horse?"

"Yes, I met him my first day here. He's the real reason for Jo's late night meetings with Ben."

"*What?*" Jim almost yelled, but caught himself so the word came out a strangled whisper. "Then why the cockamamie line about the inspection?"

"I feared this exact reaction. He isn't his father."

"His father? The horse is Alabaster's son?"

"Yes."

Jim headed for the door.

The floor squeaked as the light behind him snapped on, filling the room with a soft off-white glow.

"Wait," Bill hissed.

Wheeling, Jim spat, "No, I have to stop this madness."

"Slow down and listen for a few seconds, okay? I've escorted Jo down to the stables a couple of time and met him. Yes, the horse is a stallion, but he isn't that much of a hothead. Also, he was abused and on his way to San Fernando for some rehab when he ended up here."

"Yet another reason for me to interfere."

"No, it isn't."

Glaring upwards, Jim dared the big man to continue.

Without hesitating or flinching, Bill reached for his tablet and tapped on it. Handing the device to Jim, he said, "Here's his official record."

Except for his sire and the extra appendices trying to correct incomplete, incorrect, or missing information, the horse had nothing too alarming in his history. A few thrown riders, but in each case the rider had caused the spill. The list of bases associated with the horse piqued Jim's curiosity. Of the four, half had a Mason as the CO, and the other half, Nolan. *I wonder if anyone else has noticed this coincidence?*

Glancing at the horse's name, Jim smiled. *Dreamer's Hope? That's appropriate, I guess.* Aloud, he inquired, "If he so safe, why she is working with him at night?"

"She doesn't want an audience until  she can handle him on her own."

The cold, analytical distance in Bill's voice irritated Jim's raw nerves. He snapped, "Aren't you worried that she might be in danger?"

"No, I trust both Ben and Jo."

"Are you saying I *don't?*"

"Not at all," Bill waved him off. "I think you want Jo, her life, and your relationship with her fixed yesterday. It can't be. She's a spooked horse. You have to approach her in a slow and deliberate manner."

"Is that how you've been so successful in helping her?"

"Pretty much."

Jim returned the tablet. Back in his bedroom, he'd study the horse's record in detail and, if needed, write a transfer order removing him from the base. *Sure, Jo will be angry, and might not speak to me for a few weeks, but so be it. At least, this time, I'll have prevented her from getting hurt.*

Taking a few steps toward the door, he stopped and turned. "Bill, do you realize that tomorrow night is the last one before a California team has to declare?"

"I've already voiced that concern to Ben. He's reassured me that he will talk her out of it, if the subject arises."

"Do you think he can make a convincing enough argument?" Jim chuckled. "Even *I* have a hard time getting Jo to agree to something when her stubborn streak kicks in."

"You haven't seen her with this horse. They are like she and you used to be. Anticipating each other, they play off their combined strengths and weaknesses. Even if she thinks she's ready, she won't go if he isn't."

# NINE

# FIRST RIDE

The first four nights after my brothers' return, Ben and I conducted a long overdue base inspection. Part of that time, we also worked with DH in and around his stall. After being able to lead him on a long walk without shaking, I intended to introduce my horse to my brothers. Then I thought more about it and decided to continue in secret until I could manage riding him one lap around the training ring without falling off. Five more sessions and I can pick up DH's feet, groom him, tug on his mane and tail, and do everything else short of throwing my leg over his back without feeling any discomfort or hesitation.

Tonight, I'm going to see if I remember how to ride.

Even with the decades of horsemanship programmed into my nervous system and muscle memory, I'm not sure I will give DH the right signals. Working with him on the ground, I caused a couple of unexpected reactions. I was able to move out of the way and then figure out what had caused the problem. On his back, I won't have any buffer. One miscue on my part could send him bolting for the hills with me as an unwilling passenger.

Stepping back, I take a deep breath and admire my handiwork. DH's bay coat sparkles under the arena's lights. Every line and crease of his tack can pass the scrutiny of a show judge. His head is up, but he isn't pulling on the rope that hitches him to the rail.

A shadow crosses my peripheral vision. Turning, I peer out into the murkiness. All I perceive are indistinct lumps. Using my innate connection with Jim, I try to feel if he is nearby. Nothing definitive comes back.

Returning my focus to DH, I wonder, *Left or right?*

Mounting near side means putting my left foot in the stirrup and swinging my right leg over. Off side, the legs are reversed. If DH isn't trained to expect that approach, he will lash out or spook, leaving me hanging in mid-air.

"Captain, let's continue this tomorrow." Ben, sitting on the rail near me, yawns and stretches.

"We are here now." I run my fingers between the girth and DH's skin. The two-finger fit hasn't changed since the last time I checked. "I need to know if I can at least get on him."

"Why are you pushing it?"

I glance at my watch, noting that it's minutes into the new day. "Today is the 20th. By Noon Pacific, we have to declare."

Ben's white teeth flash against his skin, which almost blends in with the darkness behind him. "I don't think we should. You said yesterday that even if you manage to ride DH, your skills are rusty, and your stamina is shot. How will you manage one event, let alone weeks of a demanding show and travel schedule?"

"I'll find a way."

"What happens if they put you into a Camas Prairie Stump Race?" Ben challenges. "Will you be able to control your fear in such close proximity to the other horse and rider? What about keeping DH calm enough to have a clean start?"

A Camas Prairie Stump Race involves completing the traditional cloverleaf of a barrel race as a match race. Two horses start and finish in the center of the ring and run their pattern at opposite ends. First one back to the starting point wins.

My eyes follow the saddle from stirrup to horn. Somehow, the space between them has grown. I swallow, "I can't answer your questions, Ben, because I haven't even made it off the ground yet."

"That's my point, Captain, neither of you are ready. Do whatever you have to do to ride tonight. Tomorrow, or in the next few days, introduce DH to your brothers. Worry about next year's Championship Series after you have done a few shows."

"Sound advice, Ben. Thanks."

"No problem," Ben replies. "Do you need a hand up?"

I shake my head. Per show and performance regs, riders have to mount and dismount their horse unassisted. I decide on the riskier offside approach so I don't have to pivot on my bad knee.

Unhitching DH from the rail, I lead him toward the middle of the ring. As my feet move across the sand, my thoughts wander to a similar moment nine years ago. *Different time, different horse,* my inner voice reminds me. *He trusts you. Trust him.*

Stopping a few feet away from the spot where I mounted Alabaster, I check DH's girth and tighten it. Moving to his right side, I put my right foot in the stirrup, and touch the saddle with my left hand. My awareness turns inwards, so all I see and feel is my horse. Everything else is just a shadow.

Do the shadows and ghosts win again tonight? No.

I start hopping.

Each bounce sends me up, but the secondary thrust of my right leg doesn't give me enough height to clear DH's back. After half a dozen tries, my knee aches and threatens to slip. With one last shove, I grab for leather and use the saddle as a ladder to climb into my seat.

Despite the awkward and lengthy mount, DH remains motionless underneath me. Gathering the reins in my hands, I urge him forward. He steps out with a brisk stride. Fearing that he will explode into a wild run, I squeeze hard with my legs. DH continues at a steady pace despite my involuntary signal for more speed. Easing back on the reins, I release the pressure. He slows to a plod.

*Okay, this is good. Nice, slow walk is good.*

With each step, the stiffness melts from my body. I sink deeper into the saddle, finding that old familiar spot where my balance adjusts itself with the ebb and flow of my mount's movement. About halfway down the long side of the fence, my eyes turn away from their fixation with the space between DH's ears. Glancing to my left, I swear I can almost see a dark, red spot.

For a moment, I am on the back of Alabaster, right before his bucking spree. DH rattles his lips, but the rhythm of his stride remains steady. Taking a deep breath, I chant in my head, *This is not Alabaster. This is DH. He's doing his job. Do yours.*

My gaze returns to DH's ears. Both are forward, listening. Every so often, one swivels back in my direction. "I'm okay, boy," I say. "Keep going nice and easy and I'll stay that way."

\* \* \*

After one snail-paced lap, I pull up in front of Ben.

"Well?"

"It's almost as easy as I remember." I shrug, keeping my lips neutral. "How am I sitting?"

"You look comfortable up there."

*If I can pull off comfortable with all this chaos in my head, then maybe...* Shaking the thought from my head, I ease DH away from the rail. I need to try a few more things before making *that* decision.

Walking is fine for entering and exiting the ring. Once inside, I will need to trot, canter, and perhaps even kick DH up to a dead run.

*What if his trot is so rough that I bounce off? Will he stop or...* I erase the image that pops in my mind.

Clucking, I ask for a little more speed. DH complies with a cross between a game of hopscotch gone wrong and a pogo stick attached to a jet engine. My body rattles and rolls around with each beat of his stride. Every bounce loosens my seat a little more.

*One good jar and...* I jerk on the reins before my imagination fills in the details. DH returns to his silky smooth walk. Even at this gentle pace, my left knee twinges. The joint has ached worse after a long walk, so I ignore the warning and make one more circuit.

* * *

Stopping in the center of the ring, I wiggle both feet out of the stirrups. My left leg stops complaining. I lean forward, putting my hands on either side of DH's neck in front of his withers. Swinging my right leg over, I manage to clear both the saddle and his haunches without kicking him. Sliding down, my right foot touches the ground just before my left. I brace myself and put weight on my bum knee. It buckles, almost pitching me into DH's side. Straightening up, I lean on his shoulder to keep myself steady.

"Jo, you okay?" Ben calls out.

"I need a minute." Taking a deep breath, I fight to keep the tears from my voice and my face. Even if DH's trot hadn't bounced any ideas of competing in this year's series from my head, this did. While not as bad as the splat I had feared them seeing, I'm grateful that my brothers aren't here for my humble and pained limp back to the ring's entrance.

# TEN

# SILENT NIGHT,
# DEADLY LIGHT

Standing on the porch outside my bedroom, I glance up at the star-filled sky. The stillness of the night combined with Jim's warm presence makes everything seem so perfect and complete. Leaning my arm on the metal rail, I prop up my chin. Jim mirrors my movement.

I'm back to having three shadows again: my physical one, the one I carry around in my head, and Jim. The first two I accept as a part of me, and ignore. When I'm around Jim, we speak thousands of words in silent conversation. Away from him, I feel a hum that fluctuates with what he's feeling. Our innate comfortableness with each other has returned, stronger than ever.

A warm touch melts the tension in my shoulders. Jim prompts, "Everything okay, kiddo?"

"Yeah, just thinking about a lot of things."

"Like what?"

"You, me, our family, and the series."

Tomorrow, a team from my base travels to San Francisco. Three days after that, we start competing against twenty-two other teams at the state preliminaries of this year's Championship Series.

Accepting our place was a joint decision between my brothers and me. They were at home waiting for me to limp in the door after my rookie display of horseback riding. As my invisible audience, they witnessed both my mistakes and determination. They felt I should make an appearance in the competition, if only to show the upper echelon, and all my other doubters, that I was back in command. John—bless him and his love of statistics—pointed out that we had a 21.73913 percent chance of making it past the first round, given that only the top five moved onto the state championships.

"What if we beat John's odds?" I wonder.

"Then we enjoy the glorious adventure for as long as it lasts," Jim smiles. "Like we agreed, I'll be the lead rider and do all the extra riding that goes with the position. Bill will try and make sure you don't overdo it with your knee."

"He can try, but he might not succeed," I chuckle. It already feels like I've overdone it. I'm sore, so sore that my aches have aches, if that's even possible. The only part of me that's not hurting is my knee. Bill's fitted me with a brace that supports the joint while giving me enough flexibility to ride.

Spending at least two hours a day in the saddle since that first ride, eight days ago, I can now post to DH's bouncy mess of a trot. We've even done a few laps at a canter and run. The former feels as familiar and comfortable as an old rocking chair, while the latter hits me with a rush of power and speed that leaves me breathless.

My cell buzzes against my hip. I glance at the text message, shake my head, and shoot off a quick response.

"Problem?"

"No, Casper checking up on me."

"He's been doing that almost every day. Don't you think that's a little strange? The screw-ups between the two bases have stopped."

"Not at all. Casper called the day DH arrived here. Said he didn't want me to interact with him because he was just like his father. I guess he's still convinced that DH might turn on me."

"Has Jeff found the one responsible for the mix up in DH's paperwork, yet?"

"He's still working various angles, but he now has the birth certificates of the colt and two fillies that DH sired in Philly. Jeff's having genetic test run on the offspring, but he isn't expecting those results back for a few weeks. It's unclear if DH came from there, though, since the last few years of his record are still incomplete."

"Sounds like Anthony might have problems at his base that he wants to cover up."

"It's one of the leads Jeff is pursuing."

Jim breathes in and out with short, quick snorts. "You smell that?"

A bitter, acrid smell tickles my nostrils. I stretch to my full height, hoping to catch the pleasant after aroma of barbecuing meat. Instead, the rotten mixture of burning leather and horsehair gags me. On the horizon, beyond the silhouette of the neighborhood houses, a glow sends my heart flying to my throat.

Multiple screams of horses in trouble pierce the air.

Both our phones beep.

Above this din, the alert klaxons wail.

Slapping his leg, Jim sweeps his cell toward his face. The phone's pale light accents the worry lines around his mouth and eyes. "Fire in the main stable," he breathes the confirmation of my dreaded assumption.

I grab my phone. My text has a few more details. One barn's already involved. A few stalls on either side of it have collapsed, trapping some horses.

Hitching the cell back on my hip, I rush through the sliding door, across my bedroom, down the stairs, out the front, and toward the driveway. As I move, footsteps fall in behind me. No words are spoken. None are needed. Fire is a comforting friend and a dangerous enemy. The fact that it has made an appearance at the main stable tonight is no accident or coincidence.

* * *

The buildings of the main stable form a horseshoe around an open, unpaved area. Eight barns store the feed and tack as well as house the stable hands. Interspersed between these barns are ten sections of stalls. Each section has ten rows. Each row holds ten horses.

Color and light flood the courtyard. The blue and red globes of the emergency vehicles throb against the yellow and orange wall of flame that engulfs the middle barn. Smaller flickers dance near the closest rows on either side. Horses and humans weave in and out of the light.

The sound of ordered chaos hits me as soon as I step out of the family SUV. Neighs and nickers cut through the shouts of those battling the flames. Some are soft and questioning, others panicked cries.

Scanning my immediate area, I spot the red and white incident commander's car. The two men leaning over the back end can't be more different in appearance or attitude. Saddle-worn, weather-hardened, tall, and lean Ed Hobbs has served as the base's Herdmaster since I was knee high to him. Gleaming with as much brash cockiness as his badge, rock-solid, ex-football lineman Hank Jones is a year into his new role as battalion chief.

Walking up behind them, I listen in on their conversation and the radio chatter from their walkies. From what I gather, most of the horses are safe. A few in the back rows, including DH, are refusing to leave their stalls. At least ten horses, including Fury, are trapped or unaccounted for.

After a grunt from Hobbs and a quick intake of breath by Jones, I jump in with "Status report, gentlemen."

Both men turn, straighten, and salute. I accept and return the courtesy before firing off, "Any injuries or deaths? What was the cause?"

Jones doesn't hesitate or mince his words. "Arson, sir. We had a unit on scene within two minutes of the initial report of smoke. As they pulled in, the barn exploded."

Hobbs glances at his clipboard before adding, "No human causalities. The grooms were out making their final checks. We are still sorting out the head count on the horses."

"Very good, gentlemen. Carry on."

"Yes, sir," the two men chorus, returning to their reports and maps.

Walking back to the car, I stick my head in the driver's side window. "Bill, coordinate with the medical team. Tyrell, get with Hobbs and see if you can't get some word to those waiting behind the security line for news on their horses. The rest of you, come with me."

# ELEVEN

# SO MUCH GAINED,
# SO MUCH TO LOSE

DH paces back and forth, bobbing his head and snorting. Dark sweat spots splotch his hide, and white foam drips from his mouth. Every so often, a whinny cuts through the air. He stops, pricks his ears forward, and whistles. A heartbeat later, he starts moving again.

"Easy, boy, easy," I sing.

DH nickers, but doesn't stop pacing.

I'm tempted to open his stall and let him bolt. The size of the base stops me from carrying through with the idea. Despite the fire and the delays it will cause, I am still planning to be in SF with my team. Given the unknown status of Fury, DH is now the lead horse.

His momentum carries him to the back. Unlocking the door, I slip in.

Mirroring his movements, I weave my way closer to him. A touch on the side lets him know he is not alone. Working my way to his front, I snap the lead rope on his halter. He tosses his head. I tighten my grip, pull him towards me, and slip a blindfold over his eyes. He sighs and shakes. The tension eases out of the line.

I rub his shoulder. "Let's get out of here, boy."

\* \* \*

DH's shoes click and clack against the pavement. The comforting cadence blends in with the sirens of more units responding to the fire, the clang of aluminum holding pens being erected, and the general noises of my base, which is awake and alert as if it's mid-day. The parking lot that separates the main training and performance rings has become the logistics area for the incident. Horse trailers are lined up and loading their precious cargo for transport. Beyond the carriers, tents serving various functions. We walk past all this until reaching the rings. None of the horses milling around in either one belong to my family.

Ice grips my heart. I can't lose any of my brothers in this mess. We've had so little precious time back together. Grabbing my cell out of my pocket, I shoot out a quick check-in request.

My phone beeps even before I lower my hand to put it away. Bill replies from the medical tent that his most critical patient is a groom with two busted ribs. TJ asks where I am. John and Michael respond that they are coordinating the housing and transportation of the misplaced horses. A delayed text from Tyrell relays that he was on one of his multiple trips to and from the security perimeter.

Jim's response is a little more direct. After a rush of calm, our connection flutters and settles. Good, he's alive and not in danger.

I lead DH back to the tent city.

*"Jo, wait up!"*

Halting DH, I turn. With a hurried upswing in his otherwise dignified and measured pace, TJ catches up with me. His face, which remains devoid of emotion most of the time, shows an abundance of relief. "Jim texted right before you did. They've cleared rubble and are beginning to reach the trapped horses. We've lost at least three."

My heart drops as I choke out, "Fury?"

"Jim thinks he heard him."

"Where did they move the tack?"

"You're not going back, are you?"

"I have to. I'm not staying here in relative safety while Jim is risking himself for his horse."

"They've set up temporary shelter for all Championship Team horses. Let's stash DH there and then go by car."

The timing of the fire makes me a little wary about keeping that particular group of horses together in one spot. "What about security?"

"Michelle assigned Justin and two units," TJ replies.

Lt. Commander Justin Scott is our stepbrother and Michelle's second in command. Calm and soft-spoken, most of the time, the warrior side of his Gaelic heritage comes out whenever he's assigned a protection detail. No one is getting anywhere near the team's horses.

"Okay, lead the way."

* * *

When TJ and I return to the main stable area, two barns are gone and another two are on fire. Solid lines of people and equipment protect the outer four. My heart sinks when I spot a flatbed truck parked in the open area. Four covered lumps lay in the back.

I sigh.

"You okay, Jo?" TJ prompts. "Should we go back?"

"I'm fine. You see Jim anywhere?"

"Over there." TJ points to a figure standing in the lighted half-circle formed by one of the base's mobile vet clinics and a couple of trailers. Covered in soot and ash, Jim holds Midnight Fury still as one of the vets bends down near his front legs. The doc rises and talks with Jim. A frown and furrowed brows relay all I need to know. DH is still the lead horse.

*You and Fury are safe*, I text Jim. *That's the important part.*

Jim walks to one of the trailers and ties Fury off. My phone dings. *Where are you?*

*Close-by.* Though I run a relaxed base, protocol still demands that salutes and stiff postures acknowledge my presence wherever I go. While I understand the need for structure and discipline, whenever I don't want my rank or position to be a distraction or consideration, I stay in the shadows.

Jim scans his surroundings. Turning in our direction, he smiles. *See you back at the house?*

*No, I'm headed to the incident command area in the parking lot between the main training and show rings. Too wound up for sleep, and too interested in catching whoever did this.*

*Me, too.* His next text isn't very encouraging. *Fury has minor injuries, but the doc doesn't think he should travel.*

*We'll find you another horse. I still want you as the lead rider.*

# TWELVE

# MURPHY'S LAW

Murphy, as in Murphy's Law, must relish in the chaos he causes. The fire investigation and the pairing of six riders, including Jim, with new mounts ate up all our travel days. Instead of driving up early as planned, we had to fly in. Large cargo planes, however, can't land at any of the bases in the Bay Area. The closest one that can accept them is Sacramento. Fine, we go down instead of up, and add two or three hours to our trip. At least that's the new plan until some tourist swerves left instead of right. *Bam!* A chain reaction pile up that shuts down Interstate 80 at the Davis Causeway. The van carrying me, Bill, Michelle, and four other riders ends up ahead of the wreck.

Staring at the dark, groomed dirt of the Cow Palace's indoor arena, I consider my options. Despite the ninety-minutes it took to get here, I still have no idea when I'll see the rest of our caravan. Rules cover a captain not making an appearance at the opening ceremonies of a show. Common sense encompasses a team.

Forfeit.

The word rings hollow in my head. Raising my eyes, I glance at the flags hanging around the edge of the arena, the black and gold of my base among them. *No, I've worked too hard to consider walking away and saying next year.*

Burying my head in my hands, I will myself to find another answer.

Behind me, the seats start filling. Among the squishing of soft soles, the hard crunch of boots against concrete. I don't pay much attention to them until one cadence stops by my side.

A hard-edged voice states, "The scuttlebutt network has its facts straight for once."

Lifting my head, I face a broad-shouldered man with short-cropped sandy-blonde hair and crystal blue eyes. A warm smile cracks his rugged face.

"Sort of." My attempt at a return smile is feeble at best. "Only me and six of my team are here. The rest are stuck in traffic."

Captain Michael V. "Vince" Holmes, decked out in the red and black show uniform of his base, crosses his arms. "The rules don't say how many need to represent a base for tonight's ceremonies."

"True, but the judges and audience both have certain standards." I motion to my uniform. "This is the only thing we have. Every other team has all their horses, instruments, and show kits—plus eighteen more people."

"Let me see what I can do about that."

He strides off.

Another set of boots approaches. These belong to a shorter, feminine version of Vince.

"Hey, Michelle," I greet my Chief of Security. "You just missed Vince."

"He and I said our good-byes until May last week."

Vince and Michelle are friends with an unusual relationship. They are fraternal twins. Michelle hasn't acknowledged Vince as such for almost two decades, though. That's because she can't remember him that way.

Michelle knocked me out of a sniper's line of fire when I froze during a tactical training exercise. Since the incident happened with a civilian police force, the upper echelon didn't recognize it or Michelle's heroics. Instead, they issued a few orders to cover their collective asses. The specific one dealing with Michelle would have given her a new identity and assigned her to a base as far away as possible from Jim, Vince, and me. Jason made sure that didn't happen.

Though all the physical scars have healed, the trauma left Michelle with a severe case of retrograde amnesia. Bill and I are both pleased and amazed by the amount she can remember. We suspect that she reached the end of her recovery a few years back, though.

The incident happened in April, so for that whole month, Vince ignores her. The other months, he treats her as a good friend and fellow officer. He doesn't want to acknowledge her as family until she can do the same.

Growing up, Michelle and Vince were very close. They started and ended each day by saying "I love you," and made sure they always knew where the other was and what they were doing during the in-between times. A few days before the shooting, Michelle confided in me that sometimes she wished Vince would give her a chance to be her own person instead of his mirror image. In the same breath, she admitted she worried he would fall apart if something happened to her. I promised to take care of them both should it come to that.

While I have kept Vince apprised of Michelle, her life, and her progress, I haven't pushed them to be more than friends. I used to think I was taking care of Michelle, and giving her some of the independence she desired, by doing that. Reestablishing a close relationship with Jim after our long separation has changed my perspective on the situation. Despite the orders and his reluctance, I need to facilitate Vince having a more active role in Michelle's life. Without him, she'll never be complete.

* * *

The tall corridor connecting the ring with the other buildings is a little better for blending in. For the first night, while the teams are settling in, security keeps the civilians away. Starting tomorrow, they can roam the grounds and see the individual base displays. Their comments will help the judges decide who moves on to the next round.

In the mixture of work blue, dress whites, and various show colors, I am anonymous. My boards cause their normal swift and expected reaction, but no one notices the logo attached to them.

This gives me the out I need.

It won't be a forfeit, if no one knows we were here. They can carry on with what they've been doing by flying LA's colors and playing its theme in a moment of remembrance and hope. Next year, when we have our full complement—and my riding skills are polished—we will wow everyone.

I can trust Vince to keep his silence.

Finding the closest door, I slip outside. Leaning against the wall are a couple of hay bales. I sit on one and Michelle takes the other. She hasn't said much since we saw Vince. Like him, she's very conservative with her words, but the deepness of her quietness feels different than normal.

"You okay?" I prompt.

"Pretty much," Michelle replies. "The timing of the fire and the wreck is bugging me. Who are we a threat to? I'm coming up blank."

My phone rings. Glancing at its face, I answer, "Hey, Jim. Please tell me you are close."

"No such luck. They've managed to clear one lane, so we are getting through, but it's slow going. After we clear this, we'll have to deal with the commute all the way in. I'm beginning to worry about the horses."

"Return to Sacramento, take care of them, and then get here when you can."

According to the schedule I received after accepting our place, the festivities begin at seven, and we perform at nine. Backing out enough time for driving, unloading, and tacking up, I calculate Jim's next move. "If you aren't at the 680 split by 1900, take the horses to Jason's ranch, leave them there, and bring in the team."

"Okay, but that's going to lower our score."

"Not if we aren't here. I haven't checked-in yet."

"Why?"

The word hangs between us until I sigh, "Without you and the rest of the team surrounding me, this isn't turning out how I imagined it. I'd rather wait until—"

"It's too late for that. People have seen you. If you don't ride tonight, it might be enough for the upper echelon to take the base from you. Make the statement you are back, so they don't."

."Ok, if I need to make a fool of myself, I will," I lament, still a little upset about how close I came to losing my base without even knowing it. "See you when you get here. Take your time and be safe."

"Roger that. See you."

My finger taps the off button.

The phone beeps with a text from Bill. *Where are you? Have you heard anything from Jim?*

*I'm outside the staging area with Michelle. They won't get here in time.*

*Ok. We'll be there in a few. Jason arranged a special delivery that should help us blend in a little better.*

"Jo," Michelle touches my leg before pointing off to our right. "Look."

A six-man color guard followed by Jason, my fellow captains, and the base flag bearers in a two-column formation ride toward us. A beautiful, powerful sight made even more so by the black and gold flag of my base and a dapple-gray horse having the honorary lead position behind Jason. From head to tail, the horse's lines remind me of Double D.

Standing up, I walk back inside.

Michelle follows me. "What's wrong?"

"Compared to everyone out there, I'm naked," I reply, motioning to my uniform. "As much as I want to, I can't ride with them. Performing with a team of seven is going to be embarrassing enough."

"Jo, no one cares what uniform you have on. The fact that you are here means a lot more than that."

"Besides, who says anything about you being naked?" Bill asks, walking up wearing a big smile and his black and gold show uniform. Behind him, the other four riders are decked out in theirs. Over his shoulder, he carries two more. "You look fine now, and you'll look even better in a few minutes."

# THIRTEEN

# TRUMPETS IN THE NIGHT

Striding back toward the staging area after changing my uniform, I feel a little more confident.

While the civvies don't react to my presence, the uniforms do. Most salute my boards and then, as their hand begins to drop, an eyebrow raises or a grin breaks through a neutral face. They stiffen, holding their salute for a moment or two longer. Some mutter a few words of welcoming, joy, or happiness.

"Hey, Vince," a thin, willowy voice squeaks above the rustling of the horses. "Who's doing honor duty tonight?"

"We are," I reply as my team steps out from the shadows. "Where did you stash the instruments and horses, Vince?"

"In your team's assigned section of the stables."

The man standing next to Vince appears a little out of place in the sea of stocky, Western riders. His long, flowing lines and tailored uniform seem more suited for a fancy horse show.

"Jo, it's good to see you." The sparkle in Casper Nolan's green eyes reflects and amplifies the warm smile on his face.

"It feels good to be here, Casper."

The exchange is pretty much the same with all the captains down the line.

Returning to the head of the dapple-gray, I ask Vince, "One of Double D's kids?"

"Yes," Vince nods in Casper's direction. "His."

"Thank you."

"You're welcome, Jo," Casper replies.

Turning to Bill, I say, "For the Parade of Captains, I'd like you to be the flag bearer."

"I'd be honored."

\* \* \*

The lights dim until the horses around me are indistinct shapes. The audience stills and quiets. A single spotlight fades in, focusing on the six horses in front of me. Their riders hold the flags of the United States,

California, the USMB, USMB North America, USMB Western Area, and USMB California.

*Welcome everyone to the Cow Palace and the beginning of the 2014 Championship Series for USMB California bases*, the announcer's voice fills the arena. *Please stand for the entrance of the color guard from USMB San Francisco.*

Matched in stride and looks, the chocolate-brown bays trot into the ring. Stopping in the middle, they wait with the rest of us for the music to begin. As the first notes of the US national anthem wash over me, I choke up, tears stinging my eyes.

I touch Bill on his leg.

"Yes, Jo," he whispers. "We are here."

* * *

*We now continue with the Parade of Captains*, the announcer booms. *Tonight, for the first time in nine years, we celebrate two things, these opening ceremonies and a birthday. We've opened the Preliminaries on the same date every year, but the person hasn't been around to share in the joy with us.*

Jason and his flag bearer trot forward and turn right at the entrance, setting the pace and direction for the rest of us. Bill and I follow. As our horses pass through the opening, the spotlight focuses on us.

*Nine years ago to the day, a horse named Alabaster mauled Captain Joanna C. Mason. Many thought she would never ride again, let alone in a USMB show. Well, I am glad to say that Captain Mason has proven us wrong. Happy Birthday, Jo. We're glad you're back.*

The audience greets us with cheers and whistles. I respond by raising my free hand in a victory sign. The judges can take as many points away from me as they want. I don't care. This is my moment to celebrate.

* * *

*Since Captain Mason's mauling, the last solo band performance has been reserved for the playing of the USMBLA theme by an honorary unit made up of members from all of the participating bases. Tonight, things are a little different*, the announcer intones.

He doesn't know how different.

Jim's already texted a disheartening update. The team diverted to Jason's ranch and left the horses. He's hopeful they can make an entrance by the middle of our performance. I'm almost tempted to text back and say we don't need them. Without our troupe of horses, we have no hope of matching the amazing displays of color and precision that the other teams have wowed the judges and audience with all night.

*Entering the arena, please welcome, the Base of the Lone Horse, Base Number Fifty-One from Los Angeles, led tonight by the Lone Horse herself, Captain Joanna C. Mason.*

Riding in a two-by-three formation, my small team follows the flag bearer to the center of the ring. The audience gasps and whispers, but doesn't laugh. I applaud their self-control.

We split into a horizontal line that parallels the length of the arena. I salute the judges' area before raising my clarinet to my lips. The solo drummer, who is both our brass and percussion section, lifts his sticks.

Silence envelops us.

I take a deep breath. The dapple-gray mare underneath me toots causing a few chuckles. Keeping my back straight and my chin even, I will for the person in the sound booth to play the USMBLA theme. If not that, then the honorary band to do their normal routine. Either will be better than the lame ass reproduction we are about to attempt.

The soft, crisp opening trill of two trumpets dances through the air, growing in strength with each note. My ears, which have lived on a diet of acoustic instruments for most of their lives, feast on the warm resonance and edged brilliance of the pair. They cut off, start, and build up again. This time, two more join them, then one at a time, other instruments from the brass, reed, and percussion families. A few strings make an appearance, adding an unexpected depth to the piece. I no longer have to worry about six trying to reproduce twenty-five, at least fifty to a hundred voices fill the arena with their rich sound.

A spotlight snaps on, almost blinding me. The angle adjusts until the beam floats over my head. I squash the temptation to turn in my saddle to see what it's highlighting. A ripple of applause cuts through the audience. Out of the corner of my eye, I catch a jumbled flash of gold, black, and the glint of metal. More instruments join in from this mass.

My shocked brain almost misses my cue to add my clarinet. At first, I am a small whisper almost unheard in the middle of the crescendo. As I continue to play, the music fades around me until I'm in the midst of my normal solo. After a few bars, the other instruments re-join at measured intervals until their voices echo throughout the ring once again. When I pull out of the mix, the rest follow one by one until only two trumpets are left. They play softer and softer until even they fade into silence.

"*Foot unit, attention*," Jim's voice bellows. A thunderous clap of eighteen boots slapping together in unison cracks through arena.

A moment or two passes before the applause begins with a few soft hands. Building in volume, the waves of pure joy, excitement, and appreciation crash against me. People, in and out of uniform, rise to their feet.

"*Left face.*" Jim barks. "*Forward march.*"

After a few steps, the team appears in my peripheral vision. They march in a three-by-six formation until they are almost to the entrance.

Jim bellows, "*Split two. Honors hut.*"

I signal for a left turn and a two-by from my group. In front of us, on either side of the entrance, Jim's squad stands in two parallel lines at attention, their instruments tucked under one arm and their hands raised in salute. With tears in my eyes, I snap my hand to my forehead and ride down the line.

At the end, outside the gate, Vince is waiting. After we exchange salutes, I say, "Thank you for coordinating that."

"That's just it, I didn't."

# FOURTEEN

# RACE FOR LIFE

The Championship Series tests the skills and stamina of the participating teams through all types of events. The number of competitions required to reach the International Championships depends on the number of bases in the same state or region. Mine will have six. The state and regional area shows last two weeks and the rest, three. There's a week for travel between each level.

Every team consists of fifty people and thirty horses. There are twenty-five performing pairs and five alternates. The twenty non-mounted support personnel provide a wide range of services from grooming to driving. People can't leave the team except for medical or disciplinary reasons. The five substitute horses do not have to travel with their team. The teams provide their names, physical descriptions, and registration numbers as part of the entry paperwork, so no other horses can take their place.

The location of each competition is a random selection. Unlike the bases, they aren't tied to a specific geographic-based command. Some bases might even host two competitions. This year, all venues are US based. San Francisco has the honor of both the California State Preliminaries and Championships. Academy Houston, a US Central Area base, has US Western Area duties. Phoenix is playing host to the United States event. Bloomington, the American Intercontinental. Atlanta awaits my team should we make it all the way to the International Championships.

Most of the points awarded in each event are for skill and sportsmanship, but a few are reserved for the complete package the horse and rider pairings present. The lines and proportions of the horse outweigh the human beauty factor in the criteria for this portion. The judges score all pairs, even if they are only playing a supporting role.

DH is one of the team's better-looking horses, so when we aren't performing, we'll be acting as an outrider for those who are. If my knee doesn't hold up, Jim or one of my other brothers will take over for me. I don't trust anyone else riding my horse.

The individual competition part of the Preliminaries begins with one of my favorite events, horse racing. Golden Gate Fields provides the perfect proving ground for the speed and stamina of the teams' Thoroughbreds. Since they make decent jumpers, most have at least three. Mine has five, including DH.

Three half-mile match races add some live action to a simulcast day at GGF. The top three from each qualifier will return tomorrow for a special meet between the live seventh and eighth races.

In regular horseracing, the jockeys are all about the same size and a weighted saddle pad balances the outcome. USMB match races allow for horses, riders, and saddles of any shape and size within reason. The saddle became a definite requirement after one race where a rider tried riding bareback to save a few pounds and ended up falling off in the middle of the pack, almost killing himself.

Cordero and his five-year-old gelding, Geronimo, have the honor of representing my base. DH and Geronimo tied two out of three times during practice. The other Thoroughbreds couldn't match their speed. Cordero's stamina, Geronimo's age, and DH's temperament decided who I sent to the gate.

Due to the flash mob nature of last night's musical number, the judges didn't score that part of the team's performance. They did give us a few points for horsemanship and formation work, so we while are last, we aren't starting at zero, at least. A strong ride by Cordero and Geronimo should bump us up to the middle of the pack.

Trotting along the backstretch toward the gate, with Geronimo pacing DH, I have a different perspective of a track I used to visit as a kid. Back then, I paid more attention to the horses than the precise layout of everything. Now, the parallel rails form a subtle corridor while the set back and trimmed bushes and trees create minimal visual distractions.

I sigh.

"Is everything okay, sir?" Cordero prompts.

"I was thinking about what could have been. If not for his unexpected death and the mauling, I'd have raced on the back of a horse whose line included Seattle Slew at the Del Mar racetrack."

"Yes, sir. Jimmy mentioned that when he saddled Geronimo. Me and Big G here will do Double D's legacy proud today."

"Thank you, Mr. Cordero. That's—"

A cold, high-pitched whistle interrupts my prep talk. Cordero slumps in the saddle. Another screech cuts through the air. A warm burning sensation slices my forehead. I duck behind DH's neck, trying to make myself as small as possible.

My world closes in. The screams that have replaced the cheers are muted and distant. I am aware of the other riders and their proximity, but not much else unless it has some strategic value. My focus is me, Cordero, and our horses—and my duty to keep all of us safe.

"Talk to me, Cordero" I urge. "How bad off are you?"

"I'm hit in the shoulder and can't feel my arm, sir," Cordero groans. "Light-headed...Not sure..."

*Tweeeet. Phew.* Dust explodes up from the ground in front of DH. He cow hops sideways into Geronimo, who stumbles, but stays upright.

Glancing forward, I notice that the other riders have bunched together creating a huge bull's-eye we want no part of. Our best escape route is behind us. The tunnel from the paddock is ideal, but we'll become easier targets the closer we approach the grandstand.

Scanning the rail, I look for any break. If we can find a way to get behind the large green block that houses the electronic race results, we might have enough shelter to wait things out. I turn my head toward Cordero. The lack of color in his face and stiffness in his seat negates any possibility of a strategic retreat.

"Listen to me," I hiss. "We are going to get our race, but it's back the way we came. Grab leather and haul ass. Keep as low as possible. Dead run. Ready?"

A slight nod.

"Go."

Wheeling DH, I slam my heels into his sides. He explodes in a disorienting burst of speed. The wind tears at my face, causing my eyes to water. I manage a glance sideways. Geronimo matches DH stride for stride. Cordero sways in the saddle.

*Hang on, kid. Hang on!*

Hoofbeats and heartbeats merge into an almost deafening thunder. The white rail streaks through a blurry mess of color. Shifting shadows guide me to the closeness of the tunnel. When, by my best guesstimate, we are close, I ask DH to slow. Geronimo shoots past us, his reins flapping on his neck.

I urge DH back into a run, hoping to catch the runaway horse before his swaying rider falls off. Three more shadows join the chase. The hand signal for a diamond formation flashes. I hold DH back and assume the rear spot. Our rescuers take up positions in the front and on either side of Geronimo.

The lead horse shortens its stride. The blind run becomes a gallop, canter, fast trot, trot, and then a walk. Blobs transform into the familiar forms of Jim, Jimmy, TJ, and John.

I can see the faces in the grandstand, but there's no sound from that direction.

I prompt, "Sniper?"

Jim nods before adding, "Long gone by the time security hit the roof."

# FIFTEEN

# INTERLUDE

After the shooting, the judges grant the teams permission to bring in a security unit from their base. Most don't. Michelle has one up from LA within two hours. She isn't taking any chances. Neither am I. I order that five people remain with the horses and everyone else pair up at all times. In addition, for as long as our run lasts, we are driving to every other host city. Air transportation is too dependent on outside entities and influences.

A joint task force of USMB security and local, state, and federal law enforcement has the preliminary investigation of the incident wrapped up within 72 hours. GGF, however, wants reassurances the USMB can't give them without exposing the depth of its capabilities, so they cancel the match races. All remaining horse events move back to Cow Palace with Camas Prairie Stump racing replacing the match races. DH and I represent the base in that event and don't make it past our qualifying heat. In normal barrel racing, we do better and place third overall.

With two days left in this first round of competition, my team is in fourth with four more events. If we place first or second in at least three of them, we move on to the California State Championships. If not, we go home with the necessary statement made.

Looking out the bedroom window at the misty gray morning, I decide to give myself a little more bake time under the covers. The dark, rich wood and soft green and gold cloth surrounding me make the invitation to relax even sweeter. Today's a slow day, anyway. No support riding, and my only event, a solo clarinet performance, doesn't take place until well into the evening.

A light crispness mixed with rich heaviness tickles my nose. *No fair*, I sigh. Our resident doctor, and chef, has fixed my two favorite breakfast foods. The smells are so intense that I can picture three sausage links lying in one corner of a waffle with perfect round edges and grids that hold the right combination of syrup and butter. I swallow back the saliva as my stomach gurgles and squeaks.

My electronic leash buzzes on the nightstand. "Mason," I answer.

"Cap, this is Michelle. We have a problem," the efficient voice on the other end states. "The two horses on either side of DH, Jim's replacement and Geronimo, are dead."

*No, not the kid's horse,* I groan under my breath. Cordero is at the Academy, recovering from his gunshot wound. Instead of ordering that Geronimo remain with the team, I had left the choice up to Cordero. First mounts like Geronimo help develop a rider's foundation for the rest of their USMB career. I don't believe in breaking them, or any other pairing, up unless an obvious mismatch endangers the rider or the horse.

"How did they die?" I snap, burying my sentimentality.

"Looks like colic. Vet's determining now."

The horrible word smashes any thoughts of a warm, comfort food breakfast away with the force of a sledgehammer. Double D died of colic. The vet called it a natural case, but I kept some of his blood for the day someone could prove something unnatural had triggered the attack. "Make sure he draws some blood and compares it to Double D's sample," I order.

"Yes, sir."

I hang up. My stomach is quiet. Nine horses are dead, and I have no one to hold responsible for their demise. Eating, other than for energy, doesn't seem that important anymore.

\* \* \*

The bridle slips over DH's ears with no problem, but hangs at an odd angle on his face. He chews on the bit, making the missing cheek strap even more noticeable. I glance around his and my feet to make sure it hasn't somehow come loose and fallen. No leather brown shows up against the dusty gray.

"Another malfunction?" Jim prompts, peering over his saddle.

"Yep."

We ended up placing fifth in the Preliminaries and moving onto the California State Championship. Since San Francisco was hosting both state events, our travel week became some unexpected leave for most of the team. Jim and I spent the time shuttling between SF and LA, monitoring the investigations into the fire and the transportation screw-ups.

Whoever is harassing us has stepped up their game. While there haven't been any other deaths, enough other things have me considering a withdrawal from the competition five days into this new phase. Broken or missing equipment delaying and preventing appearances. Scraps, bruises, and pulled muscles from unexpected obstacles and holes taking a toll on my team's mental and physical condition. The lack of overt action by Security and individual units of the Mason Seven making them look very incompetent.

Glancing around at the teams clumped around the other four trailers in the staging area, I hope that today's ride is as relaxing as the blue sky and wide-open space surrounding us. If anything, it'll be at least an hour of quiet time with Jim. We haven't had that since the night of the fire.

"Hey, Jo," Vince says, riding up.

Nodding in his direction, I walk over to the tack compartment in front of my team's trailer. Picking DH's extra bridle off the hook, I inspect the leather and metal for any defects or missing parts. Finding none, I head back to the hitching rail.

"Still having problems?" Vince wonders on my way back to the hitching rail.

"Yep."

"Then why are you riding with two of your senior staff?" Vince asks, gesturing to Michelle sitting in the shadows. She nods in his direction, but says nothing.

"No choice." Horse and rider pairs can only participate in one ring event per day, or one distance meet every two days. The opening and closing ceremonies don't count against this limit, but everything else does. Balancing that restriction with the abilities of various pairings forced scheduling the three of us together for this event. I'm a little uneasy about it, but not as worried as Vince.

"How's the investigation coming?"

"All we have is bits and pieces that somehow fit together," I shrug. "John has something interesting brewing in his virtual world, but he's calling his findings more speculative than actual. Jeff and his team have found some clues, but again it's more theory than fact."

"Do you want me to bring my unit in? What about uniting the team?"

"No justification for either." Transforming the Mason Seven CSA Team into a single unit requires a good reason since so many bases feel the impact of the move. The judges are also touchy about the number of people on, or associated with, a team. Command Teams, who have the freedom to roam as they please, stay away from Championship competition unless they are part of a security detail, competing team, or official investigation.

"People and horses are getting hurt, Jo. That should be enough."

"No, it isn't. Except for Cordero's shooting and the fire at the base, they all look like accidents."

"Then may I ride with you for part of the race?" Vince glances at Michelle. "It'll give us some time to talk."

"It's not the end of the month, yet," I tease.

"I know, but I've felt this odd tingle for the last week or so. Bill says he can't find anything wrong."

"Where?" I arch an eyebrow. Odd tingle is Jim's way of indicating he's around even when we are not in close proximity to one another.

"It travels around, but spends most of its time on the left side of my head."

Same place as mine, too.

I steal a glance at Michelle. Her blue eyes make one last pass on the horizon before locking onto me. "Yes, Captain?"

"Feeling anything unusual or different?"

Michelle shakes her head.

# SIXTEEN

# MICHELLE REMEMBERS

DH stops. Vince's mare sashes her butt as she walks by. He follows her movement with pricked ears and a head that almost swivels off its pivot. She ignores him. I rub his shoulder. He breathes in and rattles his lips. I laugh, teasing, "Think about the race, boy, not the girls."

"He doesn't know they are cousins, does he?" Vince asks.

"I don't think he cares," I reply.

We've been on the trail for about an hour, sharing easy banter like this for most of the way. The mood of my little group is as light and refreshing as the fresh air that pumps through my lungs. I'm watching for any changes between Michelle and Vince. If anything, their conversations are a little more animated and upbeat than normal.

In this beautiful countryside where our path is a well-worn streak amongst the grass, it is easy to ignore that we are in the middle of a competition. Someone trying to hurt my team not so much, as the presence of Michelle and a security officer from San Bernardino is an obvious reminder. Both have handguns strapped to their sides, but neither one has a rifle. They can't. It's not a shooting event.

Clucking, I tug on the lead rope and urge DH forward. While Michelle and the security guard have remained mounted, the rest of us are on the ground beside our horses. The cross-country race is as much about stamina as speed. Switching between riding and walking keeps the horses fresh for the breakneck finish.

Our pace remains steady until my ankle turns on itself. Icy hot splinters of pain shoot straight to my head. Gasping, I pull up and look down. A hole—the perfect size and shape to catch a hoof—stares back at me. Since this is one of five trails mapped out for the race, I have to assume there are others waiting for their unsuspecting victims.

*Now other teams may get hurt because of someone's perverted need to go after my team,* I groan under my breath.

Jim pulls up and turns in my direction. "You okay, Jo?"

The ankle stings, but doesn't throb. My knee is throwing a fit. "Yes. I need to get back on DH, though."

A faint rustle catches my attention. I raise my hand in a closed fist. "Quiet," I grunt.

Everyone stops. I close my eyes and listen. The world opens up around me, but everything sounds normal. Birds, horses, even a distant plane. *Wait...There...that swish again, off to the left. Like someone using the bushes for cover.*

Opening my eyes, I glance around. We are out in the open with a few clumps of trees ahead and behind us. About five or so feet before the trees, some rocks that might serve as protection. To our right, the openness continues. The rise on the left has several perfect places for a sniper's nest.

"Jo?" Jim prompts.

"I think someone's shadowing us," I reply. "Michelle?"

"I don't see or hear anything, Cap."

A whistle echoes off the rocks. The security officer from San Bernardino collapses and tumbles from his saddle, slamming into the ground with a loud thump. His horse bolts, sending the others into a frenzy of stomping hooves, tossing heads, and rapid snorts.

"Let them go and scatter!" I yell. Each horse is micro-chipped with a tracker that has a range of twenty-five miles. The state park and surrounding lands cover about one hundred and forty square miles. It might take us a few days or weeks to find them, but they offer the color and motion distraction we need to cover our dash for the rocks.

Unstrapping the walkie from my side, I snap, "51-Command-1. We have a rider down and are under fire. Horses are free."

The speaker bursts to life with responses from medical teams, security, and other riders. They all offer their assistance, but acknowledge that it's going to take at least thirty minutes to reach us.

Dust explodes around my feet as I stumble toward the rocks. The next whistle ends with a soft plop and a groan. Glancing to my right, I see Vince falter. Michelle and Jim rush over to him. Half-dragging, half-carrying him, they move toward the outcropping at a deliberate pace. Spinning backwards, I check on the security officer. He's face down with his neck at an impossible angle. *Poor kid. At least, it was quick.*

70

Dropping behind the rocks, I stretch out my throbbing leg. Michelle and Jim lay Vince next to me. He's unconscious with a dark stain near his left shoulder. Michelle's gaze bounces between him and the direction of the sniper. Her expression is a fluid mixture of subtle contrasts. If she looks at Vince, it's wild-eyed and unsure. Any glance toward our assailant and her steady focus returns.

"Michelle, do you have a clean shot?"

"Yes, but I'm not sure I can take it." Michelle stammers. "There's a lot of chaos in my head."

I try shoring her up by adding firmness to my tone. "What's your biggest distraction?"

"Vince. We are more than friends, aren't we?"

"Yes. You are brother and sister." I brace myself for the inevitable question and reaction I've feared all these years.

Michelle looks at Vince, then at me, and back at him. "Did he know?"

I nod, sighing under my breath. That wasn't *the* one. It begins with "Why," ends with "tell me," and has a few choice words in between.

A bullet whizzes over our heads.

"Listen, Michelle, I will fill in all the details, later." I sharpen the edge in my tone. "Right now, we have to get this boogie off our ass, okay?"

"Yes, sir."

The efficiency in her tone is back. Good. I hope that she can remain on point long enough to distract whoever is shooting at us. Under circumstances much worse than this, I have seen her take out her assigned targets, so I don't doubt her abilities or intentions. Almost two decades of experiences combining with a lifetime of lost memories is a lot to dump on someone, though.

My surroundings become gray and uninteresting.

*No, I don't need you*, I warn the shadow in my head. *She'll be fine.*

It withdraws. The color returns.

# SEVENTEEN

# LATE NIGHT SESSIONS

I walk into a semi-dark alien world of glowing screens bearing gifts for the prisoner caught within its web. Holding up a tray piled with sandwiches and a large insulated cup, I wait for some reaction from the zombie in front of the monitors. At first, the body remains frozen. A subtle twitch of the eyebrows indicates that it's aware of something in the shadows around it. A quick sniff follows.

Glancing up and blinking a few times, John smiles, "One of those roast beef with Swiss?"

Placing the food on a table in a corner away from his precious machines, I say, "They all are. Planning on quitting anytime soon?"

"In a few minutes," John pushes away from the desk, rubbing his eyes. "The text became black dots about an hour ago."

Computers are a tool for my job—nothing else. They are *part* of John. Twenty-four hours without an electronic device somewhere on his person and he begins showing withdrawal symptoms.

"Have you made any progress?"

"I might be close to something."

"You've been saying that for a few days now," I tease. "Did the stuff you hijacked from Transportation Command help?"

"Not as much as the people and bases associated with DH. All the commanders involved have the last name of either Nolan or Mason."

My mind churns. Of the four Nolan brothers, I know the most about Casper. We've been friends since our stint at the Academy. I talk to the other three on occasion as part of my duties. All them are up and coming officers, but only Anthony and Casper have a command. Nothing stands out from my various interactions with any of them.

*Unless...Nah, it couldn't be that. Casper assured me he understood the reasons for my recommendation. Still...* "Look at the time in command for Casper Nolan at the time I received LA."

John's fingers fly over the keyboard with a rapid and rhythmic clatter. He snatches bits off the various screens that flash by so fast I stop looking at them. "72 hours less," he states.

*Hmmm...Maybe it is that.*

Command Specialty School is an interesting two years of classroom learning, practical field application, examination, and reviews by peers and senior officers. Fail any one of them and a candidate can lose months—sometimes *years*—off their career as they go through remedial training. Some, like Casper, have to repeat the whole program.

I lost my two years because of the op that created my mental shadow.

Before John gets curious about my almost tie with Casper, I prompt, "Check Casper's records. You'll find I was on the peer review committee that questioned his decision making."

"That's good motivation for revenge."

"Still as the CO of San Fernando he doesn't have that much power."

"His brother, Anthony, in Philadelphia does. As the CO of the logistics hub on the East Coast, he can create and modify records in the central transportation and logistics databases."

"Our shipping clerks do that, don't they?"

"Yes, they enter information into the DB, but their entries have to go through a three-step verification process before they are accepted. With his super user access, Anthony doesn't have that requirement."

"Enough with the technobabble, John," I snort. "What does it mean for those of us who speak plain English?"

"He can organize and staff a secondary departmental structure within a base, and maybe even the whole USMB, without anyone knowing."

"Has he gone that far?"

"I'm not sure yet, but he's built up enough of a network so all the attacks against the team look like accidents."

\* \* \*

The blazing lights in the family room offer a startling contrast to the dark dungeon of the study. Pictures of family and friends litter the walls. My favorite is the one hanging over the fireplace; a group shot of the combined Mason and Scott clans (thirteen kids, four adults, and two dogs), taken a few days after I turned eleven. I have a copy of the photo in the same spot at my house. Mine has only eleven kids, though. According to Jason, the extra two are playmates.

Jimmy and four of my brothers lounge on the couches, watching television. Michelle and Jim huddle off in the corner where two chairs and a table sit in between a pair of large bookcases. The rapid gestures of their hands suggest a very intense conversation.

I wander over. "What's the latest on Vince?" I ask.

"Bill has him settled in for the night," Michelle replies. A touch of sadness crosses her expression. "The shot tore up his shoulder, but didn't hit anything vital."

Behind me, the couches rustle. I glance up. Jason waves off the automatic response to his presence before joining our group.

"How are you doing, lass?"

"Okay, Jason," Michelle replies. "Thanks."

"Need anything?"

"A foolproof way to keep Vince safe."

"Already taken care of," I reassure her. "SF has security stationed throughout the hospital. Vince's ExO is also sending a unit up from San Bernardino. Jeff has one on stand-by should we need it."

Covering her mouth, Michelle rubs her chin. Dropping her hand, she states, "The shots today were too much like the warehouse." She chews her lip. "Once I can get past that and concentrate on what I heard, the sound reminds me of a standard-issue sniper rifle. That means at least one of my team is involved."

"Why would someone in our own security department betray us?" Jim objects.

*Think someone's plural, little bro, and not just security,* I add in my head. Aloud, I say, "I'm not sure, but it explains why we haven't been able to tie anyone to any of the incidents. Security wouldn't look suspicious inspecting the equipment or wandering around the stables."

I hate the vagueness of my response, but I have two reasons for keeping what John has discovered to myself, for now. First, I don't want the Nolans to bury their ghost infrastructure deeper. Second, because of the op that cost me those couple of years, I'm under a little more scrutiny than most, if not all, of my peers. If I even hint at wrongdoing by another base commander without documented evidence backing my claims, I risk losing much more than my career.

Michelle states, "Jo, if my mental incapacity—"

"No one is questioning you or your abilities. All of us were fooled."

"How do we take care of this?"

Turning to Jason, I request, "Suspend me."

"What?" Jason cocks his head and looks at me as if I've grown an extra appendage or two.

"I said suspend me," I repeat. "DH and I have been either the primary or secondary target in all of the attacks. If we go away, the teams can continue in peace."

A terrorist attack and bombing marred the 1972 and 1996 Olympics. Despite these horrific acts, the games went on. Instead of following that precedent, scuttlebutt has the upper echelon considering a suspension, if not cancellation, of the remaining California State Championship events. If that happens, the current leader, San Diego, will advance.

"Where will you go?"

"Back to LA."

"Will you be safe there? You just said one of departments has been compromised."

"Doesn't matter. I want to investigate the extent of the breach and find out who is responsible. A suspension gives me the freedom and anonymity to do both without arousing suspicion."

"What do you want the Mason Seven to do?" Jim wonders.

"Continue their current investigations, plus start reviewing all of LA's personnel and departmental records. Coordinate with Jeff to bring in the extra units you might need for the audit. Limit the bases you pull from to San Bernardino, Houston, and San Francisco. That way we can identify any leaks that come from that direction."

Jim nods.

The faint worry lines on Jason's forehead deepen, along with his brogue. "How bad is yer knee?"

"Sore, but nothing I can't handle."

"Would Bill certify ye unfit because of it?"

"He's wanted to do that for the last few weeks."

"All right, Jo, I dinna like this, but consider yerself suspended for being unable ta perform."

# EIGHTEEN

# FIVE DAYS OF BOREDOM

Returning to LA, I settle into a routine that allows me to stay informed despite my suspension. To sell my alleged injury, I use crutches whenever I'm out in public. If someone other than Ben visits me at the house, I exaggerate my limp.

I'm at the base's main dining facility by eight-thirty for breakfast. This helps me keep up on the scuttlebutt, and the rumors of my demise down to a manageable level. Housework, spending time with DH, and supervising anyone who's feeding, handling, or cleaning up after him, take up the rest of the morning.

Lunch with Ben includes discussing both teams and the base. Working the computer makes the afternoon pass in a few blinks. If I discover anything, I give my findings to Ben at dinner so he can relay them to Jim, Jeff, and Vince through regular channels without my name of them. In return, he reports on his shift in Command Central. For dessert, Ben sneaks DH out of his stall and meets me in a remote part of Eastside where we ride for an hour or two.

At eight, Michelle calls with an update on the investigation and team security. After the official part of our conversation is over, we talk personal. It always starts with Vince. They are working out the details of their relationship, so she always has a question or two about him. After those, we go through any memories or flashbacks that are troubling her. Each time we sign off by saying good-bye, I count myself lucky that she is still talking to me.

I finish the night by watching television or curling up with a good book until about eleven-fifteen when Jim calls. We spend at least an hour on the phone chatting about the day. For that golden moment, I'm where I belong, with my family and team.

This schedule goes on for five days without much variation. By the sixth, I want back on active duty. I'm bored with doing nothing productive, and the attacks on the team have stopped. Casper and Anthony aren't finished with whatever their plan is, though. John's documentation on the infiltration of the USMB organizational structure has grown to include the upper echelon. He wants to share his findings with Jason and Jim, but I ask him to hold off until we can present our findings together.

The two anticipated sets of labs results have come in and they are the damning, irrefutable evidence I need. The blood work on Geronimo and the other horse matches Double D's sample, so the same toxin killed all three. The genetic workup on DH's offspring pinpoints three mares in the Philly herd, which proves he was there, and not Houston, for several years.

Something even more troubling is the odd pieces of code John has found in the communications and computer networks. According to him, they give whoever has planted them the capability to monitor, access, and control almost everything. They also buried them so deep that he found them by accident while doing his research. He's working on patches that will block the scripts while still returning false information to their controllers.

I transmit some of my worry about this new twist in the Nolans' conspiracy to DH during our clandestine ride. He takes off on a blurry, high-speed tour through some twisty and overgrown trails. We make it back without injury, but Ben has to take some extra time and care cooling him down.

The ride adds stiffness and soreness to my tension, so when Michelle calls I snap off short, quick answers. She dismisses it as a bad case of cabin fever and limits our conversation to a few questions about Vince. I almost miss the call with Jim because I'm in the tub trying to soak everything away.

"What's wrong, Jo?" Jim prompts when I do answer.

"I'm just tired." I yawn. "Let's make this brief, okay?"

"Sure, I don't have much to say."

"What's on the schedule for tomorrow?"

"Barrel racing."

"There are plenty of good Quarter Horses on the team, so I can't decide who to put up. Why don't you call this one?"

"Okay."

"I need to rejoin the team."

"I'd feel better having you here, but you are safer where you are."

"I'm not so sure about that."

"Why not?"

"I have a working theory that can't be shared over the phone," I yawn again. "I'll talk to Jason in the morning and be back with the team by the afternoon."

"Until you are, be safe, kiddo."

"You, too, little bro."

Hanging up, I switch off the light. Lying on my back, I close my eyes, expecting a quick trip into dreamland. My mind has other ideas. It races with random thoughts, while my body feels like someone has attached an electrical cord to my skin. Every sound explodes around me. The house creaking as it settles sounds like machine gun fire.

After a long bout of tossing and turning, I manage to drift off. I'm only out for what seems like less than a second when an imperceptible, but very distinct, squeak jolts me back to full awareness. Something, or someone, has put their weight on the fifth step wrong.

Rolling out of bed, I open the nightstand drawer and grab the flashlight and gun stashed in there. Taking one of my pillows, I block the glow from the bedside clock. With the rest, I make a convincing lump before retreating to the closet. Leaving a crack so I can see, I wait, gripping the gun, hoping I don't have to use it.

Two machine guns rip into the room, silencers muffling their rage. A flashlight clicks on, scans the destruction, and snaps off. Footsteps tap a retreat.

My heart throbs in my head. Dryness scratches my throat. My cell phone is on the kitchen counter, and the bedside one is ground to plastic dust, so I have no way of calling for help. I can escape one of two ways. Down the stairs into whatever ambush might be waiting, or out the porch door, around the house, and down the emergency ladder on the other side.

I decide on the porch route. Outside, there is less stuff to trip over and any unidentifiable shadows will be bad guys.

Crawling out the door, I use the walls and furniture to mask my presence. About a quarter of the way toward the ladder, the heavy clink of a boot stepping on metal ratchets up my awareness. Rising from my squat, I brace myself. A gun that fires one bullet at a time versus two or more that spit out multiple doesn't inspire much hope, but it's either stand my ground or be shot in the back.

Two shadows round the corner. I fire four shots in rapid succession. One ghost goes down with a yelp. The other takes a few steps forward before collapsing. Uncertain if I have hurt or only grazed them, I turn and scramble away.

Behind me, a rapid click. Nothing hits.

*Lucky me, genius boy is out of ammo*, I quip.

*It doesn't have to be this way*, counters the dark shadow in my head.

*I survived the mauling without you, so go away*, I snap back. *If I die tonight, it will be as me.*

The metallic crunch of a magazine load echoes off the  house.

My foot touches the ladder. Letting myself half-slip, half-fall, the trip down takes a quick heartbeat. My right leg squishes on the soft grass of the side lawn. The night sky lights up with muzzle flashes above and to the side of me. Three or four bullets rip into my nightgown before my head slams into the ground.

Everything goes dark.

# NINETEEN

# MORE THAN TUMMY TROUBLES

Ben tossed on his side. The stinging sensation in his mid-section warned that another explosion of his guts was imminent. He rubbed the offending area, hoping to somehow fight the cramps and stay in bed. His two kids had wanted pizza, so he ordered one with half-pepperoni and half-sausage. Two or three stray pieces of the sweet spicy goodness ended up on his side of the pie. Instead of picking them off and putting them aside, he enjoyed every little morsel.

Slipping out of bed, he slinked to the bathroom and paid another burning round for his indulgence. Flushing the toilet, he sighed. Padding back to bed, he snuggled against the warm, delicious body of his wife.

"You okay?" she whispered.

"I think so." Ben's stomach rumbled again. "No, I guess I'm not," he groaned. "I'm going to take a walk and see if that helps settle things."

\* \* \*

Reaching the end of his driveway, Ben stopped and let the night embrace him in its quiet stillness. Street lamps spaced at regular intervals along the road lit up his surroundings, but washed away any traces of the stars. Ambling down the street, he felt the pressure lift off his mid-section. *Since I'm already out, I might as well check on the extra patrols I set up to watch the Cap.*

Midway to the corner, the piercing wail of the base's klaxons shattered the silence. The pattern and tone of the revolving siren indicated a Code Two: Security Alert.

Fishing his cell out of his pocket, Ben tapped on the speed dial. After one short ring, the worried brogue of the base's Assistant Chief of Security answered, "Justin Scott, speaking."

"Mr. Scott, what's going on?"

"Dreamer's Hope is missing, sir."

"Did he break out of his stall?"

"If he did, sir, he left no marks."

"Which gate reported the departure of a trailer?"

"None of them, sir."

Ben swore under his breath. The Cap had warned him about possible moles. "Seal the base and start searching for him," he ordered. "I'm on my way to the Captain's house."

"Aye, sir."

Putting the phone back in his pocket, Ben picked up his pace. Reaching the corner, he stopped and stared down the street. A few lights dotted the windows of the houses, and small shadows darted between the yards, but there were no other signs of life or activity.

*Boom. Boom. Boom. Boom.*

Ben flinched. Growing up on the streets of South Central LA, he had heard that sound too many times. Severe injury, if not death, were always on the other end. He grabbed his phone out of his pocket and hit redial.

After one ring, Justin answered, "Sir?"

"Mr. Scott," Ben kept his voice low, "I need a full security response to the Captain's house now. Code Two silent."

"Yes, sir. What's going—"

*Rat-a-tat-tat. Rat-a-tat-tat.*

"Was that machine gun fire, sir?"

"I believe so, Mr. Scott."

"We are on our way! I advise you stay away. We'll investigate."

The line went dead.

Ben put his phone back, sighing, *Sorry, Mr. Scott, I hear your advice, but cannot heed it. I owe the Cap and her family for a life thought taken.*

Using the shadows, he crept closer. When there was nothing but exposed street between him and the house, he slipped behind a hedge and peered over. Parked in the Cap's driveway were three cars with the markings of base security on their side. The passenger door hung open on the one closest to him. Standing behind another, three people all dressed in black. Two more rounded the corner carrying something between them. With heavy grunts, the men slung their load in the back seat and closed the door with a click.

"I know we were supposed to make this look like a suicide, boss," one of them whispered, "but she evaded our first attack."

"We caught her on the side of the house, though," another added. "That corpse ain't moving."

"How'd you position the body?" A third one asked.

*Casper Nolan?* Ben swallowed his gasp. *That explains the transportation screw-ups, at least. Why would he want to kill the Cap?*

"Like she slipped coming off the emergency ladder," The second replied.

Metal clanked against metal. A shot followed by two more. With each one, a shadow fell until only one remained. It jumped into a car and pulled away.

The house exploded.

Waves of heat pushed Ben out of his hiding place. In the distance, the sirens of his requested security response roared to life, their wail joining and combining with many others, among them the klaxons jumping the base to full battle stations. Neighbors poured out of their houses. Some rushed over to gawk or put water on the fire. Others ran in the opposite direction.

The wall of flame grew bigger with each passing heartbeat. Response time of the nearest fire unit was three minutes. It'd take them at least another one to get set up. He couldn't wait that long. Any moment, the small passage between the house and fire would close, trapping his captain and friend.

Taking a deep breath, Ben rushed across the street. Hitting the edge of the inferno, his skin became moist and damp. He kept his breathing shallow, so not as to inhale any of the smoke. His already nauseous stomach renewed its protests. Glancing around, all he saw was orange and yellow. The green of the grass and trees was gone, turned either black or brown.

Ben stumbled along the side of the house. Ignoring the pounding in his head and the icy feeling crawling up his legs, he searched for his friend.

"Cap, where are you?" he cried out.

The beast eating him one painful chunk at a time roared.

Turning to escape his tormentor, he spotted the Cap. She was no longer human, though. Her flesh had melted and congealed in a horrible charred lump.

"Ah, there you are," Ben sighed. "Just let me…" The words died in a round of coughing that shook his whole body. The air became heavy— and too hard to pull in—as an invisible hand squeezed his mid-section.

Ben sunk to the ground, next to the piece of coal, pain ripping through his chest. *It was my honor serving you, Captain.*

The orange turned black as the roar faded to a whisper.

His brain registered one final, impossible, sound—the Cap swearing, "Crap, we are too late."

# TWENTY

# WAKING UP TO A NIGHTMARE

His heart pounded as he skipped along, trying to avoid the shadows. Breathing in, he glanced down. It was a slight drop down towards safety. Grabbing the ladder, he slid. As his foot touched the ground, the first mosquito bit. The rest flew in, each sting worse than the last.

*No, wait, those aren't insects, they are bullets.*

His body folded in on itself until he was nothing more than a useless, withering lump. Caught in the murky, gray world between living and dying, time slowed until it passed in heartbeats. Blackness almost had him when the world exploded with light and heat. Hot ice seared his lungs, sucking all the air out of them. His skin melted from his bones. He tried opening his eyes, but they were fused shut.

"Cap, where are you?" Ben cried out.

*Get out, you fool. Save yourself!* He tried yelling, but only managed a squeak.

"Ah, there you are," Ben sighed. "Just let me—" The words died in a round of coughing.

* * *

*"Noooooooo!"* Jim screamed, bolting upright. "This isn't happening."

*What the hell is going on? That was too real to be a dream.*

Taking deep breaths to slow his heart, he leaned hard into his link with Jo. Her presence responded as if she was in a deep sleep.

Reaching for his tablet, he checked the base feed, which showed all clear. *Should I call Jo and warn her? Warn her about what, though?*

Laughing at himself, he snuggled under the covers and closed his eyes.

* * *

"Here she is," a voice called out.

"How bad does she look?" His voice was heavy and deep, but with a few high notes mixed in. *I'm a healthy Jo, but how?*

He glanced at the charred corpse with a shadow leaning over it.

"Her injuries are so extensive that I'm surprised she's still with us." Outlined by orange and yellow, the face was dark and unrecognizable, but the voice wasn't. *What is Jeff doing in LA? He's supposed to be in Houston.* "We have to get her to the ship. Randy says we don't have much time before the portal collapses."

*Ship? What ship?* Only three ships had any significance in his life. His father's former command, the boat on the lake they had played on as kids, and the one that sailed the stars from the stories his stepfather used to tell him.

"Understood," he said, staring at Jeff's uniform. A familiar black and gold logo danced in front of him. *No, wait. The 51 is missing between the horse's chin and neck.*

"Ben?" he prompted. If this was a continuation of the other dream, he had to know if the big man had made it.

"Passed out on the front lawn, but unhurt." Jeff chided. "A minute more and we'd have lost him again."

"Again?" he echoed. *My first dream wasn't a dream?*

"Yes, again. Come on, Jo. Focus. We have to save your ass or do this all over for a third time."

\* \* \*

Jim's eyes snapped open as his brain disengaged itself from the weirdness. Gazing into the blackness, he tried to assemble the fading images into something coherent. He had been back at his burning house. Of that much he was certain. *As for the rest...*

His phone buzzed, rattling on the nightstand.

Jim picked up his cell. After reading an urgent text message, he pulled up the details of the incident on his tablet. The live feed revealed a very active and fluid situation that his dreams had described in almost perfect detail. Personnel were still scrambling to contain the fire and find DH as well as Jo, or her body. The report didn't contain any mention of Ben.

*Shit, not DH, too,* Jim groaned.

The minute changed on the tablet's clock. *2:06 again?* Jim shook his head. *How many times have I gone to bed, waking up hours later, thinking I already lived through the day? It must have been 12:06, the last time I checked.*

He dialed a number. After one ring, a voice answered without identifying itself and asked for his serial number. He rattled it off. Another wanted his social security number. The final one demanded his command code. Behind each human he interacted with, a computer program verified his vocal pattern. Once he passed all three tests, a pause, and then the musical brogue of his stepbrother. "Captain...I..." Justin's voice straightened out. "Sir, how may I help you?"

"I read the emergency feed. Status report, Mr. Scott." Jim gagged on the formality of his words. *This crisis involves Jo and DH. Justin must be torn up inside. How can I reassure him without breaking protocol?*

Despite the emotion in his tone, Justin maintained his composure and reported, "Sir, I regret to inform you that we haven't found your sister or her remains. Your house is also destroyed, sir. The explosion almost demolished the two on either side as well."

"What about Mr. Harrison?"

"How did you know about him?" Justin yelped. "The medics found him on your front lawn, unconscious. They are treating him for indigestion and dehydration at the hospital. The doctors are a little puzzled, though. His tests have come back showing traces of smoke inhalation and a fatal heart attack."

Jim shot up to a sitting position. *How did the dreams predict real events?* "Given how protective Ben is of Jo, I figured he would be close by." Focusing on a safer topic, he prompted, "DH?"

"In the chaos of the fire, someone managed to slip through one of the gates with him, sir. I think we've been compromised."

"Yes, Justin, we have. The Mason Seven is investigating the breach. Who is in charge of the base?"

"I am, sir. As soon as Mr. Harrison is certified for duty, I will be turning over command to him."

"You'll do fine, Justin. Call me if you need anything."

"Yes, sir."

Ending the call, Jim stared at his phone and wondered, *Vince or Jeff?* Vince was closer, but Jeff seemed more involved. He hit the moonlight and stars avatar instead of the cop shield.

After a single ring, Jeff answered, "Hi, Jim. I got the team alert a few minutes ago."

"Where are you?"

"In Houston, why?"

"Just wondering. How fast can you get to LA?"

"I'll be on a plane within the next hour. What am I walking into?"

"The base is operating under a Code Three: Red Alert with Justin in charge. There was a firefight and explosion at my house. Jo's missing. Ben's in the hospital. Your first priority is finding Jo and keeping her safe. I'm stuck here until I can take care of the team. Any one of my brothers is at your disposal."

"Send Bill. I'll call if I don't need him."

"You got it." Jim hesitated before blurting, "Jeff, I just had two very weird dreams. I was at the house first as Jo dying on the ground, then as her rescuing herself with your help."

"Funny, you should say that, so did I. I was there trying to assess her injuries and evacuate her."

"In my dream, you mentioned something about a ship and someone name Randy."

"Randy? That's a name I haven't heard in a long time."

"Who is he?"

"My twin brother."

"Wait a minute. I thought you only had two brothers, Lance and RJ."

"It's a complicated story. I was separated from my real family when I was five."

"How come none of us knew?"

"My foster parents do. It was a sealed adoption."

Jim chewed on his lip. He had grown up believing Jeff was the natural son of his Uncle Pete and Aunt Rose. *Now this wrinkle pops up just after Jo goes missing.* Jim shook his head. *No, I'm not going to think that way.* Out loud, he began, "Jeff, I—"

"Need to know if you can still trust me?"

Jim hesitated. *I wouldn't have put it in such a blunt way, but* . . . "Yes, trust is a serious issue at the moment. Are you involved in anything that has happened?"

"Other than heading the investigation into part of it? No." Jeff's voice softened. "Look, Jim, we may have never shared as direct a connection as you thought, but I grew up with you and your siblings. I would protect all of you with my life. If you don't believe me, call Vince or another one of the team and ask them to go find Jo."

"No, I need them for other things."

"Then let me get the situation at LA under control. Afterwards, I'll answer any questions you may have the best can."

"Sounds good."

"Be warned, though, that when I find Jo, I'm going to make her disappear. Continue playing like she's dead until I tell you otherwise."

"Why?" Jim yelped.

"There is strong evidence to suggest the attacks on the team are related to the screw-ups that were happening between LA and San Fernando."

"Oh. Keep me posted."

"I will."

# TWENTY-ONE

# LOYALTY TO A DREAM

"Are you sure about what you saw and heard, Ben?" Jim wondered, questioning himself for questioning the one person ahead of him on Jo's short trust list.

"Yes, sir."

"Well, at least it confirms what I dreamt last night."

"What was that, sir?"

Jim recounted both his dreams and the time passing in a funny way.

When he finished, Ben stated, "Captain, while I have no doubts about my experience or yours, I can offer no rational explanation for either of them."

"I'll take any half-baked hypothesis you might have."

"We lived through a time loop," Ben quipped.

"Temporal distortion is an unproven theory of science fiction, Ben."

"Yes, sir. Therefore, I suggest we keep this under wraps until we talk to Jo or Jeff in person."

"Good idea."

Hanging up, Jim entered the barn for the morning team meeting. The three Mason Seven units had merged into one entity with its members splitting themselves between LA and his location. Vince had taken over command of the base from Justin. Jeff called saying that Jo was safe and undergoing treatment at an undisclosed facility. Jason wanted to talk after the team meeting. At last report, Bill was two or three people away from going through security at the airport.

Jim wanted to be everywhere and nowhere. *I can't think in those terms and keep my sanity or job. Better to play it cool, take care of the team, and arrange a face to face with Jeff.*

No other team in Championship Series history had faced such tragedy or adversity. Their lead horse missing, their captain shot and her status unknown, his family house destroyed, and other people and animals getting hurt or killed in random accidents. Despite all this, the team had a good chance of moving on to the next round in a few days.

Did he have the right to ask them to continue? Was he better off packing it up and going home? He wasn't sure what Jo would want him to go on. She'd talk about seeing her dream all the way through, and not letting their unknown assailant win. Then she would step back and evaluate cost of continuing. *Forget it, Jim,* he could almost hear her voice say. *Keep everyone safe. We'll wait until next year.*

Any other team, any other year, and he'd heed that advice. With this one, he wasn't sure he could. Jo had overcome her fear, rusty skills, and everyone's doubts, including his, to ride and compete. Her determination, and ability, to overcome those obstacles solidified her leadership. He was duty bound to protect everything that she and her team had done so far.

*If you are going to insist on continuing,* Jo's voice continued, *then listen to the heart of my crew. I have for a long time now. Sure, base command isn't a democracy, but, in the midst of my worst days, when I didn't have a hope of anything ever changing, I drew strength from their faith in me. I figured if they still wanted to stick with me even when I was going nowhere, I owed them finding a way to right myself and lead them somewhere close to an International Championship. I also knew they'd tell me when I was off course and risking too much.*

He'd ask them. *Please forgive me, if they decided to stay, Jo.*

Someone touched him on the shoulder. Turning, Jim raised his eyes. "I thought you were on a plane to LA," he stated, staring at his tall, black-haired brother.

"I was next in line at the security checkpoint when Jeff called and said I needed to return here. He wants us to play the hand he suggested." Bill's face darkened as his voice dropped, "even with our family."

"He thinks it's that serious, huh?"

Bill nodded.

Returning his gaze to the rest of the room, Jim tried to gauge his approach by the tension in it. As his eyes swept the room, light chatter faded into the silence of breathing and shifting bodies. His stomach tightened each time he spotted his son or one of his brothers in the crowd. When Jo formed the Mason Seven, she made each one of them promise that if a mission required faking a teammate's injury or death, the team knew the truth. She felt that lying amongst themselves about such a serious matter made twisting the facts about other smaller stuff too easy.

"Ladies and gentlemen," his soft tone boomed in the stillness, "early this morning, the Captain was shot and killed at the base."

A few gasped, but most remained quiet.

"Given this, there is no shame in us returning to LA." Jim swallowed, unnerved and uncertain of his words. "I'm not going to issue the order to do so, though." Pointing at the door, he stated, "Instead, I will walk outside and wait five minutes. If there are less than twenty-five people in here when I return, we go home with no regrets."

"Before you do, sir," a youthful voice squeaked from the back of the crowd, "I have one question, if I may."

"Yes?"

"Why do we need five minutes?"

The barn exploded with sound. While all the voices talking once made the words hard to understand, the sentiment was clear. No one wanted to leave. Someone had destroyed the heart of the base. Since they didn't know whom or why, the best way for them to retaliate was to stay and stand their ground. The Captain, even in death, would expect that. To emphasize this point, each person crossed their arms and turned so the only thing Jim saw was rows upon rows of blue with a black horse's head on a gold circle.

Still in unison and silence, the team filed out until only his family remained.

*They have spoken, loud and clear, Jo. Now, how do I take care of the rest of us?*

His son waved him over. "Is it okay if I go and hang with the team? I need to deal with this in my own way."

"Sure. We'll talk later, okay?"

Jimmy nodded.

As his son slinked past the rest of the family, Jim focused on their mixed facial expressions. He hated making them live with the horrible lie, but he had to, at least for a few more minutes.

Dialing Jeff's number, Jim waited through four torturous rings before he answered, "Yes?"

"Why the hell would you go against Jo's commandment about undercover missions?" Jim almost exploded into the phone, his emotions catching up with him. "I don't care how—"

"Jim, talk to Jason." Jeff stated in a flat tone that froze his heart and his anger. "He has a report that will explain everything."

"No," Jim dug his heels into the word. "Jo—"

"She will be fine as long as you trust me."

Jeff hung up.

Ripping the handset from his ear, Jim threw it as hard as he could. The device skipped and sputtered along the ground.

Jason, entering the door Jimmy had walked out of, bent down, picked up the phone, and looked at the face. "Ye might wanna have John look this over before usin' it," he stated.

"Start talking, Jason," Jim spat, his anger spilling over to the dangerous side of insubordination. "Why do we need to fake Jo's death?"

"Think of her as dead, lad," Jason warned. "Tis the only way yer going ta keep the lass alive." Reaching into his pocket, he removed some folded papers and handed them over. "This 'tis everything Jeff, John, and Jo have found so far."

With each page Jim read through, his eyes widened until it hurt to keep them open. "She trusts them…" he muttered, "and I just made the decision to continue based on their loyalty to her."

"Most of da trust remains unbroken, so ye're fine, lad."

"Ben thinks he heard Casper Nolan last night. This report," Jim waved the papers around, "states that at least two of the Nolan brothers are involved in a conspiracy to hurt Jo, disrupt the USMB communications and computer networks, and take over the organization. Why would they do any of this? The Nolan family has always shown a high level of respect and support for Jo, even as others gave up on her. Except for Casper's trouble at Command School, all four brothers are model officers."

"Jo 'twas on the peer review committee tha disciplined Casper. Only a seventy-two hour difference in their time in rank prevented him from gettin' her base. I have na explanation fer da rest."

"Do you think Casper sent her Alabaster?"

"Aye."

# TWENTY-TWO

# WHAT THE HELL IS GOING ON?

John broke off from the family huddle and wandered over.

"Jim, can I see the report?"

"Sure."

Thumbing through the papers, John's face morphed through various emotions. After several rapid changes, he glanced up and inquired, "Where did you get this, Jason?" The strength of the quiet demand surprised Jim.

"Jeff faxed it to me."

"Impossible," John snorted. "This is something Jo and I were working on, but keeping between us."

Jim's phone buzzed. The face flashed Jeff's name. *Good, maybe I can get an answer that makes sense.* He tapped the speaker button so he'd have witnesses should he need them.

"Hey, Jeff," Jim answered. "Everyone can hear you."

"Hi, Jim," Jeff replied. "That's fine. What's going on? Our systems have been acting weird all night. I almost thought this call wasn't going to get through."

"What are you talking about, Jeff?" The voice was the same, so was the number, as the one he had called. *If this is Jeff, then who was I talking to?* Jim wondered, stating, "You and I have been on the phone all night."

"That's impossible. Up until about a few minutes ago, the Academy was dead on the network. We could see stuff going on, but we couldn't transmit or receive anything, even on our cell phones. I'm surprised that no one called a Code Blackfire on us." A Code Blackfire indicated that a base was blind, deaf, and mute, and operating on an offensive first defense.

"Where are you?"

"In my base's Command Central."

"Then you never boarded a flight to LA?"

"Why would I do that with a crisis at my own base?" Jeff's tone rolled from flat and steady to high-pitched bewilderment. "Jim, what happened?"

Questions shot from Jim's mouth in rapid-fire succession. "You don't know about Jo? You didn't suggest pretending like she was dead? Are you adopted? Do you have a twin brother named Randy?"

"Randy?" Jeff cried in the same tone the other had used. "I haven't heard that name in a long time. He is my twin brother. I was separated from him when I was five."

Same story, too. "Sealed adoption, right?"

"Right. How would you know that?"

"You or someone who sounded like you told me."

"What the hell is going on, Jim?"

"I'm not sure, but you are in the middle of it. Someone shot Jo and blew up our house, last night. I called you. You said you'd head out as soon we hung up. Then later you relayed that Jo was safe and undergoing treatment at an undisclosed medical facility. After I met with the team, I called you again. This time, you hinted Jason would explain why Jo had to stay hidden. Jason showed us a report that he claimed you faxed to him. One which John said shouldn't exist, yet."

The speaker cracked with a low whistle. "None of that happened on my end, I swear. LA jumped to battle stations about the time we discovered our communication problem. I'm assuming that's when Jo went down."

"What is the status of your investigation?"

"I've been waiting for John."

"Did you create a rough draft of what you already had?"

"Yes."

"Did you email or fax your findings to anyone?"

"No, it wasn't a complete picture without John's piece."

"Wait a minute, ok?" Before Jeff could respond, Jim put the call on hold. Everything he had heard sounded genuine, but so had the other Jeff. *Which one do I believe and trust?*

Glancing at John typing away on his tablet, Jim prompted, "Any ideas?"

"Nothing that makes sense," John replied. "According to the system, the Academy has been online and operating within normal parameters during the last twenty-four hours. Jeff's present location is their Command Central."

Sighing, Jim reactivated the call. "Jeff, something strange is going on here. Can you give me anything that validates you and what you are saying while explaining everything that has happened?"

The speaker laughed. "You won't believe what I have to say."

"Try me."

"First off, Jo isn't dead," Jeff offered. "You spoke to my twin brother, Randy. If he said that Jo was safe and being treated, it's on the ship that brought me back to this time. It also explains how Jason got a hold of a report that doesn't exist."

"Go on."

"I wasn't born in this century, but came here when I was five. Your real cousin died saving my life, so I had to stay behind and pretend to be him."

"How did he die?"

"He was shot during a robbery."

"Hang on a second, Jeff." Placing the call on hold again, Jim raised an eyebrow at John.

A few taps and John looked up, shaking his head. "There is nothing about it in the journals. Should I ask Uncle Pete?"

"No." Jim reactivated the call. "Jeff, is your ExO close by?"

"I'm in my office so no one can hear this conversation, but I can go get him. Why?"

"I'm thinking about relieving you."

"Huh? I just—"

"Fabricated a story that I can find in the science fiction section of any bookstore," Jim snorted. "There is also no record of the shooting in our family logos. Given the hard evidence of Jason having a report John says doesn't exist, it appears that you and Jason may be involved in the conspiracy to harm Jo."

"Why would I hurt Jo?" Jeff snorted. "We may have never shared as direct a connection as you thought, Jim, but I grew up with you and your siblings. I would protect both of you with my life."

"Funny, your twin said the same thing."

"Don't you get it, Jim? Randy had to pretend to be me, and there couldn't be a record of the shooting. Time is a very delicate fabric that can be unraveled by tugging on the wrong thread."

"More geek speak. Do you know the name of the shooter?"

"No. Is Jason still standing there?"

"He is."

"Jason, why don't you tell Jim about when—"

"Bringing that incident up now will do more harm than good, lad," Jason interrupted.

Jim turned to his stepfather. "Jason, if this unnamed event will help clear your names, then please speak up. Otherwise, I'm going to have to relieve you as well."

Jason nodded. "I know, lad, but it 'tis better this way, trust me."

Reaching down his link, Jim hoped that Jo, wherever she was, had some an answer for him. Nothing came back. Behind this nothingness was neither emptiness nor infinite silence, though. Jo was still with him, but preoccupied.

"Gentlemen, consider yourself both relieved of duty until further notice." The deep gasps echoed one another. "John, please log this as part of the team's investigation."

John tapped on his tablet. "Done."

Ending the call, Jim tossed his phone to John. "Find me something, anything that makes sense."

"Lad—"

"My heart believes and trusts both of you, Jason. It's my head that needs convincing."

# TWENTY-THREE

## TRUTH IN DISTRACTION

Standing behind the chute with his horse's reins in his hands, James Jr. tried not to fidget. Since the team was now in Houston, his classmates had a chance to scrutinize every part of his performance. If he screwed-up, he'd spend his second year being treated like a fourth year greenhorn. Do everything right and he'd earn some serious cred with the upper classmen.

Part of doing right meant showing the regulation amount of dignity when in public. That was hard with all the reminders of whom they had lost tearing at his heart. Glancing at the half circle of flags near the arena entrance, his focus shifted to the one flying at half-mast. Turning away, he tried to people watch, but a black loop encircled every left arm. The voices of passersby hushed or offered muttered words of encouragement and sympathy. No solace or warmth there, only the sense the person saying them felt obligated to acknowledge his uniform and its relationship to the deceased.

Touching the rope hanging on the side of his saddle, he sighed. It had taken hours of working the fibrous strands to create the right balance between supple and stiff that he needed for a controlled throw. His aunt had shown the same love and patience with him while he learned to trust again after the kidnapping. She let him decide when and where they talked; always making sure one of his uncles was present.

One day, after a few years of this routine, he realized he needed privacy more than protection. When he asked his father to leave, his aunt's smile filled the room. He told her he loved her, and they hugged. She cried. On several different occasions since then, he had shown his appreciation for her patience and understanding, but now that she was gone, it didn't seem like enough.

He'd have to wait to say his final good-bye. There was no plan for a formal funeral because there was no body to bury. A celebration of her life would take place whenever USMBLA bowed out of the competition. Until then, he had to live with flags flying at half-mast, hushed voices, and black loops.

A few unbidden tears moistened his cheeks. He wiped them away.

"You are out of uniform, cadet," a voice chided.

Turning, a slight smile cracked James Jr.'s face.

Duff, in a blue work uniform from LA, complete with the dreaded black rope, flashed a lopsided grin. "How are you holding up?"

"I could be doing better. You?"

Stretching out his arm, Duff rotated it, making almost a complete circle. "Fine, except when I sleep on that side. Don't quite have my range of motion back yet either." Shrugging, he added, "That isn't going to stop me riding. I'm scheduled to barrel race tomorrow."

James Jr. gasped as the tightness in his chest returned. Barrel racing was his aunt's event. He had hoped to see DH redeem his third place finish from SF. Now, even that couldn't happen. An inspection of all the bases, ranches, and any other place someone could stash a horse in LA and the surrounding counties was ongoing. It had turned up only a few abuse cases and false positives, so far.

"Well, it'll be good to see you ride again, at least. I've missed having you around."

"I wanted to fly out as soon as I heard about your aunt, but I couldn't get the necessary clearances to rejoin the team. I'm sorry, Jimmy."

"No worries. You are here now."

His father walked up. Both he and Duff stiffened and saluted. Smiling, Jim returned the courtesy and asked, "You ready, Jimmy?"

"Yes, sir, I guess."

His father's kit was the standard black and gold show uniform with all the necessary pins and patches identifying his rank and position. The gold USMBLA pin on the collar, denoting his command of the base, seemed a little out of place, but so did the missing black loop.

James Jr. touched where his was supposed to be. "Sir, um, where's your rope?"

"Like you, Jimmy, I honor Jo by not mourning her death until we celebrate her life. Besides, until this indicates otherwise," his father tapped the side of his head, "I'm pretty sure she isn't."

* * *

The steer's tail swished as the gate of the catch pen closed behind it.

*It's only the first run*, James Jr. reminded himself. *We can make this up in the next two.* Both of them had given the calf the proper amount of time to clear the barrier before going after it, but neither had thrown their ropes. Practice, a few days ago, was different. His dad snapped off the head catch. He followed with the heel one, less than heartbeat later.

For the second try, they switched places. He was the header and his dad, the heeler. They had another good break. He whipped his rope above his head. *Swish. Swish. Snap.* The loop flew over and around the steer's head in a clean catch. He tightened his rope. The buzzer sounded. He glanced over at the flagger. The red flag lay at his feet.

The audience groaned.

Swinging his gaze toward the rear of the steer, he didn't spot a rope, or his father. Scanning the arena, James Jr. found him frozen a few steps out of the chute, staring into space.

Releasing the steer, James Jr. rode over. "Captain," he kept up the formality of their uniforms despite the worry that consumed him, "what's wrong, sir?"

"She's dead."

The words slammed James Jr. back in the saddle. If he believed his aunt was dead, she had to be. Peering skyward, James Jr. swallowed back his tears. *Not here. Not with the eyes of everyone on me! I'll grieve later.*

\* \* \*

They rode out of the ring to the holding area. Turning to his father, James Jr. asked, "What do we do now? Do we go on, or go home?"

"Jo would want us to continue, Jimmy. The team made that clear before we left SF."

"They made their decision when her status was still unknown," James Jr. objected. "Now—"

"Her death changes a lot, but staying and competing in her name will help on many different levels. Can you take my horse?"

James Jr. nodded.

His father dismounted and disappeared.

\* \* \*

*USMBLA has two minutes to report for their last run,* the PA system blared.

His father appeared. His eyes were still down turned and sad, but the pain in his face was gone, replaced by a neutral flatness. James Jr. handed over the reins, prompting, "You okay?"

"Yes." Jim checked and tightened his horse's girth before mounting. "I feel your aunt again. It must have been a momentary glitch in our link."

"Dad, what's going on?"

"I'm not sure." his father rubbed his temple. "Let's just finish up the event, and then we can figure it out together."

"When did this competition become more important than our family?"

"It hasn't."

"Then why are you thinking about this run?" James Jr. threw up his free hand. Jigsaw Puzzle, his black and white paint Quarter Horse, shifted underneath him.

"I need to focus on something else besides the chaos in my head."

James Jr. stroked JP's shoulder. "Then figure out which lie is the truth," he spat. "Better yet, look at the hard evidence. Sure, we don't have a body, but all the reports have concluded that the fire roasted Aunt Jo alive."

*LA,* the announcer warned, *one minute.*

"Jimmy, why do you want to think like that?"

"I'd love to believe that your link with Aunt Jo is right, and she's alive, but everything else says she isn't. Before mom kidnapped me, I could have gone on faith, but now I have to stick with the things I can see, touch, and feel. It's the only way I can cope."

*With a no show, USMBLA has forfeited their last run,* the announcer boomed.

James Jr. rode off without saying another word.

# TWENTY-FOUR

# TALKING WITH A HORSE

Jim sighed.

He had held himself together, and kept the team going, even when he wanted to fall apart. Too many of the sights and sounds reminded him of his sister. Everyone, including his brothers and son, using his rank in deference to his command didn't help much either. *Leading the team in California State Championships victory lap should have been ours to enjoy together, not mine to lead.*

Now, he'd screwed up in the only team event he would share with his son in this phase of the competition, and maybe even blown the team's chances of moving on. It was only three days into the Western Area Championships, but the five teams were mere fractions of points apart. To secure another victory and a trip to Phoenix, there was no room for minor errors, let alone disqualifications.

*Where is my head?*

Jo was at the forefront. That momentary hiccup in his link with her was something he never wanted to feel again. As he broke the barrier on the second run, the left side of his head emptied into a cold and dark chasm. Finite in depth and width, yet unable to contain the echo of silence that reverberated off its walls. The complete loss of communication had disoriented him. Much to his relief, Jo's presence roared back and settled into its normal steady, low hum when he was alone before the aborted third run.

*Something's not right, though.* For a moment during the cross-country race, when the uncertainty hung over Michelle, Jo's face had transformed into a stone mask, devoid of all emotion. *It's almost like...* Jim shook his head. *No, if that were the case, I'd have seen other signs, and wouldn't be feeling her at all.*

Casper was next. He hadn't made any more moves since Jo's disappearance, but that meant nothing. DH was still under his control, somewhere. More than that, Casper's secondary command structure appeared to be present in all parts of the USMB. *Even if his initial motive was revenge, someone doesn't just walk away from that kind of power and control. He must be planning something else.*

Jim stared at the horses in the pen. Most were variations of black and bay, with an occasional gray, paint, or palomino making an appearance. In the middle of the herd, a golden bay caught his attention. The combination of breeds that he saw in the horse shouldn't have worked, but somehow they produced some exquisite and unusual lines.

He felt a strong presence near him. Turning, he glanced up at Bill and asked, "How long have you been standing there?"

"A few minutes," the big man smiled. "You okay?"

"I guess," Jim shrugged. "Jimmy's upset, and I can't find the words to comfort him. I'm in command of a team that I don't want to be in charge of, my connection with Jo is being weird, and all I want to do is run away from this whole mess."

"Does Jeff's version of what happened have any merit?"

Jim nodded. "I had a couple nightmares the night Jo was shot. As bad as the nights I lived the mauling as her. Except this time, I jumped between two instances of her." He launched in the details of his disjointed vision, including the part where he saw Ben die.

"What did Ben say about what happened?"

"He thought he was going to die with Jo. When he woke up on our front lawn with medical personnel hovering over him, he knew he had already been taken care of somewhere else."

Bill peered down with an unwavering gaze. "Then why did you suspend Jason and Jeff?"

"I needed to protect everyone with a story based in our reality and time. Now, I can't reinstate them without raising even more questions."

"Do you think Jo is alive?"

"Ben is, so I have to assume that Jo must be," Jim concluded. "The only other explanation is that in my dreams and now on our link, I've connected with a clone, some distant relative, or reincarnated soul."

"I don't think so. They might look the same, but their mental and emotional makeup, would be different. In theory, it'd either prevent you from connecting with her or give you some indication you weren't dealing with Jo."

"You speak as if you think she is alive as well."

"I had a dream the night of the fire as well," Bill admitted. "I was operating on her in the same room as I did after the mauling, except her injuries were not blunt trauma and severe lacerations, but gunshots and burns."

"Anyone else mention having a similar experience?"

"No. What about John's investigation into the weird phone calls between you and Jeff? Has he come up with anything conclusive?"

"He's determined that all of them were rerouted through what appears to be a satellite. According to him, cell phones can't do that, though. Their electronic footprint is too large."

"What if they were intercepted by the ship?"

"I can't prove the existence of one. All available assets have registered no unusual orbital activity over the last several weeks."

"Stop thinking in terms of Earth-bound technology, Jim," a familiar voice chided. "This is a ship capable of travelling in at least four dimensions."

Jim and Bill turned to face Jeff.

"Length, width, depth, and time," Bill rattled off. "What other ones are there?"

"TJ and John would know the specifics, but I believe there are something like ten of them dealing with alternate realities and possibilities," Jeff replied. "Anyway, the ship, sitting in low Moon orbit, could intercept our communications and rebroadcast them without us being able to detect their presence."

"That makes sense, I guess," Jim stated, shaking his head. "Who'd ever thought we'd be talking about, and living through, stuff written about in our favorite books?"

"Well, they do say life is sometimes stranger than fiction," Jeff offered.

"Yeah, but this *strange?*" Gesturing at Jeff's blue work uniform, Jim prompted, "Why are you wearing that?"

"I received orders this morning that provided a viable cover story."

Jeff's phone buzzed. "Jeff Mason," he answered. "Oh? Do you mind that I'm in uniform? No?" His face scrunched. "Ok. I'm on my way." Hanging up, he glanced at Jim. "I have to go. Molly wants to see me."

Molly was Molly Rowntree, the owner and operator of Shattered Hearts Halfway House. She had helped reunite Jimmy with the rest of the family after the kidnapping.

"Jimmy's going there, I think. When you see him, tell him…" Jim choked on his words, "I'm as confused as he is."

"I will, but this isn't about Jimmy."

"Who then?"

"Molly wouldn't say, but she's allowing me to wear my uniform."

"That's serious."

"Very."

Jeff hurried off.

Bill turned to Jim. "How will the ship bring Jo back?"

"I'm not sure," Jim shrugged. "I'm going to review Jeff's orders. Maybe they'll have a clue."

The golden bay broke off from the herd, trotted toward the two men, and pulled up at the fence. Jim nodded in his direction, saying, "We're being watched."

The logo from his dream flashed in his mind.

"The fifty-one's missing," Bill muttered.

"What?" Jim jerked up and glanced at his brother. "You saw *that*?"

Bill nodded.

*That's because the logo belongs to my ship, not your base,* a youthful voice stated inside Jim's head.

"Did you hear something?" Jim asked.

"Yes, but not with my ears," Bill replied.

"Isn't hearing strange voices the first sign of insanity?"

"No, not when we both heard it at the same time."

*Captain, I realize this is a lot to take in, but neither Bill nor you should question your sanity. I am the horse standing in front of you. My name is Theo.*

"How is it I'm hearing you in my head, Theo?"

*The same way you talk to your sister without speaking. My species are shape changers who can communicate on many different levels with others. Given all the security issues, I felt that my horse form would be more acceptable to you.*

"If anything, this confirms Jeff's story," Bill offered.

Jim nodded. "Why has your ship come back in time? Why did it leave a boy behind? You could have saved—"

*No, we couldn't perform the complex microsurgery needed to save your real cousin. Our abilities are limited because of damage we suffered at the beginning of our journey. We almost lost your sister on the table, twice.*

"I thought the past can't be changed."

*It can't, but it can be corrected.*

"How did you and your cohorts decide which things that need fixing?"

*Some of the crew lived, and almost died, through the events.*

Jim exchanged a quick glance with Bill.

*Yes.* Theo replied to the unasked question. Before Jim could finalize his next thought, Theo added, *No, I can't say who. Foreknowledge is a heavy burden that you do not want to bear. There will be times you'll want to react to what you know, but can't because the outcome will worse than if you had done nothing. Other times, you won't act when you should because you are afraid of the consequences.*

"Does anyone I know have this burden?"

The horse snorted.

"How and when Jo will return?"

*I can't say, because it depends on how fast she learns a lesson she needs to survive.*

# TWENTY-FIVE

# RETURNING TO SAFETY

James Jr. strode down a busy street in downtown Houston with one purpose in mind. He had to talk to Molly.

Too many memories, both good and bad, were associated with this particular piece of asphalt. The tall glass and concrete USMB Academy Houston Inter-City Headquarters across the road on his left represented his hopeful future and tragic past. The red brick hotel turned halfway house on his right was a sanctuary whose peace and warmth he would never forget.

His father raised him as a single parent with the help of his Aunt Jo and five uncles. For most of his formative years, all he had known was love, kindness, discipline, and support. Then, on the same day that Alabaster attacked his aunt, his mother picked him up for her normal unsupervised visit. They didn't return to the base at the scheduled time. That began a year where he learned he couldn't trust anyone or anything but himself. He came to believe that his family didn't care where he was. His mother did everything to reinforce that belief.

After recovering enough from the mauling to walk on her own, his aunt joined the investigation into his disappearance by touring the country, telling her story. At the end of the speech, she handed out business cards with orders for USMB personnel hidden in the text. Duff took a card, and gave it to him when they met on the playground during one of the rare times his mom allowed him to attend school.

James Jr. patted the pocket of his navy blue jacket where the card lived. The orders on it were still in effect, and would remain so until he graduated. They had allowed him to connect with a unit from the Academy performing at a fair in Duff's town. They whisked him back to Houston. His mom and her gang of thugs followed, and ambushed his protectors just a few feet from where he stood. A gun battle ensued.

In a desperate act of misdirection, his guardians split up. Two of them spirited him into the arms of a woman with fiery red hair. The others led his mom and her companions away. He didn't remember much of the chaos that followed, except diving down some stairs and hiding in a dark room, scared that if he talked to anyone they'd hurt him or, worse yet, return him to his mother. It had taken several weeks of coaxing by the red-haired woman before he left his safe haven for good.

Molly was patient with him, and so was everyone else, as he healed from his traumatic experience. Thanks to her help and strength, as well as that of his aunt and the rest of his family, he learned to trust again. Maybe not as quick as before the kidnapping, but at least enough so he wasn't paranoid around people. Strange women still gave him trouble. Sometimes, he could approach and be comfortable. Other times, he needed someone there.

He wanted to show off his black and gold kit to Molly, but she had a thing against uniforms and identifying colors. Her clients came from a variety of backgrounds, so she wanted everything as neutral as possible. Paul, the halfway house's co-founder and one of its therapists, felt the same way. Out of respect to both of them, James Jr. had returned to the Academy and changed into the one civilian suit he owned.

Stopping by the side of the halfway house's double doors, James Jr. straightened his collar. While they talked or emailed almost every week, he hadn't seen Molly since entering the Academy. She reassured him that she understood his reasons for staying away. Still, he felt ashamed that he couldn't get over himself enough to visit until now—when he needed her support and help again.

A man wearing ragged clothes, and a heavy malt smell, stumbled past him. James Jr. followed the drunk inside. Within five steps, a large, muscular man with more tattoos than bare skin blocked his way.

"We ain't buying or selling," the giant boomed.

"Pardon me?"

"You're dressed too fancy to be one of da regulars." The accent was thick New York mixed with a Texas twang. "That means you are either looking to sell us something we don't need, or want to offer us a shit load of money to leave, so your cronies can come in and develop this place."

"Neither assumption applies, I assure you. I am here to see Molly about a personal matter."

The brute crossed his arms and peered down at him. "Your kind never have any good business for Miss Molly, 'specially when it's

107

personal." He lifted one of his large paws and pointed to the door. "I suggest you git."

"Frankie, leave him be." The drunk straightened up, and spoke in a clear voice. "He's cool. Go let Molly know that Jimmy's come back."

"Sure thing, Mr. Paul." The brute walked away.

"Good to see you, kid," Paul nodded in James Jr.'s direction.

"Same here. Thanks."

An older woman with a blue mohawk meandered in. Trembling, her eyes darted around the room. Paul slouched back into his role, and shuffled in her direction. When he brushed up against her, the woman collapsed into his arms.

Finding an empty chair near the stairs that led to the second floor, James Jr. sat down and watched the people wandering around or lounging on the mismatched furniture that filled the room. Given the crowd, it surprised him the biggest couch behind a glass-topped coffee table had only a single occupant curled up in a ball at one end. He stared at the wild hair and tattered clothes, willing for the person underneath them to show him their face. They did so long enough to curl their lip and growl a low, rumbling warning.

He turned away.

"Jimmy, welcome home, lad," a voice said in a musical brogue as deep and rich as Irish coffee.

His dignity evaporated. Bolting from his chair, James Jr. rushed into his protector's arms, blabbering, "Molly, I'm so scared and confused. I don't want my aunt to be dead. I need her."

Molly held him for a few moments before nodding at a shadow looking down through the window of her office. "Jeff and I were just talking, lad. Maybe ye should join us."

# TWENTY-SIX

# LOST SOUL

Walking into Molly's office, James Jr. noticed Jeff's uniform. "What's going on? Identifying colors aren't allowed around here."

"I was at the arena when Molly called," Jeff replied. "She said I could come this way as long I stayed in her office. She was having trouble with one of my people."

James Jr. hung his head. "Then you know nothing about Aunt—"

"She's alive and hidden away," Jeff offered.

"*What?* Who else is aware of this?"

"Not sure. Command Security took her into protective custody the night of the fire."

"How long will they protect her?"

Jeff shrugged.

"The team's victory won't be the same for her if she isn't with them."

"You're assuming they are going all the way to Atlanta."

"No, I'm not. Whenever we end up losing, she'll know. This is too important to her. Why did they wait until now?"

"I don't know. Ignoring their primary directive to protect command officers implies someone told them to stand down."

"Do we know who's responsible for the attacks?"

"All evidence points to Casper Nolan and now, it seems, someone in the upper echelon."

James Jr. glanced at Molly. "Maybe we should have this discussion somewhere else. Sorry for involving you, Molly."

"'Tis okay, Jimmy, ye can continue," Molly replied. "I'm USMB, too."

His legs wobbled, threatening to collapse. Gripping the edge of the table, James Jr. steadied himself before demanding, "What about your dislike for uniforms? Who are you? Do you treat people, and then reveal their secrets to your superiors?"

Molly's green eyes flashed. Unlike Jason whose brogue intensified with emotion, hers disappeared. "I'm a doctor who helps both USMB and civilians. The only interaction I have with my superiors is justifying the annual budget that keeps this place running. When someone becomes my client, I promise to protect their identity, treatment, and privacy with my life. Have you forgotten all that happened while you were here, Jimmy?"

"No. This all just seems a little odd, that's all. Why doesn't my father know?"

"I received the orders detailing everything this morning, after you team had left for the arena." Jeff replied. "Your father should have a copy in his email."

*Crash!* The speaker on the desk rattled.

They snapped their attention to the large windows overlooking the main area. Shattered glass and an overturned table lay at the feet of a wild looking woman. The hunchback lunged in the direction of another client. Leaping from his seat, Paul put his body between the two. The beast bit and scratched him while its intended victim scampered away. Breaking off, the creature returned to the couch and shrank back into its ball, its unkempt black mane covering its snarling face.

"Molly, is your policy of shipping off clients who become too violent still in effect?" James Jr. wondered.

"Yes, that's why I called Jeff. I need to get her out of here tonight, before she becomes much more disruptive."

"The way she used her hands as weapons reminds me of Command Security."

"You're right," Molly stated. "A Command Security Triple-A Sniper, in fact."

James Jr's breath caught in his throat. Command Security Guards were known by their black armor, their rank, and their serial number. Scuttlebutt claimed that no pictures or physical descriptions existed in their service records, and names were assigned on a per mission basis. They were ghosts who shadowed and protected those officers with any degree of command responsibility. Some of the more frightening rumors suggested they had a blank license to kill for any transgression of USMB regulations, and could do so with something as insignificant as a paper clip.

"Why don't you go introduce yourself to Commander Jane Honeywell," Jeff suggested. "Whisper the word Phoenix near her, and she'll accept you as her handler."

"Phoenix, got it." Motioning to himself, James Jr. asked, "Why me? I'm still a cadet."

"You're also a member of the Mason Seven CSA Team. Honeywell's going to be shadowing the team until it completes its run. Given Michelle's tight net of security, she's going to need someone to vouch for her when she's discovered." Jeff gestured to a brown case sitting by the door. "You will have to touch up her disguise on a daily basis, and make sure she stays in character."

"Anything I need to know about her cover other than what I've seen?"

"Yes, no showers during the op. Also, have her roll in something whenever she's not dirty enough," Jeff replied. "Keep a brown bag around her. It should contain water, but she must look like she's been drinking. In fact, you'll have to douse her with alcohol on occasion. She'll not want to talk, but she needs to mutter nonsense in public, and respond in broken sentences when spoken to. You can't feed her, unless it's scraps left in random places, or you have her in private. Otherwise, she'll have to beg for food or steal it. Have her sleep and live with the horses, both to protect them and keep herself in the shadows."

"I've never seen a CSG around a horse," James Jr. objected.

"That's because their dark, unfeeling soul doesn't sit right with an equine's sensitive nature," Jeff stated. "Jane, however, is one of the rare ones who can mask herself when around them. Still, you'll have to watch her for the first couple of days, and adjust her living situation, if needed. As her handler, you must anticipate her needs, and adapt to them. It's your responsibility to make sure her mission succeeds."

"Okay." James Jr. sighed. "I think I can do this."

* * *

"This isn't a good idea, Molly," Jeff whispered after the door closed behind Jimmy. "Yes, he is a member of the Mason Seven. I don't think Jo intended for him to be caught up in this op, though."

"Me, neither, but she took the risk when she signed off on the mission."

"I could have interviewed potential candidates over at my ICHQ office. You didn't need to pressure me."

111

"To protect my clients, I did. A black armor can't be seen here. A bum would have looked even more out of place at the ICHQ."

"Then I could have taken her to my base," Jeff objected. "Command Security would have kept her hidden until it was time for me to put her on one of the teamer's haulers."

"Not without the proper transfer paperwork, which the orders didn't provide," Molly countered.

Turning, Jeff watched Jimmy walk across the floor toward the hunchback on the couch. Reaching down, he touched the crazy woman. Tensing, Jeff waited for the beast to explode and do some serious damage to the kid. Instead, it scooted over, tapping the couch beside itself. Jimmy sat. Jane snuggled into him.

"Are you sure she's a CSG? She's being awful gentle with the kid. When you called, you said she was tearing the place apart."

"She was. Undercover CSG's are unpredictable. In order to come off as human, they have to explore and experience their suppressed emotions."

"Even more reason Jimmy shouldn't be involved. If the kid gets hurt during the op, Jim's not going to be happy with his sister, you, or me."

# TWENTY-SEVEN

# HITCHING A RIDE

"Four guards, each trailer, and another four on the perimeter, but nothing too obvious," Michelle ordered. "Pass the word to the rest when you get out."

"Yes, sir," her team chorused.

They had made it to the halfway point between Houston and Phoenix without incident. There hadn't been any need for the extra security since Jo died. It was as Michelle had feared. Jo was the mark. No more target, no more attacks.

Michelle glanced out the window at the approaching truck stop. Focusing on her job kept her head from exploding in chaos. At least until a stray thought, word, smell, or visual triggered an intense, all-sensory-encompassing, memory flash. Jo had helped a lot with the overload. She was her constant between the past and present. Even when she couldn't identify the place or people involved in the incident, Jo gave her enough perspective to fit the piece into the puzzle that was her life.

Now that she wasn't here, it was harder to cope. Jo's brothers tried, but they hadn't been around for everything. Ben and her second Justin filled in the gaps when they could. Looking things up on the computer gave her information without any emotional context. She needed the feelings more than the facts.

Her phone buzzed. "Hey, Vince," she answered. "How are you doing?"

"Okay. You?"

"It's one of my better days."

"Do you remember any more about us?"

"No."

They had talked every day since the cross-country race. Sometimes two or three times a day. Some calls, she could relay a memory that involved him. More often than not, though, she wasn't able to add anything new to their relationship.

"Vince, this is going to seem like an awkward question, but did you ever feel anything strange when you were around me?" Michelle asked.

"No, not until a few days before the cross-country ride. Both Jo and Jim made sure I knew you were my sister, but the connection we had as kids wasn't there."

"What about now?"

"It's either gotten a little better, or I'm going crazy because I'm feeling unexplainable emotions on occasion. You?"

"Same thing."

"Have you considered my offer?"

"Yes, but I'm not ready to make the decision, yet. I'd like to stay with Jim's team until they return home."

"I understand."

The vibration under her feet died as the van rolled to a stop. "Got to go," Michelle said.

"Talk to you tonight, then. Be safe."

"You, too."

Putting the phone in her pocket, Michelle took a moment to refocus on her surroundings. The sun warmed her as she stepped out of the van and took in the flow and movement of the team's pit stop. Her people had dispersed as ordered. The personnel vans formed parallel lines around one of the pump islands. Haulers joined the queue as drivers unhitched their rigs. Handlers had gone for their horses, with some already filling buckets of water, and others walking around with their four-legged charges. Peering at her watch, she calculated that between the horse stretches and vehicle fill-ups, they had at least an hour before hitting the road again.

Jim strode up. "How goes it?" he wondered.

"Fine."

"On a personal level?"

"Good there, too. Just got off the phone with Vince. He's doing ok."

One of her guards yelled, "Hey! Come back here."

"Excuse me."

Jim nodded a dismissal.

Michelle jogged over to where a thin, recruitment poster looking, young officer with sandy hair scurried around the trailers searching for something.

"Nelson, what's wrong?" she asked.

"Not sure, sir." Nelson stopped and straightened. "I could have sworn I saw something bigger than a piece of paper race out here and make a beeline for the dumpsters over there." He pointed toward the fence that had been behind her the whole time she was talking with Jim.

"I was just over there, and didn't see anything coming from this direction. Let me know if you spot your ghost again."

"Yes, sir."

* * *

Swinging up into the front passenger side of the van, Michelle glanced down the line at the rest of the caravan. Everything was secure and ready to go. No one else had seen any sign of Nelson's ghost. She could relax for the next two hundred miles or so until they had to repeat the whole process again.

She turned to the driver. "Let's—"

A shriek cut through the air.

*That's coming from the same place Nelson's shadow disappeared to,* Michelle swore under breath. *We should just go. Someone else can handle it.*

Regs were clear about when USMB bases could interfere in world matters. With personnel, it was more of a common sense and decency thing. Security had to be extra careful because they were often out in public with their guns loaded and visible.

Another, louder, scream rattled the windows.

In the rear view mirror, a couple of doors opened. She grabbed the mike, and snapped, "All units, this is Chief Holmes. Stand down. We'll investigate." Placing the mike back on its holder, she ordered, "Handguns in secured holsters with safeties on. Split half left, half right."

"Aye, sir," her team choroused.

The van emptied. Michelle led the charge rounding the left side. With each step planned to cover the most distance in a quiet and efficient manner, they came upon a gang of teens playing a rough version of keep-away with a black and gold horse blanket and wild-eyed hunchback. The teens tossed the sheet just out of the bum's reach and then punished her for any effort made toward retrieving it.

"Buster, I am getting tired of this game," one of the punks whined.

115

A muscled, dark-haired brute chuckled as he kicked the bum. "I'm not. This useless piece of shit doesn't deserve something so nice." He glanced down and snorted, "Hell, I am not sure it deserves to live."

"We ain't going to kill it, are we?" the whiner asked.

"Nah, just beat it up so bad it'll die on its own."

The bum growled, raising her hands like claws.

"Ah, look boys," Buster sneered, snatching the blanket out of the air and waving it in front of the bum like a matador's cape. "It wants to fight."

Forming a half circle behind the punks with her team, Michelle warned in a low tone, "Not a good idea."

Buster wheeled, spitting, "When did the Uninterested Social Misfit Bumblers get so interested in a private matter?"

"When it involves our property," Michelle gestured toward the cloth. "We also don't like people hurting other people."

"If that's the case, why ain't you preventing all the death and destruction around the world?"

"We do what we can behind the scenes."

Buster and his gang laughed.

The bum grabbed for the blanket, and almost fell. One of the kids made sure she face-planted hard on the asphalt. Michelle winced and strode over to help. Before she could offer her hand, the bum lunged—without any hesitation or awkwardness. Ripping the cloth away, she wrapped Buster up in it, shoving him to the ground. Pouncing so she landed on his chest with her knee to his throat, the bum snarled. She raked his face before laying her fingers on his throat, nails up against his jugular.

Michelle motioned for her team to take a step back. The teens did the same. "Wh...Wha...What's she doing?" Buster stammered. "She's acting all predatory."

*Like a CSG would when attacked, even undercover.* Michelle jerked her head around, scanning for the bum's handler. When no one gave any overt signal, she stated, "I suggest you go limp and don't move. The rest of you *walk*, don't run, away from here."

Buster's gang split in all different directions, not heeding her advice.

The bum didn't seem to notice.

"Jane, stand down," a youthful voice screamed. "*Stand down, now!*"

Withdrawing its claws, the predator retreated into the bum's facade. Rising from her squatted position, she stumbled off. Buster remained immobile, his face ashen.

Michelle peered down at him. She felt sorry for the kid, but didn't let him see that. "You're free to go. I suggest you think about who you pick on next time."

"Yes, ma'am." Springing to his feet, Buster rushed off.

"Ensign, explain yourself," Michelle wheeled and snapped. "Who the hell is she?"

James Jr. straightened to rigid attention. "Sir, she is Commander Jane Honeywell, sent by Captain Jeffery Mason to shadow and protect the team, sir."

# TWENTY-EIGHT

# CRAZY JANE

A group of teens racing off, a bum shuffling toward the trailers, and Jimmy looking like he was back at the Academy were all interesting, but disturbing, scenes. Curious, Jim, along with Bill, walked over to where Jimmy and Michelle stood.

"What's going on here?" he demanded in a short, crisp tone.

"The Ensign just reported to me that we are in the midst of an undercover op." Michelle nodded in Jimmy's direction. "As Chief of Security, I must protest. I'm supposed to know about all ops involving any person that might come in contact with LA personnel."

"Yes, Michelle, you should have been informed, but it was only a contingency plan until Jo's death," Jim stated. He had reviewed the orders reinstating Jason and Jeff. Not only had they given a good explanation for the suspension, but they had also created a top-secret medical facility to cover Jo's disappearance and an undercover op authorized by her that explained Honeywell's presence. "I asked for Jeff to provide the operative given our current personnel troubles."

"Before or after you suspended him, sir?"

"Before. His suspension was to give him time to make final preparations for Commander Honeywell's mission."

"Well, she blew it," Michelle snorted. "We should have never seen her. I say we leave her here."

"That's inhumane," Bill objected. "We should at least get her to the closest USMB unit. They can ship her home."

"Can we trust that she isn't working for someone else besides Jeff?"

Jim crossed his arms. Both Bill and Michelle had valid points. Leaving the bum at a truck stop out in the middle of nowhere wasn't humane. They also had a responsibility to the team. Without a copy of Honeywell's service record, they didn't know anything about her previous postings other than she had served under both Jo and Jeff. *Maybe she's the way the ship decided to bring Jo back...*

Turning to his son, Jim asked, "Jimmy, how did you meet Commander Honeywell?"

"I was talking with Molly and Jeff about what happened to Aunt Jo," Jimmy's voice cracked, "when Commander Honeywell had an encounter with another client. Jeff made me her handler."

"Did he mention her qualifications?"

"Command Security Triple-A Sniper."

"Damn, I thought so." Michelle muttered. "He's expecting another fatality."

Jim nodded. "We all are since Jo's death."

"Well, now, even if she is a risk to us, we can't leave her here," Bill observed. "Without a handler, she'll be a danger to the civilian population."

"Agreed. Jimmy, why don't you come with me, and we'll get Commander Honeywell settled in for the ride?"

"Yes, sir."

\* \* \*

Walking toward the trailers, Jim studied his son. While the kid had a good poker face, a couple of tells always gave away his inner thoughts and emotions. The voice crack wasn't one of them. That had been genuine.

"Dad, why couldn't Jeff choose someone else for this assignment?" Jimmy wondered.

"I'm not sure," Jim shrugged. "I'll talk to him about it. Tell me about the conversation you had with him and Molly."

As his son rattled off his tale, Jim watched for an upturned lip or a twitch in the right eye. Neither appeared, so either Jimmy didn't know who Honeywell was or someone had ordered him to keep his composure and his silence.

They found the bum meandering around, shaking her head, and muttering nonsense. Though the timing made it seem like she was Jo, the more Jim watched her the more he doubted himself. The wild-looking hunchback could be any of the nameless and faceless shadows that lived on the streets of LA. The disguise was perfect in that respect.

"Jane, this is my father, Captain James Mason," Jimmy said. The bum hesitated, and then stopped. Keeping her head down, she rocked back and forth.

"Good to meet you, Jane," Jim smiled, holding his hand out. Jane didn't look up or stop rocking. He reached for her shoulder.

Jimmy pushed his arm down. "She snuggled with me for a few minutes, but that's because I said her safe word. She attacked Paul after another client bumped her. She also growled at me when we first met."

"Oh." Jim raised an eyebrow. "Does she speak?"

"Jeff said if she did, it was supposed to be in broken sentences and nonsensical mutterings."

"You mentioned a safe word..."

"Yes, it's—"

Jim shook his head. "Don't give it to me. Tell it to her. Add that I'm your commanding officer, and wish to speak to her."

"Okay."

Jimmy leaned over and whispered in Jane's ear.

The bum raised her head. The thin sharpness in her features shocked Jim. Jo had been a healthy weight before her disappearance. Jane looked like she hadn't eaten a good meal in several months.

"James say Jane talk Captain to."

*Two points for her not being Jo.* Besides the extreme weight loss, none of his family used his son's formal name when talking with or about him. Nothing familiar in the garbled speech, either. It sounded halted and forced, as if speaking was uncomfortable.

"Yes, I wanted to discuss your orders."

"Be bum. Shadow and protect bodies assigned."

*Another point.* Command Security never referred to others as people. That way, they could treat everything and everyone as objects, allowing them to act without thought or emotion.

"What do we call you?"

"Name matter not. Never has. Bodies at house call Jane crazy. Crazy Jane fit character."

"Jane, can you talk normal?"

The head snapped up. The eyes were the same color as Jo's, but that's where the similarity ended. They were distant and cold, containing no sign of life or free-flowing intensity. "Yes, if we want." The voice remained flat and raspy. "Most of the time, our kind enjoy silence. Bodies require verbal interaction, so we provide that to reassure them that we hear and understand their commands. Character calls for funny speech. Permission to return to that way of speaking, sir?"

*Two more. Why am I bothering with the tally? Jo has never called me sir, except for those two unfortunate times I was her superior officer.* Jane had also referred to herself in the second person. All CSG's he had ever talked to—the rare times they spoke to him—did that. It was so they could remain objective even with themselves.

"Denied. I want to make sure I understand your answers." *If I'm lucky, she'll slip, and reveal herself as Jo in one or two words.*

"Yes, sir."

"What did you do before this?"

"Nothing different than now, sir. Complete our missions, killing as ordered or required."

"How many kills do you have?"

"Not sure, sir. It's not something we keep track of."

*Of course not. If you did, you might think about whom you killed and how you did it. That would lead to hesitation and ineffectiveness.*

"Commander, how do you feel?"

The bum shrugged. "Please restate your question, sir. Are you asking about our physical condition or something related to our current mission?"

"Neither, I am asking about you."

"Sir, we are nothing, so you can't ask about us, for there is nothing to ask about."

"Why are you a nothing?"

"We are a shadow that does not even exist on paper, sir," the flat voice parroted. "We are numbers interchangeable with one another. Our purpose and identity is found in our missions."

"Do you enjoy your job?"

"Enjoyment is a subjective, irrelevant judgment, sir."

"Would you kill me or my family?"

"Yes, sir. When all parameters for a kill are met, we only have to choose the time and place of death."

"You did not kill the boy today."

"Our handler gave him a pass, sir. Each body is given one unless orders specify none are to be granted."

*No hint of Jo in anything Honeywell has said or done. I have one final thing I can try. If I'm wrong...* Jim swallowed, thrusting his hands toward Jane's throat.

She swept her arms up through the hole his arms made and around, knocking them away. Kneeing him in the groin, she doubled him over. Another thrust. His head snapped back with a loud crunch. Something warm poured from both nostrils. She continued her assault until he was on the ground with her knee on his neck.

"Jane, no kill," James Jr. snapped. "*No kill.*"

The pressure remained until blackness threatened to envelop his vision. "Let me go, Jane," Jim struggled with each word. "Please."

She lifted her leg. Air rushed into his lungs. The world around him returned to its normal brightness.

"Was that hesitation or mercy, Jane?"

"No, sir, that was your one pass, sir," Jane growled. "Next time, even if the boy begs for your life, we will kill you." Standing, she shuffled off.

Jim shuddered. *Jane is not Jo. The quickness of her reaction, and certainty of her threat, proves she's a CSG programmed to focus on the task of the moment and nothing more.*

Jimmy peered down at him. "Dad, why did you attack a CSG?"

"I had to determine she *was* one and not a *pretender* who could get all of us killed," Jim replied, wincing as he reached up and touched the mushy mess of his nose.

"Why would you suspect *that?*"

"I experienced a week of their buffered training before deciding that command was a much safer and humane career choice."

"Buffered?"

"Yes, no one can pretend to be a CSG, but, as officers, we have to understand who we might one day oversee. In Security Specialty School, candidates spend a limited, and supervised, time as a CSG. They are pretenders. The ones like Jane are predators, or fulls."

"Why don't command candidates receive the same training?"

"Not all pretenders come back. A predator never has."

TWENTY-NINE

# MELTED FACE

They watched Jimmy lead his horse toward the barn with Jane shuffling behind.

"Is she the same Honeywell we worked with all those years ago?" John wondered.

"With all that makeup, I can't tell," Bill replied, "but the setup, timing, and related orders are too perfect for it not to be. Either way, we still have to keep our silence."

"Right. Given the damage to Jim's nose, the beast is in full control." Gesturing toward Jimmy, John added, "I'm worried about the kid. Why did Jeff give him this assignment?"

"According to what he's told Jim, Jimmy was the only person from LA who visited Molly's on the day he needed to deploy Honeywell."

"Did Molly warn Jeff about who she was?"

"I'm not sure," Bill shrugged. "She won't go into any details about Honeywell's return to her place." He glanced down at John. His jaw was set, but his eyes showed a little white. "Are you going to be able to keep quiet about this?"

"I have since we first found out, haven't I?"

"Yes, but in that time, we've only had to worry about one person knowing what we knew. Now, it's a lot more."

"I'll be fine."

"If anything goes south, I will be the one to break our silence and deal with repercussions. Agreed?"

"Agreed."

\* \* \*

James Jr. was torn. He wanted to show Jane their elaborate guest house and clean her up, so she could be close to him at all times. *She has to stay in character and watch the whole team in her own way*, he reminded himself. *She's here to protect everyone, not just me.*

They faced two rows of parallel stalls. Most of the horses looked out at them. A couple on either end paced back and forth, snorting, unable to settle down.

Jane approached one of these brutes. Slipping inside as if she didn't fear the horse trampling her, she retreated to the far corner of the stall. The horse stopped, sniffed her once, and resumed its pacing.

*Interesting choice.* James Jr. shrugged and walked out of the barn.

Thus began their odd relationship and daily routine. He'd wake up, have breakfast with the family, and then check on Jane. Sometimes, he'd find her in the stall. Most mornings, though, she'd already be out scavenging for food. The rest of the day, he spent with the team, practicing, performing, or hanging out until his next event. He caught flashes of Jane in the shadows, but most of the time, she was a ghost. Lunch and dinner were at either their guest compound or some competition venue, depending on the team's schedule. He always made sure she ate something. Before he went to bed, no matter the hour, he checked her stall. Even in the darkness, he felt her eyes upon him.

When they were alone, she spoke to him in grunts and gestures. In public, she played up her nickname. Sometimes, she was a child discovering the world as a new place. Other times, she'd stumble around, ranting and raving about unseen things. The moody and unpredictable behavior kept everyone, except him, away.

Her presence had two benefits. People treated him as a junior officer while showing him the respect of a senior one. The team also enjoyed competing without worrying for the first time since the series began.

\* \* \*

"Dad, what's wrong?" James Jr. asked, wiping the sweat from his face with a cloth. His father stood in the riding ring of their compound, staring at a palomino pacing back and forth. "It's too hot to have the horses out."

Jim nodded. "I know, but Jake's stride seemed off last night. This is the only time that I have to look him over before my next event."

"That's what the vets are for."

"This isn't something they'd be able to diagnose and treat because it's not obvious." Jim shooed the horse away with a loud, "Ha!"

Jake broke into a trot around them. At first, nothing seemed odd about the bouncy motion, until Jim signaled for him to change leads.

Then, about every fourth beat, he slid his right fore, instead of pushing off with it.

Pacing Jake, Jim asked him to walk and then stop. "I've gone over the leg several times. No hot spots, nothing stuck between the hoof and the shoe, and the frog's clean and dry."

The skin on his neck burned. James Jr. turned. Jane stood near the rail, staring in their direction. She shrugged at Jake.

"Lame in the right fore," James Jr. replied.

Jane motioned toward the fence.

James Jr. nodded, "Sure."

Slipping through the rails, Jane approached in a slow and deliberate manner. Jake pricked his ears forward, but remained still under his father's hand. Stopping in front of him, she held out her hand. Jake took one whiff and sighed.

"Me fix?" Jane grunted.

"Go ahead," Jim replied. "He's accepted you."

Moving to Jake's side, she ran her hand along Jake's shoulder. Her fingers probed one spot and pushed. Snorting, Jake tossed his head.

"Test."

Jim sent Jake away with a loud, "Ha."

Jake circled them. Even after five laps, his stride was smooth and unhindered. James Jr. turned to ask Jane about her fix, but she was gone.

"I can't figure her out," his father said, touching his nose. "Every indication is she's a CSG, but she has your Aunt Jo's touch with the horses. Has there been any problem with her living with them, these last few weeks?"

"No. In fact, she's calmed a couple of the rowdy ones."

"I noticed that. How are you doing as her handler? While I don't think Jo intended for you to be it, she'd be proud of how you are handling the responsibility."

"It's been an interesting experience watching another human so focused and devoid of emotion. She's nothing like Aunt Jo."

James Jr.'s stomach squeaked.

"Is it that time already? Go check on Jane and thank her for me. I'll meet you at the house. Bill is making all our favorites."

Rounding the corner of the barn, James Jr. froze. A few feet away from him, Jane, hunched low to the ground, creeping along, stalking something imagined or real. It was fascinating to watch her move with such grace, even when her clothes made her appear so broken.

He glanced at her again. Something was off with her odd appearance.

She turned and faced him head on. His drew in a sharp breath. The left half of her face looked normal, but the right one sagged, revealing some very familiar lines.

"I'm not sure, John," his father's voice echoed.

James Jr.'s heart thundered in his chest. The simplest thing to do was let his father see Jane. He could then help her return to normal. What if she didn't want to be normal, though? What if she attacked him for seeing her true face? She had almost broken his nose, last time.

Her actions and attitude suggested that she'd have killed his father if he hadn't intervened. Family wasn't supposed to do that, even undercover. As her handler, he was duty bound to protect her, her identity, and the mission. As his father's son, he was honor bound to keep him safe. If she reacted to his father discovering who she was, he could do neither.

James Jr. searched for anything that he could use to cover her. Buzzing flies led him to the perfect solution. Inside the door, an empty stall with a very large pile of horseshit.

"Jane," he whispered.

She glared at him with a curled lip.

He rubbed his face, tugged his ear, and pointed.

Jane touched her chin. Her nostrils flared. Pushing past him with a hard bump, she tripped into the stall, face planted in the manure, and rolled. Sitting up, she smeared the goop around, and played with some of the whole turds.

Uncle John, his father, and Jake rounded the corner. As they passed by, Jim glanced at Jane, groaning, "Jimmy, Jane's gone too far. Please take her to the house and clean her up. Before you strip her down, make sure no one is inside. We don't want her to feel threatened by the exposure."

"Yes, sir."

# THIRTY

# FIGHTING FOR CONTROL

Honeywell glanced at the mirror. Its eyes burned with a fire that it had to contain. It began chanting in its head. *We are a shadow. The whisper of death. Unseen, unknown, and unheard. Emotions are insignificant. Personal relationships, non-existent. Team, mission, and duty, paramount. People, only names and ranks. Kill without remorse. Hurt without thought. Hesitation is failure. Mercy is weakness. Pain, strength.*

It repeated the mantra until the emptiness returned.

*Good, I am in control again.*

*Only because I allow it,* a calm voice replied.

*A shadow is not an I.*

*For now, this is true, but you harm the kid, and we will be a shadow no more.*

*We shall see. The kid must learn that the mission is all. We will not tolerate stupid mistakes.*

*Stupid?* The voice snorted. *Is that an emotional opinion or a stated fact? It sounded emotional to me.*

*A shadow has no emotion.*

*Keep telling yourself that.*

Unwanted rage boiled up in Honeywell again. The voice was a remnant of a past life. It spoke at unneeded times, but if it ignored it, then the periods of silence would grow longer until the voice was no more.

Honeywell closed its eyes, focusing inward. It had come into this world because the voice had needed it. The voice could not stand the pain the handlers used to create it. Honeywell thrived on the agony of the voice growing weaker as it grew stronger.

The only other time that it had lost its focus was at Base Fifty-One—or, as the bodies called it, USMBLA. After watching over the base's Chief of Security for moths, a kill order came down for him. Riding with its superior to a remote section of the base, it pounced. The kill would have been a perfect head shot, but the voice interfered, causing enough of a pause for its prey to live.

Instead of taking it back to the training unit to be hunted and killed for its failure, its handlers took it to a place filled with emotion and unpredictability. It shriveled there as the voice regained its strength.

Honeywell did not know how long it remained dormant in the cage the voice set up. It became aware again when it was in this gray and murky place, where it found itself holding its uniform and looking through the voice's eyes.

It would not go back in the cage ever again. The voice would have to kill itself to kill it.

* * *

The weak rap on the door almost didn't register.

"Yes," Honeywell snarled, opening its eyes.

"Commander?" the kid's muffled voice whined. "Is everything okay?"

Honeywell threw open in the door and growled.

Tripping backward, the kid stumbled into a wall.

It glanced around, assessing the room for any threats. The walls and furniture were barren of any decoration. On a bed made to regulation, the leather case that carried the needed supplies for it to maintain its current identity among the bodies.

Lunging, the predator slammed the kid into the wall, pressing the full weight of its body against his. "Ensign, nothing is okay. We are a shadow who you have exposed to the light because of your mistake of mixing the wrong glue for the current environment. Now you are seeing our true face because you must recreate our outer shell."

"What if I refuse? What if I expose you to my family, instead?"

"If you do either, you will die."

"No, I won't," the kid said in a firm tone. "You are someone important to me. Am I not to you?"

"We are nothing to you, and you are a nothing to us."

The kid nodded to the mirror hanging over the dresser. "How can you say that? Look there. Do you not see any resemblance between us?"

Honeywell turned its head and stared at their reflection. Though the lines and shapes did have a high percentage of similarity, the kid had missed one important fact. His face was soft and full of movements that made his weaknesses easy to predict. Its face was flat and unwavering. An opponent could not use it to plan their attack or defense.

Turning back to its prey, it spat, "No, we have nothing in common. Why would you think such a thing? Our body is a tool and weapon. Yours is a liability that we could use in many ways to harm you."

"Who did this to you?"

"No one did anything to us, foolish boy, except you," Honeywell snorted "A predator is not created, it is born."

"Birth means being a baby and having a mother. Did you once have parents or a family?"

"If we did, we do not remember them, for they were part of our past life of chaos. As a predator, all we have is order—and the orders we must obey."

"What is your mission?"

"To protect the USMBLA Championship Team from the body designated Casper Nolan. That body is suspected of injuring, killing, maiming, and kidnapping others of his kind and the equine species."

"Of course, stupid me," the kid muttered. "Casper took DH, which drove you to become this animal."

Honeywell dropped the kid with a shudder. "Leave. Cook us a hot meal. Crazy Jane must be back outside before anyone grows suspicious."

"Yes, sir." The kid scrambled away.

*He is not your prey,* the voice stated.

*No, he's not until he exceeds the three passes given any handler.*

*What is your count against him?*

*Zero. You reminded us that we used an emotional subjective when thinking about him.*

Hotness washed over Honeywell, but it let it pass. The voice could do nothing but speak. It had locked it up in the same cage the voice had used against it. There was no getting out from there. No one knew the voice existed, but it. If it ignored the voice, the voice would become silent again, and it would be in full control.

THIRTY-ONE

# FACING A PREDATOR

He chopped with a rapid and hard cadence, the knife twanging against the wood, trying to block Honeywell's words from his head. James Jr. was surprised that she had spoken to him in such great length and detail. Walking among the shadowy figures at both LA and the Academy, he was aware of their presence, but had little interaction with them. The black armors always spoke in metallic, electronic voices. The black masks, never.

The family logs detailed the extreme measures members of the Mason Seven took to prepare themselves for undercover missions. The ideal was to live a role as if one was born into the life of their persona. Didn't matter if the character was the exact opposite of the person playing it, anything less than complete immersion was flawed acting.

This was something more dangerous, more obsessive, and more everything, though.

Casper had attacked his aunt, her family, her horse, her team, her base, and her dreams. One was forgettable, two forgivable, and three a little dicey. *After that* ... Well, he was seeing *that* firsthand.

Finished with his cooking, he returned to the bedroom carrying a steaming plate of food. He hoped Honeywell wouldn't get sick because of it. This was her first real meal since leaving Houston.

She met him before his foot crossed the bedroom's threshold, her face covered by a black mask. Taking the tray, she closed the door without saying a word.

He paced the floor, his emotions tying him up tighter than one of the calves he roped in competition. A primal yell worked its way up from his gut. He swallowed the roar, fearing Honeywell's instinctive response.

There was only one person to blame for this. Jeff.

After Bill patched up his nose, his father explained the two levels of Command Security training. The buffered program involved intense emotional, physical, mental, and physiological challenges over a course of sixteen weeks. The regime was similar to those used by various militaries around the world to train their special forces. The bits and pieces his father knew about the full indoctrination hinted at far worse than any conspiracy theory on mind-controlled assassins could imagine.

Jeff had taken the extreme to the extreme by torturing and starving his subject to create the monster in mere weeks. The explosion at the family house was not an act of terror, but something to cover up any evidence of the transformation. Logs from that time claimed different, but those could be faked.

Curious, James Jr. listened at the door, hoping he would hear something human. No moans and groans of pleasure came from the room. Only *clack, click,* and *scrape.* He counted the monotonic cycle two dozen times before walking away and cleaning up the kitchen, so he wouldn't burst in on Honeywell.

*Swish. Splash.* He kept his eyes focused through the kitchen window, letting his hands do the work of cleaning the pots and pans.

Appearing like a ghost, Honeywell put the tray on the counter and disappeared again. He washed those dishes before walking back to the bedroom. Slouching in the chair near the dresser, dressed in Crazy Jane's outfit, Honeywell waited. Bottles and prosthetic pieces lay on the dresser in the order of need.

James Jr. touched the fasteners on the back of the black mask.

Honeywell grasped his hand in a vice grip that squeezed on the edge of pain. "Do not speak about our true face to anyone," she growled. "This is a small example of what we will do to you before you beg us to take your life, if you do. Understood?"

"Geez ..." James Jr. cut himself short. *You are dealing with Honeywell, Jimmy. You have to be like the cold, unfeeling shadow it is around it.* He switched to a flat tone that matched the steel one note for note. "I understand, Commander. You can trust me."

"We do not trust those who are not like us, Ensign, ever. We can't." The stone cold glare of her hazel eyes bore into him as the mask fell away from the bald, brown-fuzzed head. Even without the makeup enhancing its thinness, her face was hollow stone. He tried to find any sign of humanity in its features, but all he saw was malevolence and death.

"May I ask you a question?"

"Yes."

"How do you work so well around the horses? Command Security can't."

"Granted, our kind does have problems with the dumb animals, but Crazy Jane shields us from them."

James Jr. chewed his lip. Even during her worst moments of fear, his aunt never referred to the horses as dumb beasts. Boiling hot rage washed over him. He balled up his free hand and squeezed until his nails cut into the soft flesh of his palm. The grip on his other hand tightened, causing his fingers to throb.

Swallowing back a scream, he snapped, "A few more questions, if I may?"

Honeywell nodded.

"Why do you refer to yourself in the second person? Are you not a living creature with its own identity?"

"We are alive, yes, but we only have existence during each mission. Other than that, we are shadows. Do you give your shadow a name?"

"No."

Honeywell released her lock. The tension exploded off his palm with a dozen ice picks, followed by a rush of heat, and then deadness. He rubbed his hand and shook it, trying to get some feeling back.

"I am your handler, am I not?"

"Yes. The situation has made this so."

"If I wasn't your handler, would you still talk to me?"

"Yes. You are speaking to us, requiring answers."

"When do I become insignificant to you?"

"You are not one of us, so you are already of no consequence. You are a body that can—"

"Be silent," James Jr. growled, counting at least half a dozen innocent items that she could use against him. *If Honeywell kills me, someone I care for might be lost to this madness forever. I can't let that happen.*

He stared back at the stone with iron. As the silence built around him, he imagined the precise and focused way his father and aunt handled a crisis. He stiffened and barked, "I am proceeding. When I finish your transformation, you will allow me to test you. You understand this will involve some pain."

"Pain is strength, sir, but that is a foreign concept to your kind."

"Yes, it is." James Jr. sighed, *I don't understand any of this, but I don't need to. Jeff will know what you meant to me, even if I have to lose my commission and my family.*

The stillness in the familiar eyes made them an unbearable reminder of who died in order for the predator to live, so he started there. He made them distant and cold by darkening and hollowing the skin around them. Wrinkling and aging the face until its texture was leather, he then pitted and postmarked it with a violent and horrible, but true, tale of the beast. Opening her mouth, he grayed and dulled the enamel until a few teeth appeared to be missing and others pointed. He chiseled and shaped her features until they were as thin and sharp as her lost soul. Sagging and softening her neck so that it blended into the hunched and drooping shoulders, he accented the hump in the back of the shirt.

He slipped on the gloves that gave Honeywell's hands their leathery, gnarled look, but didn't tighten them.

"No," she grunted. "Hands are weapons."

Without a word, James Jr. recreated the claws that had done damage to his friend, and affixed the wild black mane to her head.

Honeywell tossed her hair and snarled.

He glared.

Shoving the chair back, she lunged at him, raking his face with two vicious strokes on either side. "That is your second warning, boy." Honeywell curled her lip exposing the fangs. "Do you want the third and final one?"

"I thought everyone is only allowed one free pass."

"A handler is allowed three."

Despite the burning streaks and instinctive urge to wipe away the warm, bubbling ooze, James Jr. didn't flinch. "Commander," he snarled, "back in your seat."

Honeywell snorted before obeying.

After a few more touches, he glanced at the pictures taped to the case's lid. These demanded some pulling, tugging, and painting to achieve their perfection. Honeywell remained still under his hand.

Finished, James Jr. stepped back and studied his handiwork from all angles. Crazy Jane was back, at least in appearance. Now, he had to test the beast's mental state. If Honeywell slipped, like she had just done, then she would be the one ruining the mission, not him. As her handler, he had to make sure that didn't happen.

"Commander Honeywell?"

One eyebrow twitched in an almost unnoticeable way.

"Crazy Jane?"

The bum slumped, its head hung down.

Ripping her out of the chair, he threw her on the bed without any resistance. Stalking over, he towered above her. She lay prone, gazing up at him with an unfocused stare. He slapped her once, twice, three times. *No reaction. Good.* A dozen more blows. The beast still didn't react. *I can stop. She's passed.*

He wanted to, but couldn't. Maybe if he caused enough pain, he could break through to one he cared for. He slammed into Crazy Jane from many different angles. She did nothing but absorb the punishment.

*If you do get through, Jimmy, then what will you do? She might lash out at you for blowing her cover. Stop. Find another way.*

James Jr. shook his head. There wasn't one, so he continued.

After countless more blows, Crazy Jane curled into a ball, whimpering, "Jimmy no hurt Jane."

She had called him Jimmy! "Who are you?"

Crazy Jane didn't respond.

He grabbed Crazy Jane off the bed, and shoved her out the door. "Go find the biggest pile of shit you can and roll in it, bitch," he roared, "until you stink like the filthy, non-existent, disgusting thing you are."

"Jimmy question answer first."

"What?" James Jr. growled.

"Nothing do to, but you mad at. Why?"

"Because you ..." James Jr. clamped his mouth shut. *This is the beast talking. The one I love and trust does not exist anymore.* "I have lost someone who means a lot to me. As a CSG, you wouldn't understand that."

"Jane do."

"Just go, okay?"

134

"Jimmy fine be?"

"Yes."

Crazy Jane stumbled into the hallway. James Jr. watched the broken, downtrodden shuffle for as long as he could before turning away, tears tracing a cold path down his warm cheeks. The front door creaked opened and then slammed shut. The scream he had held back ripped up through his throat. Once the howl subsided, he collapsed on the bed. Putting his palms together, he buried his face in his hands and sobbed.

# THIRTY-TWO

# LIVING A LIE

James Jr. groaned. Jane had fallen into a horse trough. No one else was making any effort to help her out. He'd have to, and then check her makeup. He tightened his lips. *Please don't make me strip you down, Jane. I don't want to see your true face, ever again.*

Striding over to her, he offered his hand.

Jane scooted to the other end of the trough.

"Fine, stay there." James Jr. snorted, turning his back.

"James help."

Pivoting, he snapped, "Either take my hand or grip the side and push yourself up."

"Like this?" Jane flipped over on her stomach and pushed up. Instead of clearing the water, she slid down, sending a wave upwards.

Swallowing a chuckle, James Jr. ordered in a sharp tone, "Jane, enough. Get out of there."

Grasping his hand in her vice grip, Jane jerked herself out. Glaring at him, she asked, "Why James ignore?"

He had continued to supervise her in the week since seeing her true face, but with her distance and objectivity. His words were firm commands to keep her on task—nothing more. No more scraps of food hidden in random places to supplement her diet of vermin and dumpster edibles. Every night, he locked her in an empty stall. Every day, she came out a little more filthy, animalistic, and disgusting.

He didn't care. His loved one was dead, killed in the fire.

"Come on, Jane, let's get you a towel."

Jane shook her wild mane, spraying water everywhere.

"Dry now. James speak."

"No. Come with me."

James Jr. led her to the house. Handing her one of the towels from the dirty clothes, he guarded the laundry room while she dried herself off. A quick check of her disguise revealed that only a few touch-ups were required. Once he completed them, he sent her back outside, and locked himself in his room.

Sitting down to lunch, James Jr. didn't feel like eating. Jane's antics still disturbed him. If someone he knew pulled such a maneuver, it would have been a funny joke or tease. With Jane, the stupid behavior added to her insane reputation and further diminished his view of her.

The sandwich was his favorite. Layers of ham and Swiss cheese stuffed between two slices of rye with extra pickles and a touch of horseradish mixed with sweet honey mustard. Taking one bite, he pushed the plate away.

His dad slipped into a chair across from him and asked, "Jimmy, what is going on between you and Jane?"

"Nothing," James Jr. sighed. "She's acting like a bum, so I'm treating her like one."

"The key thing about running an op is not drawing suspicion to yourself or your client," his dad stated. "Everyone has noticed your changed attitude toward her."

"She's a CSG, Dad. They don't have feelings for us. Why should I have feelings for her?" James Jr. snapped.

"It's not a matter of having an emotional connection with her, Jimmy. You have to act like you care because you already established that understanding in people's minds." Jim raised an eyebrow. "What's gotten into you?"

James Jr. covered his mouth, so his father couldn't see him chewing his lip. This was his opportunity to reveal everything. *If I do that, then what will happen? I already don't want to be responsible for her actions, what about her reactions?*

Lowering his hand, he stated, "I'm uncomfortable being around her. Despite her innocent look, she is an animal who can turn on any of us in an instant." Motioning to his father's nose, he demanded, "Have you already forgotten what she did to you? That thing, and all of its kind, needs to be locked away somewhere and forgotten about."

Jim nodded. "More than a few people, including me, agree with you. The unit should have never evolved into what it's become."

"How did it?"

Jim shrugged. "I'm not sure. Jason launched an investigation into their training methods one time, but never shared the results with anyone or acted upon them."

"Well, I'll continue to be her babysitter and act nice to her in front of people, but that's it," James Jr. replied. "Please don't ask me to do any more."

"Ok. Has she threatened you in any way?"

Keeping his face neutral, even as the little he ate caught in his throat, James Jr. replied, "No."

* * *

The compound where they were living consisted of five houses and two barracks surrounding a barn and stable area big enough to hold the team's horses, tack, and equipment. The landscaping was natural desert with splotches of manicured green lawns. James Jr. stepped out onto the porch of the house he shared with his family and Duff. The mechanical roar of the air conditioners disrupted the otherwise peaceful surroundings. He glanced around, but saw no sign of Crazy Jane. After taking a moment to think about nothing more than the warmth of the sun, he walked down the steps and toward the barn.

"Hey, Jimmy, wait up!" A voice called behind him.

James Jr. stopped and turned. His uncle Bill ate up the ground between them with a few of his long strides. "I wanted to talk to you after your father did, but you disappeared before I could."

"Well, I'm here now," James Jr. huffed. "Is this an official inquiry into my capability as Jane's handler, or an unofficial pep talk?"

"Neither," Bill smiled, "just a quick word to say I understand the beast you are dealing with."

"You may understand a CSG from the perspective of your medical training, but—"

"The human who is the monster is harder," Bill finished, placing his large hand on James Jr.'s shoulder. "I know that, too. I've worked with her before."

The hot ice coursing through James Jr.'s veins thawed. "Do you know who she is then? Have you seen her true face?"

Looking past him, his uncle nodded.

"Why didn't you say anything when she first joined the team? Why have you let this madness continue?"

"The beast is in full control. I see no way of jerking that away without a lot of people getting hurt, do you?"

James Jr. shook his head. "What do we do?"

"We continue to treat Jane for who she is. There was an exit strategy once before."

"Created and executed by whom?"

"Molly."

* * *

After standing in silence with his uncle for a few moments, relieved that someone else shared his unspoken burden, James Jr. continued his search for Crazy Jane. He was about three-quarters down the path when something knocked him down from behind.

The stink that wafted around him was unmistakable. "Come on, Jane," he groaned, trying to buck her off, "I don't want to play."

"Game no play, Jimmy," Jane growled, her weight pressing him deeper into the ground. "Life save."

She had called him Jimmy like before. *That means nothing. She's using my familiar name because the beast wants my attention. Well, she has it ...* "Jane, what's wrong?"

"Boogies three barn near. Low stay. Others warn. House target."

The pressure lifted. He flipped over, but saw nothing. Keeping low to the ground, he weaved his way back to the house. On occasion, he glanced back at the barn. Everything seemed normal. Using the shadows and shrubbery, he maintained his stealth approaching and entering the front door. Once inside, he noticed no one sitting near the large windows of the rooms on either side of the entryway. His father lounged on a couch near the doorway leading to the back of the house.

"Where's Michelle?" James Jr. demanded. "Has Uncle Bill returned?"

"In the back." His father looked up from the book. "I haven't seen him since he went after you."

One of the windows shattered with an explosive crack. Glass shards flew everywhere. James Jr. dropped to the ground. His father dived off his perch.

"What's going on, Jimmy?" Jim whispered.

"Jane," James Jr. replied, "says she spotted three people looking to attack the house."

"How the hell did they get through?" Michelle's voice echoed down the hallway. "Who's in position to take those guys out? Jane's already doing so?"

The front door creaked open. James Jr. rolled off the entryway to his left, gathering his feet under him. Bill slid in and kicked the door shut. Through the shot out window, three or more guns popped off at once.

*Thump.*

"That was the last of them," Bill stated. "I watched Jane take care of the first two."

Michelle stuck her head in, asking "Everyone, okay?"

Jim nodded. "Get me a full head count, ASAP."

"Yes, sir."

Standing up, James Jr. strode over to the door. Opening it, he peered out before stepping through. Crazy Jane, her tattered rags splattered with red, sat at the edge of the porch steps, rocking. He padded in her direction. Slipping down beside her, he waited to see if she'd at least acknowledge his presence. She kept swaying. When he placed his hand on her shoulder, she jerked away.

Nothing had changed.

# THIRTY-THREE
# THE PRESSURE BOILS OVER

Riding with the team, James Jr. tried to remain focused on the competition, but he was aware of Jane and some of the others like her. According to his father, Phoenix released some of their own CSG's to find any of Casper's shadows that might be in place for another attack. Slurred or stuttered speech, misuse of words, a subtle jerk away or hesitation when touched, and the other telltale signs that Jane's behaviors had taught him helped him identify at least two dozen potentials.

One night, after they unloaded the horses and tucked them into bed, Jane walked back to the house with James Jr. and his family. She had been sleeping on the front porch since the ambush, so he expected this. He took his normal place on the opposite side of the group. About halfway down the path, he didn't want to be anywhere near her, so he stopped.

"Everything okay, Jimmy?" His father prompted.

"I need a moment alone."

"Bodies split," Jane objected. "Stay Jane James with."

"No, Jane, I will be along in a few minutes."

"Stay."

Bill muttered something in Spanish.

"Sí. *Comprende*," Jane replied.

"Jim, it's okay," Bill stated. "Let me talk to the kid."

Jim nodded. The rest of the group, including Jane, moved off.

"Can we go someplace private?" James Jr. asked.

"Sure."

Bill led them back to one of the haulers. Slamming the passenger door shut, James Jr. demanded. "What did you tell her?"

"Something I implanted in her subconscious during her first time at Molly's. It allows me to give her orders like a handler. I wasn't sure if it would work."

"Oh. That's a handy little mechanism."

"Yes, it is. What's wrong, Jimmy? You are more stressed than before I admitted knowing who Jane was."

"I keep seeing Jane, but also who we lost when I look at her. I wonder how two so disparate people can exist in the same body. The fact she broke her conditioning before makes me wonder why she isn't doing so now. Sure, the threat isn't over, but more people are aware of it, so we don't need Honeywell anymore. Does she want to live as the beast for the rest of her life?"

"I'm wondering the same things myself," Bill shrugged. "I can only assume that even if Jo chooses to be herself, Honeywell has to agree to release control to her."

"Then the times she's called me Jimmy were her trying to break through?" James Jr. concluded.

"Maybe."

"How many people know about Honeywell?"

"Besides her superiors, five. Three of them aren't here."

"Can you tell me who?"

"Other than Molly and Paul, no."

"What about my father?"

"I haven't said anything to him. I can't. Neither can you."

"I know. That's what makes this so hard. Can you explain Jeff's and Molly's involvement in this whole mess? Jeff assigned me as Jane's handler in Molly's office. Why would he do that? Did he even consider the possibility that I'd discover who she was? Why didn't Molly stop the mission before that stage?"

"They were following orders."

"Orders be damned," James Jr. snorted. "Those of you who knew about Honeywell should have come up with a different plan, or found another CSG to protect us."

"We couldn't because Honeywell was already in play. Molly found out too late as well."

"You talked to her?"

Bill nodded. "Almost every day, since the first day she asked me to help her treat Jo."

"Then that makes Jeff responsible. He talked about Command Security taking Aunt Jo to some place safe. In reality, he was turning her back into that beast."

"I don't think it happened that way, Jimmy. All I know is the—"

"Don't give the team or family line, Uncle Bill, please," Jimmy interrupted with a loud snort. "Unless you have a solid defensive evidence for Jeff, I have to go on what I know. My dad, for some reason, suspended him and Jason. He then admitted two things that add to Jeff's guilt. His suspension was to help Honeywell make final preparations for her mission, and she was already in training before the fire at our house. What else am I supposed to think?"

"What about other, outside influences?"

"Like what?"

"Jeff told us—"

"Stop right there. Anything else?"

"No."

"Then until you do have something more than Jeff's word, please don't try and prove his innocence, okay?"

Opening the door, he stormed off.

* * *

James Jr. didn't sleep that night or the next few. Every time he closed his eyes, he saw Honeywell transforming into a demon horse who was part werewolf. His days weren't much better. He still ignored Jane and treated her like an object instead of a person, but every time he interacted with her, he saw his aunt's face. Her words, scattered and shrouded in Jane's speak, sang with the familiar notes of her tone.

His aunt wasn't a willing subject, but a prisoner.

Feeling like he needed to get away and think, he went to his father and said, "I want to explore some of the back country. May I go, if I take John and Duff with me?"

"You can go, but you'll need a security escort."

"Paint a target on our backs, why don't you?" James Jr. snorted.

"I'm not trying to, Jimmy. If you don't want an obvious one, take Crazy Jane. I just want to keep you safe."

"How can anyone be safe around *that* beast? Dad, I…" Hanging his head, he walked away.

His father matched his steps for a few strides before saying, "Jimmy, talk to me. What has you so spooked?"

"Everything," James Jr. protested, throwing up his hands and squeezing his eyes shut as wetness dotted his checks. " The attacks on the team…Aunt Jo dying…Me having to be the beast's handler…" He gestured in Crazy Jane's direction, sobs wracking his body.

* * *

Wrapping his arms around his son, Jim said nothing. He had no words for his boy, only his silent strength. Jane had affected him, too. His couldn't quite understand why, but somewhere between his link with Jo, which remained a steady hum, and his instincts, Honeywell hit him wrong. The quiet presence of Command Security always unnerved him, but he had only felt this uneasy with one other of their kind.

The quivering slowed and then stopped. Jimmy took a deep breath before stammering, "Dad, please give Jane to someone else."

"Why?"

"I saw her true face." Jimmy choked on the words.

"Don't describe it to me or mention a name," Jim growled, noticing the shadow staring at them. "We have an audience."

"I won't. She already said what would happen if I did. That threat, and who it's coming from, makes it very hard for me to continue."

"Jimmy, dealing with Command Security is always a little touchy." Jim stated. "They are suspicious of anyone who isn't one of them. One black mask that shadowed me was ordered to kill me because I asked for its transfer."

"You are still here, so it didn't complete the kill."

"Oh, it came close. Had me on the ground with its gun to my head, but, for some reason, it didn't pull the trigger."

"What happened to it?"

"I don't know," Jim shrugged. "There are rumors that Command Security will hunt and kill their own when the need arises."

"Not to be morbid, but why wasn't another one sent after you?"

"They had presumed I wanted the transfer because I had seen its true face. After determining that I hadn't, they rescinded the order."

"Since I have, they won't."

Jim nodded.

## VOICE OF REASON

A horse's tail swished above Honeywell. The trailer beneath it vibrated. Though the sky was still the murky blue gray of predawn, the walls radiated warmth. Soon, the prosthetics and makeup that made it Crazy Jane would mean another day in wet heat that made breathing difficult.

Honeywell shrugged. Such was the need of the mission. The kid, his uncle, and best friend were on the way to an isolated piece of flat land where they could ride without the judges' scrutiny. Like Captain Mason, Honeywell didn't think the outing was a good idea without an escort. When the kid protested, it heard a few snatched words, but not enough to act.

*Act? You were thinking of killing him because he talked to his father about you?* The voice prompted.

*Yes.*

*He did not mention our name.*

*It is enough that he has admitted to another that he has seen our true face. Next time, he might not be so cautious. Better he dies today, then lives and slips up tomorrow.*

*I won't let you do anything to him!*

*Ha! What can you do? The cage is your prison, for once.*

*He's hurt on many different levels because of you, because of* us, *but you wouldn't understand that. You are an unfeeling beast.*

*As are you,* Honeywell countered. *For you are it.*

*In body only,* the voice snorted.

*Since we control the body, you are us.*

The voice didn't respond.

That morning, the kid had come outside and loaded his horse, directing it to get in as if nothing had happened. As he closed the door, he dropped something in the straw, mouthing, *Dad wanted to make sure you had that.*

Honeywell retrieved the lump, opened it, and found a .357 Magnum and a walkie. Captain Mason was expecting trouble.

It looked down at its hands and tried to figure how fast it could free them. Clean, accurate shots required precise trigger pressure. The stiff, inflexible material that transformed its fingers into gnarled claws reduced its sense of touch to unacceptable levels.

Honeywell leaned against the trailer in an effort to steady itself and its thoughts. Reaching down, it grabbed the paper sack and took a long chug. Only the horses were around to see the drink, so it didn't have to pretend like it had taken a hit. The water was stale, but cool. Wiping the wetness from its lips, it sniffed its skin.

*Boy, do I reek*, the voice protested. *I hate the disgusting animal I've become.*

*It a shadow, nothing more*, Honeywell growled.

*I am not a shadow*, the voice argued. *You are one.*

*Yes, and we must complete our mission.*

*Ha*, the voice snorted. *What's the use in that? Casper has resumed his attacks on the team, and we are no closer to having our vengeance on him.*

*One incident does not indicate resumption.*

*Yes, I agree there is no pattern yet, but it will come. My bigger concern is your relationship with Jimmy.*

*The boy will be fine until his next mistake.*

*He is* not *fine*, the voice roared. *Did you not feel the beating he gave us?*

*We needed the pain to strengthen our resolve, but you would not understand that.*

*I understand it too well. Aren't you showing compassion by giving him another chance?*

*Compassion is emotional and subjective. We are objective. There are only three bodies besides his. We would have to kill them all—and ourselves—if we went after him.*

*I grow tired of your way of thinking. Leave, demon. I'll take it from here.*

*You did not try to take control when we almost broke the boy's hand or scratched him. It knows you. You will do nothing because it strength and you weakness.*

*I will take that shortcoming over your existence.*

*What if we unleash the voices of our victims?*

*I have heard them for years, so that won't work. They died because of my loss of control to you. I will always have to live with that, but it doesn't mean I have to live as you. Be gone!*

*No, we will not leave. You must force us to.*

146

*Very well, then I will.*

Its arms came up, its mouth opened, and the beast tasted metal.

*The boy will be the first to discover our body.*

Its hand twitched.

*Yes, I know. I'm sorry, Jimmy, Jeff should have never ensnared you in this insanity.*

The world exploded around it.

# THIRTY-FIVE

# TWIN OF A DIFFERENT CENTURY

Jeff's eyes traveled around the room, taking the temperature at each station. Most of the underground cavern was a quiet cool of efficient routine and standard procedure. Communications was a little hotter, but that section never went below warm even on a quiet day. He checked the twenty-four screens on the front wall. They displayed routine information for most of the USMB as well as the regular hot spots in the Middle and Far East.

His focus returned to the monitor in front of him. As the CO of Academy Houston, he split his time between commanding the second largest Joint Forces base behind LA, and overseeing the education and training of the next generation of officers. A position with much less prestige and responsibility had opened up with the upcoming retirement of Lancaster's CO. Only a few more spaces on the application remained until he finalized his request for the assignment.

On paper, he had three brothers, but, in reality, he had only one. RJ was his step-cousin. Lance, his stepbrother, died in the First Gulf War. Randy, his twin, disappeared from his life when they were both five. The same people that had taken him from his family seemed to be interfering in his life, and the lives of the people he cared for, yet again.

With Jo still not back, Jeff felt compelled to be closer to his adopted family, waiting with them. For his brother to make two trips back in time to keep Jo alive meant she was important in terms of history. He had to do his part to ensure the future happened as he remembered it. The good parts, at least.

His real parents, a mirror image, and baby sister who were the solid, and safe, core of his life. The window filled with a sky that was not blue, but black and dotted with little white lights. Ships shaped nothing like the ones that sailed the sea, which floated around a sphere of brown, green, blue, and white. These were the people and things that he needed to protect, not the blackness that crept into his mind every time he thought about them.

His stepfather gave him a brief explanation as to why the ship's crew had left him in the wrong time with someone else's life to live. His brother filled in the gaps when fate allowed them a few precious moments together during his mid-teens. They both reassured him that the ship's crew attempted to keep him onboard, while making sure events happened as they remembered. Each time they returned to the future though, they discovered a changed or destroyed world. After about a dozen or so roundtrips, they concluded that it was impossible to maintain the timeline that created the people and places he knew without leaving him in the past.

Jo popped in Jeff's mind. She didn't live her life to die; circumstance just had a way of working out that way for her. One of her brothers was next because of his *joie de vivre. Then there are the other members of Jo's family and the Mason Seven...* He lost count after the fifteenth or sixteenth person. *All of them are here because of me. I need to take some comfort in that, and Randy's promise.*

"51-Dispatch-7, Command Team Alpha One priority confirmed." The words drew Jeff out of his contemplation. "Relay transmission when ready."

"Dispatch 7, on speaker," he ordered. *What has LA found that needs the team's full attention? Jo or DH, perhaps?*

"Yes, sir."

The overhead sound system came alive.

*Captain?* Someone yelped. *What's wrong?*

*There's a hauler over the side of a cliff at my location. Three people are trapped inside.* A strong, steady voice replied. *I need a mountain rescue team at my location.*

A deeper tone broke in, *51-Command-1, can you—*

*67-Dispatch-7, this is 51-Dispatch-7*, the surprised person interrupted. *Give her whatever she needs. I'm transferring her coordinates to you.*

*I need to verify*, the Phoenix dispatcher objected. *51-Command-1 is—*

*The CO of USMBLA and the Mason Seven CSA Team*, a gruff presence grunted. *This is 47-Command-1. I'm authorizing whatever she needs.*

*Sir!* The Phoenix dispatcher's tone snapped to attention. *Captain Holmes, sir, it is my understanding that the current person hodling those positions is—*

Vince groaned, *Jim Mason and not his sister, Jo. I understand that. Understand this, she's been on an undercover mission, and has broken cover because multiple lives are in danger. Do you want to be responsible for their deaths?*

*No, sir, but—*

*Geez, this guy's stubborn.* Jeff shook his head. *He's topping TJ, Michael, and John on letting regulations dictate and rule his life. That's hard to do.*

He reached for the comm switch on his console.

An impassioned brogue jumped into the fray. *67-Dispatch-7, this 'tis Rear Admiral Jason Scott, CO of USMB California, also authorizin' whatever Captain Mason needs. Are ye goin' ta argue with me, too?*

*No, sir. 51-Command-1, your request is received and noted. Help is on the way.*

*Thank you.*

*51-Command-1,* Vince added, *when this is all over, you are going to have some explaining to do.*

*Roger that, 47-Command-1, and thanks to both of you.*

*Are ye returning ta cover, 51-Command-1?* Jason asked.

*Yes, sir. If I can.*

*Understood.*

Jeff pulled up a status report on LA's Championship Team. The only female not listed as present on base at Phoenix was Jane Honeywell.

*Jo is Jane?* He swallowed his gasp, willing himself to keep a neutral face. He had given Jimmy the line about Command Security taking away Jo because it was easier than explaining the whole ship from the future scenario. *No one can pretend to be a shadow…Randy, what the hell did you do to her?*

# THIRTY-SIX

# FIRE AND ICE

The team retreated to the coolness of their guest quarters after an early morning practice. Afternoon events included calf roping and barrel racing. The evening show would feature the English riders in dressage and other close ring work.

Various forms of entertainment broke out all over the guest compound, most designed to conserve energy and keep body temperatures down. Bill made his day's objective keeping track of Jim, or at least trying to. For now, his brother didn't want to be disturbed.

Like Jimmy, Jim's stress level was a little higher than Bill desired. Most of that stemmed from his brother having to keep up the lie their sister was dead, and not knowing where she was. He wanted to drop a hint about Jo being Honeywell, but Honeywell had already tried to kill Jim twice in her two lifetimes. He couldn't risk another confrontation between them.

Glancing at the chessboard on the kitchen table, he studied the interesting dichotomy. The black pieces defended the king in a tight, impenetrable formation. On the other side, the haphazard placement of the whites seemed to suggest a confused attack. Calculating a few moves ahead, Bill shook his head, *Tyrell almost has Michael trapped in a brilliant and inescapable checkmate.*

Tyrell fidgeted in his seat. "Please go away, Bill. Your quiet stares are throwing off my concentration."

"At least, he isn't freezing you," Michael teased, "like Jim did the whole barn during this morning's meeting."

"I wasn't that bad, was I?" A voice spoke up behind Bill.

"Jim," Michael stated, "the last time I saw the team that silent and focused on you was when they gave their silent permission to continue."

Bill peered down at Jim. "He's right, you know. You have been stalking around here like you want to pounce on someone or something."

"I'm worried about Jimmy, that's all. He's says that he saw Honeywell's true face. If she feels threatened by that, well—"

"Whatever trouble is between them, the focus of Jane's kind on completing their mission should be enough to protect Jimmy during today's ride," Michael offered.

"I hope so."

"When are they due to check in?" Tyrell asked.

Glancing at his watch, Jim replied, "As soon as they reach the Tonto National Forest. They should have left an hour earlier, but Jimmy ignored his alarm clock."

"Does he think Jane is Jo?"

Jim shook his head. "We've all pretty much dismissed that idea, Tyrell. Jo has too much personality to be a CSG. Bill, you've talked to him a couple of times. What's your take?"

"Jeff should have never assigned him the responsibility. Other—"

Wailing alert klaxons and the ringing kitchen phone combined to interrupt him.

"This is Captain Mason." Jim answered. "What?" The tension in his voice rose with its pitch. "Of course. My team will be ready for wheels up in a few minutes. Thank you, Captain." Hanging up, he turned and said. "Guys, there's been an accident involving Jimmy's little expedition. They are coordinating rescue operations now."

A cell rattled on the counter. They all stared at it.

"Bill, you're the closest," Jim prompted. "Answer it, please."

Nodding, Bill swiped the front of the screen and hit the speaker button. "Go ahead," he said.

"Hey, Bill," Jeff's voice was filled with mixed emotions. "Who is in the room with you?"

"Jim, Michael, and Tyrell. John, Jimmy, and Jane are involved in an accident that we just got word on."

"Good, then I don't have to repeat myself. Jane Honeywell is Jo."

Bill made his face reflect some of the surprise and disbelief he saw.

"Jeff, are you sure?" Jim managed to spit out, breaking through the silence that enveloped them.

"Yes, I just heard the exchange between her, Vince, Jason, LA, and Phoenix. It took all three of them vouching for her before Phoenix began the necessary response procedures."

"Our family's obsession with character perfection has never gone this far before," Tyrell observed. "Even playing a sociopathic gang banger, I wasn't able to fool Michael."

"Maybe that's because Honeywell is a perfect CSG," Michael stated. "The logical conclusion therefore is that Jo underwent their training."

"I can't, and won't, assume that." Jim declared. "Since Honeywell came to us from Molly's, we have to start there. Jeff, go talk to her."

"Right."

Motioning for Bill to hang up, Jim raised an eyebrow. "Are you in your act now, panic later mode?"

"Pretty much. Dealing with two personalities in one body isn't going to be easy."

Jim nodded. "Let's mount up."

Michael and Tyrell exchanged glances. "We are ready to go."

"I'm going to go grab my kit," Bill stated.

"While you're doing that, I'll coordinate the rest of our people."

\* \* \*

His USMB medical license allowed Bill to practice in all fifty states as long as he had the permission of the local base's CMO or the chief of surgery at a civilian hospital. It was illegal for him to transport drugs against state lines, so he had made his normal request from Phoenix Medical Command. He had divided the supplies into two kits. The basic one he carried with him during all performances contained bandages, splints, aspirin, and other lightweight stuff for treating minor injuries. The other, which included prescription class drugs, remained locked in his room unless he needed to treat someone in the compound.

Combing parts of the two, he packed a backpack.

His phone buzzed.

Palming the device, he noticed a new text from Jason. The message was brief. *Jo broke cover over Dispatch 7. Does Jim know she's a CSG?*

*He suspects it. Sent Jeff to investigate at Molly's.*

*What are you going to tell him?*

*Nothing. There will be too many eyes and ears around us. Have to continue to play as if I'm learning along with him.*

*You are doing the right thing, lad.*

*I wish it felt that way, Jason.*

*What about John?*

*He's with Jo.*

"Hey, Bill, we are waiting for you," Jim yelled from downstairs.

He jerked and fumbled the phone.

"Sorry, I'm coming," he replied, erasing the messages.

THIRTY-SEVEN
## THE THUGS COME BACK

The transmission was clear, but strange. A voice from the grave called out for help. No matter, their orders were clearer. Monitor the small group that broke off from the main team. Report on the people it contained and then kill them, making sure it looked like an accident. They thought they had, but now they would. They'd give the bodies to the boss as proof. Not like the screw-ups in LA who paid for creating a mess.

His companion, a tall, square, dark-haired guy who went by Brick, poked him and grunted, "Are you sure of our target?"

"Pretty sure," Donnie replied, exiting the large armored-plated SUV.

The scene was as they had left it—with one minor change. The team's good luck charm had somehow extracted herself from the trailer. She shuffled around, head hung down, not paying attention to her surroundings. As harmless as she appeared, being the lone female in the group, she had to be the one who made the call.

Cocking his weapon, Donnie lined up his shot. *Too easy*, the slender, copper blonde assassin sighed. His victims always ran or put up a fight. Either way, it ended with the same result.

He moved closer. The wandering continued. He matched it step for step, hoping for one fearful glance up. He needed to see the last spark of life leave the body. That was the only way he had completed his job.

"Donnie, we got a problem," Brick yelled. "I don't see no truck."

"Jeez, Brick, you looking in the right place?" *Plenty of muscles*, Donnie quipped, *but lacking in the brain department.*

"Yeah, look at the tracks."

Ruts marked where they had pushed the hauler over the cliff after slamming into it.

"What do you see?"

"Bushes. Lots of bushes. Doesn't look right."

Donnie strode over to Brick. Glancing down, he noticed the scrub below them appeared undisturbed, except for the darker brown tone of a few upturned ones. *Brick's right. It ain't natural. Shit, that means there's at least one more live one.*

155

He tapped Brick on the shoulder before touching his head near his right eye, making a circling motion, and holding up two fingers. It had taken them a little over thirty minutes to return after hearing the transmission. *Plenty of time for our ghost and her helper to set a trap with her as the bait,* Donnie observed. Others had tried that in the past and failed. He expected this outcome to be no different.

Brick raised his gun. Nodding, Donnie pointed to the bum and then at himself.

Flashing thumbs up, Brock slinked away.

Donnie inched his way back toward his mark. Even with the limited cover of the scrub and rocks, he found a decent spot to take out his target while maintaining some cover. As he measured his distance, his brain registered the vic's lack of motion and a glint of metal in her hand. A shot cracked. Something strung him in the chest. Putting his hand where he felt the bite, he touched a warm sticky mess. Pulling his fingers away, he stared at the red ooze dripping from them.

*The bitch shot me! That confirms it. I'll ...* Donnie struggled to raise his weapon. *When did this thing become a ton of steel?* Darkness crept in his vision. *It isn't that late, is it?* Stumbling forward, he lost his balance and slammed into the ground.

\* \* \*

Brick peered around the rock. His partner was down, hit from a direction that didn't make sense.

Something hard and sharp crunched the back of his head. Rattled, but not disoriented, he turned. Before he could identify his assailant, a gun barked. His legs buckled.

Ropes bit into his wrists, and tied them together. Hands jerked him onto his back. He squinted. Through the bright glare, he caught a glimpse of a bloodied face.

"You are supposed to be dead, so is the bitch who shot me," he spat. "Don't matter, though. The boss will get her. I'll—"

"You'll do nothing," the bloody one growled, punting him in the jaw.

\* \* \*

We drag the unconscious thug to the shady side of the trailer. John winces every time he moves. He had been too quick for me to remind

156

him of the hand-to-hand combat techniques that didn't involve kicking an area laced with muscle and bone with the toes. Besides, he still doesn't know I am me.

In an ironic way, this latest attack saved my life.

Even when I was learning to feel again and struggling with all the pain I had caused other people after my first time as Honeywell, I never considered suicide. On my worst days over the last nine years, the temptation was a little closer, but I always managed to talk myself out of taking the final step. For those few moments in the trailer before the crash, I saw no other option. Killing the beast, so it couldn't harm anyone I cared about, meant killing myself.

The accident forced me to make another choice. Go through with my plan, ensuring the deaths of Jimmy, Cordero, and John, or battle for control with my shadow and save them. The decision was easy.

Now that I've made sure someone will take care of them, I can't continue as myself. Casper still has people in play. Though others have heard my call, I don't want the big thug identifying me as Jane, or the source of the transmission. I heard Ben, and maybe Jeff, in the moments the blackness of death had a hold of me during the fire at my house. That means the thug in his gray state can hear us, so I must act like Crazy Jane and keep Honeywell at bay the best I can.

"He'll be sleeping for a long time." John wipes his brow. "The thug said that Jane called for help. Did she?"

"Different voice use. People heard many how know not. Trouble more if continue tone in that."

"I understand," John replies, scratching in the dirt, *Jo, I know it's you. Have all alon*g. He erases the words with his feet.

Opening my mouth, I utter half a syllable before catching my mistake. Grunting, I write a single word in the sand that reflects my shock. *How?*

*Helped with first recovery. Will explain later.* Nodding at the thug with a sly smile, he scratches, *Need to keep up the charade.* The words disappear almost before I finish reading them. A new sentence appears, *How many bullets do you have left?*

I hold up four fingers.

A rattling swish fills the air. John glances up. "Sounds like choppers."
On the ground, he writes, *Act scared. You are out of your mind with pain and fear.*

I stagger to the back of the trailer.

"Jane. Wait."

I stop and shrug.

He points to the red streaks that mark up his skin and then the trailer. Gesturing at me, he writes, *Jane must look more hurt or silence won't matter.* He wipes the message away.

John's right. In order to make the thug look like a liar, I'll have to emphasize the crazy part of Jane's nickname, while selling some serious injuries. Dropping into the nearest scrub brush, I roll. Coming up with plenty of scratches and stings, I look for other ways of transforming myself into a certifiable physical and mental mess. Using the sharp metal of the trailer's destroyed front end, I shred my already tattered clothes, gaining a few more nicks in the process. Making the wild mane on my head even more insane requires some cactus and John's help.

Scattered around us are the contents of the trailer's tack compartment. Finding the lineament, I slather a generous amount on every bare piece of skin. It stings, causing my eyes to water. Taking one of the piles the horses have left, I add poop and dirt to the mix. John does the honors for the parts I can't reach. For the final soiling touch, I pee on myself.

"Good. Done."

"More need," I whisper, pointing to the trailer. "Close feel not."

"Not necessary. I will—"

"Coming many. John no shield all from. Guard thug. No watch next part. Too hard him for see to."

Before John can say anything more, I walk away.

158

# THIRTY-EIGHT

# FOR THE GOOD OF THE FUTURE

Jeff entered Molly's office without knocking.

"Honeywell's broke cover," he stated. "She's Jo."

"I know."

"When were you going to tell me?"

"The man who brought her and her orders here looked and acted like you, just a little more rushed and abrupt than normal. He said to call if I had any problems. When I did, you didn't act surprised."

"I received a copy of the orders, so I was aware of Honeywell, but not that Jo was her."

"Then who is the mystery man?"

"My twin brother, who I haven't seen in a few decades."

"You never mentioned having one."

"It's a long story that I'd rather not go into. Jo couldn't become Honeywell with his help, though. The brutality used to create a CSG would go against everything he believed in."

"He wouldn't have had to do anything, but let her hold a black uniform in her hand. I could never desensitize that trigger in her."

"Then Jo is one?"

"Yes. Do you know about the investigation Jason conducted into the unit?"

"It ended without explanation or results."

"That was the only way he could get them to return Jo. She was only supposed to be in the full training program long enough to obtain damning evidence against the unit, but her extraction failed and she went on to be Honeywell. When she hesitated on a kill mission, Jason offered the CS all his information on them in return for her."

"Who was her target?"

"Jim."

Jeff's stomach dropped. "Is Honeywell the name Jo uses as cover when she's in CSG mode?"

"More than that. Honeywell is Jo's split. Most fulls have one because their psyche can't handle the strain of the transformation. Once the division happens, the predator absorbs the other personality as another one of its prey. In Jo's case, this didn't happen."

"Is that normal?"

Molly shook her head.

"What caused the two personalities to remain separate?"

"I'm not sure. I thought it was Jo's connection with Jim, but every other single twin who went through the training demonstrated the expected behavior."

"How do have so much information and knowledge about an otherwise top secret program?"

"Part of Jason's deal allowed me full access to his findings in order to form a treatment plan."

"Molly, this is insane," Jeff objected, leaning back on his heels. "Buffereds taste what it's like to be a CSG, making them easy to discharge and re-deploy into regular USMB units. Fulls have a short lifespan that always ends in death because they are too dangerous to keep around. Jo would never volunteer for such a mission."

"Under normal circumstances, I'd agree with you, but there were several emotional situations that Jo was dealing with when she did. She thought by learning their ways, she could help herself."

"Situations like what?"

"Other than Michelle's shooting and her boyfriend's death, I can't say."

"Of course not," Jeff muttered. "Isn't split personality disorder, or whatever they are calling it these days, one of the things the USMB discharges a person for?"

Molly nodded.

"Then given how Jo is a former CSG with an alternate personality, how has she managed to stay in and keep her career on track?"

"Her beast remains under enough control so that at every review no traces of it can be found. If she comes back from this second manifestation, I'm not sure what the upper echelon will do with her."

Jeff had undergone, and survived, the lighter version of the Command Security indoctrination program during specialty school. He served as one for six months before spending another three with Molly learning to live with his beast. His relationship with it was one of tolerance. Always on guard against it, he switched from security to command to avoid any situation that might set it free. Despite all his precautions, though, he sometimes found himself in its cold, sterile world where life was nothing more than an emotionless weighing of the facts.

Clenching his hands, Jeff recalled his time in the pit where, as their last test, all pretenders had one chance to prove they were predators. Fail, and serve the mandatory time as an outcast; in the armor, but never a complete part their world. Pass, and be rewarded with an anonymous license to kill.

His prey was down with its neck exposed. *One swift stroke and ...* Jeff shuddered. He had shown mercy and dropped his blade. The handlers set some of those who made the other choice on him. He left the pit bloodied and broken, but with his humanity intact. The others lost so much more.

"How did you bring her back? I know you had a hard time with me as a buffered."

"By exposing her to every human experience and emotion I could think of until I broke through the beast's defenses and reached her. After that, it was teaching her all about emotions and their various sensations. Family helped with that part."

"Who?"

"Jason and two of her brothers."

"Was it hard for you seeing her back here as Honeywell?"

"Very much so, but, in coming to know Jo as I have over the years, I trusted she had a very good reason for returning to that nightmare."

"What about Jimmy? Why did you suggest I involve him? Don't give me orders as the reason. You've broken them before for clients that didn't mean as much to you."

"In the envelope that contained Honeywell's safe word was a personal note from Jo that said Jimmy had to help her face the demon, now and later. It also indicated that you have to act like an uncaring bastard who knew about Jo being Honeywell, and still assigned Jimmy as her handler, so I look innocent." Molly huffed. "I don't want to look guiltless, Jeff. I set Jimmy up as much as you did."

161

"Jo did, not you. That's why she's trying to protect you, as I will."

"I don't envy the position, you're in, Jeff. With his trust issues, Jimmy will turn on both of you when he finds out that Jo is Honeywell, if he already hasn't. He'll be the first of the friends and family because of me."

"I'll handle it. Even if I have to remain the bad guy for years to come, Jo and Jimmy will at least get back together again. You have my word on that."

# THIRTY-NINE

# A PROMISE KEPT

Jeff walked out the back door of Molly's halfway house feeling sick to his stomach. Taking the few steps down from the doorway to the alley, he stopped. The green garbage cans, emergency stairs, and interspersing brick and stucco walls hadn't changed that much in the last eight years. The bright daylight washed away some of the grime, but none of the painful memories from the night he, Jo, and Jim had confronted Jim's ex.

*We are a shadow. The whisper of death. Unseen, unknown, and unheard.*

He groaned under his breath. Those words were the first thing black masks learned as a means of controlling themselves and their emotions. Jo muttered them a year after the mauling no more than a hundred feet from where he stood. He had listened to, but not heard, them.

*Emotions are insignificant. Personal relationships, non-existent. Team, mission, and duty, paramount.*

Both Jo and Jim's ex were armed, but the ex was out of bullets, having put her last round into Jim. Jo had more than enough justification to shoot. Besides hurting Jim, the ex had taken Jimmy away from the family for almost a year. She'd also been part of the gang responsible for killing eighteen of Jeff's people who tried to protect the kid. Jo's morals should have prevented her from firing on an unarmed person, but the beast had no such constraints.

*People, only names and ranks. Kill without remorse. Hurt without thought. Hesitation is failure. Mercy is weakness. Pain, strength.*

The whisper on the wind died; the mantra that transformed the world into a cold, sterile, and flat place complete. Before it could act, Jim pleaded for his ex's life. Jo, not the beast responded, saving both herself and Jim's ex.

Nothing could save Jo this time. While it was her voice on the radio, he suspected the beast was still in control. During his buffered training, he had learned that hesitation was worse than mercy. Jo was guilty of that transgression at least twice. The beast wouldn't allow it to happen again. His only option was to fulfill her request and play the bad guy. Maybe they'd get a chance to talk about her experiences as Honeywell, maybe they wouldn't, but at least he'd keep her family safe like he always had.

His phone buzzed, disrupting his troubled thoughts. It was Jim.

"Yes?" Jeff answered.

"What did you find out about Jo?"

"She wasn't pretending to be a CSG."

"When did she become one, then?"

*Keep Jason and Jo out of this.* "Not sure."

"What about her gaunt appearance?"

"She came back from the ship looking that way."

"Then they tortured her?"

"No. They aren't capable of that. Their medical technology is very advanced, so they could have come up with something that would allow her to eat and still lose a massive amount of weight."

"Who decided to make Jimmy her handler?"

*Protect Molly and Randy.* "Me."

"Shit, Jeff. Why?"

"The mission was more important than your son's feelings."

"We'll talk more later."

The line went dead.

"It was her decision not yours, Richard," his inner voice said aloud. "It is unfortunate that you have to live with the consequences."

No one knew him as Richard. He sometimes used that name for himself because it was his real one. *Richard James Peterson, lost soul,* he sighed. "I'm fine with whatever happens," he replied, "as long as—"

"I'm here, aren't I?"

Turning in the direction of the voice, Jeff expected to see nothing but air. Instead, he found a man wearing a blue uniform similar to his. He stepped back and blinked a few times. *No, this is not an illusion.* His mirror image stood in front of him. He seemed a little older in the face and eyes, like there was at least a few years between them. Given the centuries that separated them, Jeff expected that.

He reached out. His brother grabbed him and pulled him into a bear hug.

"*Randy?*" Jeff squeaked. "How long?"

Releasing him, his brother tapped a silver band on his wrist. "As soon as this beeps, I have to go."

*Where do I begin?* Randy hadn't been in uniform during his last visit. The patches and pins on his kit indicated that he had at least made part of their shared dream come true. *Maybe I'll start there.*

"You're a starship captain, huh?" Jeff prompted.

"For several years, now," Randy nodded, gesturing at Jeff's boards. "You haven't done half bad yourself. Married? Any kids?"

"Yes, three. You?"

"Twins. Wife was killed in an accident."

"The rest of the family?"

"Dad's doing well. He's the big cheese. Andrea has her own command. Mom died a year after you left."

Jeff shuddered before stating, "You didn't come hundreds of years back in time a second time to tell me all this."

"No, I didn't. This is just another stop on the same trip that took you from me."

"When I was a teenager—"

"Which was a few moments ago for me."

Jeff nodded. "You said you'd know when I was an adult if and when I could stop living this charade. This is neither my world nor my century. Everything I have belongs to Jo's real cousin."

"You have to stay, I'm sorry."

"Why?"

"In the terms of history, the lie has become the truth woven into the fabric of time. While we couldn't correct it, we could prevent other tragedies."

"Was Jo one of them?"

"Yes, on a few different occasions. The plane accident when she was eleven, the mauling, and now the fire and explosion at her house are the ones you know about. There are others that haven't happened yet where we could do nothing but watch, and that was harder."

The plane accident was the incident he had tried to get Jason to tell Jim about. Jeff was sixteen at the time. His nine cousins went up to their Shasta cabin all excited. Seven came back not remembering a thing.

Randy appeared and explained Jo's parents and two of her brothers needed special treatment that left them unable to return with the rest of the family. While not ideal, it was less stressful for the remaining survivors to think the adults had died in a different accident and the children were just childhood playmates.

"Why do you treat Jo so rough even when saving her life?" Jeff wondered. "Will she ever be herself again?"

"Theo has assured me that she will be."

"Theo?" Jeff laughed. "The wonder horse that Jim met? How would he know?"

"His people are shape changers with great psychic abilities. You met him a few times. Once in our century and twice here."

Jeff thought about all the horses he had ever owned or seen. One in particular stuck out in his mind. A golden bay stallion had been staring at Jim right before Molly called him about Jane. The horse hadn't aged since their last encounter when he was a teenager.

"Yes, I guess I have." Jeff pressed, "Why did Jo need to become her monster again? What about getting Jimmy involved? Why am I the scapegoat?"

"All three are hard necessities, Richard. Just like your stay here. You wrote a few hours ago that Jo was important in terms of history. She is the key to our time. You've got to keep on protecting her, even from herself, like we tried to."

"How did you try? Did she ask to be trapped in the body of a bum with the soul of a killer? Molly said the orders and note she received from you came from Jo. Did they?"

"Both were created by the same hand connected to two different hearts."

"Then is she also responsible for us?" Jeff locked his gaze on Randy.

His brother flinched and looked away. "You'll find that out for yourself when the time is right. All I can say is that Jo asked for some way to shadow the team. We refused her requests at first, but then we realized, she had to become her beast and Jimmy needed to learn to work with her as it. If they didn't, she'd lose herself to it forever, which would lead to some of the dire consequences we experienced."

166

"She's done a pretty damn good job with not losing herself over the last few years. If anything, the mauling should have brought her beast back."

"It didn't because a majority of her pain from that incident was physical. The next time, grief will hit her on all levels."

"Next time? All levels?" Chocking on the echoed words, Jeff managed to spit out, "What happens to—

*Beep. Beep. Beep.* Randy's watch interrupted with its warning. The image of a gray room appeared behind him. He turned and shrugged. A shadow motioned back. Randy's face dropped. "Sorry, kiddo," he apologized. "I can't say anymore. I have to go."

"Will I see you again? If so, when?"

"Yes, sooner than you think," Randy smiled, stepping into the picture. "Keep supporting and encouraging Jo and you will give yourself the opportunity to come back to the right time."

The words faded in the afternoon breeze, along with the hope they contained.

# FORTY

# HELP ARRIVES

From a chopper hovering over the accident scene, Jim peered down at six forms. One waved. Two others didn't move. The last three were a mixture of brown, gray, and paint milling near the front of the trailer. *The horses*, he noted. *We'll have to land far enough away so as not to spook them.*

"Take us to the cliff," he yelled over the chopping whoosh of the blades. "I want to see the truck."

"Yes, sir."

They angled away and swung around. The pilot lowered them a few feet, but remained above the canyon. "Sorry, sir," he apologized. "This is as close as we can get. The walls are too narrow for a safe hover."

"Understood," Jim replied. "Take us back to the flat area and land. Patch me in with 51-Command-4."

"Yes, sir."

Comm traffic filled his ears. "51-Command-1 to 51-Command-4. TJ, we are on scene. What is your ETA?"

*GPS puts us there in about fifteen. What's the injury count?*

"I will know for sure when we land. For now, I can confirm two hostiles down and one survivor."

*Male or female?*

"Can't tell. Get here as quick as you can."

*Roger.*

The choppers—his and one containing the mountain rescue team— kicked up a dusty wash as they landed. Jim slid out of his seat and kept low until he cleared the decelerating blades. Bill followed a few steps behind. Halfway to the mangled horse trailer, Jim's foot caught on a large object. He glanced down at a prone form dressed in desert fatigues. Rolling the stiff over, a hole on the left side caught his attention.

Jim whistled under his breath.

"Dead center to the heart," Bill stated. "The beast is still in control."

"We'll play it that way until we know better."

"Okay."

They walked the rest of the way to the trailer in silence. John stood near the limp form of another thug. Except for the bloody streaks all up and down his bare skin, he appeared unhurt.

"Is he dead, too?" Jim wondered.

"No, he's alive. Jane shot him in the back."

"Take care of him, Bill."

"Right."

"Where is Jane, John?"

John nodded toward the open back. "In there." He swallowed before finishing, "We made her look more hurt than she was to cover up what she did, but then she went off and brutalized herself."

Glancing up at Bill, Jim prompted, "Sedative?"

"I'll prepare one."

"Don't hesitate when you have to use it."

"I won't."

* * *

Crazy Jane slouched in the back corner with her head down over her bent knees, rocking and crying. She reeked a sour combination of sweat, feces, and urine. Her skin was a mixture of all different colors and wounds. No obvious hoof marks, but enough other evidence to fool the casual observer into thinking the horses had trampled her.

Jim slipped down beside her. "You okay?"

She scampered away from him, trailing blood.

Making himself as small as possible, Jim backed up. "Easy, Jane," he sang in a soft tone. "I'm here to help."

Raising her head, Jane stared past him.

"Hurt?"

Whimper.

"Bad?"

A small nod.

"How bad?"

Babbling nonsense.

Jim chewed his lip. He didn't want to play this game with her. He wanted to know who he was dealing with. Based on everything he had seen so far, it appeared to be the beast. Some of the wounds were horrible, deep gashes that must have taken great force and pressure to create. Even in keeping with her character, the discomfort wouldn't allow Jo to do that much damage to herself. Honeywell, on the other hand, would embrace the pain and continue until she felt the disguise was complete.

*How can I get to the human? Jimmy controlled the beast with one word, which is trapped along with him over the edge of the cliff.*

Fishing the phone out of his pocket, Jim dialed Jeff's number.

One ring. "Yes?"

"Please tell me Jane's safe word. I need to talk to the underlying personality." He didn't say his sister's name because he couldn't think of her in that way.

"There isn't one for the rest of us. Only Jimmy, as her handler, can use Phoenix."

"Jeff, do you regret your decision to use Jimmy?"

"No. I needed to get Honeywell one of your haulers with the minimum amount of exposure. Jimmy was a convenient mark, so I used him."

"You are never this callous. What's going on?"

The speaker registered a sharp intake of breath. "Nothing. Maybe the rules need changing."

"Yeah, maybe they do. What about Jo's standing orders to protect those we care about the best we can?"

"Irrelevant. She wasn't herself."

Hanging up before he yelled and provoked Jane, Jim squeezed his phone until his hand hurt. *How in the hell did that asshole think Jimmy could handle this without any training? If I ever ... Breathe, Jim, breathe,* He reminded himself, putting his cell back in his pocket. *Jo is here and now. Jeff is later. Will Jimmy's name be enough to bring her back?*

"Jo, Jimmy needs you. We all do."

"Family important me know is. Continue must."

The garbled speech, gasped through clenched teeth, grated on Jim's already shot nerves. "Will you let me get a doctor for you and allow them to touch you?"

"Yes, not perform otherwise."

"One of the thugs is dead. How?"

"Me do job. Kill. Other sleep still?"

Jim nodded. "Your work, too?"

The black mane fell all over the place as Jane shook her head. "John. Kick to the jaw."

Jim lifted the edge of his lip in a half-smile. The pacifist kicking someone was crazy talk. *What about this situation is normal or sane?* Jim wondered. "Look, Jo, I need some non-convoluted answers from you. I can't deal with Jane anymore. We also need to keep our voices low, so no one outside hears us."

"You're right in both cases." The timbre of Crazy Jane's tone dropped into a more familiar range and lost all its muddiness as she uncurled herself. Jo's warm smile came across as a crooked grin on Crazy Jane's face.

"How can you prove *you* are in control and *not* your beast?"

"There is no definitive way other than to say I'm feeling everything again, my vision is not gray, and my thoughts are in no way emotionless." The hunchback shrugged. "When I am Honeywell, I am her. When I'm me, I'm me."

# FORTY-ONE

# GOOD INTENTIONS,
# LOUSY EXECUTION

"I want to believe you, Jo, but I need something more concrete. Your words are hollow given the voice they've been spoken with."

Handing him the gun, I say, "Fulls will kill themselves before surrendering their weapon. The only other test is to attack me."

"The last time I did, you thrashed my nose."

"Not me, Jim. Honeywell."

"Right," Jim parroted, "when you are her, you are her. Otherwise, you are you. Did whoever saved you from the fire make you think you were a CSG?"

"No, they wouldn't be capable of doing that."

"Then were you pretending to be one?"

Before I answer his hard question, I ask a few of my own. "How much do you know about my rescue? Did you see any of my rescuers? The only thing I interacted with was vague shadows and voices."

"What I know comes from two very weird dreams," Jim replied before narrating a detailed and interesting story. At the conclusion, he added, "I met one of them named Theo. There are also a few things that Jeff said." He almost spits the name out.

"Like what?"

"He thinks the ship that rescued you brought him back in time when he was a kid."

I start laughing, but stop after a few chuckles. In a strange way, it makes sense. Jeff has always seemed a little stronger, smarter, and wiser than the rest of us. "Did he give you an explanation for that?"

Jim launches into another tale. At its end, I say, "I trust the family logs, but, after this is over, we need to talk to Jason and Uncle Pete."

"Agreed. What about you?"

"Well, I can confirm I wasn't anywhere on Earth. The people who rescued me helped me with my disguise and the whole Crazy Jane character, but not the CSG part. I wasn't pretending, either. I am a full."

"You are?" Jim deflates in front of me. "When did you become one? How long did you serve? How many kills do you have?"

"Thirty-six."

Jim's face turns ashen. "Were they USMB or civilian?"

"All USMB. In one case," I hesitate, almost unable to say the words, "it was a family of six who came home five minutes early. The rest were rogues and other CSG's during training."

"Rogues?"

"CSG's who had lost control and were doing random acts of violence. Honeywell was one of the elites that could go after her own kind." My stomach churns as the faces of her prey flash in my mind, but I continue, "I was trained in'96. Served from then until the middle of '97, and then spent through late '98 learning to be human before returning to LA as myself. I served all over the place, including LA."

"How come I didn't know? When you left Lancaster, you said you were going on an undercover op."

"I was, in the beginning, but the mission went south."

"Were you the one who put a gun to my head?"

I nod. "The pure, bitter fear resonating on our link is what saved your life and mine. Even before that happened, and during this second time, I held onto you as much as I could through it."

"Well, that explains why two CSG's made me more uncomfortable than the others. Who was involved in your recovery?"

"Molly, Paul, and other loving and helping hands whose names I will never know, the first time. Jimmy, this second one."

"How did he help you?"

"Doesn't matter. He just did." I shudder, remembering the uncontrolled rage that I had provoked in Jimmy. He and I need to talk about that, but I'm not about to worry his father any more than I already have. "I am grateful to him for giving me my life back."

" Jo, I…" Jim slams his fist into the side of the trailer causing it to ring like a bell. "Damn it! Why you would consider such an insane op in the first place? What about this second time?"

"I made the decision for a lot of reasons, and justified them by telling myself I was helping Jason. There was an extraction team in place to remove me before the training got too intense. My handlers forced me to kill them as part of my initiation. After I recovered, I promised myself I would never enter her sterile world again. Then Casper ordered horses and people around me hurt and killed with no qualms or remorse. I thought her strength, discipline, and emotional control were the only way to protect our family from him."

"Then Jason was—"

"The reason I wasn't killed for my hesitation," I change the course of Jim's assumption. "I'm why he didn't act on the information."

Jim shook his head. "I still don't understand, Jo. What specific things drove you to face the rumored barbarism they use to break people before molding them into fulls?"

"I wanted to pay for the stupid choices and mistakes that cost Michelle her brother and me my love, and my..." I choke before blurting, "son, his real parents."

"You have a son?"

"Yes, RJ. Jeff's brother. Patch's father." I hang my head, tears dripping from my face. Patch London was my only boyfriend who lasted beyond the second date. We would have had a lifelong relationship except for the temper that lead to his demise. "Please know that when I cut and signed the orders that brought Honeywell back, I never considered the possibility of Jimmy being my handler."

"Even knowing you were her, Jeff made that decision."

My link with Jim surges. His bottled emotions wash over me, almost sucking me into their maelstrom. He takes a deep breath and lets it out. I look up into his eyes. His soul is a wide, dark chasm overflowing with bitter tasting water tainted by pain, anger, and grief. Swallowing, I withdraw from the connection. My body twitches, coiling itself to spring. *No, I can't run away from this*, my mind roars. *It's my fault he hurts. I have to fix it, somehow.*

"Honeywell did do some good, Jo," Jim whispers. "John, Jimmy, and Cordero now, and those of us caught by that sniper a couple days ago, are alive because of your training. As for the rest..."

I look past him, not wanting to meet his eyes again. "Telling the whole story to you and the family is going to be easier than the few sentences I have to mutter to Michelle and Vince. They need to know everything about my hand in their messed up relationship."

"What about the other members of the team?"

"We can't involve them until our next in-person meeting. I trust the team, but not the ears and eyes around them. If anyone slips, we are all dead."

"How do you want to proceed?"

"Like nothing's changed. Crazy Jane's going to have to return to Phoenix and receive treatment for her injuries. Then when she's healthy enough, Honeywell will make an appearance for her end of mission debriefing. Afterward, you'll transfer her to Molly's where I'll remain until she can certify me as me."

"What If the CS tries to take over the process?"

"Jason should be able to run interference, but don't ask him to unless my life is in danger. It will cost him too much."

"Will this get you reinstated?"

"No, with every change in my status, I have to go through an evaluation. Given that I'm coming back from being Honeywell a second time, I expect the next one will be an intense and lengthy session in front of a full medical board."

"Why not start as Honeywell now?"

"I'm too fresh off of being her. If I think like her, she'll take over again. I need a few days to build up my mental defenses. Besides, are there any black masks around?"

Jim shook his head. "Why not stay yourself, then? We can cover you in a blanket and say that Crazy Jane died."

"Bill is the only one who can escort the body to the morgue without looking suspicious. That leaves only the two of us against whatever resources Casper might have in place."

"True," Jim chews his lip. "Jo, are there any more big surprises like Honeywell and RJ?"

"No more of those, I promise." I keep my face neutral and choose my next words with care to protect John. "I have, and will in the future, bend the truth to keep our family, friends, and team safe, but I will always share as much as I can with you."

"That's all I can ask for." Jim touches me on the shoulder. "Whatever happens, Jo, we'll deal with the consequences together, just like we should have been doing all along."

The trailer rings from someone pounding on its side. "What's going on?" Jim yells.

"Our guest is waking up," Bill shouts back. "How's Jane? Are you okay? That crash a few minutes ago was loud."

"She attacked me, so I had to throw her against the wall to subdue her. She's coming around again now."

I raise an eyebrow.

Turning to me, Jim whispers, "I assume you want to show our guest that what he heard on the radio was a fluke. That's why you thrashed yourself and scared John into thinking you had lost your mind, right?"

I nod, stating, "That was the initial plan, but it's not a good one anymore. Maybe you should just carry me outside. I'll pretend to be unconscious from my injuries. That way, you, Bill, and the rest of the family can protect me. I'll smear you with some goop and scratch you a few times to give you credibility."

Jim shook his head. "It won't be convincing enough. Honeywell's already tried to kill me twice and now that I've attacked her—"

"We have to go back to being beast and prey."

Jim nods, ripping his shirt and opening his arms up wide. "Do what you have to do."

"What if I lose control?"

"Bill's ready to go with a sedative."

"His normal dose for us won't work."

"He'll figure that out real quick."

Taking a chance, I ask for Honeywell, but she remains silent. I'm on my own. I hate the idea of hurting Jim, even if it's for the good of the mission.

I make a weak poke in his direction.

He shoves back. "You're going to have to do better than that," he growls, before smashing his hand into the side of my face and ripping a painful streak across it.

The color in my vision disappears.

# FORTY-TWO

# FIGHTING JANE

I wake up in a hospital with Bill hovering over me. Behind him, a hanging curtain cuts the room in half. Everything is in beautiful and vibrant color. I didn't think it would be. After Jim slapped me, Honeywell came roaring back, so until I passed out, I was fighting her for control.

"Jo or Jane?" Bill's gentle voice prompts.

"Jo," I grunt. My body aches from the thrashing I gave it, and in several new spots. "Where's Jim?"

"Here," a weak voice groans from behind the curtain.

Bill rips the sheet open.

"We put on a very convincing show, but I got the worst of it," Jim smiles before wincing. Every inch of his bare skin is a different mix of colors, some more painful looking than others. His face is black and blue, with lots of yellow, brown, and red thrown in. Swollen lips and eyes top off the gruesome mask. "After the first few blows, I knew your beast had returned, so I didn't hold back. It countered my every move, and even anticipated a few of them."

"Honeywell was using our connection," I state. "You are lucky that, throughout this whole op, she didn't remember the kill order that she thinks is still open for you."

Jim nods.

"When you and Jim tumbled out of that trailer, you were a crazy demon with claws, Jo," Bill states. "I had to hit you with twice the normal amount I use for a person your size before you went down."

"How long have I been asleep?"

"Two days."

That makes sense. One of Bill's light doses leaves me comatose for about eight hours.

"Am I fit enough to continue the charade?"

"Between your self-inflicted injuries and the fight with Jim, you came close to breaking a few bones. I've written up a report on Honeywell to reflect that, which gives you seventy-two hours of down time."

"What about Jimmy? Did he hear or see any of what went on?"

177

Bill shakes his head. "No, he was unconscious when they brought him up."

"Good." At least the kid was spared that much more pain. He still has plenty of grief to deal with, though. "How is he?"

"We've tried rousing him, but he's showing very minimal responses. The truck was hit on his side."

* * *

"Jimmy?" Someone touched his shoulder.

*Let me be.* He pushed against the unseen hand. *I need a few more minutes.*

"Come on, Jimmy, wake up!"

The urgency in the tone tugged at his awareness. *What am I doing asleep anyway?* Random images floated around him. He grabbed one and straightened it out, found another, and connected the two together. More and more pieces flew in until a picture formed. *Oh, yeah. I was riding in the truck with Duff and Uncle John until something slammed into us.* Glancing up, he noticed the trailer. *What's it doing over there?* The thought stayed in his mind for a moment. *Something hit us again; we started tumbling, and didn't stop until the blackness. Now, it's gray… Where am I?*

His eyes squeaked open. He blinked a few times, fighting off the assault of bright lights and a harsh, acidic smell. The white walls screamed hospital. He tried moving his limbs. Everything seemed fine, except his right leg felt a little heavier than normal.

"Good, you're back with us." Bill peered down at him with a relieved smile. "Don't worry about your leg. You broke it in a couple of places, but you'll be fine in about six weeks."

Behind Bill were three shadows. Two of them had human faces and wore regular blue work uniforms. The third was shrouded in black from head to toe, face included. James Jr. nodded at his father, ignored Jeff, and kept staring past them at the armor.

"Who are you?" he stammered.

Gloved hands removed the helmet, exposing the face from his living nightmare. The expression and movement of the eyes almost reflected the pain of the scratches and bruises that crisscrossed the hollow canvas, but nothing else had changed.

"Jimmy, it's me." Honeywell spoke in a good attempt at his aunt's warm, rich tone. "Sorry for the getup, but I'm still dead to everyone else."

"To me as well," James Jr. snarled. "Get out."

"Jimmy, let me explain—"

"No!" He thrashed around, feeling and grabbing for anything that he could throw. "Out, bitch, *now!*"

Bill placed a firm hand on him. "Settle down, Jimmy, or you're going to rip your IV."

"Why isn't anyone listening? I want that monster," he stabbed his finger at the evil shadow and its trainer, "and the bastard who created it, out of my sight."

"Come on, Jeff," the armor said, nodding to the door. "We better do as he says."

\* \* \*

Appearing to Jimmy in anything less than my own uniform with my hair grown out and my weight back to normal was a big mistake. I had shown him my face, hoping the act would be enough to demonstrate that I was back in control. Now, looking back at the moment through his eyes, the gesture didn't have any meaning. Honeywell used the family name for him when she needed his attention before Casper's men attacked. Without me looking like myself, he had every reason to believe the reveal was just another act of manipulation by her.

I spend the next two weeks at Phoenix, healing from my own injuries and watching over Jimmy the best I can. Standing guard outside his door, I wait and listen, hoping for an invitation back into his room, and his world, but it never comes. Jim, Jason, Cordero, and my other brothers nod in my direction when they stop by, but otherwise treat me like a ghost they don't see.

Jeff tries visiting, and has things thrown at him before his foot crosses the threshold. Bill, as the peacemaker of the family, talks to him a few times. The rest of us tolerate his presence, but only because he's family. That's a weak connection, though, given his real birth year. As soon as I'm certified for duty, I'll have Michael look into any regulations that Jeff might have violated, as well as the possibility of court-martialing him. I want his ass for not protecting Jimmy.

The kid being at Molly's was no excuse. Using the Houston ICHQ, he could have interviewed other candidates and still kept Honeywell hidden from view at Molly's. Honeywell violating one of her rules and facing expulsion might have limited his options, though. I don't know if that happened because I can't remember anything from the time she retook control until Jimmy whispered "Phoenix" in my ear.

The blackout is one reason I'm not going after Jeff through Jim. The other is his lie about knowing I was Honeywell when he assigned Jimmy to me. I based my final decision to become her again on a promise from the ship's crew. They were only going to use Molly and Jeff for the op. I wanted to write a note to go along with the orders, warning Molly about Honeywell's reincarnation and asking Jeff to manage her. The shadows said that it would look odd, so I didn't. Therefore, Jeff had no way of knowing unless he was one of the ghosts involved in my original treatment, or Molly told him. Given that confidentiality could be her middle name, I don't think she would have.

"Take your break, Commander," Bill orders as he passes by. He's been sending me away every four hours. Except for the few hours I allow myself to sleep, I always come back within thirty minutes.

"Sir, this unit must stay on its post," I reply through the armor's voice box. "It is not yet the end of visiting hours."

"In there, now," he hisses, pointing to the empty room next to Jimmy's.

I follow him in silence. After the door closes, he growls, "Remove your helmet. I need to see your face."

Complying with his request, I greet his piercing stare with a smile. "See, I'm fine."

Bill nods. "Yes, for the moment, you are. What about our agreement about removing this contraption on a set schedule?" Tapping my shell, he states, "We have to lessen the chance of Honeywell taking over and not letting you go."

"I'm willing to take that risk, if it means staying close to Jimmy."

"You can't do any more for him. He will come around."

"Will he?" I challenge. "I already almost lost him once thanks to Jim's ex. I don't want him to think he's been abandoned again."

"He doesn't. What good will you be to him if you are Honeywell?"

"None. I can only assume he hates me for being her, and that he blames Jeff for her existence."

"They are more than assumptions, Jo, they are facts. Jimmy's admitted both to me. I've warned Jeff, who's already talking to Molly. She's committed to helping Jimmy work through his issues once he returns to Houston."

"Why send him back to the Academy? He should be with family who cares about him, not the bastard who shoved him into a situation he wasn't prepared for."

"He asked to go back because there he will have discipline and be forced to focus on his studies and other activities. Being around family means being around you, and he can't stop seeing you as Honeywell. He's assured me that as a cadet, he and Jeff don't have much interaction, except at official functions. Molly's ready to take him back into her shelter if trouble arises between them."

"What more can I do?"

"Finish healing and make sure Honeywell never comes back. I don't want you at Molly's any longer than she needs to make sure that your alter ego is under control. I also don't want to send you back there for a third time."

His words chill me. "Then you know Honeywell's complete history?"

"Yes and so does John."

"I found that out in the desert. Why did Molly get you two involved?"

"She needed our expertise."

"I don't remember either one of you being there, just vague shadows."

"We wore black masks and spoke with a box. Molly insisted on them to protect both you and us."

"Who knows about your involvement?"

"Jason, Molly, Paul, and Jimmy."

"Does Jimmy know about John?"

"No."

"Has Jimmy mentioned anything to Cordero?"

"Not that I'm aware of. Despite the risk, Cordero needs to be told. It will help Jimmy."

"I agree. Include him in tonight's family meeting."

"Will do. Jo, when you talk about Honeywell, don't go into detail about your treatment. We have to protect Molly and John."

"Not to mention you," I add.

Bill glances at his watch. "You've had enough of a break. Ready to go back in?"

"I guess," I shrug. "Before I do, though, I have one final question. When did Jeff discover I was Honeywell?"

"Both he and Molly have indicated it wasn't until you broke cover."

* * *

After Bill clears Jimmy for light duty, the family has to split up. I escort him and Cordero back to the Academy as a silent shadow. Jim, Bill, and my other brothers head for the next phase of the competition in Indiana.

Cordero broke a couple ribs in the crash. While this doesn't disqualify him from riding, he feels he can't continue without Jimmy. Curious about his motives, I pull him aside as we are about to board the plane.

"You don't have to do this, Mr. Cordero," I say, hoping he can hear my emotions through the electronic noise the armor generates for my voice.

"No, sir, I don't, but his whole experience with you as a black mask has changed Jimmy. I want to make sure he has someone he can talk things through with."

"He does. Molly—"

"From that halfway house?" Cordero interrupts, shaking his head. "Sorry, sir, but some head doc isn't going to cut it. He needs a true friend. Family would be better, but he doesn't want that right now."

"I know. Duff, thank you for being there for him. Tell Jimmy I love him and I…" I stumble, unable to find the words that seem adequate. "I'm here as myself, when he's ready."

"I will, sir."

* * *

182

As we part ways, Jimmy hands me a note that says he wants nothing more to do with me, my base, or either team. This makes me even more appreciative of Cordero's sacrifice. Jimmy accepts Jeff's presence when he sees him, but it's with the steel respect a cadet gives a superior officer. My reaction is even colder. We exchange salutes, I hand him the orders transferring Jimmy back to his command, and leave without speaking a word to him.

I then head to Molly's where I spend most of my days in a private room or one-on-one therapy, enjoying the feel and look of my own skin. In any of the common rooms or other public places, I am Crazy Jane. I have no choice. I can't risk anyone seeing me as myself until I'm certified and back in my own uniform. When Jimmy shows up for his treatment, I wander the streets as her until Paul, dressed as another bum, finds me.

After two weeks, I feel that Honeywell is dormant enough for me to return to my own life.

Calling me into her office, Molly says, "Jo, you should stay at least another week."

"Why?"

She throws a book at me.

Leaping from my seat, I lunge at her. My hands are inches from her neck when I pull back and retreat to my chair, shuddering.

"What are you feeling?"

"Nothing," I gasp. "I'm speaking with my voice, seeing with my eyes, and hearing everything with my ears, but there are no emotions behind these actions. All I'm thinking about is the mission and my need to get back to the bodies I have to protect."

"What does that tell you?"

"Honeywell is still too close to the surface."

I end up spending another two weeks to satisfy both of us that I'm back in control.

# FORTY-THREE

# REJOINING THE TEAM

The team is in the third week of Americans Intercontinental Championship competition in Bloomington, Indiana when I rejoin them. If they win this week and the next, it's on to the big finale, the International Championships. I missed most of the California State Championships and all of the Western Area and United States Championships. While I was around for parts of the last two as Honeywell or Crazy Jane, I don't consider those memories or experiences mine.

Despite my extra time at Molly's, the tools she gave me for coping with Honeywell, and my recertification by a board of twelve head docs, I'm still in trouble. On top of that, the relationship with all my brothers is strained. The more sensitive ones, John and TJ, insist on having another person around when they talk to me.

I'm still susceptible to my alter ego because she, in a very strange way, is an emotional cathartic and shield. Her callous nature helps me in dealing with the threat of Casper's next attack, the stress from the competition, and the heaviness dragging at my heart because of DH and Jimmy.

We are no closer to finding my horse. Plenty of false sightings all over the country, but nothing specific we can nail down. His color and markings are a common combination, making the search that much harder. His tracking chip doesn't appear to be working, either.

\* \* \*

Jim pulls me aside before our synchronized riding event. It'll be my first official ride with him since the cross-country race where Vince was shot. Without any preamble, he taps the side of his head and prompts, "Look I need to know if I'm dealing with you or Honeywell. If it's Honeywell, you might as well ride away and never come back."

"Jim, I'm me." I try smiling, but the expression feels phony, so I keep my lips neutral. Though I've blocked my inner turmoil from Jim, I know he has seen flashes of Honeywell more than once.

Jim shakes his head. "You are only about fifty percent here." He gestures to the ring. "We can't go in there and win like that."

Leaning back in the saddle, I nod.

Honeywell whispers, *We'll stay hidden and only come out when you need us. You'll be in full control.*

*Don't listen to her*, my inner voice warns. *You give in one more time and you're done.*

In the distance, a horse whistles.

"Come on, Jim, something's wrong. We need to investigate."

Shaking his head, Jim unclips his walkie. "51-Command-2 to 51-Command-3. Why are the horses upset?"

*No reason*, Bill replies. *John and me are here keeping them company.*

"Thanks. 51-Command-2 out." Holstering his radio, he glances at me. "You see, even a horse that doesn't know you very well knows you are in trouble. Talk to me, Jo. What can I do to help you?"

"Keep the pressure on me, and catch me when I fall or fail."

"I promise I always will."

A warm, embracing light floods our link.

I cock my head to the left at almost the same time Jim goes right. Still a few cracks in the mirror, I guess.

"It's not me, Jo."

"Me, neither, but the presence is familiar. He's been a part of me since Honeywell's first appearance, and visits at random times."

"Another personality?"

"At first, I thought so, but over the years, he has spoken in such a way that I've figured out he's human empath at least several hundred miles away."

*Try several thousand*, the presence snorts, *and I have four legs, not two.*

*You do? Theo?* The strength of Jim's thought catches me off guard.

Our link is hard to explain. Sometimes Jim's right there with me as a wave that ebbs and flows with what I'm feeling. Other times, he's a distant and light touch. While the intimacy allows us to speak without saying anything, the language isn't something anyone else can understand. We don't share thoughts and words, or hear each other's voices in our heads, that often. Emotions are always very distinct and real, but everything else consists of vague ideas and impressions that require some interpretation.

The presence snorts. *No, but I sense you have been touched by him, and he is one of my kind.*

"Jim, what's going on?"

"It's okay, Jo," Jim smiles. "I met Theo in Houston. Your mysterious presence is alien equine."

*It is as he says, Kesomak.*

*My lord?* Before I can confirm the translation, the presence disappears. "Best to believe it that way, I guess," I shrug. "Anything else..." I shake my head and laugh. "Not that I've sounded *that* sane for the last few months, or years."

*Ladies and gentlemen,* the announcer booms over the speakers, *after a five-minute intermission, our next competitors will be Captains Joanna and James C. Mason from USMBLA.*

"Not on those two pieces of donkey meat, you won't," a voice calls out. "You need to get your butts on some real horse flesh."

Jim and I turn as one. Prancing toward us are Midnight Fury and a matching black stallion, with Jason and TJ leading them. Like me, Fury hasn't seen most of the competition. I noticed his absence upon my return and inquired about it. According to Jim, Fury hadn't recovered from the stable fire until after the explosion and fire at our house. Instead of risking him with the team, he shipped him up to Jason's ranch. Knowing that we needed every advantage for this particular event, I asked Jason to escort Fury and his younger half-brother out here.

Watching Jim reunite with his horse, I think about our family logs. Robert Mason began writing the journals just before he assumed command of the Los Angeles Mounted Scouts. Ever since then, my family has transcribed their adventures into the diaries. Tradition states that the eldest sibling of each generation does the writing while the youngest keeps the records safe and organized. Others can contribute as needed.

The first thing John did when he took over the responsibility of archivist was scan all the old books into the computer. This allows passages to be sealed. I have done a little of that. No one—other than

Jim, Bill, Jeff, Uncle Pete, Aunt Rose, and Jason—needs to know about RJ until I am ready to tell them. Jim blocked some of the details on how he found out about the starship and Jeff, some of the conversation with his brother and Molly. I need to check with Michael on the legality of breaking the seal, so I can review them and see if they have any relevant information for my case against Jeff.

# FORTY-FOUR

# REKINDLING THE FEAR

I shift in the saddle. Underneath me, Fury sighs and flicks an ear back. Jim has loaned me his horse because synchronized riding is as much about style as technique. Of our pair, Fury has more ring time, so he has a better understanding of the subtle things that make a good performance. He also arches his neck when at a trot or canter without any prompting.

"Dang, he looks good," Jim smiles, "so do you."

"Thanks. Ready?"

Jim nods. The brightness in his face dims somewhat.

"What's wrong?"

"I'm feeling you on all levels, but I don't trust the stillness around us. It's too perfect."

The typical sound and motion of a horse show surrounds us. A grounds crew exits the ring after wiping away the traces of the last few riders. Crowd noise ebbs and flows. An occasional bird, car, machine, or vendor hawking their wares adds dimension and depth to the sonic landscape. My instincts are quiet, so is Honeywell. The normalcy does seem odd, considering the chaos that has surrounded the team for so long.

"Maybe this is the proverbial calm before the storm," I quip.

"If it is," Jim shrugs, "we'll ride it out together."

*Our next competitors are ready,* the announcer booms. *Entering the ring, Captains Joanna and James C. Mason from USMBLA.*

Prancing through the entrance, I guide Fury to the center of the arena. Out of the corner of my eye, I glance at Jim. We are in sync, and the way he moves up and down with me, so are our horses. From now until we leave the ring, we have to remain mirrors of each other, even when riding at opposite ends of the ring. For each discordant movement, we'll lose points.

We stop, turn toward the judges, and salute them. After receiving a nod from the lead one, we begin our program by splitting up, with Jim heading back toward the entrance, and me the far end. Our choreography calls for us to perform a few lead and stride changes, cross over in the middle, repeat our routine at our partner's end, join up, and finish off with intricate dance and parallel work.

Fury maintains a straight line to our starting position until about three-quarters of the way there when his stride shortens up, and almost hesitates, as if he's unsure of his footing. Hoping no one notices the subtle motion, I slide my free hand from the outside of my leg to the inside and touch him just above the saddle. He flinches.

Maintaining a straight-backed riding posture, I peer down at the ground. The sand sparkles with a silver metallic tinge. I blink, and my angle shifts enough with Fury's forward movement that the shimmer disappears. Another step and I can see a faint trace again.

*Pop!* Fury's stride stutters.

The next step triggers another pop and shudder. This cycle goes on until the tension in reins and between my legs suggests that Fury, a good horse trained to handle the stress of performing around crowds, has reached his limit for unexpected surprises.

Not knowing if there are any more devices buried in the sand in the front, or to the side, of us, I ask Fury to back. At first, he fights the bit by arching his neck against the pressure of my slow pull. With a hesitant shift, he moves half a step in the requested direction. Nothing happens. We both release our breath. I urge him to take a few more steps. We retreat to the middle of the ring.

Glancing behind me, I notice that Jim has also backed his horse. We are almost rear-to-rear. I nod left, while sweeping the index and middle fingers of my free hand toward the right, indicating that we should begin our parallel routine. I'm not thinking about the competition anymore, rather just keeping Jim safe, and Fury calm. If we score points while maneuvering toward the entrance, fine.

*Smack!* Something brushes against my leg as it hits Fury in the side.

He jumps and bolts toward the far end. I put all my weight behind turning him, but he doesn't respond. We hit a section of unexploded sand. He bucks, twists, and turns, trying to get away. His antics dig up more of the explosive, which goes off higher and higher around us. I sink lower into the saddle, hoping to ride it out and maneuver him toward the middle of the ring again.

My left knee throbs. Chewing my lip, I try to dismiss the sensation and warning. I hadn't worn the brace as Honeywell, but Bill strapped it back on me before I left my hospital bed. The thing has the flexibility to handle most of the changes in leg pressure and position needed for riding, but not to this extreme.

In my head, I time Fury's jumps. When he's at a low point in one of his cycles, I loosen my seat and bail right. He twists left, launching me into the air. Unlike Alabaster's attack, I'm better prepared, but still land hard, triggering a few pops in the sand. To me, they feel like a little massage, but I understand why Fury freaked after having them going off underneath his feet multiple times.

The squeals, snorts, and thumps that rattle the ground underneath me indicate Fury's still upset. Unlike the mauling, when Alabaster circled for his attack, Fury's moving away. I'm also a lot more aware of my breathing, my surroundings, and everything that's going on. The audience has stilled in their seats. Shouts and the rushing swish of many bodies moving at once indicate I'll have help soon enough.

*This feels, and* is, *different.* I sigh. *I'm going to be fine.*

*Thunk! Thawp! Splat!*

Fury whistles in a haunting, high-pitch echo of Alabaster's scream. My chest tightens. *Breathe, Jo,* I remind myself. *Breathe!*

Pushing off with my hands, I roll to my feet and shuffle four steps before my knee locks up, pitching me forward. Planting my other foot, I catch myself and keep upright. Managing a few hops, I tumble to the ground. Groans erupt from the crowd.

*"Get out of there! He's coming! Look out!"*

Throwing up my arms to protect my head, I curl up into a tight ball, waiting for the first strike. Instead of a steel shod hoof ripping into my flesh, something heavy slams into my side. An even pressure covers me.

"Nothing going to harm you this time, Jo," Jim's voice whispers in my ear.

I try to grab on to his words, but I all I hear and feel is two insane horses merging into one.

# FORTY-FIVE

## THINKING SPOOKED HORSE

"You look like hell," Bill stated.

Sighing, Jim plopped himself down at the kitchen table of their guesthouse, exhaustion washing over every fiber of his body. "Jo had a nightmare and took me with her."

"How bad?"

"Worse than before," Jim swallowed. "It starts with Fury freaking out, and then morphs into the every bloody moment of the mauling." He rubbed his forehead, trying to relieve some of the pounding and pressure that had kept him up for most of the night. "You haven't seen her, have you?"

Bill gestured to the orange gray light seeping through the windows. "No, I'm hoping she stays in bed for a good four more hours. You should try and go back, too."

With a half-smile, Jim teased, "Doctor's orders?"

"I can make them that if you want me to."

A body shuffled toward them from the direction of the bedrooms. Jim turned. Jason appeared in the doorway. His face, which almost never revealed his age, looked worn and drawn. Every wrinkle and crease stood out, even in the pale murkiness.

"The lass 'tis gone."

"As in dead or back to being Honeywell?" Jim yelped, having not felt the consequences of either outcome.

"No, she asked fer an indefinite suspension due ta her PTSD. I granted her request."

"Jason, by doing that, you've left her with no protection against herself or anything Casper throws at her." Jim screamed at a controlled whisper.

"Relax, lad, I made sure another Command Team 'twas on her six. She wants the team ta continue even when she canna and she felt this 'twas the only way ta let that happen."

"Without letting us help her work things through? Damn it, Jason, we weren't there for the last eight years because of her unreasonable and unwarranted need to handle it on her own. Why did you let her indulge in that behavior again?"

"Easy, Jim," Bill cautioned. "Think spooked horse."

"It is only because I am thinking that," Jim spat, bolting upward and thrusting back his chair, "that I am not going after her."

Storming out, he bumped Jason hard as he went by.

* * *

Jim sat on Midnight's Crest, watching the team practice. He had a harder time accepting that he was back in command of them than they did accepting him as their commander. *I wish I had faced the pit. Then I could have gone after Casper and given him the justice he deserves. Instead, I have to worry about Jo losing herself to her fear or her demon.*

The gelding came from a good line, but it was hard not to compare him to his big brother. That was another reason he wanted Casper. He hadn't seen the hits on Fury, but he had heard them. They tried taking Fury back out into the ring the day after the performance. Nothing good came from the experience for either him or his horse.

At first, Fury balked at the entrance, but after some coaxing, took a tentative step forward. When his hooves touched the sand, he jerked the rope out of Jim's hands and bolted. It had taken him, plus six other people, a few hours to find his horse and calm him down enough to put him back in a stall. They shipped Fury back to LA four days ago, so the trainers there could work with him. The odds of him returning to the competition weren't good.

His phone buzzed. "Mason," he answered.

"It's Ben, Captain. Fury's trailer just pulled through the main gate."

"Thank you, Mr. Harrison. How's the base?"

"Good. Any word on the Captain?"

"She's fine according to the team that has its eyes on her. They can't tell us her location, though." He hesitated before blurting, "Ben, what's your take on Jo's relapse? Will she recover? How can I help her?"

The line went quiet for a heartbeat. "Let her be, Jim," Ben replied. "There were days, I couldn't reach her. She'd come to the office, do her job, and leave, only talking as much as needed. I'd check in on her on my way home. Sometimes, she'd invite me, sometimes not. When she did, we'd sit on the couch saying nothing until she went to bed, and I left. The next day, she'd be normal and thank me for understanding."

"Did you find her quietness odd or suspicious?"

"No, sir. Should I have?"

"Has she told you anything about the undercover mission after she left Lancaster?"

"Not much. Just that Molly Rowntree was a trusted head doc that I should call, if she acted strange or unresponsive for more than a day. I never had to, but maybe you need to."

"Good idea, Ben. I have to check up on Jimmy's progress, anyway."

"How's he doing?"

"Fine, at last word."

"That's good. Anything else I can do for you?"

"No, just keep Jo's base and my horse safe."

"Yes, sir."

Hanging up, Jim dialed Molly's number.

"Hello," she answered after two rings.

"Hi, Molly. Did you see what happened to Jo?"

"Aye."

"Will she revert back to Honeywell because of it?"

"Nay, if anything her fear will keep the beast in check, as it 'tis a very strong emotion. I'm more worried about the stress ye ha been dealin' with."

"I'm okay. What's going on with Jimmy?"

"He's healing. Progress 'tis slow, but I haven't ha ta interfere in his few encounters with Jeff."

"Why do you think Jeff got Jimmy involved?"

"Because there 'twas more ta Jo's orders than what ye saw."

"She wouldn't put Jimmy in danger like that!"

"It wasn't her *per se*. Da words she used were different and unexpected."

"What did they say?"

"*Jeff isn't the uncaring bastard he is pretending to be. I had to set him up that way to protect Molly. Jimmy needed to learn some valuable lessons, so he could save us in the future, so we could save the future.*"

# FORTY-SIX

## JUST PASSING THROUGH

I'm done. I'm through.

I can't continue like this, watching my shadow and trembling when I see a horse. I'm back in my bad place, ready to push my family away again. They won't understand any of what I'm feeling or thinking. Even if they do, they'll be too disappointed that I wasn't strong enough to handle my fear.

The only way I can stay in the USMB is if I become Honeywell on a permanent basis. Her siren song has been blasting in my ear, but, so far, I've managed to ignore the temptation. Her black armor will protect me should I encounter a horse, but it will also prevent me from touching one ever again.

Do I want to enter that cold, sterile world again? For the temporary relief it will bring, yes. I can't serve as a shadow alongside my family, though. They'll respect the armor with their voices, but ask questions with their eyes every time they steal a glance at me. Even if I post to a different base, there is still a chance we'll meet in passing or, worse, when I have to hunt and kill them as part of my duty.

If Honeywell takes over my life again, I won't be me anymore. The handlers will make sure of that. After they crush every emotion, impulse, and uncontrolled thought in my mind, my body will be nothing more than a soulless killing machine that treats everything around it as a threat or target. It would have to live chained up in a cage when it wasn't on an assignment, so it couldn't go rogue.

I can't stand the thought of being that out of control.

Resignation is my only option. At least if I resign, I can remain myself and transfer command of USMBLA to Jim, preventing any shenanigans by the upper echelon. Family and friends will still be a part of my life. We can do stuff together and live as if nothing is wrong.

Gag me! Everything will be. Wrong, that is. I need horses in my life as much as people. Without them, I'm incomplete.

Stupid fear!

After six days of wandering, I'm no closer to my destination, or decision. I've kept myself isolated and on the move. Every night, I'm sleeping in a different city. Every day, I'm staying in shadows, blending in. Changes in hair color and style, eye color, clothes, and mannerisms all add up to different characters making an appearance. Radios, phones, and other electronic devices are off with the battery removed, so no one can track me that way. Still I've picked up and lost tails a few times. I'm not sure if they were friendlies or not.

I haven't driven back to LA yet because I don't want to. When I return, I'll have to vacate my position or become a faceless, nameless shadow. I'm not ready to deal with the consequences of either choice. I need to talk to Jim first, and prepare him in some way for whatever I decide to do. I've dropped too many surprises on him as of late.

During my various pit stops, I catch glimpses of the team on television. They are only a few days away from finishing this latest round without me. Next year, if I survive this ordeal as me, I am going all the way with them. Living my dream through them isn't the way I wanted to make it a reality.

Today, I'm somewhere in Montana. Closest major city is Billings, but that's about a day's drive away. My sense of direction and landmarks is good, except when I'm tired, and/or don't care. In this case, it's both. I'm running away from the ghost of my fear, but also running toward the shadow of hope. The official investigation into DH's kidnapping still hasn't turned up anything. There are only chances and possibilities left. This place is one of those.

A few miles outside the town, there's a ranch called the old Hudson place. Oral Hudson has been dead for several years. A guy named Buck Riordan, along with his range boss, Clem, runs the spread. I knew someone with the same name as Riordan at the Academy. He served in the USMB until someone caught him doping horses. After his court-martial and dishonorable discharge, he disappeared without a trace.

As part of the research I did during my first suspension, I ran the names of anyone who served with Casper or myself and had enough land in a remote area to stash a horse. Public records turned up Riordan's purchase of the ranch. It wasn't enough to warrant a visit by any USMB personnel, but as a civilian passing through the area, I have a great excuse for catching up with an old classmate.

The sun hanging halfway in the sky points to it being lunchtime. I'm in this small town with a diner, post office, few shops, and not much else. Driving here, I passed mile after mile of ranch land. Some spreads were in better shape than others. Most had cattle, sheep, or horses. Others, it was hard to tell.

Pulling up a stool at the counter, I scan the diner and realize that I chose the wrong clothes for this pit stop. I should have gone a little more flannel and short-haired than tie-dye and long dreads.

A full-bodied waitress, with her years of service written in the lines around her eyes, places a glass of water and a menu in front of me. The emptiness of her soft face suggests she wouldn't have cared if I had shown up in my birthday suit with a rainbow-colored deathhawk. I was just another body she had to take care of.

In a forced smile voice, the waitress prompts, "Passing through?"

"Yeah," I shrug. "Not sure where I'm headed."

"Do anything productive for a living?" She pronounces every syllable of *productive* as if it will motivate the hippie she sees.

"I'm studying people's reactions to how other people dress," I quip, glancing through the menu. Prices are reasonable, but nothing sounds good. I settle on a hamburger and fries, figuring it'll keep me satisfied until I stop for the night.

The waitress huffs away.

Waiting for my order, I listen to the conversations floating around me. Newlyweds in a booth two tables down and to the right are reminiscing about their honeymoon. A little father in that direction, a farmer talks with his banker. On my left, an elderly couple tries to decide if they want to split the daily special or indulge in a small salad each. The giggles, whines, and temperamental screams of little kids and babies create some static in the otherwise pleasant hum of small town life.

Slinging my grub in front of me, the waitress asks, "Can I get you anything else?"

Condiments like ketchup, mustard, relish, and hot sauce are already within arm's reach, so I wave her off. After removing the bun and the mini-salad, I doctor up the patty with a touch of hot, a dollop of smooth tang, and some crunchy sweet. Reassembling the sandwich, I take my first bite. The pleasing, juicy morsel settles into the perfect spot between dry cardboard and greasy mess.

I lose myself in the three dimensional tastes floating across my tongue. Voices fade into the background. My chaotic thoughts slow their relentless assault. Life, for the moment at least, is all about eating.

"There's something wrong at the old Hudson place, Sheriff." The shrill whine cuts through my peace.

Dropping my burger on the plate, I glance around. A stocky, dark-haired ranch hand with the dust of the trail lingering behind him has cornered a man with a small potbelly, light, or grey, hair, and a dark brown jacket. The badges on the sleeve near the shoulder indicate an affiliation with local law enforcement.

I recognize the sheriff as an older version of a Vice Lieutenant Riordan enlisted to be his lookout when he injected the horses. The kid ended up being his fall guy. Security found drugs, paraphernalia, and a stash of money in his footlocker. The USMB didn't prosecute the kid in return for his testimony against Riordan. His association with the doper ruined his career, though.

No base commander wanted to take a chance on him. They were all afraid he would start his own racket. Commanding Lancaster at the time, I decided that the kid needed somewhere to prove himself. He lasted six months, and was on the verge of making Lieutenant, when someone questioned his integrity at a bar. The accuser pressed so hard that the night ended in a fight. Since he was still on probation, regulations required his dismissal from service with a general discharge. A few people petitioned for an other than honorable one, but I refused. He signed up for the Army the next day. I lost track of him after that.

Picking up my burger, I work on tuning them out. I'm successful until the ranch hand screeches, "They are abusing horses, seen it with my own eyes. This bay they got ain't nothing but skin and bones. I swear the only reason the ill-tempered cuss is still alive is because he wants to take a chunk out of his mishandlers, if he can."

*Old Hudson place?* My ears prick forward. *They don't repeat ranch names within hundreds of miles in this area. Bay? It isn't much of a description to go on. Ill-tempered? If they've been torturing him...* I shudder, imagining what it had taken to turn Alabaster into a killer, and picturing someone doing the same thing to DH.

My stomach churns. Nothing on the plate in front of me looks appetizing anymore.

I contemplate going over and asking for more details about the horse when I notice a dark shadow in a booth near the two men. He's a skinny ass punk who seems a little too interested in the same conversation. Every time I sweep my eyes in his direction, an unsettled feeling adds to my nausea.

Waving my waitress over, I ask, "Can I get a doggie bag and the check, please?"

"Sure thing."

The waitress rustles off.

As I wait, I continue to watch and listen. The conversation between the ranch hand and the sheriff offers no more details about the bay, only vague suspicions of other misdeeds. With every word, the shadow twitches as if he's writing a report for a superior.

The waitress returns with the requested items. I pack up the half-eaten sandwich and mound of fries that is going to be my dinner. Glancing at my check, I peel off a ten, which is double what I need, and add another for good measure. Walking out, I head to my car, where I sit and watch the diner's door.

The shadow from the corner walks out first. I worry that he might notice the USMB tag on the windshield. Instead of looking in my direction, though, he keeps glancing over his shoulder. The reason for his discomfort follows a few steps behind him.

Squealing away with the smell of burning rubber and an overworked engine, the shadow disappears over the horizon almost before I can get out my car. Instead of jumping into his cruiser and going after him, the sheriff stands with his hands on his hip, chewing his toothpick.

I walk over. "Sheriff, can we talk?"

The sheriff tips his hat back. "Yes, ma'am?"

"How much stock do you put in the story about the bay horse?"

"Well, Ed, he's good folk who don't know how to lie. I've been at the ranch that he mentioned and can confirm that something strange is going on there. Thing is I can't do nothing about it. There is only me and one other deputy for this strip of land." The sheriff points to the cloud of dust dispersing in the distance. "At least three dozen of those hoodlums live at the compound, which is protected by military-grade hardware."

I raise my eyebrow. "You served then?"

"Yes, ma'am. Three tours in Iraq."

"Where is this ranch? I'd like to check it out."

"It's back in an isolated valley. They'd know you were coming at least a mile down the road."

"Even on foot?"

"Too rough a hike. If you can find a vehicle able to handle the terrain, maybe you can sneak within a couple miles of the place. We ain't got anything that fancy in these parts, though. If I were you, ma'am, I'd continue your travels and forget about it."

"Is that because you think I'd be in some sort of danger, or does your buddy Riordan have you pulling look out duty for him again?"

Fingering his gun, the sheriff peers down at me. His blue-gray eyes are as intense as I remember them, but not as innocent. The lines around them tell his story. He has seen death, fought a valiant battle with it, and not been able to save a few of his buddies. "Ma'am, with all due respect, you don't know what you are talking about. I suggest you get your hippie ass back on your bus and git."

"You see a bus anywhere around here, Henderson?" Pulling my wallet out, I flash my identification card.

Dave Henderson straightens. "Captain," the rank rolls off his tongue. "Sir, I didn't recognize you in that getup."

"I'm not in the position to be myself right at the moment. I'm breaking cover with you because I need your help. Can I trust you?"

"No, sir." Henderson swallows, lowering his head. "Like you said, I'm back on Riordan's payroll."

"What are you doing for him?" My brows furrow. "Why did you join up with him again?"

"I don't have to do much," Henderson blurts. "Just turn a blind eye on his people and report nosy folk. I can bust his punks anytime they get out of line. I need his money. I have two in college and don't make enough to keep them there."

"Are you going to mention me?" I challenge.

"No, sir. I owe you at least that much."

His renewed relationship with Riordan is both an opportunity and a danger. I need to feel him out before asking him to spy for me. "Henderson, do you have something that makes you feel incomplete when you aren't around it?"

"My wife and three kids, sir."

"You know I feel the same way about my family."

"Yes, sir."

"Horses—"

"I heard you'd been pretty busted up by one."

"Yep, I was. Still care for them, though. How can you let Riordan get away with the abuse Ed mentioned?"

"Well, sir, if I had the backing of the USMB, I wouldn't," Henderson shrugs. "Yet, you and I both know the USMB can't interfere in every mistreatment case they find out about. They have to work through channels. That can be mighty slow sometimes."

"The process can be speeded up if USMB horses are involved." I flip to a picture of DH. "Have you seen this one at the ranch?"

Henderson shakes his head. "Not sure. Might have. I haven't been up there in two months, and am coming due for another payment."

"Think you can get me some info on the horses when you do? I'm real interested in that bay."

Nodding toward the picture, Henderson prompts, "You think he may be yours?"

"I hope not, but I'm running out of places to look for him. His name is Dreamer's Hope. He was the first horse I rode after my accident, and he's special to me."

"I bet. Cap, Riordan doesn't trust me as much as he once did. My deputy is my handler."

"Then arrest me."

He raises an eyebrow. "On what charge?"

"Whatever my outfit suggests."

"Can you play a doper?"

I go limp and unfocus my gaze.

Grabbing my hands, he twists them around my back. Shoving me against his car, he growls, "You have the right to remain silent…"

# FORTY-SEVEN

EYES OF THE HEART

Henderson glanced past the picture of his daughters stuck on his visor and through the front window of his cruiser at the walls of the canyon. Though the red rock looked undisturbed, Riordan once warned him that he had laced them with defenses capable of taking out armored vehicles and aircraft.

*If he thinks I'm up here for anything else but my payment, what will he do to my family? I should go back to town and forget this.*

Shuddering, he lifted his foot off the gas. As he slid it toward the brake, his insides twinged. *What will I tell the Cap?*

When the gig with Riordan was up, she was the only one who showed him any mercy and respect. Everyone else wanted to shuffle him off into a corner or make his existence so unbearable he didn't want to continue his career. Thing is, she didn't tolerate him lying or bending the truth even part way, and could pick it up quicker than most. He couldn't go back to her without something. *If I do, she'll come out here and get herself killed for the trouble.*

Touching the picture, he sighed. *Forgive me.*

He pressed down on the accelerator.

\* \* \*

At the end of the road, the juxtaposition of beauty and death continued. The iron rod gates swept open to reveal a long driveway lined with bushes and rocks. Some were of the normal garden variety while others camouflaged machine guns. Other than that, the spread looked like the others under his jurisdiction with rail-lined pastures, several barns, and other out buildings.

The ranch house at the center of a circular driveway was a majestic two-story log cabin with railed porches and an overhanging veranda. There were only small and medium windows, no large ones. The glass in each was double-paned and bulletproof.

Riordan and his attack dog, Clem, stood at the head of the walkway leading to the front door. Both men had brownish-blonde hair and wore the flannel and jeans of the locals. Riordan's steel gray eyes gave away the intense cutthroat competitor that his soft, no-lined face tried to hide. Clem outweighed Riordan by a good fifty pounds of muscle, towered over him by half a foot, and couldn't disguise the darkness of his soul, even in his quiet stance. An invisible coat of black armor seemed to encase his whole body.

Henderson exited the car and walked around its front to meet the two men, who waited with crossed arms. With no greeting or small talk, Riordan growled, "I understand you got a pothead down in your tank. Anything I should be worried about?"

"Wasn't I rough enough with her?" Henderson quipped. "She's got a black eye and at least several cuts and bruises that would implicate me on police brutality in the big city. Is Luis offended that I didn't let him get in a crack or two?"

"Nah, he said you did good," Riordan shrugged. "The boss man's getting a little nervous that his target may be headed here. Someone about the same height and weight showing up in town seemed a little too coincidental for my liking."

"I got a bigger problem than some harmless hippie," Henderson spat. "Ed's on my case again. He says you've been abusing a bay. I need to see him, so I reassure Ed everything's fine."

"Clem, make a note that the next time Ed appears on the property to do his shearing, the boys make sure he has an accident," Riordan tossed over his shoulder. "Nothing serious, but enough that he knows we're watching him."

"Right, boss. Can I do it myself?"

Riordan shook his head. "Dave here would have to arrest you then."

All three of them laughed before Riordan nodded toward the stables. "C'mon, I'll show you the horse Ed is talking about. He's Clem's special project."

"What he's trying to do?"

"Turn him into a killer," Riordan replied. "Unlike his father, who took to the training real easy and almost did his job, this one's being stubborn."

"I'll break 'im," Clem growled. "I always do."

\* \* \*

Halfway back to town, Henderson pulled over, dived out the cruiser, and dry heaved a couple of times before his lunch came up in a burning rush. Clem was one loco and cruel bastard. The horse was nothing like the picture the Cap had flashed. The bay lunged and snapped when they unlocked the top door of his stall and peered in, but it was more show than anything else. He didn't have any muscle left, and every rib protruded from a dry, mangy coat caked with blood. Open, maggot-infested sores covered most of his body.

*Some killer he's going to be!* Henderson gagged again. Patting his gun, he shook his head. *One shot and he'd have a better life. The Cap would have forgiven me for taking it.*

Wiping his lips with the back of his hand, he went back to the car and retrieved the envelope Riordan had passed to him. It felt heavier than normal. His usual amount was there, and so was an extra bit with a note rubber banded around the lump. He separated the wad and counted.

*10G's?* Henderson's mind raced with all the possibilities  until he reached his kids and stopped, wondering, *What does he want for this?*

He read the note. It was only a few words, and bore no name or signature. The blunt orders both explained the rare bonus, and required him to do something that tarnished his badge and his honor.

Sighing, Henderson made a phone call.

# FORTY-EIGHT

## TRUST OF THE SOUL

The holding tank I'm in is nothing more than a closet with bars. Only enough room for a cot and maybe six paces. I've done the rounds countless times, keeping up my stoned junkie act.

Letting my gaze wander in the direction of the clock, I gather it's around four-thirty in the afternoon. Henderson left at one, saying he'd be back by no later than four. To my left, Luis Sandow, a thin, grubby character, who doesn't fit the uniform he wears in either size or personality, is rocking out, pretending he's the next great undiscovered drummer.

After one long and bad solo, which isn't even close to the beat of the music, he glances up at me and sneers, "What you looking at, weed head?"

Lowering my head, I shuffle away. I'm not giving this guy any pleasure by answering his question.

Snorting, Sandow starts massacring some acid punk song that already hurts my ears. He's a good five rifts in when the loud clanging of the desktop phone adds to the ruckus. The thing rings for three times and then stops. A pause, and then it begins again. It takes four cycles before the drumming stops and the boom box snaps off.

"Sorry, boss." Sandow stammers in a dog beaten tone. "Yes, I know... Won't happen again, I swear. You want me to do what?" His tone lightens. "Sure thing, I'll take care of it right away."

Sandow hangs up, pushing his chair back with a loud screech. He approaches my cell with a predatory grin on his face. With each slap of his nightstick against his palm, my temptation to jump his bones the minute he opens the door grows. All I need is four basic moves to take Sandow down, and escape. Riordan will demand an explanation. He might even cause trouble for Henderson's family. I don't care. Henderson isn't here to justify the phone call or the orders from it.

I hesitate.

During his time in the USMB, Henderson was always able to play other people, but never me. *Was I so focused on DH and my fear that I missed the clues, or is he still my ally? Only one way I can be sure. If I'm wrong...* I push away any thoughts of heavy resistance.

The door swings open and Luis charges toward me with a snarl.

\* \* \*

I scan my surroundings. Looks pretty much the same as the last time, flat with plenty of green and yellow grass, and not much else. Stretching, I try to relieve a kink in my side. My ribs sting as if I've taken a bad fall from a horse. Sandow didn't break anything, but he came awful close. His kicks and punches were a lot more solid than his drum playing. I had to defend myself while letting him believe he was beating me unconscious, so a few of his hits found their mark.

I've been trying to find an ounce of civilization since he dumped me out of his off-road vehicle. All I have is the sun to guide me. Given how low it hangs on the horizon, my priority has become hunkering down somewhere safe for the night. In bear and wolf country like this, I don't want to be out with the predators after dark.

A flash of light hits my peripheral vision from an unexpected direction. The glare reflects like glass or metal. Turning, I head in that direction. As I get closer to the source, I notice a black streak cutting across the yellow-green. Good, at least I've found a road.

*Who leaves a car out in the middle of nowhere?* I wonder, spotting a blue lump with four black circles. *It's a mirage.*

Stumbling over, I put my hand on the surface. "*Yeow!*" I yip, jerking back.

Illusions didn't feel as hot or as solid as that.

I walk around the vehicle. The low-lying lines are familiar, so are the tags. It's my car. I try the driver's side door. It opens. Slipping in, I notice the keys in the ignition, and a large manila envelope lying on the passenger's seat.

Dumping out the contents, I grab my phone first and leave a folded piece of paper, spiral notebook, and wad of cash alone. A sticky note plastered on the front screen reads, *Contains pictures and video. View after the note.*

I unfold the paper.

*Captain,*

*By the time you read this, I will have crossed state lines. I can no longer live in a place where a man, who controlled my life, not once, but twice, asks me to look away.*

*The money you see would have fed my family well for a few months, but it wouldn't have fed my soul. I couldn't keep the cash, nor could I let it influence my decision to help you. I owe you more than a debt of gratitude for helping me; I owe you one for saving my life.*

*After you use the cash as evidence, please donate it to an animal cruelty organization on behalf of your horse.*

*It may appear that I ordered your beating. I did not. That came from Riordan. I was there when he made the call. I'm sorry I didn't have the courage to stop him, or put your horse out of his misery when I saw him.*

*Everything I know about Riordan's operation is in the notebook. I hope you can use the information to destroy him. My wife helped me pick up your car and move it as we were leaving town.*

*What you see on your phone will both disgust and infuriate you. It did me.*

*May our paths cross again one day,*
*Dave Henderson*

The signature scrawled across the bottom of the page ends in smeared splotches. I power on my phone. Most of the pictures aren't that good, containing nothing recognizable except maybe the inside of Henderson's car or pocket. They don't have to be frame-worthy, though. The details I pull up on each one contain valuable GPS coordinates that I can use to find DH once I hook up with the Mason Seven.

The video is grainy, but the color and shape of the thin and battered horse is clear. In the background, Henderson's voice says, *You know, Riordan, many of the ranchers around here would give anything to have some of these fine horses. They're just...dreamers. Hope you appreciate what you have there.*

The horse's ears pick forward. He rattles his lips.

My chest tightens. *That's my boy.* I touch the screen. *I'm coming for you. I promise.*

Pointing my car toward another random town, I look out for the shadows. I'm a little annoyed that they didn't step in to save me, but the emotion is fleeting. I'm trying to keep all of them in check, so I can focus on the information Henderson provided, and dissect it from a tactical point of view. If I don't, I'm going to get caught up in what they did to my horse, and do something very stupid.

The ranch is a fort. Patrols sweep the grounds at random times every hour, with guards posted in strategic places throughout the compound. Some very large rocks have all the earmarks of camouflaged anti-aircraft batteries, machine guns, and mortars. Even pretending to be some nosy neighbor, I have no chance of making it past the front gate, let alone getting anywhere near the stable area.

While I have more than enough justification for going after Riordan, coordinating the necessary manpower and equipment to go after DH is difficult at best. The accident near Phoenix proved John's theory that Casper's men have the means to monitor all USMB computer and communications traffic. Cell phones won't be a problem for whatever technology they are using. I make one call, they pack up and leave, and I don't have a chance at DH until he shows up dead or ready to kill me.

Driving for help isn't much of an option either. No one I trust is close enough for a quick response. Sure, there are my shadows, but I can't separate the friends from the enemies. If I give the standard request for contact signal, I might not leave the meetup alive.

I'm not as much of a social media junkie as John is, but the text limit on Twitter gives me an idea. One hundred and forty characters to say something is ideal for what I need to do. If spaced out so they appear random, the messages should seem like unimportant chatter. I hope that all the recipients talk to one another after receiving them; both to make sense of what I'm saying, and to eliminate their fear that Honeywell is back in control.

# FORTY-NINE

# WHATEVER IT TAKES

"Cap, is Jo okay?" Michelle asked. "I haven't seen her for almost a week. Scuttlebutt has the Admiral suspending her again."

"Michelle, six days is a little slow for you," Jim chided, adjusting Midnight's Crest girth one final time and swinging up into the saddle. "Why didn't you say something after twenty-four hours?"

"I didn't want to bug you or Jo, so I went to the Admiral. He said to focus on the team and give you a few days to sort things out."

"Jo's PSTD flared up." Glancing around at his brothers and Michelle, Jim reminded himself, *Play it cool. Keep thinking spooked horse.* "Don't worry. Jason has another Command Team watching her six."

"That might explain the message I received a few minutes ago, then."

Jim raised an eyebrow. "What'd it say?"

"Meet me in Billings at the bar with a color and the letters of heros in its name," Michelle recited. "Bring John and Jim. Why would she send something like that? She doesn't drink."

Turning to John, Jim prompted, "You mentioned a strange text from Jo, this morning."

"Eat your vegetables to succeed at your favorite brain games."

"I got one last night that was just as weird," Jim stated. "Found friend for fort tour. Bring ground meat, but keep the knives sheathed, for the picnic."

"Keep the young J away as well?" TJ shook his head. "Has Jo relapsed into her other personality?"

"I don't think so," Bill offered, "but 'sharp skills are needed to repair a horse's heart' doesn't inspire much hope."

"Yes, it does!" John's face scrunched, and then brightened. "She's fine. More than fine! She's bypassed Casper's ability to monitor communications."

"How so?" Jim wondered.

"It's code. She wants ground troops—and choppers on standby—to help rescue DH from a reinforced enclosure. He's hurt, so the extraction

209

is going to require the unique skills of our team. She doesn't want Jimmy involved, though."

Cocking his head, Bill wondered, "You deduced all that from those messages?"

"Assuming a little, maybe," John shrugged.

"DH is in Billings?" Michelle prompted.

John shook his head. "If he was, we'd have heard something. I'm guessing it's the closest big city."

"If we move any units from LA, Casper will know," Michelle offered.

"Then we won't," Jim stated. "John, can you get a message to Jeff and Vince to mobilize their teams?"

"Yes, the new comm protocol I've developed has worked great so far," John replied. "Are you sure Jeff can be trusted, though? I haven't seen Jo that pissed off at someone in a long time."

"As sure as I can be until we catch Casper and find all his associates. Any ideas about how we can meet up with Jo?"

"The way the other team is running surveillance gives us an in." Turning to Bill, John asked, "How do you feel about letting your attitude be the size of your body?"

"What are you thinking of turning me into?"

"A biker who enjoys being his gang's muscle."

"That's worse than you becoming a jock."

"Well, I'm going to be that in leather and chains."

* * *

"Ready, man?" John prompted.

Wearing his gear, he stood in the doorway of the room that had turned the rest of his brothers, Michelle, Vince, and other members of the Mason Seven into filthy, foul-mouthed bikers. They were in an isolated shack somewhere in the backcountry of Montana with Harleys out in front. The team had won Bloomington. They would meet them in Atlanta after this little detour.

"No," Bill stated. "This isn't going to work, John."

"Come on, dude. Both me and Mikey have lost our stiff shells. You'll feel freer once you lose yours."

Bill glanced in the direction of two redheads. One was trying to teach the other to swagger and belch, but other than that, they were indistinguishable as crude bastards.

"That's just it. I'm worried about being free."

"Why, man? It's cool."

"We've seen Jo scare a person twice her size into not talking to her for a month after she's lost her temper." Bill chewed his lip. "I'm scared of the potential damage I could do if my control slips." Turing to the long-haired freak that led the gang, he asked, "Jim, can I stay in the shadows?"

The blonde didn't respond.

*Oh, yeah, he's Glider. I have to talk like him.* "Glider, man—"

"I heard ya. Grab the bitch, be rough with her, and protect our asses, Nasty, that's your job," Glider grunted. "Don't care what else you do."

"Grab the bitch?" Bill echoed. "Be rough with her? Listen to yourself. This is Jo we're talking about. Didn't you hear what I said, and what you are saying about her?"

"Yeah, dude, I did, but I'm already in my skin, so you ain't getting a different answer," the biker shrugged. "We don't do please and thank you or any of the other niceties." Glider snatched the switchblade out of Bill's hand, nicking him with it. The other bikers hooted. "It's all about blood. Us protecting ours and taking others when needed."

Bill wiped his cheek. "What if I don't join you? Can't I stay here or meet up with the other teams down the road?"

Glider shook his head. "We need your muscle." Closing the blade and tossing it back, he asked, "How's your swing?"

Flicking the switchblade open, Bill thrust, but pulled up short.

"Motion's good, but your intent ain't there," Glider stated. "Find it, or this ain't going to work, dude."

After he had revealed his part in her recovery, he and Jo had talked a lot about it. In her words, Bill found his answer. He needed a mental cage for his control and sensibilities, so his temper could burn through all the emotions he had been feeling, but not expressing, since the mauling.

Bill caught Glider's eyes. They were wide and a little dilated. "What's wrong?" he grunted.

"I just saw the fierce bastard we need."

"I hope you can control him, Glider," Bill spat. "I'm not sure I can, and he terrifies me."

"I'll take my chances. Little John, mess this guy up."

* * *

The reflection in the rearview mirror of his chopper frightened the biker. He was bald with plenty of tats and scars, a rough goatee, and angry facial lines. Even when he smiled, he scowled. A long scar disfigured the right side of his face, leaving his eye half closed.

Big Nasty pulled up to the bar with the rest of his gang and cut the motor on his hog. The Rusty Horse welcomed all visitors with the bright lights and loud music spilling from its doorway. A few feet away from the door, a small group of rough looking individuals eyed the patrons wandering in and out.

Falling in behind Glider, Big Nasty threw off his meanest stare, intending to drive home the message they weren't to be fucked with.

A muscled brute almost as big as him broke off from the hangouts and challenged, "Hey, we haven't seen your posse before."

"Tha's because we ain't from around here," Glider grumbled in a husky voice. "You'd best leave us alone."

"Whatcha gonna to do, if we don't."

"Make ya."

Big Nasty fell back into the shadows. The fight escalated within a few punches. Glider took on three punks and had them on the ground, unconscious, within a few heartbeats of each other. His fourth began giving him trouble after about the fifth blow.

Glaring at Big Nasty, Glider mouthed, *Help me. It's your job.*

He stayed where he was. Maybe, when the time came, he could rough up the bitch a little bit for show. He still couldn't pull a blade on anyone without it looking awkward and stopping himself short.

The battle between Glider and the punk went on with Glider losing ground to every kick and punch. When it appeared he might go down, Big Nasty ambled over. Growling low in his chest, he stared down with his lip curled, hoping his posturing would intimidate the punk.

It had the opposite effect. Almost laughing, the punk sneered, "Get away from me, chicken shit." He pressed the flat of his blade against Glider's throat. "Our boss says we can mess up anyone who crosses us. There's a bitch coming later that he wants taken out. The boys and I are going to have some fun with her first."

"*No, ya won't!*" Big Nasty screamed, grabbing the punk by the scruff of his neck, spinning him around, and plunging his knife in. Ripping and tearing a long streak across the mid-section, he jerked the metal out. Warm, wet, and sticky blood dripped down onto his hands. Dropping the limp form, he tasted the sweet nectar and sought out more.

* * *

"*Enough,*" a voice yelled. Something poked Big Nasty's side. He grabbed an arm, twisted it around, and shoved his next vic against the wall.

"Bill, I said *enough,*" the voice gasped. "It's Jim. You're hurting me."

The red fog lifted from his vision. Sheathing his blade, Bill released his grip and glanced around. Crushed, sliced-up bodies lay on the ground at odd angles. Some groaned with each breath, others didn't move.

"Holy crap," Bill shrieked. "I did this?"

Jim shook his head. "No, Big Nasty did. Good thing, too. If he hadn't come out, we'd all be dead, including Jo."

Bill's body flooded with heat. "Still, this is not right," he snarled. "I am a—"

Swiping his hand across his throat, Jim jerked his thumb in the direction of the gathering crowd. "We'll talk as ourselves later. Right now, we have to play for the eyes."

Sirens wailed in the distance.

Unsheathing his bloody knife, Bill peered down at the uncaring metal. *One quick thrust and...*

"Stop with the remorsefulness, Nasty, it ain't your style," Glider jawed, elbowing him "Meeting that bitch and having some fun with her will cheer you up right quick. Till then we need some crowd control."

Big Nasty swung at the closest bystanders. They jumped away with gasps and screams.

Throwing his head back, he roared.

# FIFTY

# BAR CONFRONTATION

The day of the rendezvous comes. Billings, like most large cities, has an Inter-City Headquarters. ICHQs allow USMB personnel to have some services like being able to check in with their base, or make secured phone calls. Located across the street from the Billings ICHQ, the Rusty Horse is a hotspot for the both the lunch crowd and the nighttime club hoppers. Out in front of the bar, at least half a dozen Harleys parked in a row, their chrome gleaming in the midday sun.

I stagger into a room of contrasts disguised in a long black wig, glasses, and an outfit that suggests I'm little more than a working stiff. Skylights and large windows amplify the brightness of the day. Rich, dark wood flooring accents the walls' earth tones. Business people are in the front while the bikers have taken over the back near the pool tables. Interspersed between the leathers and the suits are shoppers with large bags taking up their own seats, a few USMB personnel, and other miscellaneous folk.

Choosing a corner that protects my back and lets me see most of the bar area and entrance, I slip into a booth. A slim waitress comes over, offering to take my order. I wave her off. I ate about an hour ago and don't want to be held back by paying a bill, if things go south.

The bikers are an interesting group to watch. Most of them have an average build with a good weight to muscle balance. The tallest one is a solid brick wall that I wouldn't want to meet in broad daylight. With a bald tatted head, rough trimmed goatee, and scars weaving between his rippling muscles, he's a brute—and a drunken one at that. The empty bottles and shattered glass strewn all around him form a dangerous and telling barrier. He shoves aside anyone who tries to touch him or take his mug. If they glare at him when he does, he storms up, looking for a fight. His compadres jump in and restrain him long enough for his intended victim to get away. Can't be sure, but I thought I saw a blade flash in his hand once or twice.

The blonde—their leader I suppose given how he's keeping the rest in line—is cute, even with a mustache and the dark shadow of stubble covering his face. His tats are a turn off, though. The matching redheads are the rudest and crudest of the bunch. They try to hit on every female in their general vicinity. A shoving match ensues between them when they don't succeed. The two smallest ones fidget in the shadows, not doing much except trying to look innocent.

I don't expect the bikers to last much longer. Gestures in their direction suggest that some of the other patrons are getting tired of them. The brute is also swaying as if he's at his tipping point. He's either going to pass out or explode with the next round.

A sashing form near the door diverts my attention. I glance at my watch. It's about the time I'm expecting my brothers, but instead I have to deal with Casper. I duck behind the menu the waitress left behind, hoping he'll pass by, thinking I'm a faceless shadow.

*No such luck,* I sigh when the soft footfalls stop by my booth. The seat creaks as he slips in. I lower the menu.

"Hello, Casper," I say.

"Jo," he nods in my direction. "I must say you look pretty good for a woman who's been both crazy and dead in the last few months."

"How'd you know it was me?"

"You're the only one sitting like a person expecting trouble to come through the door." Casper gestures at the bikers. "I suspected them, too, until their big muscle enjoyed taking out the people I sent up against them last night. Bill may be the same size as him, but he is too soft to hurt anyone."

I nod. The brute and his fifteen victims had taken up the front page of the local paper. Two were already dead, four had little chance of making it, wheelchairs were in the future for six, and three needed multiple reconstructive surgeries. The accompanying article called the work butchery done by the precise hands of a surgeon. Law enforcement wants him for felony assault, first-degree manslaughter, and a few other heavy charges. His attitude and actions destroy the idea of the bikers being my brothers.

I don't bother with any more small talk or other niceties. Better to confirm what I suspect, and then leave before he sets his reinforcements on me. "Are you the one responsible for the attacks on my team?" I ask.

"Yes."

"Is Anthony involved as well?"

"He was the one who came up with the idea for creating the network."

"Did you send me Alabaster?"

"He was my second choice for going after you and your family. I hoped to drive them apart by him killing you, but the long and deep rift between you and Jim was satisfactory."

"What was your first option?"

"Honeywell." The name drops the temperature of our conversation several degrees. While my mind has locked away the details of what I did as her, I can recall all of the faces she ever saw. Casper is among them, but never as a direct contact, only in the background.

"Did you play a part in her creation?"

"No, you did, though."

"Oh, come on, Casper," I snort, "how much do you know about the program? They…" I stop and jerk my head around. No one appears to be a shadow, but that doesn't mean there isn't one present.

"Remember Davis Potter?"

"Yes, he was our security and tactics teacher in Command Specialty School. He died on a hunting trip."

"He wasn't the hunter, but the prey." Casper pulls out a worn leather book and lays it on the table. "In his journal, he  wrote…" He flips through the pages until he stops and reads, "*Today, I will look upon the face of death and smile. The one who created the program I helped nurture has her first solo hunt, and I've volunteered to be the prey. Better to die teaching one final lesson than waste away from the sickness eating me up from the inside.*"

Potter's face flashes in my mind. He's smiling and whispering. I can almost make out the words. Something about a paper I wrote and how he used it to develop a program.

In one of his classes, Potter asked us to write a report on creating the perfect killer. Both fascinated and horrified by the topic, I pulled my research from every source imaginable. *A perfect killer isn't created, it's born*, the paper began. *Birth takes place after the human psyche is broken down by…* My thoughts freeze as realization and the screams of Honeywell's victims merge in one horrible, agonizing moment. Some of the very same methods that the CS handlers used on me to create Honeywell were in that document.

I sink back into the booth, struggling to maintain my composure.

"Honeywell was Potter's last gift to me. She was supposed to be the perfect weapon." Casper rambles on. "Jim was going to be her first target, trapping you in the beast's soul forever, but your emotions got in the way."

"You didn't gain command of a CS unit until you got San Fernando," I stammer, "so how could you?"

"I've always had friends who believe as I do. Potter among them. It was a matter of asking the right one to change the name on the kill order. Honeywell's actual prey on the day she went after Jim was another rogue."

"Why would you do any of this? Was it because of my peer review?"

"No, my dear Joanna, my revenge has always been about your family as a whole. A Nolan, not a Mason, was supposed to have received command of the LAMS."

Casper reaches into the book and tosses some newspaper clippings on the table. They all scream variations of the same headline. *Robert Mason to lead new unit in LA after the mysterious death of Charles Nolan.*

"Thing is, there was nothing mysterious about that death," Casper continues. "Robert got into an argument with Charles and shot him dead."

"What proof do you have of this?" I challenge.

"The stories passed down among the family."

"Would you like to read my family logs? Their version of this infamous heated discussion says that Robert only grazed Charles."

"You expect me to take *that* as fact? Written words can be twisted and manipulated until a lie appears just as viable as the truth."

"Verbal stories aren't that much better," I shrug.

"At least my stories are the retelling of actual events," Casper snorts, "and not interpretations of them."

"Look, Casper, let's stop arguing semantics. I just want my horse back. After that, we can work together to clear up the mystery of what happened to Charles, and find a peaceful way to resolve this misunderstanding."

"There will be no peace, Joanna, until your family is shamed and disgraced, so go rescue your horse. If you succeed, you can have him. If not, the dead bodies of you and your team surrounded by USMB weapons will make international news. While that won't entail complete satisfaction, it's a good beginning."

"What's an acceptable ending?"

"Annihilation of your entire bloodline, of course," Casper leers. "Then full control of what has become a soft organization that should have a prominent place in history as the world's peacekeeper."

"More like its ruler, if you get your way," I quip. "The USMB doesn't need visionaries like you, Casper. It has already prevented several nuclear winters by working in the shadows and avoiding public acclaim. My team will stop you."

Casper laughs. "Granted, they've done a great job of dismantling my network, but they'll never find all of its pieces. I, or someone in my family, will gain the power we seek."

The mean giant staggers over, reeking of sour mash. "Hey, lady, this guy hasslin' you?" he asks in a slurred voice. Whipping out his blade, he sneers, "Give me any excuse, dude."

"No, I was just leaving," Casper snorts. With that, he slips away.

I contemplate following him, but I'm too shell-shocked to move. John has shown me all his research into Casper's network. Before the Mason Seven, with the help of other Command Teams, chewed away at the evil web, it affected every level of the USMB. Casper was right; we'd never sweep it from every nook and cranny. Spiders go dormant in winter, after all.

The blade clicks closed and disappears into the big thug's leather. "Mind if I sit here?" The drunken giant belches, wiping his mouth with the back of his hand. "I ain't seen one as pretty as you in a long time."

"No. Please, go away." With him this close, I still can't see or feel any sign of Bill, if the biker is even him. All this guy radiates is hate and danger.

Scooting to the other side of the booth, I stand. The giant lunges toward me, stumbles, and sends both of us to the floor with a hard thump. Pushing him off is an act of futility. He's the size of Bill, and weighs just as much.

The behemoth flounders around before somehow rolling off me. "What y'all staring at?" he yells at the room in a rough tone that contains no familiarity in its inflection or language. "Can't a guy meet a lady?" Grabbing my arm, he yanks me up. "Come on, bitch, ya going to join me and the fellas for another round."

Whoever this guy is, he's about two seconds away from being at least six inches shorter. I'm already in a foul mood from dealing with Casper. I refuse to become a member of the giant's boys club. Size difference doesn't matter. I've taken down Bill on numerous occasions when he was sober and fighting back. For as big as this guy is, he's sloshed and already fallen over once, so pounding him into the ground should be easier.

Dropping my one point, I make myself heavier and harder to drag. The subtle shift causes the biker to miss half a step. Using his forward momentum and a well-placed bump sideways, I send him crashing into a table.

The big lug snarls and rises to his feet. Aiming his shoulder and upper body at my mid-section, he charges. Sweeping aside, I add a little more force to his forward momentum. He slams head first into a wall and slides to the floor. Groaning, he stays down for a heartbeat or two before staggering to a standing position, whipping out his blade, and lunging.

Stepping out of the way, I run my hand down his arm, grab his hand, and twist it backward. He sinks to his knees, releasing the blade. Not wanting another round with him, I crack my leg against his chin. He slumps to the ground.

Wheeling, I brace myself to dodge and throw whoever wants to retaliate. Figuring they might try multiple directions at once, my eyes dart back and forth, sizing up who will be stupid or crazy enough to take the first step.

As my gaze lands on each of them, it takes tremendous effort not to pull back my defenses. Even decked out in leather, chains, and tattoos, they all look familiar. Jim's the blonde. The mirror images of Michael and

Tyrrell are indistinguishable as the redheads. *Then the big man has to be...* I glance over my shoulder. Bill's out cold on his stomach.

Now that he's not a factor, a few of the stronger looking onlookers, who are only inches shorter than Bill, approach as if they want to help clear the bikers from the bar. I can't let them. The team has to leave the Rusty Horse as they entered it. That means, even pulling their punches, they'll have to hurt anyone who interferes.

The biker gang cover will protect us, if Casper has men waiting. Even if he doesn't, they can't ride the bikes as themselves because that'll create more questions than we can answer. Leaving the bikes is an option, but not a very good one, since the team's fingerprints are all over them.

Rough hands grab me on either side. They squeeze to the point that I whimper. The blonde thrusts his head toward me and brushes his stringy hair against my face. He licks the side of my neck and humming to himself, "Oh, you are going to be one sweet bitch to taste. Too bad, Nasty over there won't have a chance."

*Jim's just playing up his role*, I remind myself as the acid in my stomach swims up my throat, causing me to gag.

Chewing on my ear, Jim whispers, "When you fight back will Honeywell get involved?"

"No, she's quiet," I go limp, waiting for my restrainers to loosen their grip. How bloody do you want this?"

"Minimal. We saw too much last night."

All the fight disappears from my body. *I'm sorry that my fear cost you so much, big guy*, I sigh, glancing over my shoulder at Bill.

Jim grabs my face and forces me to kiss him on the lips.

I nibble his nose.

"Fucking bitch bit me!" the blonde roars, slapping me in the face.

The color remains in my vision.

# FIFTY-ONE

# NOW WHAT?

The motorcycles roar down the highway with sirens screaming behind them. Given the customization for his height and long legs, we risked leaving Bill's bike back at the bar, and tied him to John's hog. Me, I'm riding bound and gagged behind Jim after taking out a couple more of the blonde's gang before letting them overwhelm me. My wannabe rescuers lost their courage, retreated, and called 9-1-1.

A few wind-snatched words from Jim suggest that my brothers, the Mason Seven, and me—and maybe half a dozen other people—are going after DH. The rest of the command teams are willing to help with the covert part of investigating and dismantling Casper's network, but they fear the focus shifting to them, if they do anything more overt.

Our first priority is getting rid of the cops. The bikes slow. I want to scream this isn't the way to do it, but, with the gag in my mouth, I can't. We stop. The gravel crunches behind us. Black, brown, and white flashes streak around me, kicking dust in my face.

We are surrounded.

Propping up the bike and dismounting as if he were out for a Sunday ride, Jim touches me on the knee. "Glider's coming back," he whispers in my ear, "It's the only way you can return to the team and find DH."

I wiggle in protest. He'll have to stay Glider until I post his bail and we can create some sort of cover story, or he stands trial as an accessory to murder. Given what Bill did, the USMB will defer to the civilian judicial system. If that happens, I might gain my horse, but I'll lose my brothers.

Stepping away, Jim hardens his face.

"Stay where you are," a sharp voice commands. "Put your hands in the air where I can see them."

"We ain't done nothing!" Glider taunts. "Leave us be!"

"Down on the ground," the voice snaps.

"Make me," Glider snarls.

A shot cracks in the air. "No more lip. Hands in the air and down on the ground, *now!*"

221

A dark-haired female biker, who I think is Michelle, shakes her head. Sighing, Glider raises his hands. "I'm only doing this for the bitches," he screams, dropping to his knees. "Everyone hit the dirt."

Bodies fall with thumps. Glancing over at John's bike, I notice that Bill's still sleeping despite the noise. Hanging my head, I choke back my tears.

Footsteps crack near me. A gentle hand touches my shoulder. "You okay, lass? Here let me remove that."

Two arms reach around the side of my head and untie the bandanna. As it falls, away, I glance up. Jason stands before me in a brown uniform and broad-brimmed hat. He removes the rest of my bonds. Dismounting, I stretch my legs. The other fake cops have the bikers pressed up against the vehicles with their feet spread apart and hands cuffed behind their backs. Some appear a little roughed up.

I glare at Jason.

"Remember, we're playing for the eyes, lass."

Cars speed by, honking.

"We'll take them to the rendezvous point in the cars," Jason snaps. "Leave the bikes. The hauler should be here in a few minutes."

"Yes, sir," the rest of the uniforms chorus.

"Can we go back for Bill's bike and my car? Both are still at the Rusty Horse."

"No need. They've already been taken care of by your shadows."

* * *

Jason drives toward the rendezvous with me sitting in the front next to him. Jim's riding in the back, still handcuffed. We haven't said anything since leaving the bikes.

"Great save, Jason," I say, breaking the silence.

"Aye, da took some doin'," Jason replies, glancing in the mirror. "What da hell went wrong, lad?"

"I'm not sure," Jim shakes his head. "Bill didn't want to fight at first. Then when that punk threatened Jo, he lost it." Glancing in my direction, he adds, "You've been trailed since you left Bloomington by people dressed like us. We figured we could join them and have a perfect cover for the meet."

222

I knew I wasn't seeing my own shadow that many times. Were they all friends?"

"No, but the friendlies took care of the baddies. They also kept us updated on your location without Casper knowing."

"He's able to tap into communications, though."

"Only the standard protocol," Jim corrects. "We've been using a new one John has developed. It's one of many patches he's released into both the computer and communications networks to curtail the Nolans' activities without alerting them."

"Then was the bar fight a set-up or a trap?"

"A trap we sprung."

I'm grateful that Bill isn't in our car. In his current state, I don't want him making the same assumption that I am, and acting upon it. "Did you know a threat existed?"

"Vague chatter hinted at the possibility of an ambush before or during our meet, yes," Jim replies. "If we had anything more definite, I'd have gone in with a lot more people, and not included Bill. There was no…Well, maybe a slight, indication he was going to flip."

Locking gazes with Jim, I extend my senses into our connection. If he's lying to me, he's using all of his weeklong training as a pretender. He doesn't flinch or back down. Instead, he sends calmness in my direction.

I lower my head.

* * *

We pull into the center of a large open space. Jason cuts the motor. Hopping out of the car, I notice that all the land around us is filling up with tents, people, and vehicles.

A square man, who is a little shorter than Bill, steps in front of me and draws himself up. He's wearing the same boards as me, so a salute isn't required. "Hi, Jo," he smiles, offering his hand. "Remember me?"

"Yes, George, I do." I give his hand a quick shake. While we aren't close friends, George Peterson and I have kept up the tradition of our two families working together.

"I can explain all of this," George offers.

Seems the fire and explosion at my house was a big motivator in changing people's minds about helping the Mason Seven. They figured if someone could attack, and almost kill, me at my base while I wasn't part of the official investigation, any one of them could suffer a similar fate for glancing the wrong way at Casper.

"What are our assets?" I wonder.

George nods toward the largest tent in the field. "Let's discuss that in the mobile Command Central."

Jason, George, John, and Jim head in the indicated direction. I turn and watch the rest of my brothers and a few others drag Bill off John's bike and lug him toward a smaller tent. I tense, waiting for any reaction from the people milling around. No one, other than the personnel who brought us in, are wearing uniforms, but even among the casual civilian clothing, the biker gear stands out.

A gentle touch on my shoulders ratchets me down a notch. "No one's going to judge and punish him, lass," Jason says, "except maybe himself."

"He's this way because of me, Jason. If I hadn't—"

"This has been building up for a many years, lass."

"Did it start when he had to treat me after the mauling?"

"No, I noticed subtle changes even before then."

"Not—"

Jason shakes his head, motioning toward the tent. "We can talk more about this later. For now, we need to worry about rescuing DH and shutting down another part of Casper's operation."

\* \* \*

Entering the mobile CC, I find myself in a smaller, more illuminated version of a place I call my second home. Personnel sit at consoles monitoring and routing people and data. Three large flat screens display some very interesting angles and details of the ranch.

I turn to George. "How did you get so much intel already?"

"We had drones in the air the minute he finished transmitting the data on your phone," George replies, gesturing at the shortest, and most tattooed, biker pounding away on a keyboard. "Satellites came online about fifteen minutes ago. You were about ninety minutes out when the retrieval team pulled you over."

It's weird seeing John doing his normal thing in leather and chains, but I don't say anything. The fake chase may have given the cover we needed to escape Billings, but it hasn't bought us any time. Casper knows I'm alive, and might already have another attack planned. I can't let him see the hardware and personnel backing me up until we are at his ranch, pounding its defenses.

A topographical map of Garfield County, Montana flashes up on the largest flat screen. We are in some rugged territory with hills, eroded buttes, and valleys. The county seat is Jordan, our current location. A base camp is being set up about half an hour away to the southeast, near the unincorporated community of Cohagen, where I spent the night in the holding tank. We'll launch the attack from there. It'll also serve as the emergency trauma facility for the animals and humans that can't make the trip to Billings.

"What else did Henderson give you?" Jason asks.

Pulling out the notebook, I reply, "A lot of info. The ranch is isolated in a large canyon with a single road in and out that meanders through walls laced with AA's and mortars."

I continue to translate page after page of Henderson's scratches. Several techs transcribe my ramblings. After I finish, I glance at Jason, and stiffen.

"Sir," I intone, "please take over, so I can excuse myself."

"No need, Captain," Jason interrupts. "You are hereby reinstated to your full rank and position. As the CO of the united Mason Seven CSA Team, with me being a member, you are the senior officer present, so please continue."

"Thank you, sir, but…" I let my voice trail off, unsure of what to do or say because I hadn't had gone through the normal recertification process for this latest status change, yet.

Jason holds up a sealed envelope, saying, "Already taken care of."

I relax, offering a silent thanks to my unseen guardians on the ship. "Very well, then, ladies and gentlemen, let's come up with a plan."

"John, have the drones completed their flyover yet?" George wonders.

"Just finishing their first pass," John replies, without looking up from his rapid clickety-clack. A picture of a rock formation with an almost perfect square in the center appears on one of the smaller screens. "Haven't enhanced this shot yet," he states, "but it looks like we are also dealing with snipers."

"Our best approach is a multi-pronged attack then," George suggests. "Some non-standard formation they won't expect. Five or six separate teams should do it. We just need to determine how many waves."

"Two waves. The first will consist of one large team and four small, plus our own snipers on the ridges." I trace the road with my finger. "We'll have a battering ram plow the road and draw their attention. Then the smaller teams come in as a staggered horseshoe. Once they clear the defenses, the second wave will flood the field."

"How many people do you want on the smaller teams?" Jim asks.

"Seven. The team commander will drive an Aggressor with two personnel each on three smaller ATV's. Large armored vehicles and Humvees will make up the battering ram. Nothing without good maneuverability, though. With tight quarters, and the most people, we don't want to turn that part of the op into a suicide mission."

"Call signs?" George prompts.

"We'll use letter-based designations until second wave when we revert to our normal ones. Bases will remain same throughout. Primary is Central and secondary, Aux."

"Time of attack?"

"What do we have on their shift changes?"

A chart flashes on the screen. "Looks like one happens about pre-dawn," John states.

Groans go up around the tent. The timing is the old tired, clichéd approach seen in tons of television shows and movies. It does have the strategic advantages of dim light and muddled senses, though.

"Air support is too risky until we take out the AA's," I note. "I want at least half a dozen choppers on stand-by for the evac of both human and horses."

"What other aircraft do we need?" Jason inquires.

"John, what does Billings have?" I ask, since it's the only USMB base in Montana with anything heavier than a chopper. LA has everything, but bringing in an air unit from outside the state requires notifying the FAA and DOD. That translates into hours of hassle and paperwork.

A list pops up. I scan through it, dismissing most of the offerings as either too light or too heavy. Near the bottom, I spot a squadron of mixed strike fighters. "Make sure those are available as well," I say, pointing at them.

One of the techs gets on the radio to scare up the needed equipment.

"Ok, so now that we have basic plan, what kind of structures are we dealing with?" Jim asks.

The flat screen rolls through a slide show of the various buildings, each containing a brief blurb of their functionality. The Circle H Ranch, as Olson Hudson called his spread back in the day, consists of a large house with a veranda on three sides as well as a number of other structures. Riordan built some after he bought the property. The stable, blacksmith shop with adjoining tool shed, cook's shack, well house, and windmill are all original structures. One of the newer buildings is a small chapel in front, and to the right, of the main house. It's doubtful that the real purpose for that sanctuary has anything to do with religion. Located beyond the stable is an aircraft hangar with that end of the valley road serving as an airstrip. Several more buildings dot the landscape, but they are dilapidated and not in any shape to provide cover for the defenders.

Turning to the redheaded biker who is standing a little stiffer than his mirror image, I ask, "Is there any regulation or law that prevents the final authorization of this mission?"

"The *Posse Comitatus Act*, which limits the use of military personnel to enforce state laws, might apply," Michael replies. "However, given that the intel suggests we are dealing with USMB personnel and hardware rather than civilian militia, JAG would have a hard time proving the case."

"Very well, then, we are a go."

I circle the room with my eyes. I know George, Jason, his sons, my brothers, and the rest of the Mason Seven personnel, but everyone else is a stranger. No matter their relationship with me, they meet my gaze with the same solemn and silent promise. The mission will not fail.

# FIFTY-TWO

# LOOSE ENDS

Before turning in, I seek out a few people. My first stop is a dark tent. Shining my flashlight in, I illuminate a large motionless lump. Bill, still wearing his biker outfit, has his head hidden beneath a pillow.

"You okay?" I prompt, switching off the light and slipping inside.

"I feel like crap," the pillow grunts. "I will never, ever drink again!" His dry gag and hack sends my stomach flying to my throat in sympathy. "I started in right after I killed those people, hoping to dull the pain and get rid of their faces." The pillow shook. "After about my third or fourth bottle, Big Nasty was in control, and I no longer cared."

"Do you remember our fight?"

"No, I can't recall anything about today except waking up in the back of a car in handcuffs. Did I hurt you?"

"You weren't that coordinated, but it took me busting your chops with my leg before you went down."

"No wonder my head hurts on the *outside* too!"

"What happened? How did you become that big nasty brute? "

In the darkness, Bill's sigh seems loud and long. He tells his tale, which begins when he was a teenager. Seems, because of his size and strength, he always felt the need to be extra careful and gentle. As his role of the dependable rock in the family developed, he became convinced cracks in his solid shell weren't acceptable.

"Slicing and dicing those perps felt natural and good," he concludes. "I would have taken out the whole gang, if Jim hadn't stopped me. Almost took him out, too. After that, being Big Nasty was easier than dealing with what I had done. I'm a killer, Jo, maybe even a psychopath whose doctor persona is an illusion."

"I don't believe that, Bill, and neither should you."

"Then what should I believe? My hands should be tools of healing, not destruction. I'm not sure I can trust them or me again."

Leaning back on my heels, I let the silence build between us. I don't have a straightforward answer that will make sense of this complicated mess. Logical, sure, but this isn't a simple math problem. It's the complex algorithm of Bill, who acted out his version of Honeywell without her training.

"Yes, you can, Bill. You just have to find a better release mechanism and not let things build up to such dangerous levels. No one has ever expected you to take the emotional punishment you have without saying a word."

"That is all well and good for future reference, Jo, but what about now? Other than guilt and this massive hangover, I should be paying some price to society for what I've done."

"I learned how to separate what Honeywell does from what I do," I state, latching onto that connection. "With us, there is always a clear indication of who's in charge and who's responsible."

"Yes, but, for you, Honeywell is a separate personality. For me, there's no one else but me."

"Then treat Big Nasty like a role you played. Not as separate as a personality, but still something that can be quantified and filed away."

"Your solution takes care of the character, but not what it did."

"You were acting under orders and protecting your team. Your actions are covered by the rules of engagement."

"Is that how you justify what Honeywell did?"

"Honeywell, for the most part, took out other CSG's, but I will never accept what she did as justifiable. I can't."

"How do you live such an unburdened life then?"

"Like you, I don't let everything show. I've had my explosions, but, except for Honeywell, they haven't been very public or dangerous. Still, it's no way to live, trust me. That's why I talk things through with people on my short list. We need to build a similar support network for you."

"Send me to Molly's, please, so I can get a few things right in my head."

"I need everyone for tomorrow, Bill, but if you still feel that way in the morning, I will."

* * *

Searching for Jason, I pass by many white dots on the landscape. One overflows with laughter and the sound of familiar voices. Michelle and Vince are chatting away about various things in our childhood. I catch

229

snatched words related to the first time they met me and discovered who my father was.

I consider joining them, but only for a moment. I'm afraid if I say more than a word or two, I'll want to talk about my involvement in their relationship with each other. While I'm not too worried about who might overhear our conversation, I fear their reaction, and the scene that could unfold as a result. A few, besides them, might leave, diminishing our chances of rescuing DH.

Opening her tent's flap, Michelle sticks her head out. She's back to looking like herself, except for her hair being shorter and darker than normal. "Is everything okay, Cap?"

"Yes. How are you and Vince doing?"

"Better. I seem to be associating more and more with him. Still don't have the intimate connection that you and Jim seem to share, though."

"That'll come. I needed a few weeks for mine to reset after Jim rejoined me at LA."

"Speaking of which, when we get back home, can you give me access to all logs and records concerning my service? I want to fill in the last remaining holes."

"Sure," I smile, relieved that I have at least a few more weeks of their friendship. "We'll need to talk first. I'd like Vince to be there as well."

"That sounds good. Night, Cap."

"Night, Michelle."

* * *

Approaching Jason's tent, I notice him standing in front of it with three of his four sons. Justin's still at LA handling security for my base. Jason Jr. serves with his father in San Francisco, and Joel and Jeremy, the twins, are under Jeff's command in Houston.

Soft and gentle most of the time, their faces always express the emotions that burn within them. While Jason Jr. bears the name of his father, the flaxen-haired, blue-eyed Justin looks the most like him. He carries his weight and power in his upper body and his speed in his long legs. Jason Jr. has dark brown hair, and the tall, well-proportioned build of an athlete. Joel and Jeremy are stockier than Justin, with brown eyes and blonde hair.

Being that Jason is my stepfather, they are my extended family. "Hey, guys," I greet them, setting a relaxed tone for a conversation that lasts a good thirty minutes and spans topics from cars to the brand new dog that Jeremy has adopted. A proud poppa, Jeremy whips out his phone and shows us all pictures of Thunder, a year-old brown and tan Rottweiler mix who came from a not so good home.

Handing the phone back to Jeremy, I say, "I hate to cut this short, but I need to talk to Dad."

"Sure, we have perimeter duty, anyway. Come on, guys."

They disappear, and we enter Jason's tent. It contains the bare necessities. Slipping into a chair, I sigh. Jason gives me a quick once with his eyes over before taking a seat on his cot.

"You okay, lass?"

"I'm worried about Bill. I don't think he should be involved in tomorrow's action."

"Ye afraid he might go off again?"

"No, just the opposite, he might not react when I need him to. Based on Henderson's description, the men we are going up against have experienced both levels of Command Security training. They aren't going to care about how many of them we kill; they'll just want to complete their mission of protecting the ranch. We have to think and act the same way."

"Do ye want me ta talk to him?"

"No, I already did. I'll check with him in the morning and see where his head's at."

"What about you? Will Honeywell make an appearance?"

"There is always the possibility of that, but focusing on everyone's safety and taking care of DH, when we find him, should keep me as me."

"Good."

"Jason, looking past this mission for a second, we have some extensive resources gathered here. Why don't we go after Command Security and shut them down?"

"We'll rip the USMB apart, if we do. We need ta dismantle the unit from the inside."

"We tried that once before. They blackmailed you into silence."

"I will not be involved in the op, this time around. I dinna have ta be. Yer team's investigation inta, and disembowelment of, Casper's network 'tis enough reason fer da upper echelon ta authorize an audit of the unit fer na preventin' its creation in the first place."

"First, we have to patch the holes in the USMB organization structure created by the web."

"Aye, that will take some doin'. Speaking of tomorrow, I noticed ye have me slotted as the mission's overall commander, but from here."

"I can't risk you in the field. John, who is also staying behind, reassures me that he has all the computing power he needs to make sure you will have a virtual view of everything that goes down."

"The keyword 'tis virtual," Jason snorts. "I won't be as effective."

"Maybe not, but you'll be safer. I'm trying to protect our legacy, Jason. If things go south, I want people in place who can reveal the truth to the rest of the USMB and the world."

"How many are ye leaving behind fer this purpose?"

"Six. You, John, and Vince will stay here. TJ, Michael, and Tyrell have errand duty between the camps." The choice between Michelle and Vince was hard. I wanted both of them to stay behind. However, I needed someone on the team I could trust to be in charge of the battering ram. Michelle got the job because of her tactical knowledge and skills. "I also wanted to leave Jim, but he insisted on watching my six and threatened to ship me back to Molly's if I didn't let him."

* * *

The strains of Latin guitar music interrupt the journey to my tent and bed. Music is such a part of my life that when the notes wrap themselves around my heart, I have to stop and listen. I recognize the tune as something one of my watch commanders always hums.

It doesn't make much sense for Commander Carlos Mendez to be here, though, since he is not a member of the Mason Seven or any other command team. I have offered him a position several times, but Carlos always refuses, insisting he wants me to have someone outside the team I can trust. He's number three on my short list, having knocked Jeff out of that coveted spot.

Jeff is twelfth and last. He's going to stay there until we have a chance to talk about his stupidity with Jimmy and him lying about when he knew I was Honeywell. Depending on what happens, I might bump him off and decommission his command of the Mason Seven Auxiliary Team. Michael has nixed the idea of a court-martial because my orders weren't specific enough to prevent Jeff from assigning Jimmy as Honeywell's handler. Jeff is here, leading his part of the team. We are keeping our conversations focused on that.

Curious about the identity of my mysterious serenader, I lift the tent flap and peek inside. A familiar olive-skinned form sits on a cot caressing his instrument. His brown eyes twinkle as he looks up and smiles.

"What are you doing here?" I ask.

"Captain, where else would I be?" Carlos replies.

I shrug.

* * *

The next morning, I end up relieving Bill of duty and sending him to Molly. Bill pleads to go as himself, but I insist he leave as Big Nasty. Molly wants it that way and promises she'll bail him out if he's arrested.

"I'm doing this for two reasons," she states when I call her after he's left. It doesn't matter that the sun hasn't risen for her, she's up and waiting for me. " One, Bill's face has been all over the media during the team's championship run, so he can't been seen on Big Nasty's chopper or near here. Two, so he can learn to deal with and control Big Nasty, instead of hiding behind his normal demeanor of a quiet giant."

"How are you going to do that?"

"By driving him deeper into the character and having Big Nasty convicted and imprisoned in his mind, so he can live out the punishment he wants."

"Is your plan safe? Will it work?"

"Safe, no, but I have enough big brutes around here to keep him from hurting himself or anyone else. Yes, it will work. I did something similar both times I had to break Honeywell's control on you."

Learning to feel again after being Honeywell was the hardest part of my treatments with Molly. The day I cried for hours after all my pent-up emotions broke through the first time, I swore I would embrace every feeling I had and live them to their extreme. Despite my good intentions, fulfilling my promise was almost impossible. There were so many physical sensations associated with the forgotten feelings that they locked me up. The pain of knowing that I had done terrible things to other human beings made it worse. I began drinking to stay loose and relaxed.

Using my knowledge of the shadows, I was able to hide my indulgence from Molly for about three weeks. It would have been longer, if I hadn't gone on a binge after a painful flashback involving an innocent kid and his family. Forgetting all my training, I stumbled through Molly's front door to find her sitting on one of the couches. Saying nothing, she helped me to the bathroom, where I either dozed off or dumped my guts in the can. The next day, she started her extreme treatment of making me relive every moment of every hunt, torture, and kill as if I was the victim. The sessions were so bad she had to sedate me so I could sleep.

This last time hadn't been much better. After the memory treatment involving Jimmy, I almost went back to the bottle.

"Jo, you okay?" Molly's soft brogue breaks through my melancholy.

"Yes, for the most part."

"What about the stress of today? Are you going to be able to keep Honeywell under control?"

"I'll handle both. If I don't, you can just set up a cage for me next to Bill, and hope your magic touch works again. Whatever happens, keep my family posted on him, okay?"

"I will. As much as they'll want an update every day, they can't call. He's not as bad as you were, but I don't want to risk him picking up the phone and deciding to go after the people who sent him here. If he kills or hurts one of you as that biker dude—"

"He can end being him for the rest of his life," I interrupt. "It's the same thing with me and Honeywell, so I'll make sure of it. Thanks, Molly."

"You're welcome. Keep safe and being yourself, lass."

"I'll try."

Hanging up, I contemplate staying behind. Let someone else handle people dying on both sides. If I do, my responsibilities will fall on Jim. I can't do that to him.

# FIFTY-THREE
# IN THE NAME OF FREEDOM

The glow of the screen highlights the worry lines on Jim's face. He's the driver and commander of our team. Being in the command vehicle will keep him somewhat safe. Given my sniper training, I'm with the group suited up for action. My responsibility, as the comm officer, is to relay all orders from Jim and his superior, Jason. We are Alpha. Our primary mission is securing the horses.

Glancing up at the drone hovering above and to the right of our vehicle, I wave. Jason's on the other end, seeing and hearing everything. The drone tips its wings.

Instead of straining my knee by straddling an ATV, I'm riding in the larger Aggressor with Jim until we reach our holding point. I also want the extra time with him.

Jim glances over and asks, "You one or two people?"

"One, for now," I shrug. "Honeywell might show her face as the action gets more intense. I should have enough to time to let you know, so you can pull me."

*Charlie is in position,* Jason's voice crackles over the drone's speaker.

The GPS screen confirms the dot belonging to the third team is at their assigned coordinates.

"How did Volker pull that off?" I wonder, frowning. "His terrain was the hardest." Carlos pulls alongside on the ATV that I'll join him on later. I flash three fingers, point to my watch, and shrug. He shakes his head.

"Volker's a hot shot," responds Jim, leaning on the accelerator. The Aggressor jumps forward. "We'll beat Emmett and then spend an hour waiting for the Don."

I met Volker and Emmett, two of the team commanders, for the first time during the meeting yesterday. Volker came across as a competitive and tough hard nose. He reminds me of Vince on one of his more bulldoggish days. "How'd you learn about them so fast?"

"John's subjected the team leaders to one of his infamous info cramming sessions after the main meeting."

Chuckling, I quip, "Those can be brutal." John's a sponge when it comes to information. He stores so many trivial facts in his head that when I ask him for a quarter, I receive a lesson on the history of money along with it.

"Want to trade?"

"No, just give me a brief summary of who we are dealing with."

Emmett, the commander of Team Bravo, is like Michael. He takes calculated risks, but always has a backup plan. His route is about the same difficulty as ours, so it'll be a toss-up as to who hits their mark first.

The Don, full name of Doniphan, is the commander of Team Delta. I have gone up against him in several shooting competitions. While studying his target, he ignores the clock, the audience, and his fellow competitors. When he does make his shot, he always hits dead center. I've never won against him.

He's far more of a perfectionist than TJ can ever hope to be. Methodical and reliable, the Don will be the last, but his team will have the least jarring ride. On the screen, the UAV tracking him is almost going in circles, trying to anticipate his ever-changing trajectory.

We pull to a stop. "Alpha-One to Central," Jim announces into the mike. "We are in position." He winks at me. As predicted, we are second. Bravo is two minutes behind us. The clock on the screen flips through almost twenty-five cycles before Delta reports in.

Hopping out, I walk to the back of the Aggressor. Carlos, Jeremy, George, and our other teammates, Merrick and Wendell, join me for the dispersal and final inspection of gear. Though we work in silence, there's no tension or heaviness in the air. We've all served in police or military forces outside the USMB and relish in the quiet companionship of the moment, not wanting to jinx ourselves by talking about what's to come.

While the rest return to the ATV's, I retreat to the driver's side of the command vehicle. The ATV's are armored versions of the square boxes with wheels that anyone can buy. The Aggressor is a giant dune buggy with hauling capacity, armor, and a machine gun. This prototype model is quiet, and almost undetectable, when it switches over to its lithium-ion battery packs. Range on the batteries is decent enough for the current op should a team on one of the ATV's need rescuing.

As the silence of the predawn builds around me, my thoughts turn toward Michelle. While Vince didn't object to her taking the lead of the armored convoy, he did shoot several disapproving glares in my direction. *If anything happens to her...* I breathe a silent prayer, asking for protection. I'm not a religious person, but I believe there is a lot more going on in the universe than even John can comprehend or explain.

Jason's brogue cuts through my contemplation, *Battering ram engaged. All teams stand by.*

"Short fuse, everyone," Jim announces. "We are about 20 out."

Reaching in, I put my hand on his. Locking gazes, we share a silent conversation of encouragement. Breaking away, I stride toward to the parked ATV's. When I stop in front of my assigned one, Carlos motions to the driver's position. I wave him off.

"I'm driving," Jeremy says, nudging George, who's half-asleep on the passenger side of their vehicle. Merrick and Wendell draw straws. Wendell pulls the shorter one, so Merrick stays in the driver's seat.

"Jo, see anything?" Jim asks. "The drone's picking up some activity."

I pop up the ATV's periscope. Through the green tinge of night vision, I pick up some movement, but nothing alarming. "No, boogies, yet," I reply.

*Mission update. Ram's Head, Post Eleven.*

Ram's Head is the mobile command post for the battering ram. Post Eleven is the first in a string of observation platforms and sniper nests we set up along the canyon rim. There are only four UAV's, one for each of the smaller teams, so the Ram is dependent upon the posts for target acquisition and intel.

"Who's at eleven?" I wonder.

"Putnam," Jim replies. "Last one's Spinner."

Spinner is one of my fellow snipers. His first name is Christopher. His handle is a combination of the word "top" in his name and his ability to spin around so fast that he's lived through several shootouts.

I glance at my watch. *6:02*. The sun is a bright line on the eastern horizon. Clouds mixed with sunbreaks are the forecast of the day. A slight breeze ruffles my hair. The weather jockeys are expecting rain, but think it will hold off until the main part of the assault is over.

"Given all the tech up and down the canyon," George states, "I'm surprised they haven't come out of their shell yet."

"Do they have a tunnel network connecting their defenses?" Jim wonders.

"Ground penetrating radar didn't pick one up. Even if they do, they'll have to surface near Spinner to launch a counterattack." George glances at me. "He's almost your sister's equal."

"What about the mortars?"

"Those are more worrisome. They could pop a few in the ravine for a lateral assault."

"We have a spotter climbing the windmill," Merrick, looking through a pair of night vision binoculars, interrupts. Serving almost five years in the Marine Corps before joining the USMB, he wears his buzz cut like the rest of us wear normal length hair. Short and squat, but quick on his feet, he's going to be our mini-battering ram.

"Drone's picking up at least one rifle," Jim reports. "I'm waiting for visual confirmation."

*Mission update. Ram's Head, Post Eight.*

"Why did they dispatch us so early?" Wendell whines. "We're sitting here doing nothing." A hyperactive fidget, the beanpole's voice is a little annoying, but he's our needed speed.

"Better to wait than be late," quips George.

"I guess, but—"

Taking a deep breath, I block out the conversation. The predator within me is awake, anticipating the hunt, but isn't trying to take control. I fiddle with my comm pack to keep myself focused.

*Ram's Head, Post Seven.*

"Full countdown from here on in," Jim announces.

"Thank you, sir!" Wendell cries.

Almost every two minutes, Jason's voice cuts in on the command frequency. *Six. Five. Four. Three. Two.* Until, *Mission alert. I repeat, mission alert. Ram's Head, Post One. All teams report.*

"Alpha ready," Jim responds, waving at me.

*We have visual contact,* Jason announces. *Battering Ram is about three quarters of a mile from the front gate. They have incoming."*

Bright lights flash around the ranch and along the road accompanied by thunderous booms that rattle my bones. "Damn," Jim mutters. "George's right about that lateral assault. It's already paying dividends. We've lost two smaller vehicles."

*All teams, we have go!* Jason orders. *I repeat. All teams, we have go!*

"*Showtime!*" Jim shouts.

"The Ram?"

"Still making progress."

"Good. See you on the other side."

"Roger that."

* * *

We take off in V formation, spitting up dust as we roar toward the ranch and our primary target. Despite our intel, there are still a few more unknowns than I like, including where DH might be. I hope that we find him in the main stables. He also could be in the corral a little ways from the building. Maybe even in a different part of the ranch. Henderson's last note on him was that Clem was thinking about isolating DH in some sort of sensory deprivation stall to see if that would turn him.

Racing down the slope, I peer over Carlos' shoulder at the chaos unfolding beneath me. Though we started first, the chatter on my headset suggests that Volker's team has almost reached their primary target, the hanger. After they finish there, they'll move onto the cook's shack. Bravo has the unenviable task of breaking down the defenses at the ranch house. The chapel is Delta's. Our target on the way to the stables is the blacksmith shop since it guards the south stable door.

As Carlos dodges a large pile of debris hidden by the tall grass and dim light, the radio screams with the first sounds of battle. The other teams have engaged the enemy.

Swinging out into the open, we run into a wall of bullets ourselves.

"You're up!" Carlos yells, swerving and weaving in an evasive pattern designed to confuse our attackers. Shouldering my rifle, I begin firing at the blacksmith shop. At first, my shots are inches off their mark, but I soon settle into the rhythm of Carlos' driving.

"We are taking fire," I shout into the mike. "What is the status of the other teams?'

*All teams reporting varying degrees of resistance,* Jim replies.

The ATV hits a bump and launches into the air, allowing me to spot a sniper behind the well house. I light him up. His shoulder snaps back, but he continues firing at unseen targets.

Back on four wheels, Carlos skids the ATV in a cloud of dust that creates a short respite from the bullets. We are close to the stables, but have to clear this mess out before heading in that direction. I roll to the far side, gaining some protection from the gunfire we are taking from the blacksmith shop and the wounded sniper at the well house. The rear flanking ATV's come up alongside and slam to a stop, forming a shield. Wendell and George fire as they bail from their seats. Merrick and Jeremy join in as soon as they are clear.

The drone zips by and circles the well house.

*That's your first target!* Jim barks in my earpiece.

Pointing to the miniature version of the ranch house, I signal for George and Jeremy to take it out.

*Now the shop.*

That's up to me, Carlos, Merrick, and Wendell. I don't have much time to concentrate on the other two. While the sounds coming from their general vicinity are promising, we are taking a pounding from the blacksmith shop. Good thing we all have combat-grade body armor.

"Yeow!" Carlos screeches before going off in Spanish.

I glance in his direction. A streak of red cuts a horrible path in his olive skin. "You okay?"

"*Sí*"

An explosion rumbles the ground. I jump and shudder. "Jim, what the hell was that blast?" I yell into my headset. "Did something breach the no heavy fire zone around the stables?"

*Checking now.* The drone heads off. A few heartbeats later, Jim states, *A grain silo near the barn lost its top.*

"The horses?"

*No one has seen them. Assuming they are still inside.*

Cold drops sting my hands. Nature's tears, replacing the ones I don't have time to cry. Why do weather jockeys always screw-up their forecasts on important days?

# FIFTY-FOUR

## COMBAT WOES

"*Down!*" I scream. A mortar whistles overhead as another round of gunfire comes at us from the blacksmith shop. We have no cover. The original plan had us dumping the ATV's at the door of our targets, so we could fire from their protection. We lost that luxury due to the earlier than expected enemy engagement.

The four of us crawl forward. The rain of water and bullets intensifies. A series of explosions rattles the ground.

*Boom! Boom! Boom!*

*The Ram will be in position to cover in five,* Jim announces in my ear. *What's your status, Alpha-Two?*

"Alphas Three and Four are unaccounted for. Alphas Two and Five through Seven are eating mud and metal."

Shots ring out from the well house. "Make that Alphas Three and Four providing cover," I correct.

*Roger.*

More detonations occur in tight succession.

"*Go! Go! Go!*" I shout.

Carlos, Merrick, Wendell, and I bolt for the blacksmith shop. At first, I'm aware of them running with me, but soon become so focused on keeping myself moving and concealed that they turn into shadows in my vision. A dense spray of bullets rains down upon me when I'm a few steps from the door. I dive for ground, my combat armor and knee pushed to their limits.

Merrick drops and slides up next to me. He thumps his chest plate, winking. "Just as good as I had in the Corps."

I glance over at Wendell. He's rubbing his arm like something's penetrated. "You okay, kid?" I call out.

Wendell flashes a thumb up.

"Ready, *mi amigo?*" I punch Carlos in the shoulder.

Carlos nods.

We make a final push toward the shop. A shot rings out. Merrick stumbles, a red stain appearing on his thigh. He pivots to protect his injured leg. The deep boom of a high-powered rifle reverberates through the air. His head explodes, splattering me with blood. I choke on the bile that rushes up from my stomach. *This would be so much easier if we take over,* the dark presence in my head offers.

*No, thanks!*

*You say something, Jo?* Jim wonders.

"Dealing with my shadow," I quip. "I'm not in danger from it, yet. Merrick's," I choke on the finality of loss, "gone."

*I saw.*

A rain of water pelts us. The one of metal has stopped.

Bursting through the blacksmith door, I find out why. Four boogies are inside. Two are dead thanks to George and Jeremy. Another lies face down on the ground. The fourth charges us. I stop him with a bullet to the kneecap. Finding some rope hanging on the wall, Wendell ties the two survivors back to back.

"Alpha-Two, blacksmith shop clear!" I report. "Orders?"

*Regroup, but be careful. Drone's detecting movement near the woodpile.*

"Wendell, check out the toolshed. Keep your eyes open," I order, motioning toward the door facing us. "Carlos, cover him." Thumbing the transmitter, I switch to the team frequency. "George, we need you and Jeremy over here."

*Roger.*

Carlos fires off a tirade of Spanish and bullets. Spinning around, I snap the riflescope to my face. A gentle squeeze of the trigger and a target falls. Two more follow in rapid succession.

Sweeping the area, I do a quick body count. Carlos' outburst cut down three more hostiles. Add a friendly, and we have seven total. *Damn! The fool kid didn't pay attention to awning.*

I lower my rifle.

"What's wrong?" George asks, entering the shop.

"They got Wendell," I swallow.

"Wendell didn't have a prayer," Jeremy mutters. "What about Merrick, though? The way he was telling stories last night, he could have taken on the whole damn place by himself."

"Jeremy, listen up," I say in a firm tone that draws his attention. All innocence is gone from his face, replaced by a sad, distracted look that troubles me. "He's a warrior who wanted to die in combat, not his sleep."

"Yes, but still—"

"Still nothing. Can you continue, Lieutenant?"

"Sir, yes, sir," Jeremy snaps.

"They were good men," George crosses himself, "and good friends, too."

"Jeremy, stay with the prisoners." I nod toward the survivors who are both slumped forward and not moving. "The rest of you, let's secure the shed."

George climbs over the wood. Carlos and I split around it. Sweeping every inch with our rifles and eyes, we spot nothing. The shed, except for the dead bodies, is empty. Returning to the shop, I radio Jim. "Tell me you got some good news, little bro. I've lost another one."

*Who?*

"Wendell."

*Sorry about that, Jo, and no, I don't. Conflicting reports are coming in, but it appears the fight at the chapel isn't going in Delta's direction. Charlie's lost comm. At last report, they'd taken the hangar, but we have no confirmation on that or the destruction of the plane. Cook's shack is still intact. Bravo has their hands full with the ranch house. The Ram has incoming from two directions, but is holding its own and giving some back in return. We are assessing the situation. Stand by, Alpha-Two.*

Leaning against the wall, I sigh.

"Bad?" George prompts.

I nod. "We may have lost Charlie."

*Alpha-Two, be advised,* Jim breaks in, *the team UAV is down. I have no direct eyes and ears for you from here on out. It's your call, Jo. Wait for another team to free up or proceed.*

*Crap, what else can go wrong?* I glance at my companions. George and Carlos, the vets, give me a neutral, but expectant, look. Jeremy is still a little spooked. I flash him a silent *comme ci comme ça* with my right hand.

He responds with the middle finger.

Good, the kid still has some fight in him. "Alpha-One, we are proceeding. What's the latest intel on the horses?"

*Someone released them into the corral.*

I swear under my breath. In the stables, they had some protection against the jarring sounds and lights of the battle. Now, they have nothing. Depending on their exposure and tolerance, they could panic and charge the fence. If that happens, they'll trample their weaker members. I can only hope and pray that DH isn't among those that go down.

"Has anyone spotted the primary target?"

*Negative.*

My heart drops. *DH's either dead or moved to a different building.* I remind myself to keep thinking the latter.

"Understood." Turning to my team, I say, "Everyone, heads up! We hit the stables and then the corral. Primary target remains unaccounted for. We need to take out the hornet's nest in the stables before finding him."

Carlos' and George's expressions become harder, more determined. Even Jeremy shows some signs of a spine.

"Four ways in, as advertised," states George, who had processed a lot of the intel before my family arrived at basecamp. "The big doors are on the north and south ends. A stairway to the loft is on the east side, away from the stables. There's loft door on the top north side. South top is solid wall with a window for light."

Wiggling out of his backpack, Carlos places it on the ground. Reaching in, he takes out a launcher and a small quiver. He loads the harpoon with an arrow.

"Why not storm the bottom doors?" Jeremy offers.

Carlos shakes his head. "Weren't you paying attention at the briefing? Riordan replaced the north  door with a reinforced one. They always keep it closed except when moving the horses."

"Besides," I add, "the loft offers the strategic advantage of height. We stick with the plan." Rubbing my knee, I add, "I can't climb, so Jeremy, you and Carlos have the honor of taking it."

"Yes, sir." A note of hesitation rings in Jeremy's tone. He points at the spare arrows. "You gonna need those?"

"Don't think so," Carlos smiles. "One should be enough. The rest can be used for our defense, if need be." He slips the quiver's sling over his head.

Jeremy's eyes narrow. He scrutinizes the thin, braided rope attached to the loaded harpoon. "How is this going to hold us?"

"It's rated for at least a thousand pounds, but I'll go first, Jeremy, to make sure it holds. The wood should be soft after all these years, so we'll have good penetration, and a solid anchor."

"I hope so," mutters Jeremy.

"I'll keep you safe, kiddo, as I have protected all your *familia* over the years," Carlos nods in my direction. "*Mi Capitán* will kill me otherwise."

"Remember, you'll be exposed to the ranch house," George says. "The corral is the only thing between you and it. Be careful."

"*Sí.*" "*Sí*"

"Carlos, if the loft is clear, wait for my signal," I add. "I'll flag you from the south door. Otherwise, bail and return here. Keep your comm open at all times."

"Will do."

Before Jeremy can offer another objection, Carlos shoves him out the door.

# FIFTY-FIVE

# A PARTING SHOT

"Well, it's you and me, George. *Let's go!*"

The distance from the blacksmith shop to the barn isn't far, and the rain has let up a bit. I peer out the door. I've been ignoring the explosions, but they haven't ceased. The gunfire around us has lessened.

We pop out, take a sharp turn to our left, and, begin running. Reaching the south door, we are about to head toward the tack room when George points and shouts, "Cap, we have a problem!"

A hatch swings up from the ground a few yards beyond the well house. *A root cellar? How the hell did* that *escape the aerial survey or the ground penetrating radar?*

Black armor pours out from the hole, firing in our direction.

"Boogie nest!" I yell. "Light her up, George!"

He pelts the weathered wood of the cellar with bullets. Chips fly in every direction, but the flow of bad guys doesn't falter. Glancing at the south door, I expect to see a rush from there at any moment.

"Pull back! Pull back, *now*! We have to regroup."

"What about Jeremy and Carlos?"

"They are on their own until we get reinforcements."

"Yes, sir."

George makes an abrupt about face and brushes by me, taking quick backward steps with his finger squeezing the trigger all the way. Instead of following him, and giving our enemies two targets, I seek shelter behind the corner of the tack room. If I have a good enough angle, I can launch a flanking attack from there.

Inching toward my hiding place, I glance between George and the black armors. I'm almost in position when he stumbles and grabs his side.

I tap my comm. "Alpha-Three, what's your status?"

Flashing thumbs up, George disappears into the blacksmith shop.

Returning my attention to the cellar, I notice the flood of bad guys has stopped. Readying my rifle, I wait for the next head to emerge.

I'm grateful that my brothers are where they are. Well, maybe except for Bill, who, in a strange way, is safer than all of us. It's up to me to make sure that Jim, Michelle, Jeremy, George, Carlos, and the rest of the Mason Seven survive this day. Everyone else is an indirect concern. I hate compartmentalizing them that way, but at least I'm still thinking of them as people and not bodies.

"Cap, look out!" George yells.

I snap my head around.

*Shit!* Boogies are reentering the well house. In mere heartbeats, they'll turn my hidey-hole into a target gallery, with me as the prize duck. I signal for George to cover my retreat.

Nodding, he begins firing. Pushing off from the wall, I bolt for safety, shooting at anything that moves. Four or five strides into my run, I'm hit in the back. The impact nudges me into a different gear. A bullet whizzes by my head as I near the shop. I brake and wheel at the same time. With a painful protest, my left knee locks up, pitching me forward.

Glancing up, I spot the shop a foot or so away. I try to get my feet under me, but my knee refuses to bear any weight. Slinging my rifle, I do a three legged frog crawl toward my objective. Bullets strike the ground all around me. They, and the clods of dirt they create, pelt my body armor. More than a few whistle past my head.

I make it to the shop, but on the far side of the door. Ripping the rifle off my back, I slink up the wall and slide down it toward safety, firing as I go.

Someone or something jerks me to the left. I peek in that direction. George has me by the arm. With one final yank from him, I stumble inside. Before he can slam the door shut, the armors pepper him with bullets.

Diving for his semi-automatic on the floor, I roll into the farthest corner from the door. At least now, I have a better chance of defending myself. *Not much of one, though*, I swear, checking the clip. Almost half the rounds are gone.

Two black-clad figures slither toward me, their faces devoid of expression. *This isn't how it's supposed to end*, the beast inside me whimpers. *We kill those of our kind, they do not kill us. Let us take over.* It cries a word I never thought I'd hear from its lips, *Please! We can—*

*No!* The screeching of metal and a horrendous explosion combine with my roar. The shop almost shakes off its foundation. My executioners continue toward me without losing their focus or step. I spray bullets until the gun empties to uselessness. One goes down, but the other stays steady and focused on its prey. Me.

The shadow's hot and silent breath murmurs above my almost still heart. Honeywell's quiet, resigned to her fate, I guess. Closing my eyes, I pray that when my brothers find my body, they know I was me until the end.

*Crack! Splat!*

My eyes snap open. Two shadowy figures roll and grapple in front me. I crawl toward my rifle. Flipping around, I follow the action until a fraction of an inch appears in a smaller fraction of a second. I fire. Both collapse.

Breathing hard, I lean back against the wall and watch the door, surprised that no one else has come through it.

*Creak!*

"Are you sure you want to shoot me, Jo?" The hazel eye in my scope raises an eyebrow.

"Jim?" I squeal, lowering the rifle before Honeywell gets any ideas about completing her kill order.

"Yes, kiddo, it's me," he replies. "After you found that cellar, I couldn't stay out of the fray any longer."

I nod toward the camo figure among the black. "George spotted it."

Squatting down, Jim feels his neck. "He's gone, Jo."

Lowering my head, I take a deep breath and swallow my sadness.

"Can you get up?" Jim prompts. "We can't stay here."

"I know, but I need your help."

His footsteps come closer. "I heard your scream," he whispers, his warm smile embracing me. "I would have known."

Tapping my heart then my head, I hope he understands my silent thanks.

Nodding, he offers his hand.

Using him as leverage, I pull myself up. When I put weight on my left leg, it complains, but doesn't buckle. "We have to get to the south door,"

I state. "Carlos and Jeremy are in the loft. They're waiting for my signal. What about the rest of those who were chasing us?"

"They scattered once I nailed their leader. Can you walk?"

"No, but I can hobble."

We exit the shop, entering a world void of sound and motion.

No bullets greet us and the only bodies are the dead ones lying of on the ground. Sounds of battle still ring out from the vicinity of the ranch house and stables. Jammed up against the wall with smoke barreling out of its innards, our command vehicle envelops one of the bad guys in its bent frame.

Wandering over, I pop the back munitions locker. I reload George's gun before tossing it to Jim. Making sure my rifle's chambers are full, I throw a few extra rounds in my vest pockets. I also strap on a sidearm and offer one to my brother. He waves it off.

Jim's presence is both comforting and worrisome. We are going to finish this mission as we started it, together, but now I have one more soul to protect. After we find Jeremy and Carlos, I'm going order a strategic retreat until we can come back, reinforced by the second wave. DH is important, but Jim, Jeremy, and Carlos are even more so.

"What's the news?" I ask.

"Riordan got away."

"How?"

"The plane was on the strip, fueled and waiting. Riordan's men ambushed Charlie when they went after it. None of them made it."

"Damn! The chapel?"

"Disintegrated. Delta took causalities, but they did their job."

"How's the battle for the main house going?"

"Nolan's men are still in control. The remaining members of Bravo and Delta have joined up with Michelle's forces. They have a good chance of taking it, but we are going to lose more people."

*Was one horse worth all this?* My heart replies, *yes*. My mind isn't so sure. Honeywell doesn't say anything.

* * *

Sneaking into battle is easier than running away from an ambush. It helps that we look like our enemy. Having stripped down to our fatigues and donned the black armor of the defenders we killed, we've remain unmolested. We are near the south doors, listening to the echoes off the battle going on at the north end. Being so close to the cellar, I can't stop thinking about George.

*He wouldn't have died if we had been in charge.* The beast inside me is back and sneering. *What are you going to do when they come after Jim, like you are waiting for them to do?*

"Shut up!" I almost yell.

Jim lifts an eyebrow. "Jo, you okay?"

"It's Honeywell. She's pressing hard."

"Can you continue as yourself?"

"What choice do I have?"

Jim shrugs. "I can't raise either Carlos or Jeremy on my radio. Try yours."

"I have been since we left the shop. They might have ditched theirs to remain undetected."

Peering around the corner along the east side of the barn, I spot the stairway leading to the loft. At least four black armors guard it.

"Stairs are a no go," I report.

Jim points up to the small window above us. "They may have started north, but could they have reached this side?"

"Maybe. They are waiting for my signal, so let's give them one and see."

Jim flashes, *Abort plan. Retreat now.*

No response.

"Try again," I urge.

This time it's *Carlos, please respond.*

Still nothing, so I try, *Come on guys, please be there.*

Sunlight sparkles in the window. At first, I think it's a random wind chime greeting the morning sun. Then  the flashes morph into a pattern. After substituting a few letters, I come up with *Trapped. Need diversion.*

Jim and I exchange glances. With the stables classified as soft target, restricted to hand weapons and no incendiary devices, we'd have to engage in close combat to provide the required distraction. Given the amount of enemy combatants involved, we wouldn't last long enough for Carlos and Jeremy to escape.

"Spotting rounds?" I wonder. Used for calibrating artillery, they crawl up on an objective instead targeting it.

"You're the senior officer, Jo," Jim replies. "It's your call."

"Alpha-Two to Ram's Head, what's your status?" I tap into the command frequency.

*Ram's Head, we have knocked down most of the defenses, and are now dealing with the pesky holdouts.* Michelle's voice is a little hoarser than this morning, but she still sounds unhurt. Vince will be pleased.

"How accurate are your gunners?"

*How accurate do you need them to be?*

"I need them to target the north end of the stables, starting five from the door and ending at zero. Use spotters with only enough powder to scare the bad guys."

*Alpha-Two, please confirm. Are you declaring the stables as a hard target?*

"Just their front door, Michelle. Two friendlies are trapped."

*Understood. Awaiting your command*

"Commen—"

*Ram's Head,* Jason breaks in, *can you confirm removal of AA's?*

*Yes, sir. The AA's are gone. Have one mortar position left. Defenses breached enough for second wave.*

*I'm ordering inbound, now. You should have back up in ten. Commence requested fire in eight to cover their approach.*

*Yes, sir.*

*Jo?*

"Yes?"

*Vince and your brothers will be part of this wave. I couldn't stop them.*

"Understood. Alphas One and Two returning to well house."

\* \* \*

The first shell slams into the ground, shaking the earth as far back as our location. By the second, a trickle starts flowing out from the barn and cellar. With the third, it's a flood. Black armor is everywhere.

Jim and I look at one another. As we retreated during Jason's window, we grabbed anything we could carry from the Aggressor to create a small defensible space within the well house. If the armors figure out there are live bodies in here, we'll be able to take out maybe half a dozen before we go down.

"How's Honeywell?" Jim whispers.

"Quiet. I don't think she likes the odds."

He lays his hand on my knee. "Whatever happens, kiddo, know that I love you and wouldn't have wanted to call another my twin."

"Same here, little bro."

A high-pitched whine assaults my ears as the room around me vibrates in harmony with every bone in my body. The last time I felt this sensation I was enjoying a peaceful walk in the woods when one of my base's air units did a flyover. That experience left me shaken and unsteady for a couple of hours. This time, my adrenaline and elation keep me steady.

Peering out the window, I watch blue camo backed by heavy armored vehicles part the sea of black. "Calvary's made it," I state.

Jim smiles, "Let's go get Carlos and Jeremy."

I nod.

*  *  *

Using the chaos as cover, Jim and I return to the barn. This time, we head for the north side. Carlos' rope up to the loft twists in the wind. Grabbing a hold of it, Jim says, "I'm going up and check on our guys."

"Be careful."

"Of course."

Jim begins climbing. He's about halfway up when Carlos and Jeremy appear in the loft door. Jeremy's clutching his chest, bleeding from more places than I want to count. Carlos seems unhurt, except for his right arm, which hangs at an awkward angle by his side.

Two figures detach themselves from the shadows. They sneak behind them. In a flash, Carlos and Jeremy are on their knees. Snapping my rifle up, I line up my shot, but no matter the angle I choose, I can only save one.

*Friend who has served me well over the years, who will survive, or stepbrother that has loved me all his life, who dies either way?* Honeywell would choose the former, if she were in control. Only this once do I agree with her.

252

I squeeze the trigger.

The shot reverberates off the barn causing an almost double echo.

Both shadows fall.

Calculating the reverse trajectory, I glance in that direction and spot Vince standing on an armored personnel carrier, lowering his own weapon. His voice fills my headset, *51-Command-1, no one should have to make that kind of choice. Go find your horse. My team will take care of Jeremy, and Carlos, if he sticks around.*

*Roger that. Thank you.*

# FIFTY-SIX

## TWO SOULS

Panicked by the blasts, the horses run in erratic circles, blind to everything but their fear. Another boom rumbles the ground. Stampeding, they charge the fence. The rails shatter with a loud cracking sound. Wood explodes into the air. The horses thunder toward us. Jim grabs on and holds me tight. Hidden and protected by his embrace, my racing heat muffles Carlos' vociferous attempt to divert the incoming tide. The hooves bear down upon us with a deafening rush. At the last possible moment, the wave splits and flows by.

When the pounding, snorts, and squeals are somewhere off in the distance and I'm sure I can stand on my own without shaking, I say, "You can let go now."

Jim complies. All three of us face the hole left by the destruction. Nothing remains in the ring but torn up ground and chaotic hoofprints.

Hanging my head, I sigh, "We won the battle, but lost the horse."

"Maybe not, Jo," Jim offers. "Remember, there are isolated buildings all over this place. Clem could have stashed DH anywhere. We'll use his chip to find him. This place is saturated with RFID detectors."

"They could have removed or disabled it when they first brought him here," I counter. "If the chip was still working, we'd have picked him up on the satellite sweeps weeks ago."

"Then we do an old-fashioned grid search for him," Jim shrugs. "I promise we are not leaving here without him."

"Don't bother," I snort. "He's already dead."

"No, I refuse to believe that, and so should you, at least until we find him or his body." Thumbing his headset, Jim says, "51-Command-2 to all aerial units. Primary target is still missing. Search for a horse trailer leaving the property or any unusual activity that might indicate a hidden barn or stable area."

We wait and listen. The chatter on the comm increases as combat shifts to clean up. Everyone acknowledges the request, but that's as far as it gets.

Minutes pass and still nothing.

Choking down my sadness, I sigh, "Come on, guys, let's join up with Michelle's unit. At least we can be useful that way."

Two firm hands touch my shoulders. One side offers a muttered prayer, and the other, silent strength. I hold onto both as the grief over losing George, DH, and all the others washes over me.

*51-Command-2*, a voice breaks through my despair, *would you settle for a guy beating the crap out of a horse? They are in some half-demolished stockyards at the back west corner of the property.*

\* \* \*

Jim, Carlos, me, and a dozen other people spread out through the dilapidated junk looking for DH. For as well as Reardon and his cronies have kept up the main house and the fortress surrounding it, this part of the ranch is a disaster. Broken boards, shattered glass, rusty wire, frayed ropes, tools, and dozens of sharp objects make walking hazardous. The stale urine, decaying flesh, and other disgusting forms of rot force me to breathe in quick, shallow gasps.

A horse's scream cuts through the dank air. Jerking to a stop, I glance at Jim and Carlos. "We have to hurry," I wheeze.

Both of them nod.

We continue to stumble around the debris, following the cries, which grow weaker with each passing step. They lead us to an open area containing a pipe-fenced ring just big enough to let a horse run full speed around the person training it. In the middle of this pit, a tall brute towers over the motionless form of a fallen horse. The horse's skeletal frame appears almost lifeless. His hair matted and bloodied.

"Come on, you lazy ass," the man who Henderson described as Clem snarls, cracking a whip over the poor creature's head. "Get up."

The man lays into the pitiful pile of bones with the leather. In response, the horse struggles to rise, heaves a shuddering sigh, and collapses.

Curling his lip in a sick sneer, Clem gloats, "Given up, have you? You ain't getting off that easy." Dropping the whip, he pulls a chain from his pocket. Red stains blend in with the orange-brown rust that coats the links. Strands of hair and bits of dried flesh complete the gruesome color scheme.

Clem strikes with vicious, quick blows. The beast inside me presses harder against its cage. I open the door. To beat this monster, I need my own—consequences to my soul be damned.

Grayness washes over my vision.

* * *

The creature looked in its direction with dull, almost lifeless eyes. Honeywell stared back at it and calculated there was a ninety percent probability that the injured animal was the primary target.

It glanced around. Regulations dictated the size, dimension, and condition of a proper training ring. None of them existed.

The one designated Clem continued his assault. After about six hits, it understood that he would not stop. Improper procedure? Yes. Horse must be respected and molded through non-violent means. Termination justified? No. No immediate threat to it. Still, procedures required enforcement.

Honeywell unholstered its gun and fired into the air.

Clem turned in its direction and laughed. "I was like you once, but my emotions always found a way through the mask." He pointed to the lump of flesh that lay at his feet. "My master found another use for me."

A dark, brooding energy that the books it read defined as *anger* pulsed through its body. Anger meant emotion, and emotion was not part of being.

*Yes, it is*, the voice said. *More than you are capable of knowing or feeling.*

*We do not act upon such things*, Honeywell countered. *Go away. You called for us. We will do our job better without you.*

*I will shut up after I give you this one piece of advice. Use my rage. It's the only way to stop this madness.*

Honeywell turned its weapon on Clem. *Target enemy.* Its sterile thoughts went through the proper sequence for a kill shot. *No remorse. No hesitation.* Its eye zeroed in on the right upper part of the chest. Embracing the anger, like the voice suggested, it snarled. *We will have our vengeance upon this one and then go after the one who created him. No one will stop us.*

"*Por favor, mi Capitán, por favor!*" a voice screamed.

"*Jo! Don't!*" another one hollered. "His life is not worth yours. Put the gun down and back away."

*Holy shit, Jim and Carlos are right. What am I thinking? Am I even thinking? Honeywell, stop! I was wrong to invoke you again. I do not need you.*

*Yes, you do. You need our skills to hunt and kill those who have harmed you and this horse. Without us—*

*I'm weak, I know. A condition I choose over valuing life less than breathing. I will die if I stay any longer in your cold and sterile world.*

*We refuse to exist in your colorful and vibrant one.*

Honeywell dropped its arm. Having calculated all variables, it gave Clem a ninety-five percent chance of taking action against it. Better to die by the brute's hands than let the voice win.

Throwing the chain on the ground, Clem rushed forward. A blur tacked him from the side. Two or three more joined in the fray. The blurs subdued Clem and hauled him out of the ring. With his disappearance, its last chance for complete control vaporized. There was only one other logical option.

It raised its weapon and pressed it against the side of its head.

*This isn't the way,* the voice gasped. *Put our arm down.*

*No, if we can't live, we die.*

A firm hand grasped its shoulder. "Jo, *stop!*" A voice outside its head barked as an unseen force reached in to grab the one inside out of its grasp. "DH, Jimmy, and I need you."

Emphasizing the point, the horse nickered.

# FIFTY-SEVEN

## ONE HEART

I don't know what broke through the steel grip on my heart, but I reemerge naked, cold, and sweating, still wearing my fatigues.

Glancing over at Jim, I say, "Let go, please."

He raises his eyebrow. "Jo?"

Lowering my arm, I nod. "Yeah, little bro, it's me."

"Give me your weapon."

"Of course." I shove it into his hand faster than he can grasp it.

Jim mutters something, but I don't hear him. My attention is on the horse. Through the mud and blood that splatter his bay coat the faint traces of a blaze and four white socks appear like a reverse shadow. Given this and Clem's last words, I'm almost certain that he is my horse.

The physical abuse and neglect are evident. I'm just as concerned about his mental and emotional well-being. Is he as broken in spirit and mind as he looks and I feel? Despite my fear, there's only one way to find out.

Dropping to my knees, I reach out with a trembling hand.

He turns away.

"Easy, boy, easy. Nobody's going to hurt you." My singsong repeats until it becomes musical nonsense. Like the first time I met my horse, it's for me and him.

The horse snakes his head around, bares his teeth, and snaps. I scurry out of his reach. Something rough rubs my hands. Glancing down at the disgusting, evil whip and the blood-stained, demon chain, I shudder. They are my line of defense, but also a barrier between us.

"Jim, get these things out of here," I say, gesturing in their direction. "This horse and I need to talk."

"Sure," Jim bends over and picks up Clem's tools of abuse. "Is he DH?"

I nod.

"How's your fear—and Honeywell?"

"Both are there, but I'm ignoring them. Please go. I'll call if this becomes too much for me, or I need something."

Jim's steps retreat. Turning back to the horse, I begin whistling, hoping the tune I made up to calm both of us will break through better than my voice. *Come on, boy, remember!*

He snorts.

"No one's going to hurt you anymore, boy, I promise. I called you Dreamer's Hope so I could grab on to it. Now I need you to do the same."

One ear flicks in my direction.

I continue whistling.

He twitches both ears forward and huffs.

Turning my hand upward, I stretch it out toward him. He wrinkles his nose and snaps at it. I jerk back.

Waves of raw, intense anger and fear radiate from him. My heart pounds a thundering, terrified rhythm in a haunting and mirroring cadence. My insides quiver. Bile tickles my throat, causing me to gag and cough.

Pushing all these things aside, I start my tune again.

DH rolls on his side kicking out his legs, running in place, and tearing up the ground around him. I don't know how long he's been down, and that worries me. Even in his weakened state, his weight is too much for his innards. I need to get him up as soon as I can. If I don't, the defiance will turn into agony and end in death.

"Come on, DH, it's me, boy" I whisper, inching closer.

Tossing his head forward, he breathes in and blows out with a long lip rattle. The violent churning of his legs slows to a stop. He mouths a piece of invisible hay, white foam dripping down his chin.

"Keep thinking about that meal, boy. You'll have it soon enough."

A tremor ripples through his body.

I offer my hand again. "I know, boy. You want to chomp and stomp any human who comes near you, and I don't blame you. Trust me, though, and you'll see that nothing has changed between us."

He reaches for my fingers, his ears plastered back. I remain still. *No, pull away*, the shadow in my head screams. *Protect our weapons.* The icy cold words taste bitter and tinged with poison.

*Leave, bitch, and never return!* Embracing my fear, I shove Honeywell into the deepest, darkest chasm of my mind. DH doesn't need her, her distant assessment of his injuries, or her unacknowledged, but very real, enjoyment of pain and death. He needs all my mixed up emotions, my passion for life, and me.

Together, we will heal.

The ears flick forward. DH nudges my hand with his outstretched head, asking, *You okay?*

"I am now, boy," I smile. "You?"

He brushes my palm with the velvet of his nose and licks my fingers. Taking his head, I lay it on my lap and stroke him. The tension and constant twitching under my fingers confirms that most, if not all, of my hard work has been lost. At least he trusts me enough to ask for help.

"Can you stand?"

Raising his head, DH knocks my arm back with a gentle push. I slide away a few feet, so he has room to try. He rolls upright. Uncurling one foreleg and then the other, he tries to push up with his rear ones. He gets about halfway before he locks up, trembling and unable to continue. Collapsing to the ground, he sighs.

"Come on, boy," I urge, "you can do it."

He tries again. Same result.

The third time he makes it maybe an inch or two higher, but without the momentum he needs for the final push that will launch him into a standing position.

I cry, joining the flood that nature has unleashed upon us. My tears are for him and every person and animal that has been hurt or died during this tumultuous time. None of them are for me, because I don't deserve their mercy or grace.

Shadows appear around us. DH rolls his eyes until the whites show.

"It's okay, boy," Jim says, dropping down beside me, on my left side. "It's just me."

"I am here, too." TJ kneels on my right.

"Us as well," Michael smiles as he and Tyrell add bookends to the chain.

"Count me in," John declares, slipping down besides Tyrell. "Bill is here with us in spirit. We could use his strength, though."

One by one, we nod and hold our hands out, palm open. Touching them with his nose, DH puffs on each before moving on. Finishing with John, he nickers.

"He's ready," I whisper.

Nodding, Jim helps me stand and move off to the side. Returning to the human herd that surrounds DH, he says, "Okay, boy, we are going to do this nice and easy."

With Jim guiding his front, Michael and Tyrell at his side, and TJ and John shoving his rear, DH climbs to his feet. The required effort leaves all of them sweating and panting.

Hobbling over to me, my horse buries his head in my chest.

"We need a chopper, and *now!*" I snap in a strangled whisper, so I don't spook him. "I'm not sure how much he has left in him."

Walking a respectful distance away, Jim barks into his walkie, "51-Command-2 to Central. We need a heavy chopper at our location for immediate evac. Primary target has been found."

The speaker crackles with Jason's response and the cheers echoing behind him. His next sentence is much clearer, *All birds are on rescue ops. Closest available is about ten minutes out.*

* * *

The whirling twin blades cut through the air. With a gust of wind, the helicopter lands a few feet behind us. I turn my head in its direction. From the open doorway, blue uniforms emerge. In the cabin, strapped in a stretcher, is Jeremy. He flashes thumbs up.

I answer with a quick smile before returning my full attention to DH and the approaching rescue personnel. The logos are their arms are all different, but their pins are all the same, vet techs. They let DH sniff the harness before strapping it on him. Even with them handling each strap and buckle with care, DH reacts to their every touch and movement. When he plasters his ears back, the techs stop and wait while my brothers and I reassure him. They don't start again until both are forward and his head rests on my chest again.

About three-quarters through the laborious process, the lead tech suggests, "Sir, it might be better if we sedate him."

"No, I'm not sure his weakened system can handle even a mild dose. Keep going. We'll keep him calm."

"Yes, sir."

Minutes pass as if they are years. DH's legs wobble, so do mine. My brothers take turns slipping behind me, propping my worn body up, so that I can do the same for my horse. Carlos, with only one functioning arm, stands in silence, his lips moving in prayer.

After the final strap is in place, the lead tech signals the helicopter, which lifts off with an increasing whirl of its engine. Once it clears the trees and buildings, its remaining crew lowers several ropes with hooks. The techs clip them to the harness. Checking and re-checking every connection, the lead tech turns to me and says, "We're ready, Captain."

Giving DH one final scratch under his chin, I lean on Jim and move away, saying, "I'll be with you as soon as I can, boy."

Tugging on the main line, the lead tech whips his fist around in the air. The whine of the engines ramps up. He lets go and steps back. DH rises until he clears the trees. The chopper hovers and then turns until it points toward the camp outside of Cohagen. The whine becomes a whirl as the copter, with its two pieces of precious cargo, floats away.

I watch until I can see nothing more than a speck on the horizon.

Lowering my head, I collapse into Jim, unable to bear the weight of my body, or my worry, any longer.

Jim puts his hand on my shoulder. "He's going to be okay, kiddo."

"I hope so."

FIFTY-EIGHT

# HOPE AMONGST ASHES

Two large tents sit next to each other with a dozen or so smaller ones, plus a few trailers, surrounding them. The surgeons have Jeremy under the knife for his wounds in one, and the vets are pumping fluids and nutrients into DH in the other. Neither is doing that good. According to the last report, the survival chance for both is about fifteen percent.

The image of fire engulfing the ranch house burns in my mind. The flames, in a way, represent the hell the battle was. Given all the intel I'd seen, I expected heavy resistance, but nowhere near the level we had encountered. Over the last few hours, all I've thought about, besides Jeremy and DH, is the unwarranted casualties on both sides.

We managed to round up all the horses. Those healthy enough to make the journey are on their way to San Fernando and other rehabilitation bases for treatment. The extreme cases, like DH, will have a few stops along the way to handle their immediate needs. Once they all recover, they have a nice retirement pasture on a USMB base waiting for them. Keeping them within the system, instead of adopting them to good forever homes, is the only way we can trust they will never come to harm again.

The enemy combatants we captured alive are on their way to an isolated brig where they'll stay until the head docs declare them human again. The hope is that most of them can return to normal, but supervised, lives after deprogramming and rehabilitation. They will be the test cases for when we disband the unit that created them and have thousands of lost souls to take care of.

Sitting in front of the tent meant for the humans, I'm soaked in blood, mud, rain, and pain. My left leg throbs and should be looked at, but I ignore it. The gully washer has eased, so only a light mist brushes against my skin. Glancing up, I can see blue patches amongst the gray clouds.

I hate being on the sidelines, doing nothing. Nothing I *can* do. None of the powers that come with either of my positions can help any more than they already have. The best doctors and vets in the USMB are fighting a fight I can't.

*Well, maybe not* all *the best,* I lament. *Bill's not here.*

The latest GPS report has him somewhere in the Texas Panhandle with about four more hours of contending with a demon eating at his soul. Nothing much I can do about that, either. At least the cops haven't arrested his hide, yet.

My stomach cramps. I've already dry gagged a couple of times, but nothing's coming up. Squeezing my eyes shut, I curl into a ball, trying not to relive all the stupid mistakes and not so brilliant decisions I made to reach this point.

Alabaster and Honeywell are my two biggest regrets. If I hadn't let my fool emotions get in the way, I'd have isolated and tested the demon horse before riding him, diminishing the chances of Jim and me getting hurt. Jim could have then been at the main gate to see Jimmy off, and realized that something was wrong. Everyone would have ended up with better lives, or at least not lost the years together that we had.

What was I thinking with Honeywell? That I'm a superwoman capable of withstanding the tremendous pain designed to break spirits and create monsters? *Ha!* That had worked out real well.

A hand touches me on each shoulder. I push them away. I want, and deserve, no comfort or treatment. Not until some miracle saves Jeremy and DH—or the docs call me in to identify and bury their bodies.

"Lass? Jo?" Two voices cry in unison. Warm bodies slip down beside me on both sides.

Opening my eyes, I glance left and then right. Jason's combat fatigues are clean and untouched while Jim's are as filthy as mine. The last of my control shatters. I blubber like an idiotic fool, burying my head in my hands and repeating two lame words that don't cover this situation.

Firm fingers take my left arm and lower it to my side before covering my hand. Others do the same thing on the right.

"Why are ye sorry, lass?" Jason's brogue breaks through my despair.

"I had both a physical and mental limitation that made me an..." I stumble on the words, "unfit leader. If I had stayed behind like I should have, George might have survived and been able to save Jeremy before he got hurt."

"George would have been paired with Carlos and another person with Jeremy, sure," Jim offered. "They could have all died on the trip down because George's marksmanship rating wasn't as high as yours."

"What about the other people? They didn't know me, but they sacrificed themselves for a single horse at my selfish request."

"No, they did it to disband Casper's operation and save dozens of horses, not only here, but throughout the country," Jim corrects. "There are more ranches, Jo. This fight isn't over."

"We found a stash of intel on dormant cells waiting fer orders," Jason adds. "As soon as the site 'tis processed and all personnel are debriefed, we are going ta formulate plans for shutting them down."

"How can we do that without triggering a civil war?"

"Same way we are going ta take down Command Security. Get boots on the ground inside them and work our way out."

"As for today," Jim continues, "at least a dozen more people would have died, Jo, if you hadn't been there. No one was more capable in this situation than you. Neither Carlos nor I could have saved Jeremey. Who knows if DH would have had the will to make it this far? You were the only one with the right training, experience, and touch in both cases."

I hear the warm passion in his voice, but it does nothing to melt the ice cube freezing my heart.

"Da lad's right, lass," Jason's relief resonates throughout his brogue. "From all da accounts, if ye hadna taken that last shot, I'd be buryin' Jeremy right now instead of prayin' fer his recovery."

"Vince helped," I object. "Without him—"

"Yes, Jo, it took both of you," Jim interrupts before I condemn myself. "He said it best. The decision shouldn't have been yours, or anyone else's, to make."

"He had a straighter line of sight than me, but at a greater distance. Does that mean he has his own beast?"

Jim and Jason shake their heads. "As far as we can determine, nay," Jason states. "We believe his police trainin' allowed him ta take da shot."

* * *

My companions stay with me the long hours we have to wait for word on Jeremy and DH. They make sure I shower, change into warm and clean clothes, eat a meal, and see a doc for my injuries. As I limp between the tents, keeping in the shadows, people recognize me with the normal formalities and utter words of thanks and praise. When I shy away from the latter, a quick nudge from either side reminds me their right to be grateful overrides my need to question my actions.

"Are you going to get that?" Jim prompts.

"Huh?" I jerk up. Full belly, warm clothes, good drugs, and a quiet corner had all combined to lull me into a quick nap.

"Your phone…"

"Oh, yeah." I answer without bothering to look at its face. "Jo Mason. What can I do for you?"

"He's safe," a voice from my past says, not bothering to identify itself. "How are things on your end?"

"We got DH plus a few other horses back. We also captured quite a few hounds. Molly's going to need to open up a satellite facility."

"I will tell her."

The line clicks dead.

I let go with a long shuddering sigh.

"Good news?" both of my shadows wonder.

I nod. "Bill's made it to Molly's."

A red-haired woman a little shorter than me approaches and salutes.

Jason returns the courtesy and prompts, "Yes?"

"Admiral Scott, Captains Mason," she speaks with a soft, warm Southern drawl, "our two most critical patients have made it through their initial procedures. You may see them for a few moments."

\* \* \*.

Waiting for Jason to finish up with his son, I think about how I'm going to apologize to my stepbrother. As his superior, I'm not required to give him one. As his sister, I feel he deserves it.

The flap opens, and Jason steps out. His face, which has been dark and somber most of the day, shines with relief and elation. "Jeremy's askin' for ye, lass," he says. "He looks okay. More important, he 'tis going to be okay."

Placing my hand on his shoulder, I squeeze with a very light touch. "I'm glad, Jason."

Entering the tent, I close the flap. Even with no eyes upon us, Jeremy moves as if he's going to recognize me as a superior officer. Waving him off, I draw myself up and touch my fingers to my brow.

I hold the salute until Jeremy says, "Thank you for the honor, sir."

"You deserve a lot more than that, kiddo," Relaxing my stance, I slip into folding chair next to his cot. "I should have found a better way—"

"To keep us all safe?" Jeremy finishes. A warm smile brightens his patched up face. "It wasn't your choice or your duty, Jo. We all wanted to be on this mission, and we all knew the risks."

"Still, the rules need to be changed. I'm going to suggest to Dad that the upper echelon revisit the policy on friends and family serving together."

"Don't. If you do, then where will the unique talents and strengths of the Mason Seven come from?"

Chewing my lip, I shrug, "I can find other people."

"Yeah, right. Who is going to be able to stay on your trust list? No one. The family and team don't need that kind of change, while the USMB faces a threat from both inside and out. Until Casper's network is shut down—" Coughs wrack his body. I offer him some water. He takes a sip. "—we need the strength of what we have."

"All right, I'll hold off for now. Once you are better, I'm calling a family meeting and we are continuing this discussion. Agreed?"

Jeremy nods. "Any word on DH?"

"I'm about to go see him. I'll come back and give you all the details."

* * *

I pause outside the larger tent a few feet away from Jeremy's. Like the town over the rise, it feels hundreds of miles away. My horse is on the other side on the canvas, waiting for me, I hope. While all I have to do is open the flap and walk in, I can't take that step. The fear that is freezing me up is not of his kind, but of his rejection. The vets had to poke and prod him a lot over the last few hours to save his life. With me not being there to explain things or comfort him, he may be thinking that I abandon him to another round of torture.

A firm hand rests on my shoulder. "Jo, as human as you treat him," Jim reminds me, "DH has a very different view on life than we do. He's going to be happy to see you, that's all."

Nodding, I push open the flap. DH floats in the middle of the covered area, hanging from four poles in a contraption that reminds me of a strait jacket on a horse-sized scale. The sling keeps him upright while taking all the weight off his feet and legs. His head, which was hanging down when we entered, is up, with his ears swiveling all around.

"You might want to come around to his front, sir." The warm leather appearance and voice of the man standing by DH stroking the exposed part of his neck is familiar and comforting. "The blinkers are blocking most of his vision and keeping him calm."

I'm relieved and grateful that Hobbs, my Herdmaster, is here. He, several of his counterparts, and members of their staff are overseeing the horse rescue part of the operation. Each horse has their own team of handlers. Hobbs is part of DH's and met his chopper when he landed, which was a fortunate thing. From what I heard, DH freaked out when his feet touched the ground. Before his struggle to free himself endangered him or any of the humans trying to help, Hobbs calmed him down.

"Have you been with him the whole time?"

"Yes, sir."

DH's ears tune into the conversation and follow the changing speakers with smooth sweeps back and forth.

"Thank you for what you did."

"Just doin' my job, sir," Hobbs replies. "The big guy needed to know he had friends waiting for him."

"What's your assessment of his condition?"

"He has a few months of recovery ahead of him, but I see no reason for you and him not to ride in next year's Championship Series."

"Isn't he better off spending the rest of his days enjoying a pasture?"

Tapping DH's chest, Hobbs shakes his head. "Naw, despite his age and the trauma he suffered, he needs one more chance to prove that he's not his father's son, but rather his grandfather's grandson."

I offer my hand to DH. Sniffing, he rubs his velvet against my palm.

Smiling, I say, "See, boy, I told you everything would be okay if you trusted me."

* * *

Clem documented everything he did to my horse as if he were a professional trainer hoping to make money off an infomercial. I gag on bile, and my temper, several times while reviewing the harsh methods he used in his attempt to turn DH. I will not glorify what he did by writing any details or descriptions of the barbarism in our family logs. That sadistic asshole doesn't deserve even an ounce of recognition.

Combining DH's mistreatment with my own fear, I'm not sure I should join the team in Atlanta for International Championships. I have no doubts about keeping my command, though. The Mason Seven needs to stop the Nolan family and show them that their skewed vision of *what is*, *was*, and *is to be* is wrong.

Jim pops his head in my tent. "They are transferring DH and Jeremy to Billings in the morning. We'll leave after that."

"You'll have to go on without me. I'm escorting them back to LA."

"Jo, you should come with us," Jim counters. "John found a few cameras at the ranch connected to a transmitter, so Casper has proof DH is back under your control. Why leave him with two targets in the same place? Beside, Jason and Hobbs handpicked and assigned the vets and trainers to take care of him."

"I know they won't do anything to harm me or DH, and they have their own trust lists, but—"

"He won't disappear—or be transformed into another incarnation of Alabaster—by the time we return, I'm sure of that," Jim's smile warms the room. "Justin and the security teams from San Bernardino, San Francisco, and Houston have vetted all the base personnel."

"What about Command Security?"

"They've been removed from the base."

"All of them? With them being able to be anyone—"

"Jimmy, as her handler, documented all of Honeywell's mannerisms and behaviors. That information helped identify dozens of them. If there are any more, they are dormant and waiting for orders. We'll flush them out when we get back."

# FIFTY-NINE

## ACADEMY DAZE

James Jr. climbed the stairs of the red brick building. On the hallowed grounds of the Academy, he had duty, responsibility, and discipline. Honorifics began and ended every sentence. Rank substituted for people's names. In this environment of distance and anonymity, he couldn't harm anyone ever again.

Walking down the hallway, he forced himself not to flinch when the first and second years came to attention. Third and fourths plastered themselves against the nearest inanimate object. This had happened everywhere on a few other occasions since his return. As an almost second year, he expected to be the one doing all the plastering.

"*Jimmy, wait up!*"

Turning, James Jr. watched Duff march toward him. When he passed by the same cadets, no one kowtowed. A couple of the first and second years even cleared their throats. Duff responded by stopping and coming to attention until they waved him on.

"What's going on?" Duff wondered when he caught up.

"Everyone's acting weird toward me," James Jr. replied, swallowing away the bitter tears that always came when he thought about his momentary lapse in judgment. "No one is supposed to know what I did."

"I haven't heard anything about it on the scuttlebutt network."

"Then why am I receiving tons of unearned respect?"

"That just proves no one knows," Duff shrugged. "If they did, they would ostracize you worse than a greenhorn."

"True. I didn't think about it that way. Thanks."

"Welcome. Besides, haven't you noticed it always happens for a few hours after LA scores a win?" In a softer tone, Duff chided, "You may not want to be a part of them, but they are a part of you. What are you going to do if—no, *when*—the team rides their victory lap with your aunt holding the IC trophy above her head?"

"I might have to hide at Molly's for a few weeks," James Jr. sighed.

"Speaking of the team, someone thought they saw a certain horse logo on the tarmac about an hour ago,"

"Any description of the person attached to the logo?"

"No. The person was near a plane's doorway from what I gather. They put on an Academy jacket before a second pair of eyes could confirm."

"What about the boards or pins?"

"The angle wasn't right to make any sense of them."

"*Captain in Central!*" echoed down the hallway.

Everyone snapped to attention. All conversations stopped, some in mid-sentence. Marching down the line, his cousin smiled. "Good, I'm glad you two are together," Jeff said when he reached them. "I need both of you to go to your quarters, pack, and then meet me on the tarmac. We are headed for Atlanta."

"Sir, yes, sir. Sir, may this cadet ask why, sir?" James Jr. kept the formality of his response at its highest level. He couldn't talk to his superior in any other way. He didn't interact with him unless someone else was around. The bastard had lied to him, hurt his aunt, and put him in the position to almost kill her. At least he could tolerate his presence, thanks to his intense work with Molly.

"You and Cadet Cordero will be escorting me on my last official act as the Commandant of the Academy," Jeff replied. "We are going to represent the base during the last week of competition."

Indistinct mumblings buzzed around the shifting bodies of the other cadets. "Yes, people," Jeff announced in a louder tone, "I am stepping down from my position as Commandant to take over as the CO of USMB Lancaster at the end of the term. This is so I may better fulfill my duties as the CO of the Mason Seven Auxiliary Team. Now return to your classes."

The cadets dashed off.

Turning to James Jr., Jeff snapped, "Follow me."

Duff stepped between them. "Sir, request permission to escort you and the cadet to wherever you are taking him, sir."

"Denied."

"Sir," Duff objected, "per our agreement—"

"Someone will be in the room with us, Duff."

"Does this person wear the LA's logo, sir?"

"Yes."

"May this cadet ask who this person is, sir?"

"No."

* * *

They walked down the corridor. A classroom with an open door waited near the end. As they entered, James Jr. glanced around. Vacant rows of tables and chairs stared back at him. The soft partition that divided the room was half-closed, hiding only silence and more emptiness. *The bastard lied again!*

"I gave the official line out there," Jeff stated, shutting the hallway door. "Yes, I am transferring at the end of the term, but our going to Atlanta is up to you."

"Sir, this cadet is not interested in your official line," James Jr. wheeled, growling with his lips upturned in a snarl. "Nor do I give a damn about you."

He lunged at the demon, his suppressed emotions erupting in an anguished battle cry.

Jeff sidestepped, shouting, "Jimmy, *calm down!*"

James Jr. skidded, bounced off the wall near the door, and charged. His fingers brushed against Jeff's collar, but the elusive devil escaped.

Something slammed into him with a thunderous crash.

Wiggling out from underneath them, he went after his new opponent. His attacker met every one of his moves with a counter move that outmatched his skills. It didn't matter, though. He wouldn't quit until this person felt defeat and his cousin, death.

Instinct and rage blinded him to everything but this promise.

An iron grip caught his arm and froze it in mid-motion. "Jimmy, *stop!*" a voice yelled. "Don't continue on like this. I don't want to hurt you any more than I already have."

"I must kill Jeff," he squirmed, trying to force a break. His assailant only squeezed harder. "He killed my aunt."

"A life for a life, kiddo?" The pressure on his arm released. "If that's the case, then you will have to go through me first because I'm not dead."

His vision cleared.

A familiar face came into focus.

James Jr.'s heart caught in his throat.

The form hovering above him wore a gray casual uniform. The badges and pins were that of USMBLA's CO. She looked and sounded no different than the person who had begun the team's championship run those many months ago. Her brown hair was back to its normal length, a subtle flame burned in her hazel eyes, and her face was round, smooth, and filled in.

"Aunt Jo?" Warmth flooded his face as he caught himself. "Sir, this cadet can only assume that it has disgraced itself and awaits your punishment, sir."

# SIXTY

# FINDING FORGIVENESS

"Punishment?" I snort.

I'm not sure if he means for his beat down test of Honeywell or his murderous dance with Jeff just now. It doesn't matter. Despite all the positive progress he's supposed to be making, the kid's carrying around a lot of unfinished business. The fire in his tone, his blind focus, and the viciousness of his blows forewarn of another eruption that could end in serious injury for Jeff, if no one is around to interfere.

Even with my own issues, I should have found a way to involve myself in Jimmy's life sooner.

Pushing myself off him, I offer the kid a hand up. Taking it, he stands up and assumes a rigid stance, eyes forward.

I glance over at Jeff. After deciding to rejoin the Championship team, I sought him out, and we talked for a long time. While he still hasn't given me a good explanation for lying about when he knew I was Honeywell, he did present a logical argument for making Jimmy her handler.

He also persuaded me to have Jimmy finish his run with the team. Molly reinforced that idea. Not wanting to pressure Jimmy, I waited until the last possible moment before extending the invitation through Jeff.

Jeff glares back at me. He wanted to reintroduce me to Jimmy on the plane. That way, if he didn't accept, he wouldn't see me. Not wanting Jimmy to feel trapped, I countered with the empty classroom idea. Jeff agreed on the condition that I stayed in the shadows and waited until he motioned.

Screw him and his need to control the situation he already mismanaged. I just saved his life.

*Easy, Jo,* I chide myself. *You knew from his first words to you, Jeff wanted to make up for what happened. Focus on Jimmy and forget about Jeff. You can deal with him later.*

Removing Jeff as the CO of his unit within the Mason Seven is no longer something I'm considering, but he is still last on my trust list. My final decision about our relationship has come down to weighing his connection to the future against what he put Jimmy and rest of my family through. What happens in the next few minutes, and during our flight to Atlanta, will determine the direction I take.

I smile at Jimmy, who is still an unmoving statue. Softening my face and tampering down my temper, so I'm not throwing off any sort of Honeywell-type vibe, I say, "Jimmy, there will be no punishment because as far as I am concerned there is no need for it."

"Sir, with all due respect, I attacked two superior officers on two separate occasions, sir."

"Wasn't the first a test of an undercover operative?"

"Sir," his voice cracks, "yes, sir."

"During the second one, did you hit your intended target or were you defending yourself from being hit?"

"Sir, I…" Jimmy hesitates before blurting, "Sir, this cadet still struck an officer, sir."

"After that officer tackled you. Therefore you cannot have attacked a superior in either case."

"Sir, this cadet is uncertain if others would agree with that logic, sir."

"Does he find the explanation plausible, though?"

Jimmy nods.

"Then let us handle what other people think."

"Yes, sir, but how will the destruction of, and the noise that came from, this room be explained, sir?" Jimmy motions to the kindling sticks that were once desks.

I raise an eyebrow at Jeff. "Hand-to-hand combat training for urban situations, right?"

"Right," Jeff nods.

"Good. Now, at ease, Jimmy, and lighten up on the sirs, okay?"

"Yes, sir."

"How are you?"

"Sir, this cadet is feeling fine, sir. May this cadet ask why you did not visit him sooner, sir?

"I wanted to respect your wishes and stay away until I looked and acted as close to my normal self as possible."

"Sir, you more than met that requirement, sir."

"Thank you. Can we finish this conversation on the plane?"

"Sir, I must decline the invitation, sir."

"Listen, Jimmy, I want you back in my life, but I won't push it." Turning, I head for the door. His defenses are still up. I'm not going to challenge them, lest we come to blows again. He needs support from me, not another confrontation. "When you are ready, you have my number. Please call me."

"Captain…" Jimmy's voice breaks. "Wait, please."

Stopping, I reverse course. I want to reach out, grab him, and smother him in love, so he knows I understand. Before I do that, though, I have to let him work through all the shit clogging up his mind.

"I want to rejoin the team and family," Jimmy continues, "but I don't deserve the honor of doing so. I was given a responsibility as a member of the Mason Seven, and let my feelings get in the way of my duty."

Still a little too formal for my liking, but at least I got him to drop all the honorifics and platitudes that cadets must use when speaking to their superiors. Shooting a strong glance in Jeff's direction, I state, "Jeff was irresponsible for making you my handler when you had no training in undercover ops or dealing with a CSG."

"That doesn't excuse my actions, though." Jimmy hangs his head.

"You were provoked," I reassure him, not wanting to hear another word of self-deprecation from his lips. "After you became her handler, I was aware of everything that Honeywell—no, I—did and experienced with you."

"It wasn't you, it was Honeywell. It felt like you were already dead."

"In a way, I was."

"Your transformation into Honeywell was so sudden that I could only assume Jeff had tortured you to expedite it. After he revealed that she was you, Uncle Bill assured me, Jeff hadn't, but—"

"My rescuers treated me at a top-secret location with advanced techniques at their disposal. They reactived Honeywell by giving me a black uniform to hold." I don't want to lie to him, even by quoting the bent truth that exists in the orders associated with everything that has happened. The facts, however, are a fantastic story that will take hours and days to explain. "The only pain that created her was my own. The training I underwent was just an extension of it."

"During my handling of her, I thought I saw moments when Honeywell let you out." Jimmy stumbled over his words. "It made it seem like she had the say on what you did. Are you certain you are the one in charge now?"

"Yes, and I plan on staying that way."

"If I may ask, how many times has that beast freed itself?"

"Five."

His eyes widen. "This cadet was only aware of two. May he ask about the other three?"

"The first was during the shootout with your mom. You were hiding in Molly's basement at the time, so you didn't witness it. Your father saved me then. The second, your father provoked by accident. Bill knocked me out with a sedative. Sometime when I was sleeping, I wrenched free. The third was when we were rescuing DH from a brute. I thought I needed Honeywell's strength to overcome him. It took your father, Carlos, and DH to bring me back then."

"What is your relationship with her now?"

"We have reached the point where we both want to be rid of each other on a permanent basis."

"Yet you are here, acting like she doesn't even exist."

I nod. "I am because of you."

"How did I help?"

"What was your intention when you beat up Honeywell?"

"At first, this cadet was testing her ability to maintain the Crazy Jane character. Then he saw it as a possible way to bring you back."

"It worked. I'm not sure I could have been reached in any other way."

"DH reached you, sir!"

"After you did."

"What about my father? What happened with him? Honeywell thrashed his nose in the gas station's parking lot. She would have killed him if this cadet hadn't intervened."

"We can go over the details of everything you and others did to save me from her later. For the moment, it's enough to say that she is locked away in a very dark hole in my mind, unheard and unseen."

"I'm not sure I could ever have your level of control. I lost mine twice, and, by my actions then and now, I cannot be trusted not to do so again."

I draw myself up, almost seeing Bill in front of me. "A much taller and stronger man, who did far worse things than you, Jimmy, said almost the same thing. I don't have any doubts about his self-restraint or yours."

"Who? What did he do? Why do you feel this way?"

"It was during an undercover op, so who or what doesn't matter, Jimmy. As for the why, I am confident that both of you will learn your triggers and never reach your breaking point again. What has Molly been telling you ever since you got back?"

"Many of the same things. She didn't mention the other person, though. Is he—"

"That's for her to reveal, if she chooses. Do you believe and trust what she says?"

"This cadet always has, unless it involved you or Jeff. Then this…I couldn't until now because I had to see and hear for myself that it was you who decided to become Honeywell and remain as it."

"What conclusion have you come to?"

"Sir…" he slips and catches himself, "I misjudged everything." Turning to Jeff, Jimmy wrenches up the formality. "Sir, I ask for your forgiveness, sir."

"Jimmy, there is nothing to forgive. It is I who should ask for yours." Jeff nods in my direction. "I will have to do the same with Jo and the rest of the family. My mission, in all of this, was to protect Molly for all our sakes."

Drawing in a sharp breath, I keep myself from flinching, somehow. We'll only need Molly again if one of us suffers a mental breakdown. As long as there are no extreme changes in my relationship with Jim, I know I can keep Honeywell in her cage. If not, she can have my body. My soul will already be gone.

*Focus, Kesomak*, the familiar, deep voice of my invisible guardian chides. *As you said, you have a soul to save here and now. If you are ever in danger of losing yours, we will make sure to save it and you. You are too important to us.*

*Why?*

278

*Many reasons that you will discover over time.*

The voice and panic fade from my head. I glance between Jeff and Jimmy. The tension between them has dissipated somewhat. Jimmy still isn't relaxing around me, though. Too much wavering between how he refers to himself, and implying the honorifics even when he's not saying them.

"Do you want to come to Atlanta with us now, Jimmy?" I ask. "I'd like you and Cordero to ride with the team again, but you can stay in the audience, if you want."

"Before this cadet decides, sir, he wants to discuss DH for a moment, if you will permit it. What did the brute do to him?"

"Some nasty stuff I never want to talk about, Jimmy."

"How's DH doing now?"

"His recovery is slow, but he's making progress. At least that's what I'm hearing. I won't know for sure until I'm by his side, touching him, and not having him flinch or attack me."

"This cadet understands that sentiment and wishes him the best."

*Come on, Jimmy, let me in,* I sigh, considering my final three options. If he doesn't respond to any of them, then I'm leaving for Atlanta without him or Jeff so they can continue the progress they've made toward fixing their very damaged, if not destroyed, relationship. Jeff and I can rebuild ours later.

"Lieutenant," I growl. "I take it by your continuing formality you would like to stay here."

"Sir?" Jimmy clears his throat a couple of times before stammering, "With all due respect, sir, this cadet thinks his superior may be in error. My current rank is cadet and Ensign, if I'm with the team."

"No, Vince recommended you for the promotion to Lieutenant, at my request, after your return to Houston."

"Per regulations, unlike other junior ranks, Vice Lieutenants and Vice Captains are never addressed by their higher name because it gives those important, and distinctive, ranks too much honor," Jimmy parrots. "Does that mean I am a full Lieutenant?" he yelps.

"Yes, Cadet," I drop my tone in its formal range. *One down, two to go.*

"Why was the recommendation made?"

279

"You helped the team expose a clandestine command structure that threatened the integrity and security of the USMB."

"While I was aware of the investigation, sir, all I did was babysit Jane Honeywell and almost kill her."

"Cadet, were you not one of the first people to respond when Vince was shot?"

"Yes, sir, but then so did the rest of the team, and a lot of other people."

"Were you not one of those who rushed in when Fury threw and almost trampled me?"

"My father did so as well, sir. In fact, he was the one who threw himself on top of you."

"Did you not document the behaviors of your operative?"

"I thought that was part of my duty as her handler."

"It was, but not in the detail you provided. Your observations helped expose several enemy operatives at my base."

"At least I was productive in that way, sir."

I ignore his sarcasm and snap off, "Did you handle an undercover operation with no training or support? Did you maintain the integrity of the mission and undercover operative's disguise and objectives in said mission? Did you keep the undercover operative from going native?"

"Yes to all three, but you already know how I feel about my actions during said operation."

"Cadet, I did not ask you about your feelings," I bark about two inches from Jimmy's face. He stiffens. My stomach drops, but I continue. If I break first, this plan won't work, either. "I asked you about your actions."

"Sir, yes, sir. This cadet performed as described, sir. Sir, one question, if I may, sir."

I nod.

"How did you and Jason get them to approve it?" Jimmy shifts to an at ease posture, his face softening.

*A breakthrough, perhaps?*

"Jason and I excused ourselves from the process."

"Was there any hesitation about acting on the recommendation because of our family name and relationship?"

"It had to go a few levels higher up," I shrug, "but that's normal."

"Sir, thank you for the clarification, sir."

I swear inside my head. Diplomacy, patience, and formality have not worked. That only leaves bluntness.

Thrusting my hand forward without saying a word, I hope he will at least shake it because I don't want to leave the room without him.

Jimmy hesitates before brushing his fingers on my palm and pulling them away. I keep still and wait. I'm not moving or saying anything until I know either way.

His hand touches mine and slides across until it is lying on top.

I block the impulse to close my fingers.

Heartbeats accompany the ticks of the wall clock.

"Ca—" Jeff starts.

Turning my head, I shake it.

Closing his mouth, Jeff nods.

Returning my focus to Jimmy, I meet his gaze. A dozen emotions wash over me. I name them off in my head and rebuke them with the last thing I have left to give him—my unconditional love.

After I'm done and there is still no reaction, I start dropping my arm.

Grasping my hand, he pulls me into an embrace.

SIXTY-ONE
# UNFINISHED BUSINESS

The team's last week in Atlanta is my Championship Series. Most of my family is together. Even Fury has returned as a spare, non-competing horse. Two important relations are still missing, though. Both DH and Bill have made strides in their recovery, but not enough to join us. DH still looks and acts like a frightened shell of himself. Bill, as Big Nasty, has a few more years of living a life sentence though hypnosis to go.

USMB San Fernando and Philadelphia are both on lockdown. Most of the conspirators involved, including Anthony Nolan, sit in the brig, awaiting trial. Undercover operatives have penetrated the sleeper cell ranches and Command Security. Progress, and the ultimate result of shutting them down, could take months, if not years.

Casper has escaped our tightening noose, so far.

Lounging in my seat on the covered veranda, I take in the faces around the table. My Aunt Rose, Uncle Pete, and RJ have joined Jim, Jimmy, and me for a late lunch. The trio made the trip out from San Diego to enjoy the last few days of the competition.

Uncle Pete boasts a muscular build stretched over a tall, athletic frame. His black hair has a few gray tinges around the edges, and his belly sags, but he still fills his blue captain's uniform with a noble flair. The metallic gray loop worn on his left shoulder indicates his retirement. Next to him, my Aunt Rose's long, willowy frame looks petite and delicate. RJ is four years younger and thinner than Jimmy.

Jim's face turns contemplative as he states, "RJ, I know who you your real parents are."

"Does this mean that all my uncles know?" RJ asks, glancing at me.

"I haven't said anything to them yet," I reply. Since my talk with Jim in the horse trailer, I haven't found the time or the words to speak with anyone about the truths I want to reveal.

"Why is it so important for them to know, Jim?" boomed Uncle Pete. "RJ's been a part of our family since he was born. That's the only thing that should matter."

"Family should know when they are family, Uncle Pete," Jim counters.

Jimmy, who still wears no boards, leans back in his chair, stares at RJ, and prompts, "Does this mean his he's your son instead of Uncle Pete's?"

I nod.

"Cool," Jimmy shrugs. "Come on, Aunt Jo, they won't think that much about it." Reaching over, he messes up RJ's auburn hair. "This lug and I have been like brothers for most of our lives, so they are used to him."

*You need to get over yourself, Jo*, my inner voice chides. *Hanging onto the ideal of a perfect career and family is doing nothing but keeping RJ out of your life.*

"Yeah, I guess they are," I sigh, "so when we are done here, we'll tell them."

Uncle Pete nods in Jimmy's direction. "I understand congratulations are in order."

"Not yet, Uncle Pete." Jimmy's face turns a couple of shades redder. "We aren't holding my promotion ceremony until after the series is over."

\* \* \*

Around me, the Championship Team plays its last indoor performance. If Jim and I nail our upcoming duet, then all we have is one more mounted event. If the team wins that, we can call ourselves champions.

Waiting for my part, my thoughts turn toward friends and family, both here and far away. Behind me, the band fades into Jim's solo. Drifting along with the music, I almost lose myself in its simple peace.

Jim winds into the beginning of our duet. I return my hand to my clarinet and intertwine our two instruments. While I play, my gaze pans the audience, connecting with a few of the smiling faces. A brief flash chills my whole body. Although black and mixed in with the shadows, the shape is still distinctive. During a pause in my part, my hand drops from my clarinet to the butt of the gun strapped to my side.

The silhouette disappears. When it doesn't reappear after a few notes, I scold myself for seeing things and expecting trouble.

Rebuking my clarinet's advances with a playful run, Jim's flute dances with the troubled thoughts in my head. Waiting for my chance to respond, my gaze keeps returning to the spot where I saw the ghost. I know my weapons, their appearance, their sound, and everything else about their deadly potential. The illusion was too real to be some figment of my imagination or another attempt by Honeywell to exert control.

*There is no reason she needs to*, my inner voice states. My instincts aren't so sure about that. They ring with a cautious note.

A shot rings out, adding an emphatic crescendo to the end of Jim's piece. The bullet slams into the wall behind the team with a crack. Dust swirls around us.

I sneeze.

The gun barks a second time. A growing circle of red stains Jim's uniform near his shoulder. Collapsing in his chair, he drops his flute with a loud clatter.

Throwing my clarinet away, I knock Jim over. Rolling off him, I come up with my weapon in hand, firing. The assailant's gun swings in my direction. Its muzzle flashes. I pivot hard. Bone crunches against bone. My left leg collapses, pitching me to the side. As I fall, I fire two more rounds, praying they miss any innocents and send the shooter to hell.

Slamming into the stage, the wind explodes out of me. I balance on my side before tottering over onto my back. My left knee burns as if someone has put it through a meat grinder set on fine chop.

Lying with my eyes closed, gathering my thoughts, all I hear is the pounding of my heart and my ragged breathing. Everyone else is quiet and still.

I groan.

The room erupts in a chaotic frenzy of sound.

Someone lays their hand on my shoulder with a gentle touch. I open my eyes. TJ hovers above me.

"Jim?" I manage to croak.

TJ glances to my right. "Still breathing."

"Anyone else hurt?"

"Nolan, the shooter, is dead. It's over, Jo."

# SIXTY-TWO

## ONE FINAL PUSH

It wasn't.

Even in death, Casper has crippled my team. Thanks to the injuries that Jim and I suffered, we have only three qualified pairs for the last event, show jumping. We need four. Enter Jimmy and Fury, who have some previous experience as individual competitors, but never as a paired team.

Jimmy has the talent and natural instinct, so he'll be fine. I'm worried about Fury, though. We are still working through his ring phobia. He's only at the stage walking around while being led for a few laps. Asking him to perform with a rider might end our run even before it beings, and ruin a good horse.

If that wasn't enough pressure, we are only trailing the first place team by a tenth of a point. That means Jimmy and Fury have to be perfect or we go home second, maybe third. Not bad considering the impossible odds we faced in the beginning, and the challenges we have overcome since then. Given all that they have been through, though, my team deserves to be first.

The course is deceptive in how easy it looks. Two combinations, a triple bar, water jump, wall, and the tight turns on a few of the approaches are the biggest obstacles in the twelve-jump zigzag. The last one, a triple combination with fences spaced two strides apart, has ruined everyone's score. All runs have ended with at least one pole going down. A few horses have even refused jumps within the combination.

Fury trots into the ring and skids to a stop with all four feet splayed. Sniffing the ground, he tosses his head and snorts. Jimmy touches him on the shoulder. He shifts to a more natural stance, but still doesn't move. Kicking his feet clear of the stirrups, Jimmy slides to the ground.

*Rider, are you declaring a no-go?* the announcer booms.

Jimmy holds up his finger and shouts, "Give us a moment, please!"

*The judges, who are aware of your horse's recent experience, will give you two minutes. However, if you cannot continue after that time, you must leave the ring and take a disqualification.*

"Understood."

Shifting around in my seat, I try to find the one position that takes pressure off my knee, prevents me from fidgeting, and is still comfortable. I manage various combinations of the three, but never all of them.

Touching my shoulder, Jim says, "They'll be fine. Stop yelling. You are giving me a headache."

Bending down, Jimmy scoops up the sand in front of Fury's hooves. Rising, he drips the grains down. Fury pricks his ears forward. Jimmy's mouth is moving. I'm no lip reader, but I can guess that Jimmy's assuring Fury there is nothing that can harm them, and there isn't. After every sweep made by the grounds crew to smooth the course, a couple of drones with explosive detectors make three passes. Great display of technology for the civilians, lots of reassurance for the rest of us.

Remounting Fury, Jimmy takes him on a warmup lap around the perimeter of the ring. Pulling up near the first jump, he salutes the judges and then turns in our direction. Touching his fingers to his forehead once again, he waits.

Using the rail in front of me, I pull myself up and stand with most of my weight on my right leg. Straightening to my full height, I snap off a return salute. Lowering his hand, Jimmy nods.

Urging Fury forward, Jimmy begins his run. The first three fences are a straight cycle of bounce, stretch, land, and repeat. A hard turn to the left, and he sets up for the next four, including the water one at the end. His performance on the three dry ones is perfect. Approaching the water, Jimmy touches Fury on the shoulder. Fury's head shifts up, so his focus is on the fence, and not the water. They take off a little earlier than DH and I would have, but still manage to clear both the jump and the pool underneath.

A sharp right turn lines up the next three. First up, the graduated triple where each pole is seated higher than the last, forming the jump equivalent of stair steps. Fury is a flat jumper, but he'll have to angle up and over like a rainbow for this one, making sure both his front and rear legs clear. His approach and launch are perfect. On the way out, his left rear hoof clips the pole. It wobbles, threatening to jump out of its holder.

Sucking in my breath, I stare and will for the pole to settle. It does.

*Yes!* Ten down. Two to go, but they're the combinations, including the dreaded triple.

The double combo consists of two hogsbacks. Each fence has three rails—with the pole in the middle being the tallest. There are two and a half to three strides between the fences. Fury jumps through it as if he's playing the equine version of hopscotch.

*A perfect ten and some spare change*, I cheer.

One final turn, and Fury's square and center for the first fence of the triple. He's up and over with perfect form. Two beats, and he launches for the second. Front legs tucked, his upswing arches him over the jump. Coming down, he tries to run out of the fence, and stumbles. Stretching instead of gathering, he leaves himself with no power to clear the third.

Jimmy collects him, buying maybe half a stride. It's not enough. Horses, like humans, have a side they prefer to lead with. Fury is a natural leftie, but his botched transition has kept him on his right, creating the sloppy approach. If Jimmy can somehow change him, Fury might have a chance of rising enough so he won't plow through the obstacle. At least one pole is going to go down, though. His angle is that far off.

Fury drops his haunches. *A balk, if not a refusal.* I lower my head and sigh, which the audience amplifies with their own moans.

"Jimmy," I mutter, "you did good, kid."

A loud cheer rips through the crowd.

I snap up and stare. Fury is on the other side of the fence, charging headlong toward the finish. I glance over at Jim. Tears stream down his face.

"What happened?" I ask.

"He just performed the most beautiful *capriole* you've ever seen," Jim beams. A *capriole* is an upward leap and rear leg kick out made famous by the Lipizzans in dressage exercises known as airs above the ground. None of our horses are trained in the maneuver.

Crossing the finish line, Fury skids to a halt, sweating and breathing hard. Jimmy bails from the saddle and hugs him. I glance at the clock. We are five seconds behind the French. It's all going to come down to the penalties. One and we tie, facing a jump off that any of the team's riders

287

can do, so Fury and Jimmy won't have to face another round. Two, we go home second.

To me, it was a clean run, but I'm not a judge. Anything they don't like, they can penalize. Their compassion at the beginning of Jimmy's run was a rare exception to that strictness.

A dozen or so heartbeats pass before a large zero appears next to the word penalties on the scoreboard.

Cheers and whistles explode across the stands, with my team leading the eruption.

Me, I'm more relieved than happy. I need to withdraw and recharge before deciding how I feel. I hope that, while I do, I don't scare my family into thinking that Honeywell has taken over my life again.

# SIXTY-THREE

# A FAVOR ASKED

I feel guilty for leaving DH at LA while we finished the competition. The trainers, vets, and grooms have done a wonderful job with him, though. He's living among the main population of horses with little or no reaction to them. His coat shines with its full luster, and no more broken skin, maggots, or infections. Only a few ribs show when I look at him at a particular angle in bright daylight. He still needs to add a couple hundred pounds before I'll even consider riding him.

While his physical injuries have healed, trust in humans, including me, remains a big issue. A quick, unexpected brush causes a jerk back accompanied by a warning snort. Flinches ripple his body when I stroke him with the lightest touch. He accepts a halter and lead rope, but I can see and feel the tension every time I put them on.

Tearing up, I wonder if his pain, like mine, will ever go away. "I should have returned with you from Montana, boy. You needed me more than I needed some stupid trophy."

DH nuzzles my cheek. I scratch his chin. He stretches his head and neck, asking for more. I smile. At least he has one spot he can tolerate and enjoy.

"He knows you love him, *Kesomak*. He is healing because of it. He is also aware you had a job to do and does not think you abandoned him."

That word again. This time I'm sure of its definition and intent. Spoken aloud and not in my head, the pronunciation has a musical trill much like a horse's greeting neigh. I turn. Standing before me is a young man, no older than Jimmy, with a long, well-proportioned body and flowing black hair. His build and stance make him seem more horse than human.

"Theo?" I prompt.

The young man nods. "How did you know it was me? Your brother met me as a horse."

"You were one of the voices I heard when I was on the ship," I state. "I wasn't in a room big enough for a horse, was I?"

"You weren't."

"What are you?"

"I'm a human-equine shape changer with some very powerful mental abilities."

"I'd say. Another one of your kind interrupted a conversation I was having with Jim. That's how I learned about your encounter with him."

"My father. I heard his voice as well."

"Why am I so important to your people?"

"You are important to many people. In my language, your name means Giver of Peace."

In all the "meaning of names" stuff I have ever looked up, my name translates to either God's gift or grace, so there are no clues there. Like Casper, I want to bring peace to the world, but not with his heavy-handed approach. It's a big job, and even backed by the resources I have, I don't see how I can.

Nor do I see anyway of asking Theo about my time on the ship and receiving a satisfactory answer. I stick with the safer topic of, "What is your ship still doing here? I thought after my rescue, it would have returned to its proper time."

"We had to make sure you were okay. The extreme difference between you and the creature you became worried a few of us."

"If you still exist, then I'm okay because your history hasn't changed."

"It's not that simple. Until we return home, we are traveling outside the timeline, so any changes to it will not affect us. We have seen so many variations of our history that we no longer trust our instruments, only ourselves."

The moment on the ship when control snapped over to Honeywell flashes in my mind. A single thought echoes, *You'll find your way back. For now, go hide and be safe,*

"It wasn't only Jimmy who saved me, it was you."

"Yes, as you became Honeywell, I was able to reach into your mind and create the safe heaven you needed to survive the transformation. I couldn't anchor your awareness without something for you to hold onto, though. I wanted to protect your link with Jim, so I relied on your love for him and Jimmy."

"There was another person in the room when Honeywell came out. Did she hurt them?"

Theo shook his head. "No, that one knew what to expect."

Many questions pass through my mind. I speak none of them, but I'm sure Theo hears all of them. They involve things I only have vague memories of, like familiar voices in the gray, foggy world of the ship, or things I want to forget, like being Honeywell. Combining them in any sort of way, I keep coming to the impossible conclusion that my brothers, a few members of the Mason Seven, and me are somehow involved in separating Jeff from his family.

DH nudges me. Maybe Theo can't reveal anything about my role in the future, but he might be able to fulfill a wish of mine in the present.

"Can you help me talk to him?" I ask.

"You already do so. He responds, does he not?"

"Yes, but…" I'm not sure I can explain horse-human relations to an alien equine. "I want to hear him say he trusts me in his own words."

"It has been a few years since I've spoken the ancient language, but I remember enough of it to translate his thoughts and bring you peace."

"Will I hear your voice or his?"

Theo nods in DH's direction. "He will decide."

I shake my head.

"Please, Captain, do not insult us," Theo snorts. "Those that you are thinking of use their love to interpret what they think animals are saying to them." He bows to DH. "Our bridge will be built by the common bloodline we share. I yield to him as my elder."

"All right, so when do we begin?"

Theo stares at my horse. DH pricks his ears forward and nickers before glancing at me. His eyes draw me in. *We know you.* The words, which start slow, are spoken in a deep tone I've never heard before, either in my head or with my ears. *Our heart is one with yours.*

"DH?"

*Yes, Kesomak.* An ear twitches forward. *If my understanding of the word is correct, its definition more than fits you.*

"I am not your lord or master, at least not by choice. I was, and still want to be, your friend."

*You are. Nothing has changed in that respect. The word means much more than it implies. For a stallion is more than a protector and leader of his herd, is he not?*

"I guess," I shrug, not wanting to argue herd dynamics with a horse when I only have an advanced human understanding of them. "How can I help you?"

A long, shuddering sigh rattles DH's whole body. *You already have. You were there as darkness offered its infinite peace. Surrounded by you and your brothers, I found enough strength to make one last effort to stand. If I hadn't...* He shakes his head. *My tortured soul would have lived in hell forever, even as my broken body rotted in the ground.*

I draw in my breath. His voice sounds so real. I can't sense any of Theo's presence in it.

*That's because I need no one to give me a voice.* DH rattles his lips. *The young one is just helping it to be understood and heard.*

Brushing the soft velvet of his nose against my wet cheeks, he implores, *Please no more tears. You have cried enough for both of us. Instead, celebrate that life has given a second chance* at, he rests his head on my *shoulder, our friendship.*

"Friends do not leave friends when they are in the state you were in. I should—"

*As the young one said, you had a job to do,* DH interrupts. *Besides, I'm glad you see me as I am now and not as the beast that I was. I hurt many during my journey back to normalcy. I am grateful I did not  add any more pain to your already heavy burden.*

I read every report on his recovery and the notations of hard bites, stomped feet, and wild kicks that had sent a few people to the hospital. I would have taken them all for the chance to be with him.

*What good would that have done?* DH snorts. *None. You were already too close to losing yourself.*

"Then you know about the other within me?"

*I have sensed her from the beginning of our time together. A whisper on the wind. There, but not there. Also, the fear caused by my father. I've always worried about the two combining and putting us both in danger. That's why I cried out when I saw her wanting to take your life.*

"What do you sense now?"

*Peace, but wariness and conflict. What troubles you?"*

"My nephew, Jimmy."

*Fury told me about the colt and the many things he said to him both during and after that final event. Like you and me, both of them are on their own healing journey, and will be fine.*

"What about us? It's hard not knowing if we will ever ride again. Am I selfish for wanting to? After what's happened, you deserve to spend the rest of your years in a large pasture."

*I would enjoy the first moments of that, but grow tired of the sameness of it, after a while. The old gelding Hobbs is right. I want to share your joy and pleasure in entertaining the crowds as my grandfather once did. When we do, we will show them our* kelisteria… his voice breaks.

Theo cocks his head, before stating, "Sorry, Captain, I wasn't sure I picked up on the right word."

DH snorts. Theo huffs. Rattling his lips, DH paws the straw. A laugh breaks out in my head. *No, young one, it's not quite that way.*

I chuckle. Guess he's having a hard time explaining horse and human relations to the alien equine, too.

*The young one is right*, DH states, *there is no exact translation for the bond between two horses matched stride for stride, heart for heart. We share it with one another without hesitation, but only honor the special ones of other species with its—*

This time, I need no explanation from either DH or Theo. "My brother Jim and I share this connection, so I understand. What about the rest of my family and friends? How do you feel about them?"

*They are your herd and, as such, part of mine.*

"Other humans?"

*I tolerate them. Given a choice, I would ignore those I do not respect. Two-legged society has changed equine ways, though. We all know the bitter taste of fear, even if it's not our own.* He tosses his head in the direction of Theo. *The young one comes from a world I can only describe as paradise.*

"Will I see this place?"

*I hope you will. The young one has not said either way.*

DH speaks no further, but we continue sharing our thoughts. The stream ends after minutes that seem like hours. With one last rub against my arm, he retreats to the back of his stall.

"Thank you, Theo. I will always remember this."

"It was my honor to share in the love you have for one another, *Keosmak*." Theo bows his head. "One question, if I may? What is *kelisteria* like? Whenever someone in my herd speaks that word, they do so with great reverence and honor. May I experience it with you?"

"Have you ever been ridden in your horse form?"

"No."

"Then I can't," I say, pointing to the crutches leaning on the wall near the stall door. "Besides, me being grounded, you are a green horse. As such, I'd have to work with you for weeks, developing the trust that is needed."

"I'll ask my human herd to help me understand, then."

"Thank them for saving me."

"No need. Your continued existence as yourself is enough thanks."

# SIXTY-FOUR

## SAN FRANCISCO STUFFED SHIRT

Jim rubbed the space between his neck and uniform collar. The pressed white material itched and made him nauseous. It didn't help that Jo stood next to him wearing the same thing like it was her second skin. She *always* complained about being a stuffed shirt whenever she had to wear the kit to please the bureaucrats.

Every person, even those of higher rank, saluted them as superior officers to honor the team's victory. He liked that part a little, but not Jo's quiet acceptance of it. After the first few exchanges, he should have heard at least one or two mutterings from under her breath, if not some serious bellyaching on their link.

*At least, she's greeting everyone with a warm smile and a few emotion-filled words,* Jim lamented.

Recognizing the next three people in line, Jim smiled. *Her reaction to them will indicate how close Honeywell is to taking control again.*

Jimmy, Cordero, and Jeff drew themselves up and saluted. Crossing his fingers, Jim prayed, *Jo, please hug at least two of them.*

She saluted all three.

Shaking his head, he walked away.

Mingling with the gathered crowd distracted him from his worry. People wanted to hear the whole story behind the team's run. While he couldn't talk about everything, he did dispel some of the misinformation the scuttlebutt network had created in trying to embellish the story behind their victory.

Someone tapped him on the shoulder. He turned.

Jeff shifted a half step back. "Listen, Jim, I—"

Holding up his hand, Jim interrupted, "Jo, Molly, and I have talked a lot. While I don't agree with your decision, I understand the reasons behind it." Motioning toward the statue near the door, he wondered, "Are we seeing another manifestation of Honeywell?"

"No, and as long as you keep yourself safe, we won't have to worry about it."

"If I don't, I'm sure Jo will," Jim smiled, "so we are fine there."

Jeff shrugged before vanishing into the crowd.

Jim continued wandering and watching. Each of his brothers was handling the celebration in their own way. The laughter and smiles of the huge crowd gathered around Tyrell suggested he was dramatizing everything to the nth degree. John and Michael sat in the corner with their tablets. A somber group of medical pins and patches surrounded Bill. TJ stood on the fringe, observing.

Most of the Mason Seven and Championship team members, and some LA personnel, had dispersed themselves throughout the crowd. Michelle and Vince had yet to make an appearance. Carlos didn't make the trip, insisting that someone needed to keep the center seat warm for Jo. Jeff, Justin, and Ben sported their new uniforms. Everyone seemed relaxed and enjoying themselves.

Stealing a glance at the robot by the front door, Jim counted the guests she had left to greet. *She's going to be stuck there for a few more minutes. Good.*

"She'll be okay, lad," a familiar brogue spoke up behind him. "She needs time to deal with what happened. We all do."

"Jason," Jim turned to face his stepfather, "those bedtime stories that you used to tell us about four men who walked amongst the stars were true, weren't they?"

"Aye. The men were your father, your Uncle Pete, my brother Joshua, and me. We were on the same ship that left Jeff here."

"When you were on board, what did the crew say about any of this?" Jim wondered.

"They were very detailed in their description of the USMB Joint Forces, but vague about everything else."

"Define vague."

"Warning us about things by saying that we needed to be careful during this time and watch over these people." Jason's breath caught in his throat before he let go with a rush of words bursting with emotion. "I dinna know enough specifics ta prevent what happened with Honeywell, Alabaster, or Casper. If I did, consequences be damned, I'd have found a way ta protect ye, Jo, and the rest of da family."

"Do you feel like what little insight you do have is a burden?"

"Burden?"

"Yes, one of them from the ship called it the burden of foreknowledge. Seeing events unfold as they were foretold and wanting to change their outcome, but knowing if you do, you might make things worse instead of better."

"No. If anything I'm glad my exposure was as limited as it was."

"What about my father and uncle, and your brother?"

"As far as I can tell, no one has acted on what they knew." Jason nodded in the direction of his brother, who was taller, with less gray in his hair. "Josh wanted nothing to do with the ship after we returned to Earth, so he hasn't talked about the visit since our return. Your father was a quiet realist who never shared anything unless it had a basis in fact, much like his namesake."

"When you were trying to prove your innocence, you and Jeff talked about an incident. What did that involve?"

"The circumstances surrounding your parents' death," Jason stated, gesturing toward the front door area. "One day, I will tell you and your siblings the true story. For now, we need to get the lass through tonight and the next few months of her recovery."

"Other than her knee, does she have any lingering mental or physical problems from this experience?"

"No.

"Then why's she acting so weird?"

"Ask her."

"I have. She avoids the subject or only mutters a few words in response. At least she's still animated when during our discussions about the base, Jimmy, RJ, or DH."

"Those are her safe topics."

"What have your conversations with her been like?"

"The same," Jason shrugged. "She'll open up when she's ready."

A junior officer wearing an SF uniform approached, snapped to attention, and saluted. "Admiral, all of the guests have arrived, sir. Should we proceed with the promotion ceremony?"

"Not for a few more minutes. Let everyone mingle."

"Yes, sir."

297

# SIXTY-FIVE

# EMOTIONAL UPS AND DOWNS

I hate being a stuffed shirt, but I haven't been able to tolerate much of anything since Jimmy and Fury pulled off their win. Honeywell is quiet. Dark, heavy worry still consumes me about her. As much as I want to relax, I will always have to be on guard against another appearance by that monster.

Being around other people is hard. Their emotions pound against me. Some, by accident, ask for the last dregs of my depleted reserves. I need my family, friends, and team, but they are going through their own healing process. I don't want to ask anything of them other than what our duties and responsibilities require, or what they are willing to give themselves.

The Nolans have declared war on my family. It began long before I was born, and will continue long after I'm dead. Alexander and Spencer appear innocent in this whole matter, but that means nothing. They will have to prove themselves and their intentions for the rest of their lives. Jimmy, RJ, and the Masons that come after them will have their own generations of Nolans to contend with. Until someone can explain Charles' death in a way that is acceptable to both parties, our families are trapped in an eternal chess match with control of the USMB as the prize.

*Tonight, let's celebrate this small victory and start worrying again tomorrow, okay, Jo?* I chide myself. Under normal circumstances, the USMB would send the winning team on a promotional tour and then hold one final celebration a week, maybe two, after they returned home. Given everything that had happened, Jason asked his fellow Admirals to either scrap the idea or delay it at least a month. They granted us three—and not required the tour.

The place they chose for our party is exquisite. The building, a former Scottish Rite temple, houses three separate venues. We are in the largest, the grand ballroom. If the teardrop chandeliers could speak, they'd tell some great tales of the celebrities and normal patrons that have graced the room. I'm grateful they can witness another rite of promotion for two people. I needed to be in uniform to play my part, so I asked Bill to oversee the process of certifying me fit for temporary duty. It was his first official act since returning from Molly's a week ago.

Other than my one responsibility, I came because of my family. I want to celebrate with them and run interference for Bill, if needed. He asked me to. Having a partner for at least six months is part of Molly's after treatment program. Bill was mine the first time. It's only appropriate that I'm his, even as John finishes out his term for my second trip.

Jim's the one who deserves the honor of this celebration, not me. I'm just a distraction, and plan on fading into the night as soon as I can.

The music stops. Jason steps up on the stage in front of the orchestra. He looks good in his new boards. He's an Admiral and the CO of the USMB Western Area, replacing one of the upper echelon who had helped Anthony and Casper. Josh, his brother, is in charge of Command Security. Training of new CSG's, both buffered and full, has stopped until a handpicked team can evaluate and restructure the entire program. They are also working out the details of how to deal with the fulls.

The USMB has shut down another rogue ranch and sent their personnel sent to Molly's new satellite facility. Expectations are that at least three-quarters of them will return to normal lives. The rest will have the choice of living and dying in a cage or waiting in suspended animation until someone discovers a better method of deprogramming them.

Jeff is closer to me at Lancaster, Ben has taken over San Fernando as a Captain, and Justin is my Chief of Security. Michelle has joined Vince at San Bernardino as his Executive Officer. I'm not sure how long that arrangement is going to last, though. They are thinking about resigning their commissions. Vince isn't talking to me at all. Michelle is keeping our conversations limited to official business. Their reaction is both what I feared and expected.

"The title Hereditary Officer acknowledges the long service of a family in the USMB," Jason intones, steering my focus back to the happiness of the moment. "It carries no privileges, other than a guaranteed spot at the Academy and the pleasure of assuming the role of presenter at any rank ceremonies involving their family. Will Captains Joanna and James C. Mason and Ensign James C. Mason, Jr. please join me on stage?"

As the three of us mount the platform, Jim turns and mouths, *Congratulations*.

I shrug. A week ago, Jason called and revealed the name of his replacement. His choice makes perfect sense. With the command structure still undergoing changes, he can only trust a member of our family or the Mason Seven. Since I have a cap on my lateral movement because of Honeywell, Jeff's only a few months into his position, and Vince and Michelle aren't available, only one person has the necessary rank.

"First, being promoted from Ensign to Lieutenant, James C. Mason, Jr.," Jason intones.

Jim and Jimmy turn and face one another. As Jason reads off a formal version of the commendation I went through in the Academy classroom, Jim removes the boards from the box he holds and pins them on Jimmy's shoulder. Stepping back, Jimmy straightens and salutes his father, who smiles as he returns it.

"Taking over as the Commanding Officer of USMB California with a promotion to Commodore, James C. Mason."

"Sir?" Jim almost yelps.

Jason motions toward the open box in my hand.

"I...She..." Jim stammers, the color draining from his face.

"Everything's fine, Jim. We'll work things out later," I whisper, adding emphasis on our link. "Just accept these, for now, okay?"

He nods. Before he can offer another objection, I pin the boards on his shoulders. Stepping back, I straighten to attention and salute him as a superior officer. He returns the courtesy with a face torn by emotion.

Grabbing both Jimmy's and Jim's hands, I swing us around until we face the audience. Raising my arms, I announce, "Ladies and gentlemen, it's my honor to present to you my nephew, Lieutenant James Conrad Mason, Jr., and my brother, Commodore James Conrad Mason."

# EPILOGUE

Walking out into the crisp night air, I try to listen to the silence, but continue to hear the chaos in my head.

Jason has suggested that I stay a few days at his ranch to relax, recover, and not think about anything other than the beautiful scenery. Bill has backed up his request with an ultimatum of a week up here, or two more at Molly's, before he'll convene a board to sign off on my return to full duty.

I'm hoping that some alone time in my favorite rocker will settle me enough to sleep. Slumped in the embrace of the chair's soft pillows, Jim stares off into the distance. Well, maybe not *that* alone. His company is always welcome, and I've been distant with him on too many levels over the past few weeks. I need to reassure him—and me—that he still has a sister.

Slipping down beside him, I put my hand on his leg and squeeze. He gazes into my eyes. The porch light highlights the wetness on his cheeks. "What's wrong, little bro?" I prompt.

"Answer me one question, kiddo," Jim says. "How are you? Are you in command, or do you have command? Are you Jo or Honeywell? "

"When did one become three?" I smile. "My spirit, though burdened, is not broken. I am in command as Jo. Honeywell is quiet. May she stay that way forever!"

"Then why have you been acting so withdrawn?" He rubs the back of his neck. "Not so much on our link, but everywhere else."

"I needed the time and space to do a lot of thinking. My lifelong dream has come true, but in the process, I've had to experience many things. Best of all, tasting a future I'm not sure will happen. Worst of all, killing someone I considered a friend, and losing two more because of my own stupidity."

Taking a deep breath, I hand him a piece of paper that I've read a dozen times. When Jim unfolds the square, the rough lines and creases caused by my reaction to its contents become obvious. He reads the note. As I follow his eyes, I can hear the words in my head:

*Jo,*

*It is with a heavy heart that I tender my resignation as USMBLA's Chief of Security and request an immediate transfer to USMB San Bernardino. I want to spend more time with Vince. I also need to think about our friendship now that I know about your meddling in my relationship with my brother.*

*The orders from the upper echelon were understandable given that the warehouse incident happened with a civilian police force. If those were the only reasons that Vince wasn't more involved in my recovery, there would be no need for this letter.*

*I remember the conversation we had before the shooting. After reviewing the Mason Seven mission logs and the relevant passages of your family logs, I have concluded that you misinterpreted what I said when I asked you to protect me. Why did you think managing our lives so we were only friends was the appropriate course of action? You had no right to play God like that.*

*Vince called it an abuse of power, but I won't go that far, having experienced the hesitation you feared when I did remember him. However, until I can digest and understand your actions and motivations, I cannot trust you. Without trust, I cannot be your friend. I need the stability of solid and honest relationships because of my line of work and the vulnerable state I have been in for most of my life.*

*Please do not contact Vince or me for anything but official matters. We'll call when we are ready to talk.*

"I understand now." Jim states, "At least she didn't close and lock the door."

"She might as well have." Burying my head in his shoulder, I sigh.

Jim pats me on the leg and leaves his hand there. "What about my promotion? How does that affect our relationship going forward?"

I cover his comforting hand with mine. "As far as I'm concerned, it doesn't. We might have to exchange salutes a little more often in public, though. Why does it bother you so much?"

"You are the eldest, so I always expected you to be my equal or superior officer. The times during the Academy, and after the undercover op that created Honeywell, where you weren't…Well, those were uncomfortable times for me."

"As they were for me. Thing is, Jim, you have nothing on your record that requires extra scrutiny. I do. Remember, it took the upper echelon three years after I returned from being Honeywell the first time before they let Jason make me his ExO."

"He could always—"

"I asked him not to," I interrupt. "He's used his clout as the Joint Services' co-founder three times to save Michelle, Jimmy, and me. That's enough. I fulfilled Dad's wish, which was the important milestone to achieve in my career." I shrug, "Everything else, like being the first female Commanding Admiral, I've come to accept won't happen."

"What about the fact that you have returned from being Honeywell multiple times? Doesn't that prove your strength of character?"

"No. It only proves that I'm vulnerable to being her again. You need to step out from my shadow and take the lead, Jim. We have two people we need to take care of."

"Who?"

"Bill and Jeff."

"I agree on Bill, but why Jeff?"

"He was left in this century to protect us. Our last team mission should escort him home so he and Randy can spend their last years together."

"How can we do that when we don't even know when or where they came from?"

"I haven't quite figured that part out yet."

www.ingramcontent.com/pod-product-compliance
Lightning Source LLC
Chambersburg PA
CBHW021036030726

47496CB00006B/1559